Hearts of Darkness

By Paul Lawrence

The Sweet Smell of Decay
A Plague of Sinners
Hearts of Darkness

Hearts of Darkness

The Chronicles of Harry Lytle

PAUL LAWRENCE

Allison & Busby Limited
12 Fitzroy Mews
London W1T 6DW
www.allisonandbusby.com

First published in Great Britain by Allison & Busby in 2014.

A CIP catalogue record for this book is available from
the British Library.

First Edition

ISBN 978-0-7490-1527-5

Typeset in 11/17 pt Sabon by
Allison & Busby Ltd.

The paper used for this Allison & Busby publication
has been produced from trees that have been legally sourced
from well-managed and credibly certified forests.

Printed and bound by
CPI Group (UK) Ltd, Croydon, CR0 4YY

For Ruth, Charlotte, Callum, Cameron and Ashleigh

Chapter One

We write of the year 1666 in which, according unto the expectations of many, very miraculous accidents shall happen.

Astrological Judgments for the year 1666

I poked the rancid beef about my plate, suppressing a desire to run from this place, dancing and singing, all the way to the Mermaid. For that afternoon I made a momentous decision, the most important decision a man makes, for I decided what to do with the rest of my life. I was going to become an apothecary. I wanted to celebrate, tell the whole world, and drink a toast to myself. Instead I withered beneath the stony glare of Mrs Collis, who stared like she suspected me of a great crime, her face glowing a shade of pale green in the candlelight.

The cesspit overflowed. We had sidestepped a shallow pool of thin, brown soup on the way to the dining room, seeping from beneath the cellar door. It stank so foul I could taste it at the back of my throat. It coated my tongue. Every morsel of food on the table, every mouthful, tasted the same as the air smelt: rank and putrid.

You could tell who were the butchers sat around the table. They were the ones munching slowly with the monotonous rhythm of contented cows, happily oblivious. Of them all, Dowling was the largest and seemingly most satisfied. Square-shouldered as a dray mare, his head resembled a boulder on a beach, grey and craggy, coated with a thin layer of spiky, white bristle.

John Collis sat at the end of the table, he whose wedding it was. His ruddy, blotched face stared out unhappily from beneath a stiff, tangled mess of brown goat hair, a stray lump of periwig fallen precarious over his right eye. I never saw a butcher in a wig before. I had met him but two or three times, for he was Dowling's friend, not mine. I was surprised he invited me to his wedding dinner.

Fourteen of us sat round the long table, the backs of our chairs pressed up against the plaster walls. Bride and groom sat next to each other at the head, flanked by a bridesman and two bridesmaids. Collis sat with shoulders petrified, only his jowls hanging loose and floppy, while his bride scrutinised the rest of us like we were strangers, peering beady-eyed through the darkening gloom.

The pile of cakes and biscuits at the centre of the table stood modest, for the butchers all brought meat instead. The taller the pile, the brighter the prospect of the couple, which signified a life of hardship for these two.

The church ceremony had passed cheerfully enough. Though a second marriage, Mr and Mrs Collis nevertheless chose to marry in public, an option neglected by many for fear of mockery and sabotage. The vulgar guardians of social sensibilities made special effort to attend such occasions, to whistle and jeer at the reading of the banns, then to follow the newly wedded couple back to their house, to make uproarious din as they prepared to consummate their union. Today's congregation participated with sombre respect, for everyone knew these two suffered grievous loss during the plague. Collis lost his wife and all three children; Mrs Collis lost a husband and two sons. Collis managed a smile or two, but the bride scowled, with a permanently wrinkled nose.

The last of the daylight slipped away, leaving us to the mercy of the long thin candles lined up down the centre of the table. The pocks upon Collis's face turned black.

'I am thinking of becoming an apothecary,' I said to Dowling, louder than I intended.

Dowling stopped chewing, and regarded me like I was drunk. 'Making drugs and selling them in bottles? You have no training as an apothecary.'

I stuck out my chin, determined he would not dishearten me. 'I will learn.'

Dowling sighed like I was his errant son. Few men had taken as many wrong turns as I. First my father sent me to Cambridge to study theology, where I learnt only that I would never be a religious man. Then I endured years of abject misery as a clerk at the Wakefield Tower, sorting an endless stream of old documents and records, feeling my soul leak steadily from my fingertips into cracked, yellow parchment. Finally I accepted a post in Lord Arlington's intelligence service. Anticipating a life of derring-do and glorious adventure, instead I found myself performing more tedious, clerical duties, until Dowling and I were finally instructed to investigate the death of Thomas Wharton, Earl of St Albans.

'I have nightmares, Davy,' I whispered, staring out the window into the dusk. Of the night I led one of Wharton's violent accomplices into the churchyard at St Vedast's. In the dream, I sat alone upon the stone bench beneath the giant oak, staring into the pitch-black night, listening to the screams of a man being tortured to death somewhere betwixt the gravestones. Then the screaming stopped and all fell silent. My heart beat loud against my ribs, drumming out a deafening rhythm for the murderer to hear. I didn't move, terrified, unable to tell whether anyone approached. Then a vicious, young face appeared before me, looming from the darkness, lips curled in hungry satisfaction.

'God help me!' I slapped my palm against my chest, for the same face suddenly appeared framed in the window afore me before disappearing just as quick.

Dowling shifted his weight and thrust his face next to mine.

'I thought I saw Withypoll,' I gasped.

'Withypoll is dead, Harry.'

So he was; he died a year ago. I left him lain upon the floor of the King's wardrobe tied to the corpse of a dead woman, a woman killed by plague. It was not me who bound him, but I who left him, for fear he would kill me if released.

'My nightmares are impatient.' I tried to laugh. 'Now they don't wait for me to fall asleep.'

'Too much ale,' Dowling muttered. 'Now, tell me how you plan to become an apothecary.'

I bowed my head, afraid to look again out of the window. I regarded my hand instead, flat against the thick grain of the sturdy oak table. 'When I was at Cambridge I attended some lectures about plants, and the healing properties of several sorts. Don't you remember I prepared your thumb with fleabane?'

'You bought some powdered fleabane at the market and bandaged my thumb,' Dowling said, gently. 'Which ability doesn't make you an apothecary.'

'No,' I agreed. 'But I know an old man who owns a shop on Walbrook Street. His son died of plague, as did his wife. I spoke to him today about buying his business, upon condition he teaches me first.'

Dowling grunted. 'Do you have any money left?'

I snorted. 'Barely.' For Arlington never paid us, and my hard-earned savings were dwindling fast. 'But yes, I do have enough, and once I am established I will earn a good living.' My heart surged with new conviction. 'Now is the time,' I declared, 'before it's too late.'

'My wife died of plague as well,' piped up the stringy fellow to my right, leaning over, eager to engage in conversation. 'With some it was quick and painless. I saw a man walk down the street, swinging his arms and tipping his hat, all smiles and "how-do-you-do's". Then he stopped and clasped a hand to his chest, like you just did.' He stared, eyes wide as soup bowls. 'Then he fell forwards, dead. When they rolled him over they found tokens on his chest.'

I nodded, thinking of a medic I watched fall face forwards into his dinner. 'I once beheld a similar thing.'

'Aye, well, he was lucky.' The man stuck out his lower lip and banged his small fist upon the table. 'My wife suffered six days afore she died. Awful to behold, the agony she endured. The night before Death took her, I had to fetch her from the river. She leapt from the window and ran naked down Creed Lane and on towards the river. She jumped in and I had to leap in after to fetch her out.'

'She was hot, I suppose,' I heard myself say.

The man's little face collapsed in a fierce glare. 'Aye, she was hot, of course she was hot. Why else should she jump in the river?'

11

'For in much wisdom is much grief, and he that increaseth knowledge, increaseth sorrow.' Dowling leant over and patted the man's hand, which action seemed to frighten the poor fellow, for he sat back and regarded Dowling with timorous eye.

Did John Collis's wife jump into the river? Behind each shadowed face around this table hid a lifetime of experience, tales of tragedy and joy, darkness and hope, few clues of which manifested themselves in tired expressions.

Not every man became wiser with sorrow. Some became angry and bitter. The world was a different place since the plague's grim visitation. The King's return to Whitehall symbolised a new beginning, yet the shadow of the Pest stretched long. Dead relatives, lost friends, missing neighbours. Though the City simmered quiet, behind that melancholy facade lurked fury. You heard it in the words of those who spoke of King and Parliament, of others that spoke of the Dutch with whom we were at war, or the Catholic French, or even God.

I was more afeared than angry, afeared of Lord Arlington. Officially, I still reported to him. He was an evil fellow, who plotted to kill us both at St Albans. Instead I saved his life and he hadn't spoken to me since. I bided my time nestled in the sweet arms of the Mermaid every afternoon, not leaving while still I could walk. I shook my head and determined to think only happy thoughts.

'How is Jane?' asked Dowling.

'She is well,' I replied thoughtfully. 'Her usual noxious self. When the plague arrived in London she nagged me incessantly to leave; after we left she nagged me incessantly to return. Now she complains that all men are self-pitying miseries.' Me mostly.

Jane was my house servant. I fetched her to Cocksmouth out of the goodness of my big heart. There my mother lived in a small house with her brother Robert and several pigs. They invited me to sleep in my dead grandmother's room, out back, and arranged for Jane to live with an elderly woman in the village, who walked in her sleep and dribbled constantly out the side of her mouth. A dreadful place, yet the only safe haven I had access to. We lived in Purgatory for six months, with only each other to rely on for sane conversation. Though she maintained her usual foul temper with effortless ease, something stirred between us, something mysterious I could not yet comprehend. All I knew for sure was that we ended up in a warm, sticky embrace one quiet afternoon, the consequences of which were still to play themselves out.

'We lay together,' I whispered.

'Lay where?' he asked, hoarse.

'Upon my jacket to begin with,' I replied. 'Though she quickly pulled me over onto the grass.'

'You *lay* with her?' Dowling hissed, spittle spraying against my ear.

'I didn't mean to,' I protested. 'Nor did she.'

I blamed six months in Cocksmouth. Six months safe from plague but not so safe from a more insidious infection that penetrated a man's skull and caused it to gently rot. Boredom. Never was I so bored in all my life. Isolated from tavern, playhouse and every other occupation man invented to keep himself entertained. Except one.

A strange, guttural whine emanated from Dowling's open mouth. I barely smothered a loud laugh upon contemplating his horrified expression. Instead I snorted beer out of both nostrils.

He jabbed my shoulder with iron forefinger. 'And when Shechem the son of Hamor the Hivite saw her, he took her, and lay with her, and defiled her.'

'Who was Shechem, son of Hamor the Hivite?' I struggled to recall.

13

'He defiled Dinah, daughter of Jacob,' Dowling kept poking me. 'And in return the sons of Jacob insisted that every man in the city be circumcised, and when they had done it they came upon the city and slew every male.'

I nudged his finger away. 'I did not defile her. We defiled each other.'

'You are the master and she the servant,' Dowling whispered a little too loud. John Collis turned his head slowly towards us. His wife already watched wide-eyed, repulsed. I tried to smile.

'We shall talk about it later,' I said, firmly. 'When ye may circumcise me at your will.'

Dowling simmered, like a cauldron of hot water.

I bent my head towards him. 'What is it like to be married?' I whispered, regarding Collis and his wife out the corner of my eye. I saw no sign of celebration upon *his* ruddy chops. What force inspired him to enter into such intimate union with so little enthusiasm? 'You've been married many years.'

Dowling perked up. 'You are getting married?'

'I didn't say that,' I answered quickly, rubbing my sore arm.

In truth, I didn't know what I thought. I always maintained a strange fancy for Jane despite her constant ferocity, for I reckoned she couldn't possibly be so angry with me unless she nurtured a passion that matched the intensity of her fury. If that passion was hatred, then why did she stay with me? A question I asked myself constantly. Yet before we travelled to Cocksmouth, never had I touched even a hair on her head with the end of my finger. To do so would have invited a swift and painful retribution. In Cocksmouth, though, she shared with me a different passion entirely.

'I don't think she would marry me,' I said, for once we returned

14

to my little house on Bread Street she returned to old behaviours. I tried to stroke her hair once and she almost cut off one of my fingers with a chopping knife. I showed the finger to Dowling, the scar still angry and red.

I wondered, though. Would she marry me if I became an apothecary? A happy apothecary, who didn't go to the Mermaid more than once or twice a week?

The stringy fellow stared. Collis watched me too, stiff-necked and mournful. There would be no flinging of the stocking tonight, nor escorting of the newly wedded to their bedchamber. Not by me anyway.

I thought of Jane again. Today was Thursday and Thursday brings crosses, I thought, becoming gloomy. God save us from more of those. Red crosses on doors marked whole streets at the worst of it. When Jane became infected, someone painted *my* door. A faint outline remained, despite my best efforts to brush every mark of it away. The legacy of plague would never be wholly removed.

I reached across to pour myself another cup of warm beer but Dowling pushed the jug away. 'Slothfulness casteth into a deep sleep and an idle soul shall suffer hunger.'

Hunger perhaps, but not thirst. He was still cross with me.

Collis's wife put a hand to her mouth and bowed her head afore suddenly running from the room, gagging. I saw a glint upon her finger. 'He gave her a posy ring,' I noticed. Now she had left, perhaps I might too.

Dowling watched, concerned. 'Inscribed *faithless to none yet faithful to one.*'

I regarded the groom with new respect. Poetry indeed.

'It is a shame this place stinks so bad,' I reflected, 'but perhaps it is

15

a good sign. It's good luck when the bride sheds tears, which she shall surely do when she vomits.'

Dowling clicked his tongue and crossed his arms.

'Whoever wed in August be, many a change is sure to see,' I said. 'For them today may mark a change in fortune.'

'Not this year,' the man to my right chirped again. 'The people will be generally troubled and the King shall be subject to internal scheming.'

A pessimist then. I ignored him.

Collis rubbed his lips together and stretched his neck towards the door, eager it seemed to relocate his wife, though not so eager he considered getting to his feet. The bridesman to his left rubbed his hands together and showed his teeth in nervous smile. He searched the room for a kindred spirit to join him in lifting the mood. None offered. Collis raised himself to his feet at last, sheepish expression upon his fleshy face, and walked unsteadily out the room, waddling like a duck. I scanned the serious faces about me, each staring into space like their heads slept.

I felt suddenly sanguine, blood coursing through my veins, heart pumping. Now Collis and his bride were gone I felt free to make my own farewells. I swigged a deep draught of ale while Dowling nodded politely at an old man sat opposite. The old man sneered, sniffed loudly and continued to chew upon the inside of his mouth. The mood of this dull gathering matched the mood of London itself, still mourning its dead, wallowing in lethargic woe. A melancholy humour infecting us all. It would not affect me. Time to stop moping about the house in daytime, and drinking myself into senseless oblivion at night. I would become an apothecary, whatever scepticism I might face, and I would start the journey tomorrow. No Mermaid for me tonight, nor the next.

'I'm going home,' I announced to Dowling, pushing the ale jug away. 'I will not remain mired in this foul stink.' I eyed my mug still half full. 'I will see you soon. If ye'd be so good as to tell Collis I can abide the smell of it no longer. Tell him I am taken sick.' I drained the mug, for there seemed no point in wasting it, and stood up straight, bursting with intent. And I would ask Jane to marry me. Maybe.

The corridor was quiet, save for the sound of a low buzzing behind the cellar door. I stepped out onto the street, savouring the slight summer breeze blowing across the black night air.

'Lytle,' a quiet voice sounded close to my ear.

I swivelled upon my heel, stumbling against the wall. A tall shadow stood against the pale moon, tall and broad.

'You cannot know how much it pleases me to renew your acquaintance,' the voice declared.

I held my breath as the figure stepped forward. I tried to speak, but managed just a gurgle. My nightmare stood afront of me, mouth grinning wide, eyes fixed upon me like a giant cat. He looked the same as he did before, save for the pockmarks upon his young face.

'Forman died,' he said, voice thick with hatred, as if it was me who killed him.

Forman had been his partner, an older man, just as vicious, but calmer and more measured.

'Wharton tied you both up,' I croaked. 'He killed the others, besides.'

'And you killed Wharton,' Withypoll nodded slowly. 'I know. And you left me bound to a dead woman. You knew she was plagued.' The cruel smile evaporated. 'I recall now the moment you saw her infection. You fell back onto the floor, staring at her neck. I didn't realise it at the time, but I remembered it afterwards. And

17

when you saw it, you left us there, trapped.'

'Because you tried to kill me!' I protested. 'You would have killed me at the Three Cranes, you would have killed me at St Vedast.'

Withypoll nodded. 'Would have, but failed.' He drew a long silver blade from the inside of his coat and held the tip afront of my eyes. 'I will not fail again.'

I thought to run, down the street or back into the house, but he stepped to his left, blocking my passage back towards the wedding party. Then he raised a languid brow, daring me to turn and flee.

'Today, though, I must take you to Lord Arlington.' He lowered the knife. 'You and Dowling; he wants to see you.' He smiled again, like he recalled a favourite joke.

My heart sank, all optimism dispersed. 'You work for Arlington now?'

'Aye,' he replied. 'Just me alone. Forman died.'

Which was the second time he told me.

He snapped and clicked his fingers. 'Fetch Dowling. Your life is about to change.'

Chapter Two

It, viz. the year 1666, hath been ushered in with three preceding Comets, or Blazing Stars; and as unto us in England it's attended with a grievous and consuming Plague or Pestilence, concomitant with a chargeable war against the Hollanders.

Dust stung my eyes, dancing thick in the musty air. Rubble lay strewn across the floor and thick webs curtained the corners. A single narrow slit in the wall admitted a light breeze. The Develin Tower had been boarded up for years, a ruinous mess upon the west wall of the Tower of London.

A stout man slouched in the middle of the room, hand tied to a wooden block nailed to a table. A fleshy fellow, well fed and prosperous, light-brown hair streaked with grey. Sweat beaded in small drops at his temples and his hair stuck to his forehead, plastered with blood. A purple lump bulged above his right eyelid. He watched us through his left eye, silent and bewildered.

Lord Arlington leant upon an upturned barrel, mouth pinched, brow hanging heavy. He stood when we entered, approaching with outstretched arms, cold face split by a false, yellow smile. I thought for a moment he would envelop me in the folds of his brown, silk jacket, but he stopped short, still smiling, eyes dark and fishy. I tried not to stare at the black plaster across the bridge of his nose, memento of an old battle.

'Such a long time since last we met,' he exclaimed. 'St Albans, wasn't it?'

'Aye, your lordship,' I replied, dry-mouthed.

He tucked his arms behind his back and cocked his head. 'Remind me,' he said. 'What happened that day?'

I glanced sideways at Dowling, but he stood frozen. Withypoll sauntered into the room, stopping behind Arlington's shoulder, face twisted in delighted expectation of chewing on my heart.

'You helped us realise Wharton wasn't dead,' I began, sidling closer to Dowling. 'You led us to St Albans to arrest him, where he attacked us.'

'So he did,' Arlington nodded slowly. 'I do recall.'

'You and he locked in combat,' I continued, mouth dry. 'You were on the verge of defeating him, when I slew him from behind.'

Arlington wrinkled his nose, unimpressed. He wiped dust from his shoulder and coughed. Truth was he betrayed us. He left us to travel to St Albans by ourselves, then arrived with a band of French soldiers to kill everyone, including us. Wharton outwitted him and I saved his rotten life.

'Have I not remembered well?' I asked.

'I had him at my mercy, Lytle,' said Arlington, pointing. 'I would have fetched him back to London to stand trial, but you struck him from behind with a butcher's knife.'

A grave misrepresentation. Had I not thrown the cleaver at Wharton's head then Arlington would have died.

Arlington turned to Dowling. 'Was it not so, Dowling?'

Dowling hadn't even been there. He had arrived later. Now he stared forward, unwilling to tell the lie.

'It was,' I lied on his behalf. 'Yet we served you as best we could. If our efforts were not good enough, we humbly accept our dismissal.'

Arlington frowned. 'Dismissal?'

Withypoll shook his head slow, an expression of regret.

Arlington glowered. 'Some demanded you be put to death for the unlawful killing of nobility, but I insisted on lenience. I protected you.'

I doubted it. 'So we are in your debt?'

'You owe me your lives.'

I nodded at Withypoll. 'How long has he been working for you?'

'Since he escaped from where you left him bound,' said Arlington, disapprovingly. 'I find it difficult to credit how cruel must have been your humour, Lytle. To leave a man bound to an infected corpse.'

I closed my eyes. There was little to be gained in attempting to explain the events of a year ago. Arlington had already decided our fate, and no words of mine would change that. When I said nothing, he grunted, then waved at the stout man bound in the middle of the room. 'I should like to introduce you to Edward Josselin.'

The stout man blinked at the mention of his name and jerked his hand against the bindings.

'His son is another ungrateful wretch,' Arlington sneered. 'A traitor and a coward, fled into hiding.'

The older man's jaw dropped, as if to say something, but he stopped himself in time. He bowed his head like he feared being struck, and cast a frightened glance at Withypoll.

Arlington clicked a finger at Withypoll. 'Give me the knife.'

Withypoll dug into his jacket and withdrew a square-bladed cleaver. He handed it to Arlington, who handed it to me.

'Chop off his finger,' Arlington commanded.

My arm fell to my side, weak as a child's. I prayed he intended only to intimidate me, yet he and Withypoll watched expectantly, unsmiling and intense. Edward Josselin blinked and tugged sharply again at his trapped hand. I looked down at the knife, a broad-bladed carving knife with weathered, wooden handle. I opened my fingers and dropped it clattering onto the stone floor.

A small smile appeared upon Arlington's lips. 'Do you not recognise it? It's the knife you used to kill Thomas Wharton.'

Dowling bent down and picked it up. 'Neither of us will cut off this man's finger,' he growled, clenching the handle of the knife tight in his fist.

Arlington drew the rapier from his belt and levelled it at Dowling's throat. 'Cut off his finger, Lytle, else I will stick that blade in the back of your skull, same as you did to Wharton.'

Josselin wriggled and squirmed, whimpering. I wanted to reassure him, release him from the restraints that bound him, but Withypoll stood at my elbow. Josselin's hand was pegged out flat, leaving bare his first knuckles. Only his little finger wriggled free, untied. Torture was illegal in England, and those found guilty of committing such atrocities risked being hanged by the neck, and sliced from sternum to groin. If I chopped off Josselin's finger, I would be a party to torture.

'Might I know why?' I asked, scalp prickling.

'Edward Josselin is a traitor,' said Arlington, pricking Dowling's throat with his blade. 'A traitor to King and country.'

'I am not a traitor,' Josselin whispered, eyes wide. 'I have been loyal to the King all my life. My son too.'

Arlington snorted. 'Your son is a spy and betrayed us all. You chose to veil his treachery. Your country or your kin, and you chose your perfidious kin.'

Josselin sunk in his chair; heavy, old head slumped upon his chest. 'I don't know what you're talking about.'

Which made two of us.

'Your son killed the Earl of Berkshire and fled to Essex,' Arlington spat.

'Whoever murdered the Earl of Berkshire, it was not my son,' Josselin insisted, emphatic, momentarily unafraid.

'Cut off his finger, Lytle,' Arlington growled. 'I won't tell you again.'

I took a deep breath and exhaled through my nose. My head swam and I placed my legs apart so I wouldn't fall over. His little finger trembled like a trapped mouse, the only finger I could possibly sever without risk of chopping two or even three. I ran my own fingers across my forehead, through a thick sheen of sweat. My first thought was to raise the blade and take a swing, but what if I missed? I might cut off his whole hand. It would be safer to place the tip of the blade in the wood of the table and lever it down slowly.

'Why?' I asked. 'What purpose will it serve?'

'Cut off his finger or I will cut off your head,' Withypoll's voice sounded, wet in my ear.

I thought for a moment to slice the knife across Withypoll's throat instead. Yet that would still leave Arlington alive, and he could conjure up a thousand other Withypolls. Josselin stared, pleading, desperate to read my intent. Withypoll stretched out a hand towards the cleaver. If I let him prise it from my grasp, then he would use it on me. My life or Josselin's finger. I stepped to the table and positioned the knife.

'May God forgive me,' I whispered, feeling my veins rush with strange energy. I stared into Josselin's bewildered eyes. 'Don't move.' Then I brought the blade down swiftly afore he could think.

He screamed and yanked at his hand. For a moment I saw flesh and bone, a perfect section, afore thick red blood welled forth like hot jam inside a pudding. He didn't scream again, just watched agape, the blood draining from his face faster than it bled from his finger. Bile surged into my throat, my skin burnt, and the room seemed to ripple.

Withypoll leant forward and prodded at the small piece of digit lain lonely upon the wood, barely big enough to pick up. 'His Lordship told you to cut off his finger.'

I threw the blade on the table. 'Aye, and so I did, and I'm not cutting off any more.' My body trembled and I felt sickness in my stomach. I couldn't stop my hand from shaking.

Arlington shook his head and lowered his sword, afore nodding gently at Withypoll. Withypoll picked up the cleaver and cut off the rest of Josselin's small finger like he was slicing sausage. This time Josselin screamed with all his lungs.

I grabbed an old mouchoir from the bottom of my pocket and tried to quell the river of blood streaming across the surface of the table. 'What would you have him tell you?' I shouted. Blood soaked through four layers of cloth in a second. The severed finger lay by itself, a most unnatural apparition. Dowling seized the old man's hand and pushed the mouchoir firmly against the wound.

Arlington watched our efforts, amused. 'What will you do, Lytle, when we hew off his hand? Will you take off your shirt?'

'Why should you hew off his hand?' I demanded, heart pounding.

'My son is not a spy,' wailed Josselin, torso folded over upon the table, drool dripping from the corners of his mouth.

Arlington pushed me backwards, towards the wall. Dust billowed about our heads, prickling at my nose and throat. 'You asked to work for me, did you not?'

My face must have appeared blank.

'You asked Dowling to promote your cause.' Arlington jerked his chin upwards. 'Is that not so?'

I watched Dowling's back as he held Josselin's hand tight. Indeed it was true, back in the days when I thought it would be a noble occupation. Why had Dowling not warned me off?

'Well here we are,' Arlington hissed. 'And this is what we do. It is my job to protect the citizens of this country and the King himself. If you doubt my sincerity, then consider what happened to our King's own father, executed by his people.' He breathed hard through his nose, black plaster rising and falling. 'I carry an enormous responsibility, as does every man that works for me, and every man that works for me should be strong enough to carry that burden. Do you understand?'

I understood. Withypoll well enough to know murder was no hardship, and Arlington well enough to know he cared nothing for the citizenry. I nodded, for I could not bring myself to speak. He wanted me dead, I was sure of it. So why did he not just instruct Withypoll to be done with it?

Josselin groaned loudly.

'This man's son is a spy and a murderer, Lytle, and his treachery has put at risk any chance of peace with the Dutch.' Arlington wrapped his fingers about my neck. 'So save your pity and your tears. There can be no mercy.'

'How do you know James Josselin killed Berkshire?' Dowling demanded, pale-faced, regarding Arlington as he would a beast.

Arlington waved a hand in front of his nose as if bothered by the smell of blood. 'They found Josselin's blade sticking out of Berkshire's chest, pinning him to the chair in which he sat, and Josselin ran away.'

'Perhaps he took fright,' I ventured. 'Else was abducted by the murderers.'

Arlington released his grip and scowled. 'I have not summoned you here to debate the man's guilt. Mine own intelligence network confirms his treachery. I have spies in all places, here and in Holland. We will win the war because of it.' He puffed out his chest and stared down his nose. Dowling's baggy eyes narrowed.

'My son is not a traitor, nor a murderer,' cried Josselin.

Arlington slammed a fist down upon the table. 'Shake your head, you villainous rogue,' he roared. 'No man here is touched by your wickedness!'

Josselin said nothing, just lay his head upon his arm, staring at his mutilated hand like it was his son, an intimate gaze of infinite sadness. A tear rolled down his cheek.

'Enough of this, Withypoll,' Arlington exclaimed, as if we ruined his day. 'End it.'

Arlington pulled from his coat a thin, short blade, a bright, shiny spike mounted upon a leather-clad handle, and handed it to his covetous accomplice. Withypoll took the strange weapon in his palm and regarded it as if it was a great jewel. Then he seized Josselin by the hair, lifted him up and wrenched his body backwards, plunging the blade so deep into his heart the handle stuck in his ribs. Josselin's eyelids fluttered a brief moment, then he lay motionless, sprawled back upon his chair, hand still bound to the block. A small circle of blood formed upon his chest.

From Dowling's mouth emanated a sigh of utter sadness and misery. Withypoll rubbed his hands together, smug satisfaction etched upon his vile features. Arlington scowled. Dowling and I stared, stunned and appalled. The blood seeped quickly outwards.

'I am disappointed in you both.' Arlington spoke to Dowling this time. 'You killed Wharton's wife, did you not? And a Frenchman. Yet you baulk at the killing of a traitor.'

Withypoll picked at the knife handle with his fingertips, oblivious to the oozing blood, but it stuck fast. He would need another knife to dig that one loose.

'The Earl of Berkshire was a man of peace,' Arlington declared. 'An envoy to the Dutch when we sought reconciliation. His efforts were scorned. Now he is dead.' He stared at me like *I* was a Dutchman. 'The Four Day Battle was no victory.'

He said it as if it was a great secret. Though instructions were issued to light bonfires and celebrate, every man in London knew we were annihilated. Rupert took half the fleet to Plymouth to watch for the French, rumoured to be heading for Ireland, leaving Albemarle to fight the Dutch by himself. It transpired the French had no intention of invading Ireland, an error attributed by some to Arlington and his flawed intelligence, the same network that said this man's son was a traitor. The same network that condemned Edward Josselin to death.

Dowling stroked the dead man's hair, a strange look upon his face, angry and sad at the same time.

'James Josselin worked for me,' said Arlington. 'He was privy

27

to the most secret of intelligence and I trusted him. *He* swore his allegiance too, Lytle.'

'Why do you question *my* allegiance?' I snapped, anger provoked. Little good ever came of giving it voice, but my mouth was busy. 'I pursued Wharton to St Albans. I killed him when I thought he endangered your life.'

Arlington smiled. 'I am happy to hear you confirm your loyalty.' He placed his hands behind his back and leant forward. 'You will go to Essex,' he said, daring me to protest. 'Withypoll will go with you as far as Colchester.'

So that was it. The thin, puckered face of the man who sat next to me at dinner formed before me, the grating sound of his shrill voice echoing in my ear. He said 1666 would be a sickly year, a year when the plague would slither out of London to wreak its evil upon other towns and cities. London was free at last, like a great old bear, beaten to its knees, bloody but unbowed. The worst was over, the Pestilence gone, in search of new feeding grounds, bounteous and plentiful, and Essex was where it went, Colchester the worst afflicted. Arlington sent us back to Hell.

'Why?' I asked.

'Because that is where James Josselin fled,' Arlington replied. 'To Shyam, where none will follow.'

'Where is Shyam?'

'Shyam is a small village,' Dowling spoke up. 'Where the plague has chosen to make its home. Three hundred people lived there before the Pest began its killings. They have closed their boundaries and allow no man in nor out.'

'You are well informed, Dowling,' Arlington noted approvingly. 'The Reverend of Shyam persuaded them all to stay, so as not to infect other villages to the north and east. Any man that ventures within its boundaries is obliged to remain until the plague is gone.' He gazed admiringly into the gloom. 'What a man he must be, that influences men to lay down their lives for others, especially the rude sort of fellow that lives in such places.'

'You want us to go to this Shyam?' I exclaimed, aghast.

Arlington nodded. 'To fetch James Josselin. Alive.'

Withypoll sat on the table, grinning with all his sharp teeth. He was sent to Colchester; not a much better prospect, but he survived the plague once already. He clearly believed himself immune to further infection.

Arlington's eyes were unrepentant. He did not expect us to return. If we did, he would kill us later. I looked to Dowling. His face was set, hard as stone.

'Very well,' I said. 'We will make preparations.' Preparations to flee, for nothing would entice me eastward.

Arlington pointed to Josselin's dead body, mouth open, dull eyes staring at the ceiling. 'First you will dispose of that, and dispose of it well.'

He nodded at Withypoll, who stretched his arms wide and yawned. 'Tomorrow you take them to Whitehall, so they may see the scene of Berkshire's murder.'

Withypoll nodded, like he had it already planned.

Arlington headed for the door. 'Fail and you will both rot in Hell,' he called over his shoulder as he left the room. Withypoll followed with languid stride. Josselin's finger rolled gently off the table and landed on the floor with a soft thud, coming to a rest next to my heavy heart.

I thought I left such villainy behind on my way to becoming a

29

happily married apothecary. Instead I cut off the tip of a man's finger and faced a journey back into the Hell of plague. I escaped Death last year. To court him twice was madness.

Josselin stared at the wall with dull grey eyes.

'What now, Davy?' I said at last.

'God will guide us,' he replied. With less mischief than he had done thus far, I hoped. The grey pallor painted upon Dowling's craggy face betrayed uncertainty of faith. I had never seen him so undone.

'What shall we do with the body?' he asked, picking at the bindings about the dead man's hand.

I was sick of bodies.

'I know a place,' I muttered. 'I used to work here, remember?'

Chapter Three

Comets are to be observed; usually they produce such effects as are the nature of Mars and Mercury, and there signifies Wars, hot, turbulent commotions.

Jane's green eyes burnt into my cheek as I entered the front door and removed my jacket. The tip of her finger stabbed into my midriff when I forgot to shake the dirt from my shoes.

'It's dark,' she snapped. 'Why are you returned so late? You said it would be a dull affair.' She stood upon her tiptoes and tried to sniff my breath.

She meant the wedding, I realised. 'So it was,' I answered. It seemed so long ago now. I couldn't recall the last time I returned so late, so sober.

She directed her attentions to Dowling, who followed me over the threshold. 'What are you doing here?'

'I came to pay my regards,' he replied slow, unable to stop staring.

'I haven't seen you in a while.'

I attempted to lose him twice upon the way home, but he wouldn't be deterred.

'Aye, well here I am,' she frowned, perplexed, sniffing the air again. 'Now tell me where you have been so late?'

My mind's eye still watched Josselin's body slowly sinking into the water. I had little appetite for one of Jane's sermons. I needed a drink and headed for the kitchen in search of ale. I wondered how to tell her of our journey east. 'Come, and I will tell you.'

'You plan to talk to me?' she declared in mock astonishment, following with quick steps. 'Why so wormy-tongued? I have no dinner for ye, and no speech will persuade me to cook at this late hour.'

I wasn't hungry. 'We have been set a puzzle that may be beyond our capacity to resolve.'

She snorted. 'If that were a reason for talking, we would spend *every* evening at the table.' She scowled at Dowling, who would not take his eyes off her. 'Will you have an ale, butcher? You look like you are about to faint.'

'No, no.' He waved a hand. 'I will just sit a while.'

Jane clicked her tongue and eyed him, suspicious, afore fetching a jug of ale, a cup and a dish of oysters. 'Tell me your tale, and spin it fast, for I would go to bed.'

Dowling smiled, hiding the expression quickly before she could spot it.

'We must go away tomorrow,' I told her, already feeling the need to defend myself. 'And though I cannot think why I feel so obliged, I will leave you instruction should I not return for a while.'

She leant forwards and wrinkled her small freckled nose. 'You

32

will leave me instruction? That assumes there is something you are qualified to instruct me upon. Since I have no desire to emulate your enviable ability to piss with one hand and drink with the other, I wonder what other *instruction* you feel compelled to share with me.'

'Do you always talk to me like this when I come home late at night?' I struggled to recall. 'Perhaps you forget, you are my servant.'

'No servant of yours could ever forget it,' Jane growled, cheeks flushed. 'Not the day of the appointment, nor the detail of each day subsequent.'

'Most servants would be glad to have me as their master,' I protested. 'I pay you well. I send money to your brother, to the brother of your sister's husband, and to your uncle with the swollen head. Indeed I have never declined to help any member of your family, though they are legion. Yet you talk about me as if I am the Devil incarnate.' I suddenly remembered. 'And I saved your life.'

'You don't send money to my uncle, for he died more than a year ago,' she retorted. 'And you didn't save my life.' She leant back and folded her arms against her plump breasts. 'Ruth saved my life. You took the opportunity to gaze upon my naked body, and do not think I have forgiven you for it.'

I sighed, sat down and filled my cup. We had debated many times before. In fact it *was* I, at great risk to myself, who entered my house when she suffered plague and tended to her while a drunken nurse lay slobbering and snoring downstairs. I changed Jane's clothes when she lay in her own foulness. It was I who ejected the wretched harridan and found a new one, this Ruth.

'You have gazed upon my naked body too, I reckon,' I replied.

'Aye, bathed in sweat and stinking of ale,' she snapped. 'For which task I could never be adequately rewarded.' She peered out from behind strands of blazing red hair, green eyes sparkling. She was beautiful and I didn't want to leave her.

'Anyway.' I slumped back in my chair. 'Tomorrow we must go to Essex.' I gazed back into her bright eyes, when usually I would look away. 'To some small village north of Colchester.'

Her top lip jumped up to her nose, revealing sharp white teeth. 'Is this a riddle? You take me for a fool and I will poke out your eye.'

'No riddle.' I drained my cup and filled it again. 'Lord Arlington summoned us this afternoon and issued those orders. We are to leave in the morning. Ask him.' I attempted to divert her attention towards Dowling.

Dowling buried his nose in an oyster shell.

'What did you do?' she exclaimed. 'Spit in the King's dinner? He might as well send you to Tyburn. I thought Arlington was your great new benefactor, your passage to wealth and fortune.'

'So did I,' I reflected.

'Tell me, then!'

I ducked quick to avoid the arm she flung at me. 'I hoped he would be grateful I saved his life.'

Jane glowered. 'You stripped him naked and gazed upon his body too?'

'No,' I replied, fist clenched. 'I saved his life. Yet he doesn't trust me. He is afraid I might divulge the truth of his devious, black soul.'

'As would I be if I were him, the amount of time you spend at the Mermaid lain drunk upon the floor.' Jane raised her brows like I was a great fool. It was a good point I had not considered.

She prodded Dowling's shoulder. 'So he has sent you both on some strange pilgrimage of repentance.'

'Whether we repent or not is of no interest to him,' Dowling replied. 'He wants us to find a man called James Josselin.'

I watched the two candles flicker in a sudden breeze that invaded from the corridor. Jane shook her head, lips pinched tight. 'If you two ninnies wander woolly-headed into Essex then you will both die. The plague is worse there than it was here. They say half Colchester is dead already. For what did we spend six months living with pigs if it was not to escape the Pest?' I saw tears in the corners of her eyes and felt my own eyes burning.

'If we do not go, Arlington will have us killed.'

'Who is this James Josselin?'

'Arlington says he is a murderer, though Dowling and I have our doubts.'

'Ha!' Jane exclaimed. 'You have your doubts. So you will ask this renegade the truth of it and he will confide all in you two? I think not.' She pulled a face like she sucked upon a lemon. '"*Excuse me, sir,*" says the butcher. "*Wilt thou reveal unto me whether or not you be a murderer, that we may inform the Honourable Lord Arlington, that doth search for you?*" The gentleman thinketh.' Jane frowned and looked to the ceiling. '"*Why do you hesitate, good man?*" enquires the short fellow that doth nothing but drink. "*Do ye not trust our good intent?*" With that the short fellow doth belch loudly, thus convincing the man who doth doubt his integrity, that these two good fellows are deserving of his trust.'

Dowling laughed out loud until he met her gimlet eye.

I saw she was afraid. Strange how quick I recognised it these days.

'We have to attempt it else he will have us killed anyway.' I said.

'We are to go to Shyam and fetch Josselin back to London, with the help of one of Arlington's agents, a murderous dog.'

'If Arlington and his agent know where this man skulks, then what use are you two buffoons?'

'Josselin has taken refuge in a small village where the plague is rife, where the villagers have closed their boundaries,' I answered. 'We are appointed to fetch him out.'

She dropped her hands and stared, speechless. A rare event.

'So the instruction I would leave you relates to the disposal of my estate,' I said, soft.

'Your estate!' she exclaimed. 'Why tell me of your estate?'

'Because I have no one else to leave it to,' I replied. 'I might as well leave the house and monies to you.'

She stood bolt upright, shoulders hunched about her ears, arms held out stiff like the wings of a tall, wading bird. 'To me?' Her voice echoed strangely deep, like the uttering of a demon.

'Aye.' I watched nervous as she stepped closer. 'I have no one else to leave it to.'

She lowered her face and breathed over my nose. She smelt of sage and mint, just as she had that afternoon in Cocksmouth. 'Leave it to your mother,' she hissed. 'Or leave it to her brother. But don't you dare try and leave it to me.'

'You don't want it?'

'You tell me you are sent to Essex.' Her hand shot out towards my neck and I caught it just in time. 'That you will likely die.' Her voice tremored and tears gathered in long pools above her lower lashes. I hadn't seen her weep before.

'I didn't say I would likely die,' I protested. 'You did.'

She screamed loudly into my face, sweet lips wide apart, head thrust forward like an angry rooster. Once all the breath was blown from her body she fell back onto her heels and gazed, wide-eyed and bewildered.

Dowling lumbered to his feet and attempted to wrap an arm about her shoulder. 'I will look after him.'

'What!' She pushed away his arm and peered into his great blank face. 'You will defend him from the plague will you, butcher? Methinks not. And why do you sit there all moonfaced, anyway?' Her eyes widened and she turned to me. My heart sunk to somewhere close to my toes and I wished I had not admitted him into the house.

'You told him,' she whispered. 'You told him!'

I opened my mouth and prayed for words of wisdom. Nothing happened.

'We were at a wedding,' Dowling ventured bravely. 'He asked me what it was like being married.'

She stared at me, green eyes flashing.

'He said I was like Shechem, son of Hamor the Hivite,' I added, unable to think of anything sensible to say.

Her top lip peeled back slowly from her teeth. I wondered where to put my hands. I edged about the wall of my kitchen heading for the door, but afore I could escape she flung herself at me and wrapped her arms about my back in iron embrace. I grimaced in anticipation of being bitten on the neck, but instead I felt hot, wet breath somewhere close to my ear. I shivered and held her afront of me. She ducked her head to hide her eyes, then flung herself at me again, lifting her head and gazing up. Her lips parted and I felt something stir deep within. And something else, not so deep within.

'I'll keep my estate, Jane, and be back in a week,' I assured her, feeling helpless.

At which she chewed her lip, scowled like Dowling, and stomped down the corridor and up the stairs. Leaving me stood in the kitchen in a state of complete confusion. Women speak two languages, quoth the Bard, one of which is verbal. The other I did not understand.

I followed her upstairs and knocked gently upon the door of her room, leaving Dowling to let himself out.

Chapter Four

These blazing stars appear but seldom, they without all doubt portend very great Calamities.

Next morning we met Withypoll at Whitehall.

All that remained of Berkshire's body was a wide black stain upon the rich yellow fabric of an intricately carved, upholstered chair. All about was deathly quiet. I scanned the small room: polished walls, squat French console with legs bowed like a bulldog, a tall walnut chest of drawers. All positioned about the edge of a fine, oriental rug laid precisely upon the wooden floor. I stole a glance out the window towards the river, saw the boats meandering well away from the well-guarded jetty. Behind us lay the Privy Garden, the King's private place of reflection and repose.

'Arlington said they found him pinned by James Josselin's blade,' I recalled. 'How did he know it was Josselin's blade?'

Withypoll sauntered across the marquetry floor of the panelled room like a prudish heron. Circling the chair, he opened the door of a tall, narrow cupboard. He reached inside, turned quick and tossed a sword at me. I leapt backwards as the weapon clattered to the floor. Its steel blade stretched two feet long, shiny at the tip, scarlet stain along its shaft. Two intertwined letter 'J's formed the bar cage, intricate and beautiful.

'The scabbard is missing,' said Withypoll. 'But the weapon is Josselin's. Every man at court would swear it.'

'So Josselin marched into the heart of the palace, killed a man with his own blade, then left it for all to see,' I said.

'Marching into the palace was simple,' said Withypoll. 'He came here often. He was obviously interrupted and ran away. It matters not whether he left his blade or not. He was caught in the act.'

'Who interrupted him?' Dowling growled.

'The guards, a servant, whoever was around,' Withypoll replied, dismissively. 'It is of no import. Arlington told me to show you the scene of his death, not to answer foolish questions.'

'Seen and chased then.' I moved slowly back to the door and looked out. 'Across the courtyard and out into the gallery.'

Withypoll glided into a position behind my right shoulder. 'So I presume.'

'You presume a lot.'

'Talk to me again like that, Lytle,' Withypoll hissed into my ear, 'and I shall prick your tiny heart.'

His warm breath lingered upon my neck and I felt my face flush. I determined to keep my mouth closed.

Dowling dropped to his knees in front of the chair and sniffed at the dried blood like a dog. He poked his finger into the torn cloth, wriggled it, then stood up and twisted the heavy chair about with one hand, revealing a long, ragged tear. 'No blood at the back.' He dropped the chair, pulled the edges of the material apart, and invited us to peer within.

'The blood poured out of his chest, butcher,' Withypoll retorted. 'Not his back.'

'Aye,' Dowling nodded. 'But when a blade cuts through a piece of meat it carries the blood with it. Unless the blade is swung fast and with great force.'

'I have never heard of a man stabbing another man to death *slowly*,' said Withypoll.

'Indeed,' Dowling conceded. 'But by the time a sword reaches a man's spine it runs slow, unless the man that plunged it is uncommonly strong.'

'Then James Josselin is uncommonly strong,' said Withypoll.

Dowling grunted. 'Who was here at the time?'

Withypoll smiled. 'The Duke of York? Prince Rupert? The Duchess of Portsmouth?'

'All of them?'

'I don't know.' Withypoll drifted out towards the gallery, suddenly bored. 'Nor will I enquire. We're here because Arlington told me to bring you here. He wanted you to see the scene of the killing so you might set about your task with fire in your bellies. He didn't give you permission to interview the King's court. Berkshire is dead and Josselin is the murderer.'

We stood at the heart of the King's domain, not fifty paces from the King's own quarters, his bedchamber, bathroom and laboratory. We loitered like flies that tiptoed across the sticky strands of some intricate web without being snared. Were we wise, we should count our fortune fast, afore spreading our tiny wings and seeking safe passage before the spider arrived.

41

'I would like to see his corpse,' said Dowling.

Withypoll laughed. 'Berkshire's body lies in state. You think his family will tolerate your intrusions? A butcher and a . . .' He stared at me with black eyes.

I ran my fingers across the woven coat of arms at the head of the chair, bloodied, ruined. Pomp, majesty and circumstance, all signifying nothing. Few cared who killed Berkshire, I realised, only that someone be executed for the deed.

Withypoll removed his beaver hat and rubbed his fingers through damp yellow hair. He bent over and picked up Josselin's sword. 'You have seen the blood; you have seen the weapon. Even you dull fools must see what happened here.' He replaced the sword in the cupboard. 'Now we leave. I will not waste any more time on you two.'

He clicked his fingers and waved his arm, bidding us to trot out the door like King Spaniels.

We followed him back along the Stone Gallery out towards Pebble Court, past a long file of stiff, silent statues contorted in classical pose upon the matted floor. Behind the doors upon our left resided the King's most favourite courtiers, each enjoying a view out onto the Privy Garden. Strange the King allowed himself to be so constantly the subject of others' attentions. He held regular court in his bedroom, supposedly.

'Hurry up, Lytle.' Withypoll waited at the top of the new stone staircase. 'Afore someone wonders why I roam the palace with tradesmen.' He bustled us downstairs and out into the summer air.

'So, then.' He faced us, drawing himself straight and imperious, for the benefit of those others wandering the courtyard. 'You have witnessed the scene of Berkshire's execution and are suitably impressed.'

'I want to talk to Josselin's wife,' said Dowling.

Withypoll frowned. 'He doesn't have a wife.'

'Edward Josselin's wife, I mean.'

Withypoll blinked. 'How many times do I need to remind you that you have one sole purpose in this affair, and that is to fetch James Josselin out of Shyam?' He placed the fur hat back upon his head and twisted it slowly until content with the balance. 'Meet me at Bishopsgate, at six tomorrow morning,' he snapped, afore casting upon me one last poisonous stare. Then he was gone, long strides carrying him across the face of the Banqueting House back to King Street.

'I don't know why he looks at *me* like that,' I said, most offended. 'It was you provoked him.'

Dowling watched Withypoll disappear. 'Arlington put him in a black mood, not I. He didn't want to bring us here at all.'

'Aye, well I see little point of it myself,' I replied. 'We came to view a body and saw a chair.'

Dowling started walking slowly after Withypoll. 'Something is amiss. It's not possible to thrust a sword that deep into a man and yet leave no blood at the point of departure.'

'Berkshire had thick blood?'

Dowling shook his head. 'And how did Josselin escape? There are sentries in the Stone Gallery. Why didn't they stop him?'

Why, indeed.

He clicked his tongue against the roof of his mouth. 'Arlington thinks we are simpletons, which is good for us, but Withypoll does not. He will go back to Arlington now and tell him what we said. We should have acted as if we believed every word of it.'

'We should go and speak to Josselin's wife, anyway,' I said, feeling brave.

'Aye.' Dowling placed a hairy arm about my shoulder and squeezed me hard. 'While Withypoll trots back to his master.'

There was always God to protect us. Dowling slapped me across the top of the head when I started to hum a hymn, suspecting me of mockery. So I sang instead, until the strain I heard in my own voice left me too sad to continue. I felt trapped. If we went with Withypoll we faced probable death, but if we refused, our death was certain.

Chapter Fiue

So it warily adviseth them of great care and provision for their personal safeties in all troublesome engagements.

Later that day we walked the cobbled streets beneath a dying, orange sun. London blossomed like a spring day after a harsh winter. No red crosses upon the doors, no death-carts, the church bells quiet. Yet the streets emptied fast once darkness descended, for the night welcomed poisonous airs, and many feared the plague still lingered.

The Josselins lived in a large house close to Aldgate. We decided I would enter alone, so not to frighten the widow. I was shorter than Dowling and more presentable. He waited outside.

The house stood three-and-a-half storeys high, a veritable castle. The front windows projected over the street in a great curve, framed in oak panels. Each storey leant out a little further than the one below, pressing forward, obliging the passer-by to acknowledge the proud lines of heraldic coats of arms. Up and down each side of the house paraded a line of grotesque gargoyles with what looked like women's breasts; a facade befitting the importance of the man inside. Not important enough to dissuade Arlington from killing him.

My heart pounded in time with my fist as I knocked upon the oaken doors standing almost twice my height. Dowling watched from across the street, arms folded.

A slim woman opened the door, head bowed. She carried a bundle of black knitting wool in her right hand. We only disposed of the body a few hours ago. Had news travelled so fast? I caught my breath and tried to swallow my anxiety.

She wore the rough, plain clothes of a servant and stood upon the threshold staring resolutely at my feet. When she didn't look up or otherwise acknowledge my presence, I cleared my tight throat and told her I worked for the King, whereupon she lifted her head, revealing a pale face with large, strange-shaped freckles. She mumbled something and faced back into the house. Though she was no more than twenty years old, she walked with the slow solemnity of an old woman.

She led me past a narrow wooden staircase, twisting up into the eaves of the great house, and into a long room, wood-panelled from floor to ceiling with a great fireplace at the far end. The white plaster ceiling was carved with yet more coats of arms. Left on my own, I paid particular attention to a painting hung between two windows on the far wall. A bowl of fruit, a loaf of bread, a cup of wine and a plate of grapes.

A husky voice sounded from behind. 'Good afternoon.' A handsome lady of mature years, grey hair drawn into a bun at the crown of her head. She wore a plain, woollen dress and clutched her hands before her. Despite the laugh lines about her eyes and mouth, she regarded me warily, lips held tight. Behind her trailed a younger woman, wearing a turquoise bodice and full-flowing skirt, slightly worn and colours bleached, dragging noisily upon the floor. She hovered, pale-faced and anxious, the skin about her eyes twitching gently. The room smelt damp.

I bowed. 'Good morning, Mrs Josselin. My name is Harry Lytle. Thank you for receiving me.' I pointed to the food and drink, unable to contain my curiosity. 'This painting. Is it Dutch?'

She attempted a smile. 'Do you like paintings, Mr Lytle?'

'I like what I like,' I replied, glad to have something to talk about. 'This one is good.' I narrowed my eyes and peered at the signature. 'Is it an original?'

'Yes,' she replied. 'Painted by a young artist. Abraham Mignon.'

'Mignon,' I repeated, admiringly, before turning to face her. 'Where did you get it?'

'My husband. He bought it from a dealer in the City.' A line appeared across her forehead. Beads of sweat formed upon the top lip of her younger companion. I hadn't made a good start. I looked about the room, eager for something else trivial to discuss.

'What do you want, Mr Lytle?' she asked.

'Where is your son?' I asked frankly, unable to think what else to say.

I noticed the quick widening of the eyes and dropping of her jaw, a momentary expression of panic she rapidly concealed. The young woman clutched at a fragment of lacy cloth.

'I don't know where he is,' Mrs Josselin replied, terse. 'He is missing these last four days. My husband told me I should not worry.'

The husband she would not see again. I tried to blank the image of his dead body from my mind. I felt my head jerk and my body shiver.

Mrs Josselin tried to catch my eye. 'Are you well, Mr Lytle?'

'Well enough, Mrs Josselin,' I replied. Healthier than her husband. I determined not to allow my heart to thaw until after I left. 'Did you know James is in trouble?'

'No,' she breathed.

I stared into her beautiful, dark-blue eyes, and noticed the few strands of fair hair that remained amongst the grey. 'I can help your son, Mrs Josselin,' I said. 'If you permit me.'

She recoiled, mouth curling. 'Why should he need your help?'

'You must tell me about him, what he does, who he spends time with.'

Her expression remained stoic.

'Mrs Josselin, if you do not permit me, he will likely be tried for murder.'

The young woman gasped, clasping her hands to her mouth, bending forwards like she had a bellyache.

'Are you his sister?' I asked.

'Eliza is his betrothed,' Mrs Josselin replied, as if I said something disgusting.

Betrothed to a man who fled into the heart of pestilence. Her eyes shone wet and she bit on a thick, red lip with moon-white teeth.

'How long are you engaged?' I asked.

'Almost a year,' Eliza replied, eyes searching mine. Long, black hair hung dishevelled about her pale, oval face. 'You speak of murder.' She covered her mouth with one hand as soon as the words escaped. New tears appeared upon her cheeks.

'Lord Arlington says he killed the Earl of Berkshire,' I answered.

'Nonsense,' Mrs Josselin exclaimed. 'Charles Howard is James's best friend. I don't believe you.'

The younger woman did though. Her face crumpled into a scarlet mess.

Mrs Josselin leant forwards, smile sculpted on her face. 'My son serves Lord Arlington. Why should his lordship say such a thing?'

Because he was a black-hearted demon. 'Arlington says he sabotaged a peace mission, besides,' I revealed. 'Which accusation by itself is serious.' Serious enough to see him executed.

Mrs Josselin stamped her foot upon the wooden floor. 'My son is neither a murderer nor a traitor. The idea is absurd. What evidence do you bring with you to support such an accusation?'

'None at all.' I spread my hands. 'For it is not my accusation. You may ask Lord Arlington yourself, though I would not advise it.'

The young woman buried her head in her hands and began to wail, a mournful sound that spoke of fractured anguish. Discouraging besides, for I fancied she might know more of his movements than the mother. Mrs Josselin stood erect, eyes darting side to side. Embarrassed, I realised, to be presented with such grave news by one so common.

'Would that my husband were here,' she said, voice choking. 'He would tell you of this family's loyalty to King and country. He should *whip* you with it.' She quivered with angry indignation.

'He would be wasting his time,' I sighed. 'I have not challenged his loyalty, nor yours, nor your son's.' I held up my hand as her brow fell over her eyes. 'For he is accused. He has fled into Essex and will be pursued. If he is innocent then there is foul trickery at play, which I am not a part of.'

Mrs Josselin stepped towards me, eyes narrowed. 'Why else would you be here?' she demanded, while her young companion continued to bawl. 'Perhaps to prise stories from us you can use against him.'

I sat down heavily upon a well-worn chair with frayed upholstery. She descended upon me like a great spider and thrust her beautiful, old face into mine. It was like donning a pair of spectacles, the delicate lines that ridged her scrubbed skin loomed sharply into focus.

She cocked her head like she intended to peck out my eyes. 'My husband is missing, not only my son,' she said, slowly. 'What do you know of that?'

I knew my face betrayed my unease. 'I heard he was arrested,' I admitted, 'by those keen to prove your son's guilt. Think on it, Mrs Josselin. If your son is innocent, then someone else killed Berkshire and accuses him of treachery. That person will do everything they can to ensure the lie is not discovered.'

'Who arrested him?'

'Arlington.'

'Do you work for Lord Arlington?' she asked, eyes sharp and piercing.

'Yes,' I nodded. 'He commands this investigation.'

'You said you wanted to help us,' she said. 'Yet you work for Lord Arlington and I know Arlington for what he is. If he has decided my son is guilty, it is because it is politic to do so. He wastes no energy in pursuit of the truth.'

'You know him better than I, then,' I answered, dry-mouthed.

'Say you,' she snapped. 'Come now, Eliza.' She withdrew, watching me like she would a snake.

Eliza stared at me with red-rimmed eyes sunk painfully within a snotty face, more like a young girl than a full-grown woman. As she opened her mouth I watched a strand of saliva stretch from top lip to bottom. I could not imagine James Josselin confiding anything of

50

importance to such an innocent. Mrs Josselin took her arm and pulled her away.

'I am leaving tomorrow, Mrs Josselin,' I told her calmly. 'If you tell me nothing, then I cannot help you, and I can assure you no one else will, unless you count the King a fond acquaintance.'

She stopped her passage out of the room. 'What would you have me tell you, Mr Lytle? What evidence do you think I might offer you? You, who come here to help, you who asks me questions about the Dutch paintings on our walls.'

'Anything to disprove his guilt,' I replied, standing. 'You said Berkshire was his friend.'

'I said his *best* friend, Mr Lytle.' Mrs Josselin stabbed her long thin finger into my chest. 'A friendship you could never understand. They are two fine men.'

'Aye,' I replied, angered by the contempt with which she smothered me. 'So fine he fled. I have never met your fine son, nor the Earl of Berkshire, yet I must risk my life to find him, else Arlington will have me killed.' I felt my face flush.

Mrs Josselin recoiled as if I'd slapped her, anger draining from her leathery face, replaced with abject fear. 'You say my son sabotaged a peace accord. My son was determined England should make peace with the Dutch. Two great Protestant nations,' she said. 'I don't understand.'

'No.' I bowed my head. 'Well, neither do I. Yet I would agree with your summation of Arlington's character. I don't know who else will help your son if not us.'

Her lips pursed again. 'Us?'

'There are two of us.' I decided to tell her all. 'Myself and David Dowling. He is a butcher. We both work for Lord Arlington, neither of us willingly. We've seen what he is capable of.'

Eliza started weeping again, a whining noise with a life of its own, thin and ethereal.

'I don't know what I can tell you,' Mrs Josselin replied.

'Where he was four nights ago. What business he conducted on behalf of Arlington. Anything that proves he is not a traitor.'

'I don't know where he was four nights ago, for he stays often at the palace,' she answered. 'And I don't know what business he conducts for Lord Arlington, for he doesn't share royal secrets with his mother. What I will tell you is that this family has a proud history of loyalty to the King. Were the King to sit back and allow my son to be persecuted, then it would be a disgrace upon his crown.' Her body trembled with indignation. 'I was at the siege of Colchester in 1648, nearly twenty years ago. So was Edward, so was James. I will not tell you what indignities we suffered, but I will tell you one thing if you don't know it already.' She held up a trembling hand. 'My son was but nine years old in 1648, and yet he volunteered to carry a message out to the King's men, without my knowledge nor Edward's.' She pointed at my forehead. 'They captured him and tortured him, yet he told them nothing. A nine-year-old boy.'

A fine tale, I conceded, yet it held little relevance to current events. My face must have betrayed my disappointment, for she shot me a venomous glance of ripe disgust and turned away.

'Mr Lytle.' Eliza shot forward and dropped to her knees at my feet. 'You must bring him back to us. You must *promise* to do that.' She seized my right hand with both of hers and dug her nails into my skin.

'I promise to try,' I replied. 'Though I would gladly hear what else you might tell me of him, for I have never met him.'

'Stand up, Eliza,' Mrs Josselin scolded her.

'He is a brave man,' Eliza declared, gazing earnestly into my eyes. 'He is quite tall and very noble. He has long, dark hair and talks all the time about fighting for his King. He yearns only to kill Dutchmen, Frenchmen or Spaniards.' She pursed her lips, holding back the tears.

'Aye, then,' I answered, slipping my hand free and helping her to her feet. 'At least I will recognise him now.' A tall lunatic killing anyone who looks foreign.

'But your promise.' She snatched back my hand again. 'You must promise to bring him back, not merely to try.'

'Come, Eliza.' Mrs Josselin tugged gently at her sleeve. 'If he is a worthy man no promise is necessary. If he is not, his promise holds no value.'

The young betrothed allowed herself to be led from the room, still staring, seeking assurance desperately.

I was left alone, black-hearted and dejected. I could barely summon the energy to breathe, I felt so rotten. The young woman, so fearful she might not see her betrothed again. Likely she would not, and I knew it. Josselin's wife, so suspicious and angry. I glimpsed the desperation hidden behind that proud mask and hated myself for seeing it. Whatever vision she nurtured, it wasn't the one that appeared in my head; her husband lain sprawled, Arlington's strange blade protruding from his ribs.

Another woman entered the room, another knitter, though older than the last. A stout woman with a stiff white hat upon her head and a large, black wart nestled upon her cheek. She knitted as she walked, shuffling forwards, head down.

'What are you knitting?' I asked.

'A pall,' she smiled, placid.

A pall? Did she mean a robe, a cloak, or a coffin shroud? I thought to enquire further, but couldn't find the words. A long cold finger crept slowly up my spine. I exclaimed aloud, which sudden noise caused the old woman to jump in the air. I apologised and followed her back to the street.

Dowling emerged from the shadows, shoulders hunched. 'What did you discover?'

'Arlington just killed one of the King's most loyal subjects,' I replied, glum, 'and James Josselin is betrothed to a child.'

It was all madness.

I thought of Eliza and Jane. 'I will tell *my* betrothed everything before we leave,' I determined.

Dowling frowned, puzzled. 'Your betrothed?'

'My housemaid,' I corrected myself. 'Come on. I have things to do before we must leave.'

Chapter Six

It points out elderly men, or one man old.

I leant my shoulder against the shop door and forced it open. A cloud of dust billowed out onto the street, dry and choking. The windows hadn't been cleaned for many years, a thick layer of grease and dirt holding the light at bay. The air smelt green, like a long-buried coffin. An angular figure lurked in the far corner, head ducked, face invisible in the gloom.

'Culpepper?' I called, stepping into the shop. Shelves covered the left wall, tall chests with tiny drawers the other wall. A large mortar and pestle sat upon the desk behind which Culpepper quietly dozed, next to a pile of dirty pots and pans.

I watched him sleeping, a frayed, old wig slipped forward upon his brow so I couldn't see his eyes. I took the opportunity to wander the shop, imagining for a few sweet moments it was mine already, relishing the chance to inspect the place unmolested. Every other time I visited,

Culpepper hovered at my elbow, fussing like an old goose, forbidding me to touch any of the jars and implements. Now I knew why, for several of the jars were cracked and broken, their contents mouldy and shrivelled.

His body rumbled as he snored. Culpepper was past seventy, and newly prone to inopportune remarks since the deaths of his aged wife and ill-tempered son. I wondered if he was capable of passing on his knowledge to me.

His lower lip hung loose from the rest of his mouth, revealing dark, shrivelled gums. Just two teeth protruded from his lower jaw, yellowed and worn. He sat with legs akimbo, tight belly sunk low into his groin. A pungent odour escaped from his clothes. He hadn't washed in a long time.

Sad how the spirit of a man disappeared beneath a layer of rotting flesh. Culpepper established this shop more than forty years ago, preparing lozenges and pastes from local-grown herbs and treating the poor for free. He condemned his fellow physicians for their greed, incurring the wrath of the Society of Apothecaries because he insisted on selling cheap herbal remedies instead of their more expensive concoctions. Yet he would not be cowed, and so was frequently imprisoned, confined in conditions that slowly ate at his health and good mind. Once famous, now forgotten, a relic in his own museum.

I opened one of the tiny drawers in the great chest. Behind me Culpepper snorted like an old horse and embarked on a long coughing fit. In the drawer lay a dead cockroach on its back.

'Lytle,' Culpepper growled. 'What are you doing here? Today is Friday.'

I closed the drawer and turned to face him. He peered at me

through rheumy eyes, breathing hoarse. His wig perched crooked upon his old head.

'I have to postpone our arrangement,' I said. 'I must go away for a few days.'

'Go away?' Culpepper jerked his wig straight. 'Are you reneging on your promise?'

'No.' I assured him. 'Lord Arlington has sent me east, on a mission.'

Culpepper clicked his tongue. 'I thought you turned your back on that business. Perhaps I should find another who would learn my trade.'

'I *have* turned my back,' I protested. 'But Arlington is a difficult man to turn your back upon. He has set us one more task and I am not free to refuse.'

'Hah!' Culpepper scowled. 'How many times will he set you one more task you cannot refuse? Either you wish to become an apothecary or you do not.'

'I am determined,' I said. 'Have we not signed a contract? I will honour that contract.'

'If you live.' Culpepper's eyes narrowed. 'They still have plague in Essex, do they not?'

'Aye.' I nodded. 'Which is why Arlington sends us. We have to fetch a man from Colchester.'

Culpepper stayed sat upon his big chair, one brow raised, the other lowered, regarding me with big bleary eyes, lower lip protruding like he prepared to break wind. 'Half of Colchester is dead, and the Pest shows no sign of abating.' He wiped his nose on his sleeve. 'Lord Arlington doesn't like you.'

'No,' I agreed.

Culpepper dug a finger in his ear. 'I give you a week, else our agreement is void. I have two more offers for this business and will not be cheated. I don't expect to live much longer.' He struggled to his feet. 'Though longer than you, perhaps.'

'Thank you, Nicholas.' I bowed my head. 'Rest assured. I am determined to make a success of this business.'

'Good luck,' he muttered. 'The road to Colchester is well guarded.' He cleared his throat and steadied himself. 'Wait a moment.'

He supported himself on his desk with one hand and eyed the chest against the wall, breathing deep, preparing himself for the short walk from one side of the room to the other before shuffling off with great intent.

He grasped the tall cabinet as soon as it was in reach, pulling out a little drawer a couple of rows higher than the one that contained the dead insect. He extracted a packet the size of his fist and held it out for me to take.

I poked a finger into the mass of dried leaves, close-packed within. I pinched a few leaves between finger and thumb and stuck them up my nostril. 'What are they?'

He staggered back to his seat. 'They will protect you.'

Protect me from plague, I assumed, along with a hundred other concoctions peddled about the City, all of them useless.

'They say it's like sage,' he wheezed. 'It doesn't grow in Europe. I paid a lot of money.'

'How much do you want for it?' I asked, grudgingly.

He shook his head. 'A gift.'

'Thank you,' I replied, surprised. 'What do I do with it?'

'Smoke it.' He raised a wizened finger. 'In the morning and at night. Do that and maybe I will see you again.'

'Thank you.' For the thought, at least. I suppose he sought to protect his investment.

'Be mindful, Harry. The man who commits a sin worthy of death shall be put to death and hanged from a tree.' He regarded me with such utter seriousness I felt obliged to bow my head, as if the words made sense.

I edged backwards. 'Until next week.'

I turned and left my shop behind. Just for a week.

Chapter Seuen

Mankind, or the generality of men, shall suffer abundance
of sorrow and affliction.

Culpepper's leaves weighed heavy against my thigh. I had smoked
a pipe already that morning, a giddy experience that left my head
floating a few inches above my body. If I closed my eyes I could feel
Jane walking beside me in a white, shimmering dress. I opened them
again after I tripped over Dowling's foot and landed face first on the
cobbles. With my eyes open I felt extraordinary lonely. Shyam was
Hell, and I was afraid. Jane's voice sounded in my ear, tickling like a
fly.

I rubbed the dirt from my cheek. 'Jane was right. If Josselin fled all
the way to Shyam, what can we say to persuade him to return? That
all is forgiven and we promise safe passage?'

'He ran because he was afraid,' Dowling replied, marching across
the cobbles. 'He will not prove his innocence hiding in Shyam. By the

time we find him his temperament may have righted.'

'What do we know of his temperament?' I grumbled. 'His mother told us nothing, his betrothed told us less. I pray *someone* might tell us of the man.'

'God will watch over us,' said Dowling with customary simple-mindedness.

'Then may he strike down Withypoll with a thunderbolt,' I exclaimed.

'The Lord our God is righteous in all his works which he doeth.'

Righteous and vindictive it seemed to me, but I said nothing. If we were to negotiate this journey without losing our lives, we would need to be mindful as well as hopeful. I resolved to manage my fear as well I could, to ensure I didn't become distracted. Culpepper's leaves seemed to help.

Withypoll waited at Bishopsgate perched atop of a great, black mare, grinning like it was the best day of his life. Relieved, no doubt, we hadn't scuttled from the City in the middle of the night. The first glinting of sun shone red behind the back of his head, bathing us all in orange glow.

Two more horses stood soft shouldered, noses to the cobbles, one dark brown, the smaller one white. I prayed mine was sweet-tempered.

I recalled the day, two years ago, when soldiers fetched me to Tyburn in the back of a cart. How the terror spread from my belly to my fingers and toes as we neared Tyburn Hill. The cruel smirks upon the faces of the spectators who lined the streets, waiting for us to try and escape, ready to throw us back. Today Withypoll was the crowd and that twitchy-looking beast was the cart. I inhaled a deep breath and walked calm.

'Good morning, rogues,' Withypoll hailed us hearty. 'Why so

61

glum? Today we renew acquaintance with an old friend.' He laughed at his own joke while his horse snorted and rolled its eyes like it would trample us to death.

I slung my pack upon my steed's saddle, filled with all the bread and meat Jane had in the pantry and two gourds of fresh water. The horse looked up, only faintly interested, as I hauled myself upon its back and concentrated on sitting straight.

There were few folks around to watch us leave, just a thin procession of tradesmen braving the end of the night, scuttling through the shadows as if afraid of being seen. Out of London we saw no one at all, just the long road east stretching ahead, deserted and overgrown.

Birds sang from the forest and the undergrowth shifted occasionally in response to the sound of the horses' heavy hooves. I felt like *I* was Death, riding towards a place of hopelessness and misery, avoided by all that breathed.

Once the air warmed, I slung my jacket across the horse's broad shoulders, clinging with my thighs to its back, trying not to look down. Dowling rode alongside breathing heavier than his steed, resenting the presence of Withypoll behind.

We reached the Ilford turnpike mid morning. A dilapidated gate hung unsteady on a rotting timber framework, supported by a pile of rocks and stones. Three stools lined up in a row, all empty. Withypoll kicked the gate and it toppled over, leaving us open passage. So much for local diligence. All turnpikes were supposed to be manned with armed men. I had been counting on one of those armed men to take umbrage at Withypoll's arrogance and shoot him dead.

A hundred yards past the turnpike we came across a coach lain upon its side in a ditch. It looked like it rested here several days, the fabric across the canopy peeling and rotten.

Faint scrabbling noises sounded from within. We stopped our horses upon the other side of the road, Withypoll as curious as us. Dowling swung himself to the ground and approached.

A pale face emerged into the sunshine from out the coach window, blinking, followed by a long, thin body, unravelling itself awkwardly. Two smaller heads popped up and down, children watching their father's every move. His trousers were soiled and stained, shirt torn, jacket shrunk so small it barely reached his elbows. My heart groaned a mournful wail when I saw the familiar growth pushing through the skin of his neck. A bubo. This one was white, the most deadly kind, meaning he would certainly die. He stared, long face haggard, brow dripping. Not an old man, I realised with a jolt, just withered.

He stretched out a hand, trembling on spindly legs. Dowling stepped away as the man staggered towards him. The two little heads protruded farther now, necks stretched. Their father lowered his hand and made a sad noise, words I supposed, though I couldn't discern them. What he sought of us I couldn't tell, but Dowling dug into his pocket and pulled out some coins. Much good money would do him.

Before Dowling or I could move, Withypoll kicked his big horse forwards and brought his blade slashing down upon the infected man's neck. Blood arched in a great spray upon the road. The man shuffled in a tight circle, clutching at his throat, eyes wide, afore falling to his knees and then his side. The heads disappeared.

'Did you not see the children?' Dowling roared, grabbing at Withypoll's bridle. A long line of blood marked Dowling's shirt and trousers, from chest down to his knee.

'He would have died before sunset anyway,' Withypoll sneered. 'It eases your conscience to leave children in the company of a corpse-to-be, rather than a corpse? You won't be able to look away so easily where we're going.' He wiped the blade of his sword against his saddle. 'Get back on your horse.'

Dowling turned his back and strode deliberately to the coach. He climbed up onto its side and peered down into the box below before jerking up straight with his hands to his mouth, almost losing his balance. He crouched frozen a moment, before slithering back to the ground, breathing deeply, face flushed.

'What will you do now, butcher?' Withypoll laughed. 'Cure them with a touch of your finger?'

Dowling ignored him. He rummaged in his saddle and withdrew a round pie and full gourd. He returned to the coach, climbed up again on its side and held out the food. Children's hands reached up, took the provisions and disappeared. Dowling took one last look at what he saw below, grey-faced and stiff-shouldered, then returned to his mount.

'It's a hot day, butcher.' Withypoll gesticulated at the sky. 'May you drink from the trough like the horses, for you'll have no water of mine.'

The dead man lay still upon the floor, flies crawling over the bleeding gash.

'We cannot leave him here,' I said.

'Touch that body and I will slice off your hand,' Withypoll barked, a cruel smile evaporated from his long, brutal face. 'We have wasted enough time.'

Dowling's heavy-lidded expression betrayed an inner torment. He glanced at the body but left it alone. He remounted and kicked his horse forwards. I waited for Withypoll to pull away ahead of us, far enough in front that I could talk to Dowling unheard. I drew up alongside and cast him what was intended to be an inquisitive gaze.

'The mother's been dead a few days,' he muttered. 'One of the children is dead, the other two infected.'

Which few words created in my mind a vision so terrible I reined back, fearing he might share more. Withypoll's back bobbed up and down, body moving easily with his steed, oblivious to the smell of death that followed us in long plume. How confident he was, mindless of the possibility we might knife him from behind. Well he knew us.

Ahead squatted a low stone bridge, beyond it the sound of chains clinking. A black silhouette appeared on the bridge, advancing slowly in our direction, shuffling in rhythm with the rattle of chains. As it approached I saw it was a man, and behind him two more men, two women, and a boy. A tall fellow wearing a brown leather coat followed, poking them periodically with a long stick. A long sword at his belt dragged in the dirt.

The man at the front stared to the ground, round-shouldered and hopeless, an empty hollowness that spoke of despair. His shirt hung in tatters about his chest, barely covering his bony ribs. Though it was sunny, a fresh breeze kept the air cool, yet they all dripped sweat like they walked for hours.

'What is going on?' Dowling called.

The man in the leather coat peered up. 'What business is it of yours? You shouldn't be here.'

'King's men,' Withypoll replied, leaning forwards on the horn of his saddle. 'Answer the question.'

'They come from Chelmsford,' the man answered, jabbing one of the women viciously in the back of the thigh. She stumbled a moment, but recovered. 'They tried to cross the turnpike. When we refused them passage they said they would walk through the fields at night, so we arrested them, for at least one has plague, and if one has plague, likely they all do.'

'Where are you taking them?' Dowling demanded.

'To Cutler's barn,' the warden replied. 'We'll lock them up for forty days, and if they still live when we open the door, they may proceed on their way.'

'You'll feed them?' growled Dowling.

'They'll get food and water,' the man replied. 'For as long as they need it.'

'Stop a moment.' I jumped from the back of my horse. 'I want to talk to them.'

The man with the stick eyed me suspiciously, but struck the boy on his ankles, forcing him to stop.

I tried to catch the eye of any one of them, but they all gazed at their feet. 'When did you leave Chelmsford?' I asked, keeping my distance.

None responded.

'Did you come across a fellow travelling in the opposite direction?' I asked. 'A tall fellow, James Josselin.'

One of the women raised her head. Her eyes shined, yet failed to focus. The bones in her face stuck out sharp and her cheeks were gaunt. If she didn't die of plague, likely she would die of hunger.

I approached her closer. 'You saw Josselin?'

She nodded quickly. 'Before Witham,' she whispered. 'He spoke to us. We were so happy when he told us who he was.'

'You know him?' I asked.

'Of course,' she replied, voice trembling. 'Every man knows James

66

Josselin. That he returns to Colchester is a great sign, a miracle.'

'How was he?'

'A handsome man,' she said.

'Was he ill?'

She shook her head. 'He rode a black horse, tall and proud, like the gentleman he is. He gave us his food and shared kind words.'

'And he headed for Colchester?'

She nodded again. 'As I said.'

'What else do you know of him?'

She looked to the man with the stick, bewildered. 'He is James Josselin,' she said. 'A great man.' She bowed her head as if afraid of being struck.

'In what state is Colchester?' asked Dowling, changing the subject, much to my frustration.

'Half the town is dead, the other half waits,' she replied in dull monotone.

Though I imagined nothing less, still my heart stiffened inside my chest.

'We must go,' said the man with the stick, gruff.

Withypoll snorted. 'Locking them in a barn will not deter anyone,' he said. 'You should shoot them through the head and string them from gibbets.'

The six in chains appeared not to hear his cruel words, but I yearned to punish him. Instead we watched the procession renew its miserable passage.

Over the bridge more people stopped to watch, dull-faced and laggardly, like their heads slept atop their walking bodies. All was silent, as if the villagers swore an oath never to speak. Withypoll rode oblivious, staring with undisguised contempt. I felt uneasy and kicked my horse, but it refused to respond, maintaining the same pace as Withypoll's mount.

A wild-eyed fellow stepped in front of us, waving a musket. 'Who are you?' he shouted. 'You cannot pass through here. Go back the way you came.'

Two more men emerged from the gathering, both carrying thick staves.

'We have credentials,' Withypoll replied, staring down his nose. 'Get out of our way, else suffer the consequences.'

The wild-eyed fellow stayed his ground, staring expressionlessly. Only his lips moved, twitching in spasm. Withypoll snorted, then spurred his horse straight at him, the great, ugly steed sending the wild fellow sprawling to the dirt. I wondered if he died, but he rolled over, groaning. Withypoll sneered just afore one of the other men hit him on the back of the head with a long stick. He fell sideways off his horse, crashing onto the road and landing on one shoulder. Blood trickled into the dirt from a gash on the back of his head and he didn't move. God spake, I thought, the hairs on my neck prickling with excitement. Withypoll's assailants stood around him in a circle, sticks raised above their heads, madness in their eyes. I held my breath. If he wasn't dead, then surely they would finish him.

'What is going on?' a voice called.

A smart fellow marched towards us, clean-shaven chin perched high upon a stiff, white collar, hair smeared with some kind of oil to keep his hair straight. He spoke with rounded vowels and carried one arm held out in front of him parallel to the ground, hand hanging limp. 'You men. Step aside.'

His head jerked like a rooster, twitching at every movement, like he feared being assaulted. The men with sticks lowered them to the ground, shoulders softening, and the moment was gone.

'Who are you?' the strange man asked, standing over Withypoll, but looking to me and Dowling. 'What have you done?'

Withypoll groaned. I stepped sideways just as his black eyes settled upon mine. He stared with burning hatred as if it was me that struck him and breathed hard as he struggled to his feet, clutching his left shoulder with his right hand.

'We are on King's business,' I answered, afraid what Withypoll might do. 'We are on our way to Colchester. We have papers.'

'As I told these men,' Withypoll crouched, teeth bared. 'Before they struck me down.'

The man with oily hair turned to Withypoll's assailants, pointing his arm at them. 'Why did you strike him?'

'He tried to kill us with his horse,' the wild-eyed fellow snarled. He and Withypoll eyed each other like dogs.

'Take the papers from my jacket, Lytle,' Withypoll commanded. I tried to avoid his eye as I fumbled in his coat. I could feel his heart beating inside his shirt, pounding hard and fast against his ribs as if it would break out. He grimaced, inspecting his shoulder. 'To strike a King's agent is treason, and the punishment for treason is death.' He looked up at the man whose intervention saved his life. 'What will you do?'

'Ah!' The man's finger began to twitch and draw circles in the air. 'I am the financier, you see. It is my job to organise things.'

'The turnpike is broken and no one guards it,' said Withypoll. His face was white, like a dead man risen.

'I manage the money,' the fellow protested. 'I am the accountant. It is the constable's job to manage the turnpikes.'

Withypoll scanned the small gathering that watched from a distance. 'And where is he?'

The accountant straightened his jacket and raised his chin, watching a rivulet of blood trickle down Withypoll's cheek and drip onto his collar. 'He died last week and no one has replaced him. Let me take you to my house and mend that wound.'

Withypoll eyed the three men with staves as if contemplating their immediate execution, but instead allowed himself to be led away by the accountant who dared hold him by the arm.

I lingered a moment, asking the crowd who remained if any knew Josselin, but they dispersed like leaves in the breeze, and soon we stood alone as the villagers withdrew again into their shells.

God teased us.

Chapter Eight

It prenotes much juggling and under-hand dealing in all manner of Negotiations.

A fire blazed inside the accountant's house. The acrid smell of tar and rosin pervaded every inch of the immaculate room. The accountant waved an arm, eyeing our muddy shoes anxiously. 'Sit down, gentlemen, please.'

Withypoll threw his jacket to the floor and headed for the biggest chair, next to the fire. 'Your wife is diligent,' he said. 'I have never seen such a tidy house.' He poked at three tiny figurines lined up in a perfect row on the mantle above the fireplace.

'I have no wife,' the accountant replied, picking up the jacket and moving the figurines to precisely where they had been before. 'It is I who like things to be in order. Sit on the chair please and I will wash your head.'

Withypoll tried to lift his left shoulder, wincing in pain. 'I will see those fellows hang,' he said, as the accountant approached with a bowl of honey and two white linen cloths.

'I cannot excuse their behaviour,' the accountant replied. 'Bend your head forwards please, sir, so I might see the wound.'

With one of the cloths the accountant attempted to wipe the dirt from the gash. He dabbed and patted, exposing a two-inch cut, deep and angry, with purple edges. Withypoll said nothing as he worked, made not a sound. Once the accountant was satisfied, he took a spoonful of honey, and let it drip from one edge of the wound to the other. Then he lay the second cloth across the top of the sticky mess.

'Is that it?' asked Dowling, watching as the accountant tried to rub a small patch of honey from his fingers.

'An ancient remedy,' the accountant replied. '*Vis medicatrix naturae.*' He picked up the honey bowl gingerly, with just four fingers, and took it back to the kitchen. When he returned he puffed out his chest and smiled.

'You are the first happy man I have seen this day,' said Withypoll.

'Happy?' The accountant blinked. 'How could a man be happy? Yet I do of my best, for the Lord God watches, and I believe he hath sent me here for such an occasion.' He stepped to a desk stood beneath the main window, upon which rested a thick ledger.

He tapped the cover of the book with a forefinger. 'I keep a record of every man and woman in this town, every child. Through good planning and expert organisation we have raised sufficient sums to provide everyone with adequate provision, including those we hold at Cutler's barn. Everyone pays his share of tax, and we have raised contributions from the towns about that are not so afflicted. We will survive this pestilence, even should it destroy every living soul within our boundaries.'

Withypoll laughed out loud.

'What of the dead and the dying?' asked Dowling.

The accountant frowned. 'The groans of the sick are a distraction, but I persevere.'

Withypoll grinned broadly and Dowling shook his big head.

'We are searching for James Josselin,' I changed the subject. 'We have a message for him from the King. Has he passed this way?'

The accountant's bright face registered strange joy, like he experienced a holy vision. 'Indeed he has, though he didn't stop.'

'What do you know of him?' I asked.

'He is a great man,' the accountant replied. 'You know what he did at Colchester?'

'We heard something of it,' I answered doubtfully. 'It was a long time ago.'

The accountant rubbed his hands and filled his lungs. 'Long ago, aye, but to understand the man, you must understand the child. Josselin's childhood defines him.'

Withypoll rubbed his palm upon the arm of the chair. 'I have little appetite for detail. Make this a short history.'

The accountant froze, enthusiasm pricked, but I made encouraging noises and his hands began to move again. 'Then I will assume you are familiar with the history of the Siege of Colchester. What you may not have heard, for the story was suppressed, are the lengths to which General Fairfax went to try to persuade the Royalists to surrender. Every man knows they persevered for three months before they starved. But the full story of the barbarity has never properly been told.'

Withypoll fidgeted. 'Tell it quick.'

The accountant turned to me, in search of a more appreciative audience. 'Before the siege was over Fairfax killed and tortured prisoners. He cut off their hands and fingers to obtain confessions, and distributed their rings to his men.' He paused for effect. 'He broke into the house of Sir John Lucas, whose house lay outside the city wall, and plundered the family vault, smashing coffins and scattering bones. His soldiers tore hair from the corpses of women and wore it in their hats as trophies, including the hair of Sir John's poor dead wife.'

He paused again, but I offered him no encouragement, for I had heard this tale before and loathed it.

The accountant shook his head, as if in sadness. 'The citizens of Colchester were not even Royalist, most of them. Yet when the Royalists invited the women to leave, Fairfax stripped them of their clothes and chased them back to the closed gates, where his men brutalised them.' He shook his head again, though I saw no tears. 'Then he starved us. First we ate the horses' fodder, then the thatch from the houses. When that ran out we ate the horses. When we ate all the horses we ate the cats and the dogs.'

'You were there?' I asked.

'Not in body,' he replied. 'Though yes, in spirit, for I am a loyal subject of this nation, and several of the villagers *were* there. What Fairfax did to the people of Colchester, Cromwell inflicted upon us all.'

God save us. 'All of this is well known.' I swallowed my irritation. 'What of Josselin?'

The accountant frowned. 'You cannot hope to understand Josselin's bravery without appreciating Fairfax's barbarity. Norwich needed reinforcement quickly if he was to survive Fairfax's siege. So he determined to send a message to Marmaduke Langdale. But Fairfax guarded every exit, and lit up the walls at night so none could escape. James Josselin went to the Moot Hall, evaded the guard, and ran up to Norwich to offer his services.'

Withypoll snorted. 'To a nine-year-old boy it would have seemed a great adventure.'

'A boy, true,' said the accountant. 'But everyone within the walls knew what Fairfax did. The sight of his men parading the bones of the dead would terrify a nine-year-old more than a full-grown man. Of course, Norwich sent him back to his family.'

Withypoll sighed. 'Then he leapt the wall of his own accord and set off to find Langdale I suppose?'

'Yes,' the accountant answered. 'He did.'

Withypoll curled his lip. 'So he tried to escape, they caught him, and Fairfax's men treated him rough.'

'They held his hand and burnt his fingers with matches.' The accountant's voice rose an octave. 'When he refused to talk they sliced off his nails. If you look at his hands you may still see the scars. He screamed and he cried, but he told them nothing of Norwich's plans.'

'Unlikely,' Withypoll muttered.

'I will not argue with *you*.' The accountant lifted his chin and wrinkled his nose. 'For I know James Josselin, and when you look in his eyes, you see it to be true. For not only may you see courage in those eyes, but also strangeness. He grew up a strange man, and I credit that to Fairfax.'

In my mind I saw a small boy, surrounded by brute soldiers. I saw one of them grasp his small hand and hold a flame to it, a cruel smile upon his lips. I felt my own hair prickle at the thought of it, and could scarce imagine how it must have appeared to a child. Like the worst vision of Hell, I supposed, a terrifying shattering of young assumptions.

Dowling bowed his head.

'He is headed for Colchester,' said the accountant. 'He didn't say so, but when he heard of the misery that envelops that place, I know he would be compelled to return.'

Withypoll sighed. 'How do you know that?'

'I know the man.' The accountant shrugged. 'He is drawn there by old ties. Why you follow him I cannot divine. You must have as much courage as he.'

His words chilled the air and I shivered. Josselin ventured deep into the abyss, and we pursued on his coat-tails.

'You said he is strange,' I said. 'In what way strange?'

The accountant put a finger to his lips. 'Ah! Distant, I would say. You look into his eyes and he stares at something a long way away, behind your back. He seems unaffected by the things that he sees.'

'What else do you know of him?'

The accountant pursed his lips and lowered his brow, in concentration. 'He has a good friend who lives in Chelmsford, a fellow called Thyme. If you wish to know the man, find Thyme.'

'How do you know?'

'Thyme is a friend of mine besides. He manages Chelmsford's accounts. He grew up with Josselin, in Colchester.'

Withypoll grunted. 'We must go.' He pulled himself up to his feet and again tested his shoulder.

'You should rest,' the accountant exclaimed, but his eyes gleamed bright.

'We will reach Chelmsford before nightfall,' Withypoll replied. 'You may tell those three men I will be bringing soldiers with me upon my return. If I have to build the gallows myself, then you shall be one of those that swings from it.'

The accountant looked to his ledger as if alarmed it was not budgeted for, but otherwise seemed unperturbed. I imagined he nurtured as little hope as us at the prospect of our safe return.

We retrieved our horses and resumed our journey, deeper into plague country. I tried to picture Josselin the man, to imagine what he looked like now, this strangeness in his eyes. A great man, everyone said. Hardly the murderer and traitor that Arlington described. I watched Withypoll stare ahead, and realised, reluctant, that Dowling and I were all that stood between Josselin and death. Why me? I was just an apothecary.

Chapter Nine

We conceive this present year will be fickly, and that the Pestilence,
or some such like raging Infirmity will afflict the more remote parts
from London.

Withypoll rode well ahead, unconcerned it seemed whether we followed or not. He held the reins in his right hand and leant towards his left. The cloth upon his head stuck like a strange cap, the edges of it flapping about a green stain of honey, blood and pus. Yet he steered his horse in a straight line with no sign of flagging.

As the afternoon began to wane we reached a crossroads, a bleak piece of moorland betwixt the forests. Each road stretched straight over the horizon, barren and deserted. A man stood up as we neared, an old soldier with tatty unbuttoned jacket, hair grown wild about a naked crown. Three bottles nestled in the yellow grass, one upside down, another unstoppered.

He threw his arms up to the sides. 'Which way will ye go?'

'Chelmsford,' replied Withypoll, eyes half lidded.

The old soldier pointed left and right. 'Waltham and Billericay. I should advise you to take one or other of those roads, but not the road to Chelmsford.' He stuck out a trembling hand. 'Whiche'er way you choose, you must pay me, for I am responsible for maintenance.'

Grass grew long as far as the eye could see. I feared Withypoll's wrath, but he slumped silent.

'We'll not pay you for something you've not done,' I replied.

The soldier reached for his sword, scrabbling at his waist afore he realised he had left the weapon on the ground, next to his drink.

'When did James Josselin pass through?' I asked. 'Tell us that and we might give you something.'

The drunken soldier rubbed his eyes and pushed the matted hair off his forehead. 'Two weeks ago.'

'How can you be so sure?' Dowling demanded, sceptical.

The soldier stuck out his chest. 'He gave me three pennies and I asked him what day it was. He told me it was the 11th August and I told him that was the day my son was born. Then he gave me a fourth penny.'

'Josselin left London on the 18th of August,' I said, recalling Arlington's account.

'I don't know when he left London,' the old soldier licked his lips. 'I only know when he came through here.'

'What else did he say to you?' I asked.

The soldier screwed up his nose. 'He asked me if I fought, and I said I didn't fight because all the battles were at sea. Said I'd *like* to fight. He told me to save meself for the French because to fight the Dutch was like to fight your own brother.'

'Which proves his treachery,' Withypoll growled. 'Now get out of our way.'

I threw the soldier a penny before he got himself killed.

He bowed. 'You need not demand it, sir. Pass with my blessing if it be your intent. I only pray you is well informed, and that you are all aware of the dangers you will find on this road.'

Withypoll kicked his horse forward. 'Praying is a waste of time.'

We reached the Moulsham turnpike two hours later. Like the Ilford turnpike it stood unmanned, gate unlatched. Someone had painted the gatepost bright red and tried to daub a large, red cross upon the road. It lay there undisturbed, untouched by horse's hoof.

I spoke my fears aloud. 'Does it mean the entire village is infected?'

'Someone paints a gatepost and you assume the worst,' said Withypoll. 'What dangers can there be to three men on horseback? We are not stopping.' Yet he steered his horse from the highway and waited for me to go first.

Half-timbered two-storey buildings lined either side of the high street, jetties protruding over the street, blocking the sun. Many doors bore the red cross, others were nailed closed. To keep the inhabitants within, or to deter thieves. I wondered which. An eerie silence engulfed us, broken only by the sound of hoof on dirt.

A figure emerged from a shadow twenty yards ahead. It stopped stock-still when it saw us, then ran across the street and disappeared. Like a rat afraid of being trapped.

Ahead loomed another turnpike, a well-fortified barricade built from planks and posts. Ten men barred passage, armed with swords, sticks and a musket. The gate was narrow, through which might barely pass a small cart. Beyond it a stone bridge, a precarious structure with broken walls arching over the River Can and into Chelmsford.

'We come in the name of the King,' called Withypoll, as we approached. 'Let us through.'

'We will not!' cried a stout fellow, shorter even than me. 'Why do you seek entry to our poor town? We are grievously afflicted. Go back from where you came.'

Withypoll clenched his fists. 'We are following a man who has travelled this way already. Since you granted *him* access, you will grant *us* access.'

'What man?'

'James Josselin.' Withypoll spat the words out like orange pips.

The man turned to his colleagues. They made appreciative noises and nodded their heads keenly. The stout fellow turned back to us. 'James Josselin is from these parts, but you are strangers. What is your business with James Josselin?'

Withypoll swept back his jacket to reveal his shining sword. 'Read our credentials and allow us passage, else I shall knock over your poor barricade and chase you into the river.'

The short man produced a musket and levelled it at Withypoll. 'You are a rude fellow,' he remarked, calmly. 'Show me your credentials.'

I prayed Withypoll would try and knock down the barricade, but instead he leant down, shoulder stiff, and handed over the King's seal.

The short fellow handed his gun to a colleague and took the letter in both hands afore rubbing a fingertip across the wax. 'This may be the King's seal,' he acknowledged, 'but it says nothing of travelling through Chelmsford, nor of James Josselin. It is not adequate authorisation.'

'What authorisation did Josselin produce?' demanded Withypoll.

'He requires no authorisation,' the short man replied. 'He lives in Colchester, and is on his way back to see family. He is a great man.'

Withypoll's cheeks reddened. 'His family lives in London. He is no more from Colchester than I.'

'And who *are* you, sir?' the man asked. 'Where do you come from?'

'I am a King's agent from Whitehall Palace,' Withypoll replied through clenched teeth. 'Now open the gate afore I run my sword through your belly.'

'I will summon the churchwarden,' the short man replied, sourcing a greater courage than I had access to. He slid sideways out of our view, replaced by a taller man with red hair about his head and face. The new fellow stared silently, lips permanently pursed like he sucked a lemon as a baby and ne'er forgot the taste.

Withypoll dismounted and approached the gate, ignoring the musket pointed at his chest. I held my breath as the sentry's finger twitched.

'Sirs,' called a new voice, belonging to a wizened old man with bent back. 'My name is Lewis Duttman, an overseer. I am told you seek sanction to pass through to Colchester.'

'We'll pass, whether you sanction it or not,' Withypoll replied. 'We are pursuing James Josselin in the name of the King.'

Duttman's eyes narrowed. 'Why do you pursue him?'

'We carry a message,' I called, tiring of Withypoll's foul mood. 'If it were not important, we would not have ventured this far. We must deliver the message, collect his reply, and return to London soonest.'

Duttman nodded thoughtfully, eyeing the soiled cloth that still clung to Withypoll's head. 'I will take you to George Jefferies. He is chief warden and knows Josselin better than any man.'

'Better than Thyme?'

Duttman said nothing.

'Your accountant, Thyme. Where may we find him?'

'I pray you don't seek to meddle in our affairs,' Duttman answered. 'I'll thank you to dismount, gentlemen, and we will walk through town.'

I did as I was told, puzzled, and waited for the red-haired man to open the padlock and unwind the chain. A narrow bridge led over the river. We trod carefully, for the wall fell into the water. The horses manoeuvred crumbling potholes, pulling at the reins and rolling their eyes.

Duttman led us past two cavernous inns; the Red Lion on the left side and the Cock on the right. Both vast establishments, three storeys high, long half-timbered buildings with stables to the rear. Rows of chimneys spewed forth black smoke all through the winter, as travellers betwixt London and Colchester sought accommodation for the evening. Tonight, though, the huge buildings loomed dark and empty. The sun sank low, back west towards London, and a chill bit at the air.

'Where shall we sleep?' Withypoll asked Duttman.

'You plan to stop here?' Duttman asked startled. 'Then I don't know. Mr Jefferies ordered all the inns closed.'

Withypoll grunted.

At the toll house, buildings crowded in from all sides, two narrow alleys leading onwards. Duttman chose the west passage, called Back Street, down the middle of which flowed an open stream, thick and filthy. The heat of the day warmed the foul brew, yielding a stink that rivalled Fleet Ditch. We passed the Unicorn, the Rose, the Three Arrows, the Bull, the Talbot and the Angel, middling-size inns all as empty as the Red Lion and the Cock. The Bull and the Talbot bore red crosses.

'No watchers?' I asked Duttman.

'This isn't London,' Duttman replied. 'We know who is sick and who isn't.' He nodded his head towards a small stone dome ahead of us. 'Any infected who try to leave their house, we lock them in the cage.'

I heard a low howl escape that same dome, thin and rasping.

'There is someone in there now?' I asked.

'Aye,' Duttman replied, avoiding my eye. 'He won't stay in his house no matter how many times we find him outside. He says he is clean of infection, yet every night he runs naked down to the river and jumps in.'

'He is in pain,' I protested.

'He is in anguish,' said Duttman. 'His wife and child died two weeks ago.'

We turned the corner into the town square. Ahead of us crouched a peculiar structure, a house with no walls, constructed around eight oak pillars. The pillars supported a tiled roof, the inside bathed in a deep, red light, strange shadows, a familiar, sick, sweet smell. My eyes accustomed to the dusky light and I recognised corpses lain upon the floor, more than a dozen of them.

Dowling regarded Duttman severely. 'That smell would drive any man to anguish. Were his wife and child laid here after they died?'

'We lay everyone here after they die, until nightfall,' Duttman replied.

The man in the cage groaned again, a mournful dirge, deep and sorrowful. 'His house is nearby,' I guessed.

'Just there.' Duttman pointed to a row of shops to the left of the south gate. 'How did you know?'

I recalled the smell of my house when Jane lay there sick, her aunt's dead body in the other bedroom. 'It is why he runs to the river. He smells their death, breathes it into his lungs. He runs to the river to cleanse himself.'

'You talk like a woman, Lytle,' said Withypoll, wrinkling his nose. He turned to Duttman. 'Where is Jefferies?'

Duttman pointed again, at a large house just past the cage. 'Just here. Likely he is at home.'

I caught a glimpse of the churchyard, through the south gate, of men digging a great hole. 'How many have died?' I asked.

'Sixty-two,' Duttman replied. 'More than thirty this last month alone. There must always be holes.'

Tears pricked my eyes. Jane and I left London before the plague fully penetrated the City wall. I didn't see the worst of it.

Duttman entered Jefferies' house without knocking and led us across the threshold into another stifling hot room. A round table filled the space, five chairs tucked neatly beneath it. A tall, lithe fellow sat in the corner, nestled snug within the depths of a deep, cushioned chair, feet up before a fire, over which burnt a chaffing dish of tar, frankincense and resin. The flames lit his face up orange, illuminating an expression I found difficult to read. His eyes were icy blue, and something happened to his lips. It was as if he smiled, but not quite. He wore his shirt open about his chest and lay with his shoes on, varnished boots of the finest leather in which the flames danced clearly. He didn't move from his seat, unperturbed by Withypoll's stern gaze of admonishment.

'I hear you are King's men,' said Jefferies. He gestured to the round table. 'Sit down.'

Dowling ran his hand over the new polished wood. 'An unusual table.'

'Aye,' said Jefferies, joining us. 'I had it built especially. When the plague first struck, all the wardens argued, bickering as to who should have the grandest title, the most money to spend. I am the chief constable, the others are all constables, and we sit in a circle.'

'You meet here, in your house?' said Dowling.

Jefferies lips changed form, though I couldn't tell what emotion played out on his face. 'I paid for the table.'

Withypoll sneered.

Jefferies watched Withypoll, without fear or concern. 'Chelmsford is such a town, gentlemen. Before the plague, all curried favour with Lord Mildmay. After he fled they sought to establish a new hierarchy. Meantime men are dying.'

'Duttman told us you know James Josselin,' I said, keen to find out all I could. 'You and a fellow called Thyme.'

Did Jefferies smile? 'If you are looking for Thyme, then you have found him already.'

'You?' I asked, confused.

He shook his head. 'The man whose voice you hear singing sweet songs from within the cage.'

I listened intent. 'Can I talk to him?'

Jefferies' lips changed again. 'You may talk to him, but he won't talk to you. He hasn't spoken a sensible word since his wife died.'

I cursed inwardly. 'Then what can *you* tell us of Josselin?'

He leant back and folded his arms. 'I know him quite well, and have always found him to be a sensible fellow. A bit quiet, perhaps. But he was strange last time he was here.'

'When was he here?' I asked.

'Ten days or so,' Jefferies replied. 'Ask Duttman. He has a better memory than I.'

'Why do you say he was strange?'

Jefferies steepled his fingers in front of his chin. 'Any man is strange that journeys to Colchester from London these days, but he was distracted. He knows Thyme well. They are friends. Yet when he learnt what had happened, he barely acknowledged it. Just raised a brow and shook his head. I'm not sure he understood.'

'Did he tell you why he travelled east?'

'In the name of his brother, who is dead,' he said.

'He has a brother?' Withypoll asked, eyes bright.

Jefferies shook his head. 'He has no brother.'

'That's all you can tell us?' I asked.

'All I can think of,' Jefferies replied. 'Now it gets dark, and you plan to sleep here the night.'

'Somewhere clean and untouched,' said Withypoll. 'As far away from this stink as we are able.'

Jefferies nodded. 'I will take you to the Feathers. It's furthest out of the town, close to Treen Bridge.'

Out on the street the last light faded. Candles speckled the sides of the road ahead of us, marking those houses where still folks lived. Three or four braziers burnt saltpetre and oil. It had been a long, hot day and my head throbbed like I was kicked by a cow.

Withypoll seized my elbow as Jefferies marched ahead. 'Josselin is a cowardly fellow, Lytle. He flees to Colchester for one reason, and one reason only.'

'What reason?' I asked, detesting how close he stood to me.

'Because he has nowhere else to go. And because it's plague country he assumes no one will follow. It is as clear as that. With no thought as to those he left behind.' He released my elbow and lay a hand on my sleeve. 'Remember that, Lytle,' he leered. 'For you have left your servant behind, have you not? Of whom you are very fond.'

He winked before striding after Jefferies, leaving me speechless and terrified all over again. Dowling laid a heavy arm across my shoulder and we trudged miserably through this black wasteland, my soul wriggling in frenzied anxiety of what lay in store for us in Shyam and what might lie in store for Jane back in London.

The evening air rang out with the sound of cruel laughter as Withypoll and Jefferies made friends; one devil with another. What chance of discovering an avenging angel out here in plague country?

I pulled my pipe out from my pocket and smoked more of Culpepper's leaves. Six days until I had to be back in London.

Chapter Ten

It's true, his Majesties Royal City of London hath in 1665 been sore afflicted with the Plague and Pestilence, and it may also much spread into several other parts of his Dominions.

Early next afternoon we reached the top of a rise and looked down upon Colchester, tucked into a long, winding bend of the River Colne. The castle perched atop a great mound of earth overshadowing all. It reminded me of London; tall stone walls dividing the town's densely housed heart from sprawling surrounds. More houses huddled together in a great spiral, from city wall down to Hythe harbour.

We lingered a while, seeking to orient ourselves with the misery below, but we were too far away to discern anything but peaceful urbanity, serene upon a lush, green plain beneath blue skies. Birds sang unnaturally loud from deep within the darkness of the green forest surrounding. It was said the swallows left London months afore the plague, sensing its arrival. Yet the birds that remained thrived oblivious. Why did the plague not affect them? Why did the birds not fall from the sky and land upon our heads?

Tension welled within me, urging me to turn my horse away from the horror I knew lurked beneath us. Dowling, though, seemed reconciled. He rode as a pilgrim, straight-backed, faithful, and free of doubt, or so he would have us believe. Withypoll sniffled and coughed, red-eyed and shivery. Perhaps an angel travelled with us, after all. He coughed through the night, and I determined to stay as far away from him as possible. He reckoned he couldn't contract the plague twice, but I knew of men who had.

'For who do you wait?' growled Withypoll, wiping his sleeve across his nose. His brow glistened and sweat soaked the front of his shirt. A new, green stain soiled the new, white cloth upon his head.

'Look by the abbey,' said Dowling, voice low.

The abbey stood closest to us, next to St Giles' church, both structures nestling within the same low-walled compound. The church lay in ruins. All that remained of the abbey was its great gatehouse, both buildings victims of Fairfax's siege. My eye swept across scattered rubble and broken walls, missing initially the square black hole, stark against the long grass. Next to it movement, what looked like two carts.

'A pit,' I realised.

'A pit,' Withypoll repeated with disdain. 'The town is riddled with plague; of course it has a pit. Now we must go.'

'Why go through it?' I asked. 'Why not go round?'

'The road to Shyam goes through the town,' Withypoll replied. 'There is no other way. Now gird your limp loins.'

Four drunk soldiers manned the turnpike on Malden Road, dressed in ragged red tunics and armed with guns. They slumped in a line, backs to the gate, legs spread-eagled. Two slept, snoring loudly, mouths wide open.

'Hoy!' one cried, without standing. 'Welcome to Colchester. *Ad multos et faustissimos annos.*' He raised a bottle and poured a long measure down his throat. 'Why would ye enter this cursed place?'

Withypoll leant down, sweat dripping from his chin. 'We are King's men. Open the gate.'

'The gate is already open,' the drunk soldier replied. 'I don't contest your right to pass, only your good reason.' He squinted at Withypoll's swollen, red nose. 'Are you devils?'

'Who commands you?' Withypoll demanded, jumping to the ground.

'Captain Scotschurch,' the man slurred.

Withypoll kicked him in the thigh. 'Scotschurch?'

'Aye.' The drunk soldier frowned and waved an arm towards his gun.

Withypoll seized the weapon and threw it onto the road. 'Where will we find this Captain Scotschurch?'

'On the ship.' The drunkard blinked slowly and belched. 'At Hythe. Go ye there and talk to him if you will.' He waved a hand and stared away into space, much offended it seemed.

Withypoll climbed back into his saddle and spurred his horse on through the gateway, allowing the beast to tread perilously close to the drunken soldier's hand. The abbey and its grounds stood away to our right, the pit hidden behind a short wall, overgrown with ivy. I nudged my own steed towards the left side of the street.

The road led us up to the town wall, to a row of houses built just a few steps aside from it. Head Gate was barred afront of us, thick oaken door firmly closed. Two soldiers slouched against the wall, one each side of it, both armed. A townsman watched us approach with a grim face and said something to one of the soldiers. They looked up, the townsman's face lined with thick, angry furrows, the soldiers' indifferent.

Every house at each corner of the crossroads bore a red painted cross. Some were brown, old and faded, others brighter. The plague resided here a while. One of the houses appeared abandoned, broken door hung crooked on its hinges. Open windows exposed a derelict interior.

Ignoring the townsman we headed east along the front of the wall, coming next to a narrow passage, dark and quiet. I peered into the gloom and made out another gate, smaller, also barred. 'This is like London,' I realised. 'They lock the gates to keep out the Pest.'

'Which be their business,' Withypoll grunted. 'We have no need to enter the town yet. The soldier said the Captain was at Hythe.'

Two men walked out from behind an arch. The gate closed afore we reached it.

'Hoy!' I cried, but they hurried away, disappearing into a clutch of houses opposite the wreckage of a priory. One enormous wall was all that remained, its edges chewed away as if by a giant rat.

I heard the wheels of a cart. At first I thought it to be a tradesman, but I turned to see a grey fellow sat huddled and hunched, clothes hanging from his slight frame like he shrunk. Two soldiers followed thirty paces behind, maintaining their distance. The carter's brown eyes conveyed a madness that pricked my soul and made it scream. He opened his small round mouth, revealing blue gums bereft of teeth. 'Bring out your dead,' his weak voice shrilled.

The cart trundled past. Three bodies lay in the back of it; two long and one short, each wrapped in a rough, brown shroud. They collected the dead during the day! I watched over my shoulder as the cart turned down a narrow alley and froze when the little fellow looked deep into the midst of my being. Like Death, sizing up my soul.

Withypoll noticed my discomfort and smiled his cruel grin afore again wiping his nose upon his shirt. 'This is no time to fear death, Lytle, nor is it the place. He will come for you soon enough.' Would that it *was* the plague he suffered from, I thought, immediately feeling guilty.

The road to Hythe wound down the hill, cutting a swathe through tight-massed suburbs. Bells pealed from a church somewhere ahead; signifying another death if the practice was the same as London. More red crosses marked the doors down either side. The air hung heavy with tar smoke, enveloping my eyes and making them itch, and burning the back of my throat.

From astride my horse, I could see down into front rooms, and up into bedrooms of the larger two-storeyed houses. Some were quiet and still, no sign of life. From others the familiar, pitiful sounds of pain and death; shrill screams and mournful dirge. One man perched upon a chair with his knees held close together, neither moving nor speaking as we passed, just staring straight ahead. Another man clutched an infant to his chest, too close for it to breathe, rivers of tears flowing either side of his streaming nose.

The bells rang louder as we neared the sharp spire of a church. A man with a shovel upon his shoulder strode across our path, ragged clothes caked in a thick coating of dried brown mud. He whistled a merry tune, an unnatural sound amidst such misery. Then at last we reached the harbour, a long stretch of dry bank looking out upon the river, teeming with soldiers, staggering about in circles or lay spread-eagled upon the ground. None of them looked like a captain.

Withypoll slipped from the back of his horse and approached a sober looking fellow with a fat, red sty in one eye. 'Where is Captain Scotschurch?'

The balding man turned his head so he could see us each in turn with his one good eye, before pointing to a caravel moored out in the middle of the river, sails lowered. 'He's on the *Enterprise*. Doesn't leave it.'

'Take us there,' Withypoll demanded.

'He receives no man,' the soldier replied. 'He fears the plague. If I took you, they would shoot us from the main deck.'

'Someone must go,' I said. 'Who takes him food and water?'

'He has supplies,' the soldier answered, trudging away. 'If you would go, go yourself.'

Withypoll's hand tightened upon the hilt of his sword as he watched the soldier walk away. If he attacked the soldier, the rest of the company would surely retaliate. But he wiped his forehead upon his soaking sleeve and took a deep breath, face shining white, gleaming in the sun.

I turned my attention to three boats moored upon the bank, each with oars laid flat down the keel.

'If we fly a white flag we should at least gain the opportunity to show our credentials,' I said.

'Get in the boat,' Withypoll ordered. 'And take off your shirt.'

The ship anchored no more than fifty yards offshore. Sliding one of the boats into the river presented no problem, and it proved easy to row. I took off my white shirt and felt the hot sun burn pleasantly upon my shoulders.

Three men watched from the ship, muskets trained upon us.

'We are King's men,' I shouted, nervous they might aim first at the man with the flag. 'Sent by the King to find James Josselin.'

'King's men or Arlington's men?' one shouted back.

I prodded Withypoll in the midriff that he might show his letter. 'Both.'

'Aye, then,' cried the soldier. 'Then ye should retrieve him, but you cannot come on board.'

'We must talk to Captain Scotschurch,' I protested.

'We may not leave the boat, and none may board,' the soldier replied.

'Tell them we insist,' Withypoll whispered to me. 'Else we shall return to London and inform the King himself of this treachery.'

'Refuse us boarding, you refuse the King,' I shouted. 'For we represent him in this matter.'

The soldier tapped his finger to his brow. 'I will confer.'

We waited on the boat, gently rocking on the Colne. Withypoll looked worse, eyelids heavy and jaw sagging like he found it difficult to breathe. Dowling watched him stony-eyed, grievously offended by something.

'Hoy!' the soldier called, once he returned. 'One of you may board.'

'What treachery is this?' Withypoll spluttered, saliva flying in all directions. 'Did you not hear what he said?'

'Aye, so I did,' the soldier grinned, blinking. He appeared drunk. 'The Captain said there is but one King, and so he would admit but one of you in his place.'

Withypoll breathed deep and stood up. 'Very well.' He stepped towards the rigging causing the boat to lurch violently.

'Not you.' The soldier raised his gun. 'I told him you look sick.' He turned to me and pointed. 'The little fellow. He may board.'

95

Withypoll eyed the rigging with teeth bared, as if contemplating besieging the ship alone. Then he fell back onto his seat and focussed his red-eyed gaze upon me. 'Find out what is going on, Lytle, and make sure you gain assurance you will be admitted to Shyam.' He wiped the palm of his hand against his hair.

'Why do you not come with us to Shyam?' I asked. 'You say you are unafraid of the plague.'

'I don't fear the plague,' Withypoll snarled, 'but those are Arlington's instructions.' His face relaxed once more. 'Besides, there is more than the plague in Shyam, Lytle, as you will discover.' He rubbed his puffy eyes. 'Make sure you succeed, Lytle, for if I have to storm this ridiculous ship myself, I will slice off a piece of you first.'

What else could be in Shyam, worse than plague? My spirits sunk lower than ever before. I contemplated asking this captain to sail me to Holland, else borrowing one of those muskets and shooting Withypoll from the safety of the ship. Tell Arlington it was a drunken sailor did it. But I was not a murderer. Dowling stood, legs astride, and helped steady me as I grasped for the rigging.

The three soldiers were indeed drunk. Bored, I supposed, but what captain would allow such debauchery right under his nose? A drunk captain, I discovered, upon being shown into his cabin.

He slouched upon a carved wooden chair, painted gold like a throne, wide enough to seat two men. Lions' paws were carved into the bottom of each leg and lions' heads upon the handles. This fellow resembled no captain I had ever seen. Short hair, black and straggly, grew wild about his scalp. Three weeks of bristle sprouted upon his big, round face. Small, dark eyes wandered about his head like he couldn't see straight. Painted below his nose was a wide, foolish smile, revealing short, peg-like teeth, most of them rotten. He slumped in the chair like his back was broken, and clutched its arms as if he feared falling from it.

'Who are you?' he slurred, grin intact. 'You don't look like one of Arlington's agents to me.'

'I am Harry Lytle,' I replied. 'And I am dressed so not to attract attention.'

Captain Scotschurch belched. 'I wasn't talking about your clothes. What do you want?'

'We have come to fetch James Josselin from Shyam,' I answered. 'Two of us will go in and find him, while Withypoll waits for us in Colchester.'

Scotschurch shook his head. 'Madness, but I wish you well. Rid us of Josselin and we can all go home.' He rearranged his mouth and let his eyes hang heavy such that I feared he might fall asleep.

I cleared my throat. 'The town gates are all locked.'

'Aye, Mayor Flanner insists, and I don't blame him,' Scotschurch exclaimed, eyes open wide for a moment. 'They seek to keep the Pest at bay. He has walls and I have a river.' He leant over the right arm of his chair and groped for a bottle. 'He controls the road to Shyam besides. They know you are coming and plan to deny you passage.'

'How will they prevent us?' I asked, hopeful.

Scotschurch snorted, spitting wine onto his shirt. 'With fine words and sound argument. They have been practising.'

'Practising? We received our orders just three days ago.'

'Aye, so you found out three days ago.' The captain lifted the bottle to his lips and took a mighty draught. 'Doesn't mean it wasn't decided beforehand.'

'But Josselin fled London only a week ago.'

'Josselin's been in there two weeks,' Scotschurch replied, releasing a great sigh of strong fumes. He noticed me flinch. 'Strong drink protects against the plague,' he mumbled. 'Which be why I encourage all my men to consume as much as they are able. Four have died since we came here, and none of them drank sufficient.'

If the townsmen tried to deny us passage, then Withypoll might attack them. 'Do they have arms?'

'Aye, so they do,' Scotschurch nodded. 'And mad men commit mad deeds, but Arlington insists you must go to Shyam and so we will enforce it. My men will escort you to the barricade.'

I scowled. 'You saw Josselin yourself?'

Scotschurch shook his bleary head. 'Before we arrived,' he answered.

'You have men in the town?'

He shook his head again. 'The townspeople are terrified that any man who enters will transport the Pest with him, and that includes my men. If I needed to gain entry I could, but I don't wish to stir them up. Flanner is an unpleasant fellow.' He belched again. 'So I leave them alone.'

'How do you know Josselin isn't in there with them?'

The captain shrugged. 'Because he is at Shyam. He cannot be in two places at once.'

'The Mayor would deny us passage,' I considered. 'Suppose he denies us access for fear we would discover that Josselin is not in Shyam at all. Perhaps Josselin hides in Colchester. They talk of him as a hero in these parts. Of course they would shelter him.'

The captain plunged his thumb up his nose and stretched out his nostril. 'Aye,' he conceded. 'Could be. I don't know where he is, nor do I much care, so long as you fetch him out.'

'Then we must search the town and make sure he's not hiding,' I insisted.

'Flanner won't like it.' The captain pursed his lips. 'But that's for you and he to debate. Tell Benjamin you wish to enter the town and that he is to take you there.' He held up the bottle, half full of what looked like claret. 'I will write it down as an order to give to him.'

'Who is Benjamin?'

Scotschurch scratched his groin and reached for quill, paper and seal. 'You will find him on the shore.' He took his time scratching out his command in loose, spidery hand. Then he waved a hand and settled back in his chair with his eyes closed. He lifted his leg and broke wind, emitting the foulest of smells. 'Good fortune and farewell.'

Good fortune indeed if Josselin was hiding in Colchester.

Chapter Eleven

Men shall be apt to put confidence in feigned friendships which shall profit them nothing.

I clambered back into the boat flushed with a sense of wild optimism. Josselin's sole objective was to hide from Arlington. What better strategy than to persuade the townsfolk of Colchester to spread false rumour as to his whereabouts?

My excitement lacked contagion. Withypoll interrogated me with derision, snorting like a sneezy goat when I told him of my idea. He settled back, contenting himself with a long stare, huddled up beneath his jacket, shivering. Dowling sat silent, as he had been most of the day.

Back on shore I walked next to Dowling, seeking an opportunity to poke him in the ribs and discover what ailed him, but Withypoll stayed too close.

The first couple of soldiers we spoke to were too fuddled to think. The third tottered about in an unsteady circle squinting into the distance against the sun, gaze fixed on someone in the distance. Following his stare I spotted the soldier we encountered before, the fellow with a sty so large he couldn't see out of his left eye. He caught me staring and ducked out of sight.

'Hoy!' Withypoll saw him too and took off. We followed through the crowd, spotting the tail of his coat disappear up Magdalen Street. Strands of long, black hair bounced upon his head and flapped about his ears. He was the only sober soldier in the harbour, the only man capable of running without falling over.

'Stop, Benjamin,' Withypoll shouted. 'Stop where you stand, else I shall slice off your ears.'

Benjamin ran on awkwardly, short legs struggling to carry his substantial bulk. Halfway up the hill he gave up and turned to face us, still grasping the barrel of his musket. His face glowed so bright I feared he might collapse at our feet. 'What do you want?' he panted.

Withypoll handed him the directive with moist palm. 'You will escort us into the town,' he said, prodding his sword into Benjamin's belly. 'Take us past the gates.'

Benjamin frowned, attempted to ignore the weapon, and took the letter.

'Why did you run?' I asked, wiping sweat from my own dripping brow.

'I've had enough,' he snapped, angry, still reading. Two more soldiers wandered down the hill, blank expressions on dull faces. Benjamin looked up and scowled. 'Everyone is drunk and Scotschurch is the drunkest. None of us are allowed into the town. No one is posted to watch who enters or who leaves.'

'Read the orders,' Withypoll commanded, his body waving gently from side to side. I wondered if he was about to drop dead on the spot.

'Your company is here to make sure James Josselin doesn't leave,' I explained. 'Now we've come to collect him. You will be sent home soon.'

Benjamin shrugged, a thoughtful expression clouding his eyes. 'Not I. I live here. When the army leaves I stay behind.' He glanced at Withypoll. 'Why do you want to enter the gates? To go to Shyam?'

'Lytle here persuaded your captain Josselin might be inside the town,' Withypoll replied. 'What do you think of that?'

Benjamin stared at me like I was a strange prophet.

'Scotschurch said you arrived after Josselin entered Shyam,' I said. 'Maybe he didn't go to Shyam at all.'

'I didn't arrive after Josselin,' said Benjamin. 'I was here already, but I didn't see Josselin arrive. I heard about it next day. Josselin persuaded Flanner to allow him passage to Shyam is what they said.'

'Would the townspeople protect him?' I asked, excited.

'Aye,' Benjamin nodded, pensive. 'He always was a liar. All this nonsense about wriggling through walls and withstanding torture. He was nine years old; he carried no special message. They tortured him, but he didn't know what to tell them, else he would have told them in the twitch of a mouse's whisker. The rest is nonsense and allowed him to take advantage of every gullible fool who heard the story.'

'You were one of those fools, I suppose,' Withypoll mocked him.

'Not I,' Benjamin replied, clenching his fists. 'But I watched him at work. His family lived here for ten years while his father sought to regain his estates. It wasn't until the Restoration that the family's fortunes improved. James Josselin is the most idle man I ever met.

He thrived upon the generosity of those who believed the tale he cultivated.'

I wondered if Benjamin was religious. The overly religious accused every man of idleness, as I knew from personal experience. 'He is accused of murder,' I said.

'I know,' Benjamin replied. 'And if you ask me do I think he is capable, then yes he is. He has no moral compass. If he killed a man, this is where he would come, knowing these people would protect him without question.'

I felt even more determined to penetrate the town walls, certain Josselin skulked in there somewhere.

Benjamin spoke louder, good eye open wide. 'When the other strangers were admitted I asked Captain Scotschurch if we might enter too, but he refused me.'

'What other strangers?' Withypoll demanded.

'Four men entered last week, none of them from hereabouts. They dressed strange, like dignitaries, but not English. Scotschurch wasn't interested.'

'Dutchmen,' Withypoll exclaimed, a glint in his eye.

'Perhaps,' Benjamin replied. He blinked furiously and rubbed at the sty with dirty finger afore leading the way back up the hill. 'That's for you to find out.'

'First we must fetch our horses,' Dowling reminded us all. 'You walk, Benjamin. We will meet you at Botolph's.'

Back at the harbour our horses stepped nervous from foot to foot, surrounded by a gaggle of bleary admirers. Withypoll cut them short thrift. I looked back at the ship anchored out in the river, lonely and forlorn. Scotschurch didn't drink to ward off the plague, else he would assume his responsibilities on shore. He drank to ward off the fear, and allowed his men to do the same so they would not revolt. Pestilence had many ways to beat a man. The drunken wretches that pawed and slobbered at our legs were no less defeated, their muskets a stark reminder of their sad demise.

My horse fidgeted, skittish and tense, and I had to pull hard on his reins to stop him dashing south along the river bank. We pushed through the swaying masses, out into clean space away from the harbour. The bells of St Leonard's pealed as we passed the church, as if signalling us to retreat. Another cart trundled westward, tarpaulin covering a heavy load.

Benjamin stood waiting at Botolph's Gate afront of two sombre-looking fellows with hands on hips. 'They want to see the captain's orders,' he said.

'Captain's orders and King's orders.' Withypoll swung himself to the ground. 'Open the gate or I'll open your guts.' He pushed one of them back against the thick stone wall. 'In the name of Charles the Second.'

'Mayor Flanner said none may enter,' the older man said, dancing on his toes with one arm held up against Withypoll's blade.

'Make your choice,' Withypoll leered, his nose still red. 'My blade or Flanner's.'

For a moment it seemed like the sentry might take him on, encouraged by Withypoll's wan complexion and stooped gait, but then Benjamin placed a hand on the older man's shoulder. The old man caught the warning in his eyes and dipped into his pocket to retrieve a heavy key, with which he opened the grand doors.

We hurried over the threshold as Death turned its head slowly towards the light, momentarily distracted from the scenes of torment. The two guards hurried after, eager to close the door behind us. What sort of townspeople were these who left their brethren to fall upon the ground?

We emerged on foot opposite a low, green field, overgrown and deserted. The site of Botolph's Fair, if my bearings proved right, now covered with empty tenter frames. Colchester was famous for its wool, but no one would be buying Colchester bays again for a while. Yet these two fellows looked fat enough.

I couldn't resist asking. 'How do you survive behind the walls?'

'Taxes,' one replied. 'There is a tax levied on every village within five miles.'

Benjamin scanned the surroundings, lips drawn tight, face white. Then we followed our guides to a small crossroads; ancient, square-towered churches on three corners, like some sort of celestial vestibule.

'Mayor Flanner will not be happy,' the younger man whispered to Benjamin, watching Withypoll stagger down the empty marketplace. Assuredly he would not. Withypoll walked like an obstinate corpse.

Low, flat, marble steps led into the bowels of the crooked Moot Hall. An enormous, wooden coat of arms hung from the uneven roof above grand, oak doors. A row of chimney stacks stood leaning at strange angles.

One guide pointed afore the two hurried away back the way they'd come. 'You'll find Mayor Flanner in there.'

The entrance led to a wood-panelled hall. From our left came a faint, scratching noise, sound of quill on paper. It stopped suddenly. Footsteps sounded sharp upon floorboards.

A middle-sized man of ordinary build stared at us with cold blue eyes. 'Benjamin!'

Benjamin bowed his head afore Flanner's trenchant stare. 'You don't have the authority to keep them out, Flanner.'

Flanner smiled, crookedly. 'You have come to find James Josselin, but you will fail.'

'It is the King's mission.' Withypoll smiled back unpleasantly. 'To prevent us would be treason.'

'Treason.' Flanner repeated, standing well back from Withypoll. 'Then I will show you about the town before you leave.' He stepped past us and back out onto the street.

'The Dutch Quarter first,' Withypoll called.

Flanner turned to confront him. 'Why?'

Withypoll stepped towards Flanner and laid a hand upon his shoulder. 'All you good country folk adopt a simple outlook on life,' he said, as Flanner shrank from his touch. 'Josselin is a full-grown man, yet you poor bumpkins cannot see beyond the boy. Why would I waste my time explaining to you that Josselin stabbed a lord through the chest? That Josselin is a traitor who spoils our parley with the Dutch? Yet I have pledged an oath to the King in the service of my country, so must pursue the truth anyway, whatever inconvenience it may present to the Mayor of Little Bumpkintown.'

Flanner's sharp blue eyes settled upon Benjamin. 'There were always those among us who envied James his situation,' he said. 'For some a bright star is something to be coveted. If the boy is courageous then so will be the man; that is evident.' He pulled away from Withypoll's grasp. 'You gentlemen, I assume, have never met James Josselin.'

Withypoll waved an airy arm. 'Nor do we need to. We found Berkshire's body with Josselin's sword protruding from his chest. Others saw him running with blood upon his hands. Seems he didn't stop until he reached here.'

Flanner shook his head and pointed. 'The Dutch Quarter.'

The houses seemed the same as any other, same half-timbered

structures with impenetrable, dark windows.

'I don't know what you expect to see.' Flanner stopped. 'Most of these people were born here, as were their fathers before them. The first arrived more than a century ago, chased from Flanders by the Spanish.'

Withypoll grunted and stalked up East Stockwell Street beneath the great shadow of the castle. 'What do they do now they cannot make cloth?' he asked.

'The town is half empty,' Flanner replied. 'Many left before the Pest established itself. Those that remain keep this town going. The neighbouring villages provide us with monies by which we ensure everyone is fed, but still we must arrange to buy provisions. The town must be kept clean, the sick cared for, law maintained.' He looked to the castle. 'We have had to lock up six families so far, who tried to visit their relatives outside the walls. Such selfish behaviour puts us all at risk.'

Withypoll turned, blocking Flanner's path. 'What of the Dutchmen who arrived last week?'

Flanner halted in his tracks, face frozen. 'I don't know what you mean.'

Withypoll tilted his head. 'And your mother was my father.' He drew his sword. 'You speak to me as if I am your enemy, when I come from the King. Lie and I will cut you from belly to chin.'

'There are no Dutchmen here,' Flanner insisted, yet his blue eyes darted from me to Dowling, seeking salvation. 'Kill me if you will, it will not change the fact.'

Withypoll lifted the shining steel into the sunlight. 'Benjamin saw them.'

'I did not say Dutchmen,' Benjamin protested. 'I said they dressed strange.'

Flanner breathed deep and slow. 'Those were churchwardens from the villages. They came with the taxes they raised.' He glared at Benjamin. 'Brave men to venture into Colchester, wouldn't you say?'

'They didn't look like churchwardens,' Benjamin said, blushing.

Flanner said nothing, just waited for Withypoll to lower his sword, staring with a burning hatred. Yet if they were churchwardens, why did he become so strange? Flanner lied to us about something.

'We must go to Shyam,' I said, watching his response.

'No man may go to Shyam,' he replied, still unbalanced. 'They will admit no man. It is forbidden.'

'Yet we will go,' I replied. 'We cannot leave Essex without finding Josselin. We must ask him some questions. If he is at Shyam, then we must go to Shyam.'

'If you go to Shyam, you will die,' Flanner replied, voice choked. 'You don't know what has become of that village.'

'Yet you allowed Josselin to go?' I said. 'The beloved son of this fair town.'

'Josselin is a great man,' Flanner replied carefully, 'and his situation is grave, very grave.'

'Indeed it is,' Withypoll agreed. 'Yours besides, for if Lytle and Dowling here go to Shyam and die, and it turns out that Josselin was hiding here all the while, then both he and you, and anyone else found to be harbouring him, will be found guilty of murder and treason.'

'Josselin is not in Colchester,' Flanner muttered.

The sound of donkeys braying broke the silence. Flanner cursed and ran his fingers through his hair, a gesture that did not escape Withypoll's attentions. The noise came from the east, round the base of the great mound upon which the castle stood majestic. We strode quickly through the streets, the sound of braying deafening to our ears, until we came to the ruins of the East Gate.

Six donkeys stood in a circle, each burdened with heavy load, heads raised to the skies crying harshly to the heavens, white teeth shining in the sun. About them gathered four men in dark trousers and loose, light shirts, all wearing tan shoes. They checked each donkey's pack and pulled at various straps and fastenings.

'The East Gate is the way to Shyam,' said Benjamin, staring at Flanner.

'They are on a mission of mercy,' Flanner explained, perspiration forming upon his brow in heavy drops. 'They are God's men, all of them brave.'

'Brave or foolish?' I asked him. 'Did you not say they will die?'

'God will watch over them,' Flanner replied, though his body spoke with less confidence than his mouth. 'They have heard the terrible tales that come from Shyam, stories of hopelessness and evil. They have pledged to purge the village of sin in the name of the Lord.'

None of which made sense. If Josselin fled London and found sanctuary between the clean walls of Colchester, then why should he make the perilous trip to Shyam? Josselin hid in Colchester, I was sure of it.

The four men finished making their last adjustments and the donkeys ceased their protests. Each man appeared grimly resolute, yet terrified besides. A dangerous addiction, the Bible. Every man sought the best of himself amongst its pages and determined to live up to that lofty ambition. Yet we were none of us so strong, nor so bold. Now these fellows realised they were just poor mortals like the rest of us, yet had created for themselves a braver man's destiny. The donkeys seemed keenest, tempted by the long, open track and the sight of fresh, green grass. At last the men could linger no more, and the small band picked its way through the rubble of the gate and set off for Shyam.

'If they can go, then Lytle and Dowling can go,' Withypoll told Flanner, smiling at me.

He surely saw the fear in my eyes. What if Josselin was in Shyam after all? Like Withypoll, perhaps he imagined some false immunity. Perhaps for him Shyam *was* a real sanctuary, a place no man might reach him, a place he might command the poor afflicted inhabitants.

'What else would you see?' Flanner asked.

'Your best inn,' Withypoll demanded. 'If we must stay the night in this cursed place, then we will stay within the walls.'

'I will take you to the Red Lion.' Flanner beckoned. 'I assume *you* will return from whence you came,' he said, spitting the words at Benjamin.

Benjamin reddened, turned on his heel, and strode back towards Botolph's Gate without a word.

If Josselin was in Colchester, we had little time to find him, for nothing would deprive Withypoll of the pleasure of seeing us step out the gate upon that sinister road to Shyam.

Curious faces stared out from the windows as we passed, and as I met the stares of men, women and children, I realised that Benjamin had been the only one of us that knew for sure what Josselin looked like.

Chapter Twelve

*The position of Mars in the 7th and in Virgo signifieth
effusion of bloods.*

As the bells rang out for evening prayer, Dowling and I prepared
to venture forth. At these times, with plague knocking upon
the town gates, every man would go to church. If we wanted
clear view of the remaining townsfolk, now presented the best
opportunity.

Withypoll slouched in a large chair, in front of the empty fireplace,
wrapped in a blanket, though the air was warm. His hair lay in wet
tangles, plastered to his head, the ugly wound now open to the air.
A small table stood at his elbow, upon it a jug of ale. 'Tomorrow
Shyam,' he said, raising a mug, his words echoing about the large,
empty room, worn timber walls, bare floor.

I thought to argue with him, but his eyes gleamed, feverish. With any
luck he might be dead tomorrow. The landlady watched, curious, from

the doorway. Her head darted like a great chicken with a faint, black moustache.

She waited for us to walk past her afore she spoke. 'Why do you plan to go to Shyam?' she demanded, tugging at my sleeve.

'To find James Josselin,' I replied.

'Josselin is not at Shyam,' she snorted. 'Who told you that?'

'Where is he, then?' I asked, ears pricked.

'I don't know where he is, but he would ne'er venture into Shyam.' She spat on the floor and wiped her mouth on her sleeve. 'First, it is worse plagued than even outside our own walls. Second, he would ne'er go to Shyam, for that is where Thomas Elks lives.'

The bells continued ringing. Churches would be starting to fill.

'Who is Thomas Elks?'

'Thomas Elks is Hugh Elks' brother, and Hugh Elks is dead.' She spat again upon the floor, a small, brown puddle of something sticky. 'Thomas Elks blamed James Josselin, and swore to kill him for it.'

'When was this?' I asked.

'Ten years ago.' She tapped me on the chest and stared, her rough, weathered face smelling strangely damp. 'Tell me why James Josselin would go back to Shyam when Thomas Elks is waiting there to kill him? Thomas Elks is as black-hearted as ever his brother was, and his brother was an evil sinner.'

'Tell us the story quickly, woman,' I urged her. 'We must get to church.'

'I must get to church besides,' she replied indignant. 'I need not tell you the story at all.'

'Tell us, please,' Dowling said, soft.

'Well, then.' She wrinkled her nose in my direction afore turning to Dowling. 'Hugh Elks was an idle fellow, like all his kin. Another man, name of William Braine, sold all his stock at market and planned to leave Shyam to go to Ipswich, I think.' She spat a third time, this time close to my boot. 'One day, at the time of morning prayer, a man entered William Braine's house with a visor upon his face. Braine's daughter was there alone, for she was sick, making cheese.'

'God save us,' Dowling muttered.

'Aye, God save us,' the old woman agreed. 'When the thief saw the daughter, he must have panicked. Perhaps she recognised him.' Her shiny, black eyes narrowed. 'Hugh Elks arrived at church very late, exceedingly sweaty, said he had been working in the field. When William Braine arrived home, he found his daughter lain on the floor with her throat cut, and a dog eating the cheese.'

'Elks' dog?'

'Aye, Elks' dog. He said his dog escaped its leash, and that the presence of his dog didn't signify that he killed Braine's daughter, and none could prove otherwise.'

'Though all suspected it?'

'Not all.' The old woman sighed deep. 'For not everyone liked William Braine, and not everyone was agin' Hugh Elks, for Elks had a large family. Half the village is related to an Elks in some way.'

'Josselin proved Elks killed the girl, and Thomas Elks hates him for it,' I deduced.

The old woman ignored me. 'When Elks arrived at church, sweat poured from his head like he had stuck it in a bucket. His face was red, his skin hot, yet Josselin noticed his shirt was clean.'

The old lady gazed up into Dowling's serious face. 'There were three or four spots where the sweat soaked through in circles, growing fast. It was a new shirt, else it would have been wet all over, like his body.'

'For someone who wasn't there, you tell a good story,' I said.

She grimaced and turned again to Dowling. 'Josselin walked the path between Braine's house and the church. Elks' house lay between the two. Past Elks' house stood a thicket. Josselin took the dog into the thicket and found a shirt, covered in blood, in thin streams where it sprayed when he cut the girl's throat.'

'God's teeth,' I muttered.

'Elks said it wasn't his shirt, but the dog picked it up and ran to him with it. Then others from the village swore they had seen him wearing it earlier that day. I don't know if they spoke truth or told lies to condemn him, but it was enough to see him hanged at Ipswich.' The old lady turned to face me. 'Some thanked Josselin for it; others blamed him for Hugh Elks' death, accusing him of bearing false witness. When Josselin found his own horse dead one day, here at Colchester, throat cut with a wire, he knew Thomas Elks did it.'

'Thomas Elks may be dead,' I pointed out. 'Half Shyam is dead, so they say.'

'More than half,' the old lady replied, 'and none of them is Thomas Elks. We see the list every Friday, and his name has not yet been on it. So you tell me why James Josselin would venture into Shyam, and tell me then why you venture into Shyam. Though having met you I am inclined to send you on your way.' She stuck out her chin.

'All good questions,' I assured her. 'We would talk more to you later, but now we must go.'

'*I* must go,' she corrected me, 'and I don't know that I have the inclination to talk to you more.' She spat one last time upon the floorboards before shuffling off.

'How sweet are thy words unto my taste! Yea, sweeter than honey to my mouth!' Dowling grasped my shoulder. 'We should inspect the latest list afore we leave.'

I didn't honour him with a reply, for we dawdled too long if we wanted to arrive before the churches filled.

Dowling reckoned there were nine churches in Colchester. We couldn't cover them all. If Josselin had indeed come here to meet the Dutch then St Martin's was the most likely, an old Norman church inside the Dutch Quarter, deformed and stunted, its tower destroyed by Fairfax's cannons.

We arrived at the door in sufficient time, for the streets were still filling. The sun still shone, which made it difficult to stand inconspicuous. By now word would have spread that three strangers roamed the town in search of Josselin and his four Dutch spies. Josselin may have been warned of our presence. Damn Withypoll for declaring our intentions so bold. I fetched in my pocket for my pipe and Culpepper's leaves.

I offered the packet to Dowling. 'Will you share my remedy?'

He shook his head, scowling.

'Why so quiet, Davy?' I asked him, packing the bowl. 'You've barely said a word all day.'

He snorted and shook his head. 'Does it not pain ye, Harry,' he said. 'That outside the walls men lie dying? Yet in here they feed themselves, watch over themselves, then rush to church to pray for their own lives.' He shook his head again. 'The end of all flesh is come before me; for the earth is filled with violence through them; and,

115

behold, I will destroy them with the earth.'

'God is angry you reckon?'

'Angry with us all,' Dowling replied, voice thick with fear and disgust. 'God looked upon the earth, and behold, it was corrupt; for all flesh had corrupted his way upon the earth. Who says the plague has left London, Harry? Who says it will not return?'

'Where is your belief, Davy?' I asked, shaken to my soul, for I never suspected Dowling's faith was pregnable.

'None of us know God's intent,' he answered. 'For without controversy great is the mystery of godliness.'

'Amen to that,' I said, thinking of Shyam and watching the last of the congregation file in through the doors. 'Though I reckon God would have us persuade Scotschurch to search this town from door to door, despite what Withypoll says.'

'Withypoll cares little about Josselin,' said Dowling. 'All this talk of treason and treachery is but part of the act behind which Withypoll masquerades to achieve his true intention. And his true intention is to see you die, Harry, and me too, I suppose.'

I thought of London, the noise, the throngs, the sound of life. 'Is now the time to flee then?' I stepped across the road to light my pipe from a brazier full of coals. I sucked hard, feeling the smoke deep in my lungs. The colours about me intensified, coals burning like little suns.

'If Withypoll reports we failed upon our obligation, Lucy may be killed, and Jane besides,' Dowling reminded me, terse.

'I know.' I stumbled on my words. 'I thought we could ride faster than Withypoll, seize Lucy and Jane, and carry them away.'

Dowling sniffed the air and regarded me, suspiciously. 'Arlington has spies all over the country, people like us who live in fear of failure.'

The church filled now, a low, buzzing noise sounding from behind the two, sturdy doors.

'No sign of Josselin,' I noted. 'Unless he arrived early.'

'I will go and see,' Dowling declared, striding towards the open doorway. 'You wait here.'

Brave of him, I thought, watching his great, broad shoulders disappear into the blurriness of the dark church. Every man would stare at him when he entered, stranger that he was. I waited in the fading sun for the service to end, watching the white clouds racing across the scarlet sky, dark and shimmering. I leant against the wall to steady myself.

At last the townspeople emerged, in twos and threes, sombre and cheerless, no doubt reminded again of the plague and the sinful excesses that were supposed to have incited it. That would have cheered Dowling up.

Three men lingered upon exiting, stood in a tight circle, backs to each other, watching out onto the street. Well for me, I stood in the alley from where I could observe unnoticed. Three more men came out soon after, plain brown jackets woven from fine cloth in foreign style. They must be the men Benjamin saw. They didn't look like churchwardens, nor behave like churchwardens either, skulking about the streets like criminals. I wondered where Dowling had got to.

I shook my head in an attempt to return the world to normal, but still the colours burnt. The little group headed east, as yellow became burnt orange, and so I followed, braving the open streets. At the end of the road they turned north, towards a large wide house, timber-framed with candles in all the windows already. They disappeared inside and closed the door behind.

'Six men and more,' I said to myself. 'And three of them are neither of these parts, nor are they churchwardens.' I stepped across the street towards the brightest window and peered in.

Twelve men or more sat around a long table. All the six I followed and a half-dozen more. Their demeanour was serious and businesslike. They took their instruction from the head of the table, to my left, but I couldn't see the speaker's face. I ducked my head and shuffled along to another window from where I could see every man. All twelve and the man at the head besides. A familiar face. My heart pounded hard enough to break my ribs.

I looked around for Dowling, but couldn't see him anywhere. I tried running back the way I came but it seemed I left my legs behind.

'Calm,' I urged myself, leaning against a wall. 'No one is following.' I took small steps.

Dowling appeared from somewhere, face white and hair black. I had never seen him with black hair before. 'Harry!' he exclaimed.

I leant back against a pillar staring at a face, a chipped stone face I recognised from St Martin's. 'You know who I saw?' I whispered hoarse.

'I told you to wait,' Dowling growled. 'Where did you go?'

'I saw *him*,' I said. Familiar stern face, scathing and terrible, the skin upon his neck now hung in a long fold that quivered as he spoke. Yellowing eyes, like a great rat. His silver-tipped cane leant against his chair. 'The Earl of Shrewsbury.'

Dowling cupped my chin in his hands. 'Shrewsbury?'

'Aye, Shrewsbury. The murderous devil that would have seen me hanged at Tyburn.' I struggled to stand up straight and dug my heels into the paving stones. 'I'm going back.'

Dowling laid an arm across my shoulders, heavy as a log. 'No.'

I felt my knees buckle. 'He killed my father.'

Dowling gazed down upon me like he was my father instead. 'Shrewsbury sits there with twelve men. What is your grand plan?'

'To stick his cane down his throat.' Gratifying but not grand.

'By yourself?' Dowling frowned. 'We need help, Harry, and Withypoll is the only one I can think can provide it.'

We hurried back to the Red Lion.

'What church did you go to?' the old lady demanded as soon as we stepped over the threshold. 'I did not see you there.'

I ignored her and headed straight for the table upon which Withypoll leant forwards, wet head rested on his arms.

I slapped my hands down upon the thick wood. 'Things have changed.'

Withypoll pushed himself up, scowling. 'Aye, the moon has risen and you are frightened.' He shivered. 'A change for the better.'

'No.' I said. 'We found the Dutchmen.'

Withypoll raised his brows and endeavoured to look impressed. 'Well, sit thee down and let's partake of an ale, to celebrate your fine achievement.'

I banged the table again. 'The Earl of Shrewsbury was among them.'

Withypoll pursed his lips. 'A trick, Lytle? For if it is your intention to weave some fine tale that will excuse you your voyage into Shyam, then you are wasting your breath.'

'No trick,' I snapped. 'We will take you to the house now, where you may see it with your own eyes. If any man is a traitor, it's Shrewsbury. What business does he have in Colchester with a table full of Dutchmen? He is involved in this, somehow or other.

There is no point in going to Shyam. Josselin is obviously here in the town.'

'You saw Josselin with Shrewsbury?' Withypoll wiped his brow. 'That is what you would have me believe?'

I breathed deep. 'I don't try and have you believe anything except that Shrewsbury is here. Come and we will show you.'

'Very well.' Withypoll clambered to his feet, breathing ale fumes into my face. 'Show me.'

The house was but three minutes away, yet from fifty yards I felt my hopes dashed against stone walls, for all the lights were dark.

Withypoll nodded at the house. 'Shrewsbury is there you say? Hiding in the dark.'

'He sat there with a dozen others not ten minutes ago,' I said. 'We followed from St Martin's.'

Withypoll wiped at his face in displeasure. 'Clearly they had little to discuss.'

'Else they saw us,' I said.

Withypoll turned upon me. 'Well they will not see you again for a while, Lytle.' Not a muscle of his hard face moved. 'You and the butcher will go into Shyam tomorrow and look for Josselin. You won't come back without him.'

'What if he isn't there?'

Withypoll forced himself to smile. 'Then bring evidence of it, else I shall assume you are lying.'

I stood my ground. 'We are not going to Shyam when it is obvious Josselin is in Colchester.'

Withypoll regarded me strangely then turned to Dowling. 'You saw Shrewsbury alone, butcher, or you saw Josselin with him?'

Dowling's eyes opened wide, like he had been slapped across the face.

'Speak up,' Withypoll snapped.

'He didn't see either of them.' I saved Dowling the lie. 'I saw Shrewsbury by myself.'

Withypoll sighed deep and a ball of anger rose within my throat, but before I could open my mouth, the noise of braying donkeys shrilled through the quiet night air. Men hurried east, towards the broken gate. The donkeys cantered towards us in one great grey huddle, eyes wide, foam flying from their lips. Six donkeys, no loads, no men.

'This one is bleeding,' a man cried, grabbing one about the neck. 'Teethmarks, look!'

'Let me see.' Dowling stepped forward, gripping the beast firm about its head. He probed the wound with thick finger. 'Aye,' he said. 'Dog's teeth.'

The donkey kicked out hard and tugged at its head, trying to bite Dowling. The rest of the herd evaded capture, kicking frantically at any that neared. They kept on running, west down the high street. Dowling let go, and the last donkey galloped with all its might until it rejoined the group.

Dowling's companion stared after the beasts. 'They were terrified. We won't catch them 'til morning.'

Withypoll said, appearing at my shoulder, 'You won't be here in the morning. I have arranged for you to leave just before dawn. I will see you by the door at five o'clock.' He turned on his heel and wandered unsteadily back towards the Red Lion, the crowd opening up before him, fear upon their faces.

'How is your faith now?' I asked the butcher.

But Dowling walked slow, lost in thought, grey-faced and sombre, eyes wet with old man's tears. I suddenly recalled Withypoll breathing on my face, the rotten smell of his breath, and I resolved to smoke another pipe before going to bed. Another day gone. Five days now to get back to London, else lose my shop.

If the donkeys didn't bray all night beneath my window, then I must have dreamt it.

Chapter Thirteen

As the tail of the first Comet did verge North-west, viz. towards England, so hath the Plague or Pestilence, or both, most sorrowfully wasted some thousands.

Two crows perched upon the brickwork, jerking their heads up and down, regarding us sideways like we were new carrion. A sleepy-looking guard unlocked one of the great wooden doors and pushed it open, inviting us to step outside this safe haven onto the lane that led to Shyam. Withypoll stood watching, wrapped up warm in his big coat, checking we suffered no sudden loss of nerve.

The track was narrow and covered with leaves, though we were still in summer. Grass grew high as my knees in places, and we allowed the horses to take their time. The forest confronted us from all sides, deep and impenetrable. Birds sang loud, the effect sinister, unnatural and isolating.

Shyam was but three miles away, such a short distance. Each steady step seemed to carry us there with dizzying pace. I was relieved when Dowling pulled his horse up sharp a mile or so in, pointing to the edge of the forest. A hut stood at the edge of the treeline, built from sticks and branches. A pole protruded out the top, with a dirty white flag hanging limp at its tip.

Dowling clambered to the ground. 'Every strange thing, I would know what it means.'

A neatly stacked woodpile stood in front of the hut, and upon the woodpile lay a flat piece of board, with words written in chalk.

'Wood for thee. Hurry up. Approach with caution,' I read aloud. 'What does that mean?'

'He shall kill the bullock before the Lord,' Dowling recited. 'He shall flay the burnt offering, and cut it into pieces. And the sons of Aaron the priest shall put fire upon the altar, and lay the wood in order upon the fire. Then the priests shall lay the parts, the head, and the fat, in order upon the wood that is on the fire which is upon the altar.'

Which left me none the wiser.

I joined Dowling on the forest floor and approached the hut, cautious. A scrap of red twill hung from the doorframe. Inside, some animal had been scavenging. A rudimentary table lay upon its side, and bits of chair lay scattered about the floor. The spine of a book protruded from a pile of rotting leaves, the leather red and water-stained. Too thin to be a Bible. '*Astrological Judgments for the Year 1666*,' I read.

Though the book felt damp, I could turn the pages and read without difficulty. Some passages were marked with ink. 'It is most certain,' I read, 'that when the dregs of the first comet are ended, the

Hollander shall pay the piper, and sing lacrima; in a manner even to their final and utter destruction. They shall be able to send forth no more than a small company of little pimping ships, neither well-manned nor equipped.'

I flicked the pages. 'As for the second comet, it may inform us, that after many casualties, losses, damages, and enormities received from the several navies and ships of his Majesty of Great Britain, the Hollanders may again upon humble addresses make first unto his Majesty, with their submission besides for peace.'

I turned to the next marked passage. 'The figure of the Sun giveth warning unto the monarch of Great Britain, both of external and internal plots and designs against his peace and government, yet with no success to the undertakers.'

'Astrology.' Dowling shrugged, unimpressed. 'Does the book have a name in it?'

I turned to the front of the book, which was wettest. A name and a date were penned in smudged ink. Ne'ertheless, the name was clear enough. James Josselin.

'Whether he went to Shyam or not, he came this far,' said Dowling. 'Leaving signs that all who pass further should take wood with them.'

'To build their own altar, you say.'

Dowling shrugged. 'I don't know, but I think we should do as the sign suggests and take the wood.'

What did wood have to do with anything? Did they not have wood in Shyam? The forest stretched as far as the eye could see. I felt a sense of deep disquiet. Though it was a summer day, the air grew colder. The birds stopped singing. About our heads and shoulders sunk a white fog, so thick it resembled something solid.

'Dowling,' I called out, for I couldn't see him.

'Fetch your horse,' his voice sounded close by.

I did as he suggested and stood upon the track unable to see in any direction. The horse snorted and shook its head, like it sought to clear the mists from inside its skull.

'What do we do?' I shouted.

'There's nothing we can do,' Dowling said, emerging from the whiteness. 'We cannot walk in any direction. This part of the world is stopped until the fog is lifted.'

So we sat upon the dry ground, holding the reins of our horses, afraid of losing ourselves. Peculiar how sharp a man's hearing becomes when his eyes are blinded. I felt my senses reach out into the thick blanket about us, searching for the faintest sound. The fog created strange shapes, mysterious figures drifting in the mists.

I fought to keep the tremor from my voice. 'What will we find, Davy?'

'The dead and the dying,' he replied. 'As we did in London, as we did in Chelmsford, as we did in Colchester. Nothing we haven't seen before.'

'A sign from God,' I said. 'He doesn't want us to go.'

'O full of all subtlety and mischief, thou child of the Devil, wilt thou not cease to pervert the right ways of the Lord?' Dowling mused. 'And now the hand of the Lord is upon thee, and thou shalt be blind. And immediately there fell on him a mist and a darkness.'

I found myself whispering, it was so quiet. I waited for hands to spring from the surrounds and seize me. 'I have no desire to pervert the right ways of the Lord.'

'You haven't perverted the ways of the Lord any more than usual,' Dowling replied. 'This fog may not be for your benefit, Harry. God has others in his sights besides.'

We sat there another hour or so, the odd sensation of nothing happening. Then the fog felt warmer and assumed a yellow tinge. At last it began to clear, not much, just enough to see the ground ahead of our feet.

The fog gave way to a swirling mist, blinding us one moment, blowing aside the next, giving us unbroken perspective twenty or more yards ahead. The dirt track gave way to stones and pebble, twisting downward between giant boulders and ancient trees. Cliffs climbed high above us, in and out of view. A thin stream wound its way about the valley floor, creating small pools about which grew bright flowers, white and violet. At the bottom of the valley the water formed a pool, green and still.

In the distance a great, flat rock lay upon a ledge, like a table balanced upon a giant boulder. Three baskets sat upon it, all empty.

I stared up at the cliffs, searching for faces, then into the trees. 'This must be the boundary.'

'Someone from Colchester rides up here every day to leave provisions,' said Dowling.

'Then let's wait,' I suggested eagerly. 'Wait for someone to leave the food and the villagers to come and collect it. The villagers can tell us if Josselin is in there or not and we don't have to go into Shyam at all.'

'There are nearly three hundred dead in there, Harry, barely a hundred left alive.' Dowling pushed me forwards. 'This is the work of God, that ye believe in him whom he hath sent. You are sent by Him, and I believe in you.'

What an extraordinary thing to say. Was the butcher deranged? I followed him betwixt the great boulders, still leading my reluctant steed. We came to a small, wooden bridge, beneath which trickled a narrow stream. Beyond the stream we found a well-worn path, broad and bare, of grass. To our left, visible around the corner, tucked into a cluster of sycamores, stood three cottages in a line, walls and roofs covered in ivy.

'This is the Town-head,' Dowling murmured, standing still. 'The western end of the village.'

'You've been here before?' I asked.

'I read a map.'

No one moved, no one called out. We approached the front door of the first cottage, Dowling calling out cautiously. No one replied. He pushed the door with his finger and it creaked slowly open. Dowling poked his head in, then withdrew.

'Empty,' he announced. 'And a mess besides. Someone has ransacked the place.'

He walked to the next house, again announcing his presence before opening the door. And the third.

'Empty.' He turned to face me. 'I wonder if they have abandoned the whole village after all.'

We headed east, back past the bridge. It didn't look abandoned to me. Deep ridges carved through the soil, freshly cut. We passed another six cottages, still and quiet, all of them empty.

We came to a church, grey tower partially hidden within a ring of linden trees, like an army of grim angels guarding the passage within. We walked the path between gravestones, many of which appeared freshly chiselled, the ground trimmed short. A small porch framed the door, upon which perched a small cross. Dowling stepped inside while I waited, listening for any strange noise amidst the cacophony of nature. Dowling tried opening the door.

'It's locked,' he frowned.

'If there were a hundred alive last Friday, who is to say they have not all died by now?' I hated the fog and the mist. I yearned to be able to see what might be hiding in the distance. I thought I heard a man's voice, distant and pitiful.

'The food baskets were empty,' said Dowling.

'Animals,' I replied.

'Animals,' Dowling repeated, catching sight of something. 'There is a pool or a pond over there, with trees around it.'

But they were not trees.

Around Shyam pond, someone had erected steel cages, each one made of thick iron, the shape of a birdcage hanging from a seven-foot wooden pole. And in each one a man, crouched with knees up to chest, for there was little room inside the dreadful contraptions.

Twelve of them stood in a great circle about the green water. Flies enveloped the first, crawling about the dead body inside with great intent. The flesh already peeled from the skin of its cheekbone, revealing a pocket of ripe, squirming maggots. The next few were also dead, in varying stages of decomposition. In the fifth cage was a woman, her green dress sodden and rotting. She too had been in here for several weeks at least. A great, black cockroach emerged from her yellow hair, an unnatural sight triggering unusual cramps within my stomach.

I heard someone groan, then saw a movement from across the pond. Not all of these people were dead. I rushed about the circle. A thin man lifted his chin and squinted against the white sky. His eyes were dull and unseeing, lips cracked and dry. The next two were living too, though barely.

'What black deed is this?' I exclaimed, bile rising in my throat. The fog clung like a shroud, hiding what other atrocities? I fought to stop myself from running back the way we came.

'Someone did this to deter others,' Dowling's voice sounded unusually shrill. 'We are in the centre of the village.'

'Well, at least we must release those that still live.' I grasped for the lock of the nearest cage.

'We keep that locked,' a voice called from our right. Out of the fog stepped a man of ordinary height, lank brown hair streaked upon a long, suspicious face. Some kind of festering sore enveloped half his bottom lip. The muscles about his mouth were hard and tense. 'Who are you?'

'My name is Buxton,' I replied, remembering the name we saw in the records the night before. 'My brother is Robert Buxton.'

'Robert Buxton,' he repeated, thoughtful. 'You look young to be his brother.'

'Aye.' My mind froze. 'I was born at Colchester.' Else he could check his own church records for evidence of my birth. 'I have not seen him for several years. I came when I heard his life might be in danger.'

He stepped towards me and stared deeper into my eyes. I felt my soul writhe beneath his gaze. So this was what the devil looked like. 'How did you get in?'

'We came through a valley, past a large rock.'

'I see.' He nodded, sombre. 'I wish you had come about the main street, for then we might have given ye the opportunity to turn back.' He nodded at Dowling. 'Who are you?'

'I am his uncle,' Dowling growled. 'What is this atrocity?'

'These are sinners that sought to expedite the Devil's work,' the man replied. 'I am Thomas Elks and this is my parish. These wretches attempted to leave our boundaries though they vowed against it.'

The mists still rolled about our ears, a deathly thing, and I found myself wondering if we wandered into a world of ghosts. This Elks spoke with strange graces, like he was the guardian of this earth.

'You are the Reverend?' asked Dowling.

'Mompesson is the Reverend,' Elks replied. 'He stays in the church.'

'The church door is locked,' Dowling said, suspicious.

'Aye,' said Elks. 'He locks himself inside.'

What sort of Reverend locked himself inside a church and his parishioners out?

'These vowed not to leave this parish, you say,' Dowling stepped towards him, 'then changed their minds. For that you have done this to them?'

Elks scratched at his chest. 'When the plague struck our village, every man agreed we would remain within the parish boundaries so we don't carry the plague further into the country. It was Mompesson's idea.'

A light breeze blew across the pond, and the cages swung from the top of the poles, creaking.

'You deny them decent burial,' Dowling hissed betwixt old teeth. 'Thou shalt fear the Lord thy God, and serve him, and shalt swear by his name. Is it you that does this terrible thing?'

'The Devil hath tempted them to run amok,' Elks explained, as if to a child. 'He hath persuaded them to listen to his voice, and now sends them forth to spew death upon the masses. Mompesson decreed they will hang here until the evil hath vanished from their bodies, and in the meantime the sight of their poor, black souls may deter others from succumbing unto the same temptation.' He stepped closer to Dowling so that the two men stood nose to nose. 'No man may leave here.'

As he spoke, a light breeze blew the mists away across the fields, unveiling a large, square contraption upon a grassy green square in front of a small church. It looked like a cage with bodies in it. Elks saw me stare.

'That is the cage,' he said. 'For those who must wait their turn.'

It was indeed a cage, fabricated of flattened iron bars, no more than four feet tall and eight feet long. Six men sat cramped within it, including four familiar faces. Dowling strode forward with furious stride, gripping the bars like he would pull them apart with his bare hands. Two of the six men staggered to their feet and thrust their own dirty fingers through the gaps. I reached Dowling's shoulder just as the shorter of the two pushed his face up as close to the bars as he could manage. Thick streaks of dirt coated his face like he had dragged through mud. He cast a pleading gaze upon us both, desperation writ deep upon his filthy brow.

'You must leave,' he whispered, hoarse. 'Else ye shall be brought down to Hell, to the sides of the pit.'

'Are those not the men we saw leave Colchester yesterday?' I asked, for indeed I was sure I recognised their distinctive tan shoes.

'They insisted upon entering before any could explain the consequences of it,' Elks spoke with a soft voice that belied his steely gaze. 'They said their mission was to bring God into our lives, to share with us their medicines, and then begone. I said unto them as I say unto you: no man may leave here.' The shorter cleric buried his face in his hands like he feared Elks' judgement. 'Then they said it was their duty to take away the sick, unto the Pesthouse at Colchester.'

'A noble quest,' Dowling observed.

'A proud quest,' Elks corrected him, cheeks reddening. 'And everyone that is proud in heart is an abomination to the Lord, whatever may be

132

their expressed intent. Bring God into our lives, indeed. So God is not here already?' His voice thundered and the prisoners cowered. He lowered his brow and cast his wrath upon Dowling and his wanton mouth. 'We swore an oath that no man would leave here, that we would trust our own lives unto God, and under no circumstance would we assist the evil plague in its quest to roam further abroad. We swore an oath unto God, and we will abide by it whatever the temptation.' He breathed loudly in and out of his nose, face suffused with blood, mouth clamped firmly closed.

'I understand that,' I said, praying Dowling would hold his tongue. 'It is a noble thing, and one that any man should respect. I assume my brother took the oath.' I fervently hoped so, anyway.

'He did.' Elks replied, the scarlet of his face subsiding to a gentler pink. 'Before he entered the Kingdom of God.'

I let my lower jaw drop an inch and did my best to appear mortified.

Elks narrowed his eyes. 'Your brother is dead. He died two days ago. Did they not tell you in Colchester?'

'No,' I answered with cracked voice. 'I came to support him in his hour of need.'

'I am sorry you arrived too late.' Elks stared. 'Rest assured he died a good man.'

I found a tear from somewhere and smeared it across my cheek.

'Brave of you to come here,' said Elks, curious.

I opened my mouth and searched for a convincing platitude.

'God shall watch over us for so long as we remain virtuous,' Dowling growled.

'I am sorry you did not enter by the street, for we could have told you of his fate and you might have left freely,' said Elks. 'They buried your brother yesterday.'

I bowed my head to hide my face, praying Dowling might follow my lead. I sensed he readied to seize Elks by the neck and throttle him.

'Will you stay or will you go?' Elks asked, softly. I heard the faint edge in his voice, and recognised immediately the choice he presented.

'We will stay, of course,' I answered afore Dowling could speak. 'For we must abide by your oath, and I would spend some time in the house of my brother.'

'Ah, very good,' Elks nodded slowly. 'And so you would take the oath yourself?'

'As God is my witness,' I assured him. 'I pledge an oath to remain within these village boundaries until the Pest has departed.'

Elks muttered something, apparently satisfied, afore turning to Dowling.

'I swear unto you, I shall stay,' Dowling growled.

'Before God, please,' Elks insisted.

Dowling scratched at his nose and looked upon the heads of the four poor clerics. 'I swear unto thee and before God, that I shall not leave this village until the plague has finished killing the good men that abide here.'

'Very well,' Elks nodded. 'Then you are free to live among us as you will.' If his words spoke of trust, his eyes did not. 'Do you know the way to your brother's house?' he asked, strange gleam in those foul eyes.

'It lies up towards Town End,' said Dowling.

Elks' eyes narrowed. 'You remember.'

'Aye,' Dowling nodded. 'But we will need help to find it in this fog.'

Elks nodded his head, curtly, and beckoned us forward into the mists, away from the horrors about the village pond. The bank of fog loomed sinister and mysterious, hiding what other monstrosities, I couldn't imagine. It seemed we were in Hell, and as we followed Elks, I feared these would be our last steps and we would never get out of this place alive.

Chapter Fourteen

Because Virgo is an earthly barren sign; great mortality amongst their greater Cattle.

Elks strode fast through the white wall of fog, like he carried a map of the place in his head. The road led us down into a freezing valley before climbing back up to where the air was thinner. Thin enough to make out a square, stone cottage with grey, slate roof.

Elks stopped at the gate. 'When did you last see your brother?' he demanded.

'Three years ago,' I improvised. 'In Colchester.'

Elks shook his head, slowly. 'I don't remember Robert leaving Shyam in all my life.'

'Aye,' I replied, doing my best to appear upon the verge of new tears. 'He hated to travel.'

Elks grunted. 'No matter. Buxton had nothing of value, as you may see for yourself.' He rubbed his nose upon the back of his sleeve and stared out darkly from beneath a greasy brow. 'Be sure not to wander.' He considered us a little while longer before marching off, back into the mists.

I realised I'd stopped breathing. Thank the Lord he hadn't asked me what Buxton looked like.

The door to the cottage stood ajar. The smell of something sweet and fetid lurked within. I sought reassurance before pushing at the door. 'Elks did say they buried him?'

The door stuck. A fly buzzed around my ear then landed inside my nostril, a foul tickle.

Dowling leant against it with his shoulder. The door remained stubbornly unmoving despite Dowling's best efforts. 'Whatever it is, it's heavier than me,' he panted.

I followed the edge of the house round to the left and into the fog. I spotted a window halfway down the wall, a piece of linen soaked in linseed oil, sagging and loose. I pulled at one corner and tore it from the frame. The stink was overpowering, the steady drone of flies belying the carnage within.

'God save us,' I exclaimed, pulling away into the fresh moist air.

'And the beasts of the fields.' Dowling took my place and scanned the scene. 'It's a cow, wandered into the house and dropped dead against the door.'

I imagined what Jane would say if she found a dead cow inside our house. 'Then we may as well leave it there. We cannot live with a dead cow.'

Dowling raised an eyebrow. 'Unless you have another relative here, I don't know where else we'll sleep.'

Sleep meant another day away from London, an unsettling thought. I turned away and gazed into the gloom. The yellow mists began to thin.

Apple trees emerged, tall, dark and spectral. We were in an orchard, apples still forming, not yet ripe. Likely the harvest would fall to the ground and rot. Between the trees nothing moved, save the swirling vapours.

Suddenly I couldn't catch a breath. I felt drawn into the orchard, compelled to keep walking in a straight line until Shyam was far behind. Fear of this place clutched at my heart, a dread of Elks and the gruesome spectacle about the village pond. I longed to go home.

'I see someone,' Dowling whispered from behind my shoulder.

I shivered, the mist chilling the naked skin about my neck and chest. I followed his gaze, my heart frozen. A woman and two children, pale-faced and motionless, three ghosts, victims of the pestilence, stood the other side of a long dark mound. They watched us as close as we watched them.

Dowling tugged at my coat. 'Come on.'

My feet stuck to the floor like tree trunks, until torn from their roots by the butcher.

'Stop there!' the woman cried, voice shrill. The two children burrowed deeper into her skirts. 'Who are you?'

I held up my hands. 'Robert Buxton's brother,' I called. I would have to find myself a name.

She pulled the children in tight and stared down at the freshly-dug grave. When she glanced up, as if expecting me to collapse in a paroxysm of tears, I ducked my head and looked for sadness. I found it quickly. We stood in silence, while I imagined my father lain beneath that earth. I had known him as well as this fictional brother would have known Buxton.

'You are Robert's brother?' the woman asked, peering closer when I lifted my head.

138

'His younger brother,' I claimed again, little confidence this pretence would survive the morning.

'You are shorter than he,' she said, doubtful. 'You don't have his long nose, nor his brown eyes.'

'You thought him handsome, then?' I asked.

'He was seventy years old,' she declared. 'No man is handsome at that age. He couldn't see or hear well, but he had a kind heart, I suppose.' She seemed uncertain.

I would have to change the subject. 'Why is Robert buried here and not in the graveyard?' I asked.

She cocked her head and looked like she would cry. 'The Reverend no longer allows burials at the church. We must bury our own on our own land, and Marshall Howe buries the last to die.'

One of the children started to cry, hiding his face in the folds of his mother's dress. She placed a hand on his head and stroked his hair. 'I'm sorry, John,' she spoke soft.

I met her eye. 'What's happening here?'

She scanned the trees and squirmed, like she would rather be anywhere else. 'It started at Edward Cooper's house. He received some fabrics from London which were wet. He hung them out to dry and died next day.'

'Then the whole village took an oath to stay,' I replied. 'That is what Thomas Elks would have us believe. It seems unlikely.'

She edged sideways. 'We must go now.'

'Help us,' I pleaded, cursing my sharp tongue. 'Help us understand. Robert is dead, yet we are told we cannot leave.'

She leant forward and whispered, as if she didn't want the children to hear. 'It started at Edward Cooper's house, as I said. Everyone took fright, and several people left. The Reverend Mompesson urged his

139

own wife to take away his children, but she wouldn't go.'

I frowned. 'The Reverend is married?'

I stepped left and she stepped right, carefully maintaining the distance between us. 'Yes, he is married. Catherine is kindly. Since the plague, though, she has been sickly and weak. I think she mourns her children.' She read our faces, quickly. 'They are not dead. The Reverend sent them away before the quarantine.'

'He sent away his children and ruled no one else could leave,' I snorted.

She shook her head. 'He didn't rule it. He spoke to us in church one Sunday. He had already consulted with the Mayor of Colchester, who agreed to provide us with supplies if we pledged to remain within the village boundaries. He persuaded us it was our Christian duty, told us God would look kindly upon us.' She bowed her head again in sadness.

'Who then hath forsaken him?' Dowling asked, bemused. 'For doth he not smite ye all down?'

'Not all of us,' she snapped back, eyes wide and white. Her lip trembled and her body shook. Tears flowed like streams. 'My family remains faithful to our Lord. We pray to him morn and night. We came here to Robert's grave. We have been to the grave of every person who died in Shyam.'

'Edward Cooper died more than a year ago,' I said softly, willing her to be calm.

As she nodded, I saw in her eyes the extent to which the last twelve months wore at her spirit. 'It changed the day the Reverend closed the church,' she spoke at last. 'More than twenty died in October. Reverend Mompesson said we should no longer congregate in the church. He said we should come together once a week, out in the open air where we can maintain distance between us, where the wind blows through us. He said the graveyard was full and we should bury our own on our own land, and should mourn our own, on our own.'

And so the community began to die.

'The Reverend stayed in his house,' she said. 'No one knew what was going on in the village, for Thomas Elks told everyone to stay at home. I went to Town Head one day, when I heard a rumour John Smythe had died. Thomas Elks stopped me before Fiddler's Bridge and made me turn around. Said he would put me in the cage if he saw me again so far from home.'

An apple hit the ground, making me jump. The little boy forgot his fear and ran over to pick up the fruit. He bit into it before anyone could stop him. His face lit up and juice dripped from the side of his mouth. My soul cried out, though I knew not why. The boy gazed towards us, stood by himself apart from his mother.

'Edward Thornley was afraid,' she exclaimed. 'It was his only sin. His wife and seven children all died and he buried them himself. All he had left was his daughter.' She looked up at Dowling. 'Didn't he deserve compassion?'

Dowling nodded, solemn.

'Mompesson said he must go in the cage. The day they imprisoned him, six others tried to escape, the Thorpes and the Talbots. The sight of Edward, sat squashed inside those iron bars, like some dreadful criminal. That was when we knew the evil was entirely upon us, that God had indeed forsaken us.'

'What reason did Mompesson give?' I asked.

'He said nothing,' she said. 'We see him only once a week when he delivers the service at the Delf. Catherine sits at the front and never takes her eyes off him. He speaks, but not to us.'

'He speaks to God, then.' Dowling nodded. 'Afraid to ask what sin he committed, for fear of the Lord's vengeance.'

She reached for her son, who finished the apple. 'You are right, sir. He fears God has forsaken him, so do we all. More than forty people have died this month already, twenty this week. At this rate we shall all be dead by the middle of October.' She gripped her apron in her hands, tears welling in her eyes. 'I have six children.'

'What is your name?' I asked.

'Mary Hancock,' she replied. 'My son, John. My daughter, Elizabeth.'

'Where is your husband?' Dowling asked.

'At home,' she replied, lifting her chin. 'He is a gentle man, a good man. He is strong and will lead us through this.'

Eight of them, I calculated, of a hundred who still lived.

Tears filled her eyes and she fell to her knees, head in her hands. The two children knelt down next to her and stroked her arms. Dowling crouched on his haunches and tried to catch her attention.

She looked up at him, eyes shining. 'Katherine Talbot was my sister. I saw her in the cage this morning, dead.'

I couldn't think of a single thing to say. The mists rolled down the slope. The sun shone yellow through the canopy. I saw a shadow next to a tree, twenty yards away, a man watching.

'Someone else arrived here two weeks ago,' I said quickly. 'James Josselin?'

She didn't reply, just wept, shoulders heaving. The figure sidled forwards into the light.

'Mary!' a reedy voice shrilled. Not the voice of a man, nor the voice of a woman.

As he drew closer we saw his body, crooked, twisted and bent. His

142

eyes boggled, wild and darting, rimmed thick red. His mouth hung half open and his shoulders twitched. Black hair hung lank in the cold, moist air, shapeless and uneven. He approached Mary Hancock in a long arc, avoiding our presence.

'Mary,' he whispered, stepping forwards and backwards, dancing upon a small spot of ground. Her husband, I supposed. A gentle man indeed, but what strength he once possessed departed long ago.

I looked away, discomfited by their awkward intimacy.

Mary Hancock looked up from the ground, eyes bright. 'Why do you ask of James Josselin?'

'We heard he came here,' I replied, noticing something protruding from the dirt.

'James Josselin has not been here for ten years,' she replied, accepting the dishevelled fellow's assistance in climbing back to her feet. 'You say he is returned?' She seemed to grow afore us, body unwinding from the cramped strictures with which she bound herself.

'So it is rumoured,' I answered, afraid I might raise new expectation.

'Then we are saved,' she exclaimed, clutching at the man's shirt. 'James Josselin is a saint. He saved Colchester from Cromwell, and will save us from Thomas Elks.'

'Shh!' The man tugged at her sleeve, scanning the trees with frightened eyes.

'Hush to you,' she retorted, pulling herself free of his grasping hands. 'Thomas Elks will frighten us no more. We must make ready to leave.'

I thought to clarify that mine was a question, not a promise, but she bustled and twitched with a mad hope that would not be satisfied by cold reason. She dragged her family back towards the thick brume.

'Where does Elks live?' I called after her.

'At his brother's house, past the church, by Fiddler's Bridge.'

She turned and disappeared into the white wall, dragging her family with her. The last I saw of them were the two little children, legs pumping as they struggled to keep up.

Dowling grunted, poking in the dirt of the grave with his finger. Then he exclaimed a short growl of quiet satisfaction. 'This is what distracted you.' He held forth the battered petals of a red rose, tied to a short wooden cross. 'The cross is the crucifixion,' he said. 'The rose signifies the five wounds of Christ.'

I trawled my memory. 'A Roman thing.'

'Rome come to Shyam,' Dowling mused, prodding at the velvet petals with monstrous finger. 'The evil unto Eden.'

Chapter Fifteen

The figure of the Sun giveth warning both of
external and internal plots.

Within an hour the fog lifted, revealing the full splendour of the imposing forest surrounds. Buxton's house nestled at the top of a small green field above an orchard below. Further down the hill ran another field before a bank of forest. It appeared Robert Buxton had owned just the one cow, for the field stood empty, save for a wide bare trough.

Behind us the field narrowed towards a wooden gate, surrounded on both sides by thick blackberry bushes. Birds sang and the sun shone bright amidst a new, blue sky, an innocent backdrop to the malevolent drama in which we were embroiled. Behind the gate the high street, dry, dusty, and silent.

I walked up the slope and peered over the gate. 'Elks did say we might live freely.'

Dowling squeezed past and stepped onto the road, facing west. 'I say we talk to Elks.'

'Did you not hear Mary Hancock?' I protested. 'He will lock us in the cage. I say we go everywhere *except* Elks' house. Speak to others in the village and ask if they have seen Josselin.'

'Harry.' Dowling said my name like he spoke to a small child. 'The village is plagued and you would wander the streets knocking on doors? There is no better method I can think of by which to find the Pest.'

'We must avoid Elks at all costs,' I replied, angered.

'Yet he is the first we shall meet if we follow your plan.' Dowling spoke so sweet I felt like punching him on the nose.

'Then what is your idea?' I answered, angry.

Dowling sighed. 'If Josselin is in Shyam, then likely Elks is the only one who knows it,' he argued. 'Josselin is a hero in these parts. If they thought he resided here, they would react same as Mary Hancock. Elks knows that. So if Josselin came to Shyam seeking sanctuary, and Elks saw him first, then . . .' He shrugged.

'If Elks killed Josselin he is unlikely to confess it to us,' I retorted.

'He may not confess it, but it would be interesting to see his response.'

I scratched my head, uncertain what to do. 'About as interesting as renewing acquaintance with Withypoll.'

'We will go to Elks' house, at least,' Dowling insisted. 'If he is there, we can turn back. If not, at least we might find some sign that Josselin's been this way.'

Had we not found Josselin's book upon the road this puzzle would seem simpler. 'We don't know where to find Elks' house.'

'We will find it,' Dowling declared, striding off down the middle of the street.

I hurried after him, casting glances at the shadowy buildings looming out of the thinning mists. No one moved or made a sound. Were the occupants of all these houses dead?

At my insistence we left the road once we neared the church, following the graveyard wall round and into the trees. The forest closed in upon us once more. Trees reached over gravestones, protecting them from the worst of the summer heat. Long tendrils of ivy crept silently up and over the wall, entangling whole stones in their stifling embrace. There appeared no clear path for us to follow. Dowling burrowed through the undergrowth, rattling trees and destroying bushes. If there was anyone even close to the church they could not help but notice our presence.

At last we emerged upon the other side of the village, scratched and dishevelled, in a small clearing not ten paces from the road. Another path led off to the left.

I recalled the words of the landlady who spat upon my shoes. 'Past Elks' house is a thicket. His house stands halfway between the church and William Braine's house,' I remembered. 'Braine's house cannot be far if Town Head is just over the bridge. So Elks' house must be close, and we must be close to the thicket.'

'I reckon we're in the thicket,' said Dowling. 'So we take the path to the left and watch for cottages.'

'It leads down to the Delf,' I realised. 'Out of the village. They will arrest us if we are caught.'

'You prefer the road?'

'No,' I snapped. 'I was just saying.'

'Stop!' Dowling held up a hand. He lifted his nose to the air and narrowed his eyes, listening to the wind in the trees.

I heard nothing, nor smelt anything.

'Someone is following us,' he said at last. 'He hangs back behind, watching.'

'How do you know?'

'I hear him shuffling.'

I strained my own ears but could hear nothing specific. 'A bird or an animal.'

Dowling shook his head.

'Who, then?' I wondered, nervous. 'It can't be Elks; he would have arrested us as soon as we set foot on that path.'

Dowling stared thoughtfully towards the road. 'I doubt he will show himself.'

To return the way we came would be pointless. To step out on the road so close to the church would attract the attention of all. 'We carry on,' I decided.

Dowling headed left, sweeping aside loose branches clawing at his clothes. I followed, bracing myself against surprise attack.

The path fell off steeply and I almost tripped as we clambered down a bank, tearing the skin of my face against a stray thorn, but then it flattened and broadened out onto the forest floor. The tangled bushes disappeared, replaced by a wide expanse of trees, the ground between them covered only with leaves and low scrub.

'Come on,' Dowling beckoned, pointing to a fallen trunk. 'We'll lie behind it and see who comes.'

I hurried after him and lay against the grassy floor. I watched from between a cleft in the dead wood at one end of the log, Dowling watched from the other.

'This must be where Josselin brought Elks' dog,' I whispered.

'If that is indeed what happened,' Dowling replied, gruff. 'We have only the word of a foul-tempered landlady.'

A large spider stepped onto my sleeve and crept carefully across my wrist.

'There,' Dowling whispered. 'Someone has reached the edge of the bushes.'

I saw nothing. Perhaps the bushes trembled a bit.

'He's not sure,' Dowling said.

His eyes were at least twenty years older than mine, so how could he see what I couldn't? Maybe he was going mad. I eyed him sideways, saw him squinting intently.

'It can't be anyone local,' I said. 'They wouldn't dare descend into the Delf.'

'It's a man,' Dowling murmured. 'Dressed a bit like you.'

Then I saw him, a lean fellow with cropped scalp, wearing a linen shirt and close-fitting breeches above brown, leather riding boots. A simple costume well cut. A sword hung from his belt, gleaming dull in the low light beneath the forest canopy. He stepped out onto the leafy floor like a mouse venturing from beneath a cupboard, then scanned the scene afore him before hurrying down the track.

'Who the devil is it?' Dowling muttered. 'Some trick of Arlington's?'

'Most likely,' I replied. 'Send two spies in to do a job, then another spy to spy on the spies.'

'Perhaps,' said Dowling. 'Yet he treads less fearfully than we do. Why does he not worry about Elks?'

'Because he works for Elks.'

'Then why does he not rally reinforcements to catch us before we make an escape through the Delf?' He shook his head. 'It makes no sense.'

149

'We should follow him and find out,' I suggested, heart pounding.

'He will hear you coming a hundred yards away,' said Dowling, which remark left me speechless, coming from such a great elephant.

We lay there upon the forest floor for another hour or more, waiting to see if he would return, which he did not.

By the time I stood, I was soaked to the skin with morning dew. Dowling staggered to his feet like an old man, and we crept down the same path where walked the stranger. The village lay off to our right, hidden behind a thick row of more linden trees. Another fifty yards on the path led downwards again, into the depths of the green dell.

I turned back. 'We have come too far. The house must be closer to the street than we hoped.'

Dowling took a few steps off the track. 'It cannot be too far, else Josselin would not have thought to bring the dog here. There must be a cottage just inside the row of trees with easy passage out into the forest. We just need to look closer.' He led us up to the treeline and we backtracked towards the church.

Not more than twenty strides back we found the passage, branches from either side grown into each other to form a tight tunnel. The entrance was overgrown and the pathway covered in long grass. The cottage sat tucked inside the trees, perched upon a shallow rise. All was quiet.

I felt naked when we stepped out onto the grass and scampered to the rear of the building, away from the windows. Dowling followed, crouched over like a great bear.

'I cannot think he would be at home,' I said, hopefully.

'He has to sleep some time,' Dowling replied.

I edged closer to the glass window and plucked up courage to peer through it. I had an unblocked view from the back of house through to the front. In front of a fireplace, to my right, stood a single, wooden chair with tall back and no discernible legs, like it had been hewn from a single stump of wood. To the left, two long, wooden shelves bearing various pots and plates. Further to the left a narrow, wooden staircase led upstairs. If Elks was here, he would be in bed. A long, wooden chest sat low under the window ahead of me, next to the front door.

'The kitchen table is clear,' I said. 'If he has just gone to bed, I reckon he would have eaten something first and left it to later to clear up.'

'Not everyone is like you, Harry,' Dowling replied.

He reminded me of Jane. It was she who cleared up after me, she who kept me fed and watered. I considered again her strange behaviour the night I left. I had never seen her cry before, not even in Cocksmouth. When I went to her room she insisted I lie next to her and let her rest her head on my arm.

Dowling nudged me aside and peered through the window himself. 'No one has been home for several days,' he said, confident. 'I wonder if we have the right house.'

He headed round to the front of the building and I followed close behind. The main street hid from view behind high bushes, taller than a man. Such a peaceful little cottage, I reflected. Not how I would have imagined the house of Hugh Elks, nor his brother after him.

The front door creaked upon its hinges as Dowling pushed it, unlocked.

'I will go upstairs,' Dowling volunteered in a low growl.

'We will go together,' I insisted, 'but you may go first if it pleases you.'

The stairs squeaked louder than the door, but no one rushed to apprehend us. In one room stood a single wooden bed with simple tester and next to it a chair.

Dowling placed a hand flat upon the naked straw mattress. 'If Elks lived here before, he is living elsewhere now. No one has slept here for at least four or five days.'

'About the time Josselin is supposed to have arrived.' I wandered into the empty, second room and stared out the window. I could see over the hedge and into the window of the cottage opposite. Elks stood with arms folded staring straight back. I gasped and slapped my palm against my chest.

'We have to leave,' I cried, rushing back into the first bedroom, but Dowling was gone.

I crashed down the stairs, oblivious to creaking floorboards, just as Dowling lowered the lid of the chest. He stared at me with pale face and wide eyes.

'Elks is just across the street.' I grabbed for the door, but too late. Three men walked down the path, Elks in the middle, each leading a squat black dog. I stepped backwards into the kitchen afore calming myself enough to stop quaking. The door opened slowly and Elks stepped over the threshold. His dog stopped panting and growled, sharp, yellow teeth protruding from betwixt black gums.

Elks eyed Dowling with malevolent stare. 'What are you doing?'

The two fellows that followed towered over him, one a young man with thick arms and shiny bald head, the other leaner with bright-orange hair. One dog barked, the other simmered like a boiling pot. I thought of Mary Hancock and her new-found intent to leave Shyam with all six children. God help her.

'We came to see you,' I lied.

'Why?' he sneered, yanking at the rope that restrained his dog.

'There is a dead cow in my brother's house and we cannot open the door,' I explained. 'The carcass is covered in flies and the cow has destroyed all the furniture. We hoped you might suggest somewhere else we might stay, at least for a night.'

'Why so?' he scowled. 'You have all day to clean up the house. You come here instead? And how did you find me?'

'We asked directions,' I replied, which was not a lie.

He beckoned to his companions with a forefinger, that they might stand betwixt us and the door. 'Of whom?'

'We didn't ask a name,' I answered, not wanting to divert Elks' attentions to the restless Hancocks.

Elks shook his head, disgusted. 'What mysterious fellows you are,' he declared. 'A man or a woman?'

'A woman,' I replied quickly. 'We found her close to the church.'

Elks laughed low, a bitter cackle, bereft of humour. His two companions joined in. 'You met a woman close to the church who told you where I live?'

'No,' Dowling intervened. 'We met the woman at Buxton's house who told us you live close to the church. She was dark-haired with two children. I think she lives close by.'

I felt stunned, shocked he betrayed the Hancocks.

'Mary Hancock,' said the bald man. 'But she has six children.'

'She spoke of six children,' Dowling confirmed, 'but had only two of them with her, a boy and a girl. They paid their respects at Robert's grave and we shared with them our predicament.'

'Why did you say you found her close to the church?' Elks asked me, allowing his grip upon the dog's leash to slip a few inches. The dog pulled forwards, straining.

'It is not so far,' I replied, attention upon the hound. 'She spoke of the church, told us it's closed.'

'And so you came straight here,' said Elks.

'We came from the back of the church,' Dowling replied quickly. 'We saw another fellow wandering there and thought to ask him exactly where you lived. We followed him down into the thicket but lost him.'

'A fine story,' Elks sneered. 'Now tell me who you really are.'

'We have told you already,' Dowling answered calm. 'He is Robert's brother and I am his uncle.'

'Aye, as you told me already.' Elks turned to me again, sensing my lack of conviction. I loathed dogs. 'What is your name, Robert Buxton's brother?'

'Harry,' I replied, for it was easy to remember.

'And tell me of Buxton.' Elks let the dog slip another inch. 'What did he look like? What was his trade?'

I recalled Mary Hancock's words. 'Taller than I, with a large nose and green eyes. He became short-tempered in later life, but was a good man beneath it.'

'He was foul-tempered all his life,' exclaimed the bald fellow. 'Ever since I was a child.'

I frowned as if offended. 'He was a weaver,' I said to Elks, recalling the broken loom I saw smashed upon the cottage floor. 'It was not easy for him when his eyes began to fail.'

Elks growled louder than his dog, suspecting he had been outwitted. Good luck more than wit, I reckoned, and prayed for the conversation to end.

'Why else would they come to Shyam, Thomas?' asked the ginger fellow.

'It's what I ask myself,' Elks replied, 'but this fellow doesn't look like a relative of Robert Buxton.' He shook his head, slow. 'Him, yes.' He cocked his head at Dowling. 'But this fellow wears fine clothes.'

The ginger man wrinkled his nose, eyeing my ruined breeches, wet and wrinkled from lying on the forest floor for an hour.

'Where do you live, *Buxton*?' Elks demanded.

'London,' I replied, for I could spin few tales of any other place. Cocksmouth, perhaps. 'I journeyed there when I was young. I became a cobbler.'

Elks looked down at my feet. 'You make shoes?'

'I do,' I lied again, though I knew how to make shoes, having spent hours enough watching my father at his trade.

'Well, we may put you to the test yet.' Elks stared into my eyes. 'Though I reckon you would pass it. You're a sly fellow.'

'I want to know how you persuaded them to let you pass through Colchester,' the bald man pondered. 'Mayor Flanner told us he would admit none. Yet in the last two days we have had four men on donkeys and you two.'

'And James Josselin,' I dared remark. 'That is when I protested to Flanner and insisted we be allowed passage. Josselin may be well loved in this village, but he has no relatives.'

'James Josselin,' the bald man exclaimed with genuine puzzlement, exchanging glances with the ginger fellow. 'James Josselin would be welcome, but he is not here, nor do we expect him. What reason would James Josselin have for coming to Shyam?'

'Mayor Flanner himself confirmed it,' I insisted. 'Everyone at Colchester says it is so. We found trace of him on the road betwixt here and there – a book with his name in it.'

'Mayor Flanner may say as he wishes,' said the bald man, 'and for whatever reason it pleases him, but I assure you James Josselin has not come to Shyam. More's the pity.'

'Right,' Elks agreed, heavy browed and solemn. 'Josselin and I are not best of friends, but that is our affair. The rest of this village adores him. If he was here then we would know it.' His eyes spoke of dark, murderous deeds, but he closed his mouth tight.

'Well, Harry Buxton.' The ginger man wrapped the leash another loop around his wrist, pulling the dog closer. 'Now you're here, you are in the same boat as us.'

Elks spat upon the floor. 'And you will abide by the same rules. If you spoke to Mary Hancock then she should have told you to stay at home. We will deliver food after we collect it from the plague stone. If we find you loose again, we will lock you in the cage.'

The bald fellow frowned, taken aback, it seemed, by his companion's anger.

'You told us we may live freely,' I protested.

'You may live freely as us all,' Elks replied, 'which is not the same as roaming where your will takes you. If every man were to wander, then every man would die. There is plague in this village, and we will not survive it unless every man abides by the code.'

'Except for you three,' said Dowling.

'Us six,' Elks corrected. 'There are three more wardens you haven't met. We guard the boundaries to make sure no man escapes, in accordance with the oath every man has taken. We do so at great risk to ourselves.'

156

'We understand,' I assured him. 'We will clean up Buxton's house ourselves this very day.'

Elks scowled like he would gladly loose the black hounds. Indeed I saw his fingers twitch, but after staring at me for longer than I thought I could bear, he pulled in the leash and dismissed us with a curt nod of his head.

'You betrayed Mary Hancock!' I exclaimed as soon as the bald fellow left us alone in Buxton's field. 'And what about the man we followed? He may be innocent.'

Dowling poked a finger too close to my eye. 'I told them nothing they didn't know already, Harry, and saved our lives besides.' He grimaced. 'You must clear your head of morning fog, else we will not survive much longer.' He shook his big head. 'Elks thought he had you, Harry.'

'What do you mean?'

'The dogs, Harry, the dogs. They followed our trail from here to there, every step we took. And if the dogs picked up our scent then they picked up the scent of the other fellow besides.'

'Oh,' I exclaimed, before falling silent. The dogs. 'Well then,' I said, pulling at my sleeves. 'As well you were there.'

'As well I was,' Dowling declared, eyes gleaming. 'For now we know where James Josselin is.'

I stared at him blankly.

He grasped my shoulders. 'In the chest. I found a pair of leather boots, a long black coat and a monogrammed mouchoir.' He shook me. 'J.J., Harry, J.J.'

'Judge John Jefferies?' I wondered.

'I think not, Harry.' Dowling let me go. 'Now I will go warn the

Hancocks they may expect a visit from Elks, while you start thinking how we'll shift that cow.'

With which he stomped off into the orchard.

Why he left me with the cow, I couldn't fathom. He was the butcher, not I. I sat down against an apple tree and lit my pipe.

Chapter Sixteen

Nothing but Contentions, Contradictions in all or most matters.

Clambering through the window into Buxton's house was like breaking into a mortuary. Flies swarmed about the eyes and mouth of the dead brown cow, and every other orifice besides. They crawled; fat, sluggish and oblivious, the low buzzing noise a sound of deep contentment. The air stank of turd and the sweet smell of corporeal decay. I held my arm to my nose and mouth so nothing could fly in.

Dowling threw the rope, broom and two sharp knives onto the floor, equipment he borrowed from the Hancocks. He rolled up his sleeves and nodded at the cow's forelegs. 'Come on, Harry. Hold your breath.'

The stink was too foul to bear, but I complied with his instruction and seized one of the cow's legs. It slithered between my hands, covered in slime. The flies buzzed angrily about my head, bumping against my bare skin as we succeeded in shifting the beast clear of the door with two almighty heaves. I caught sight of the cow's dull eyes, sunken into their sockets, maggots writhing in great wriggling masses around one eyeball.

Dowling grunted, staggering backwards out onto the grass. 'Fetch the rope and the knife.'

I hurried after him, rope in hand, sucking in great lungfuls of clean air to calm the cramping of my stomach. A shovel leant against the nearest tree. 'You thought of everything,' I said, the breeze cooling my prickling brow.

Dowling nodded. 'The Hancocks were most helpful. They seem to believe we are Josselin's disciples. When I told them we suspected Josselin might be here, they went to great lengths to describe the layout of the village, and where some of the more isolated houses may be found.'

'Good work,' I exclaimed, fresh hope of walking away alive sprouting in my soul.

'Aye,' Dowling muttered. 'Now grab onto this rope and we'll shift that cow.'

Once we removed the carcass the worst of the smell went with it from the house. All that remained was a wide sticky pool of putrid body fluids and a long smear of excrement.

Dowling was the butcher, so to him fell the task of disposing of the cow's corpse while I set about tidying the cottage. Jane would be proud, I thought, else incredulous.

The front room was in predictable disarray. The kitchen table stood lopsided with one broken leg, pots and plates lay strewn about the floor, smashed and broken.

There was a pattern to the chaos, I realised as I swept. A tall, wide dresser lay face first upon the floor, but the drawers were flung about all over the room. Papers, trinkets and some ancient items of women's jewellery peppered the floorboards.

I ventured towards the back of the cottage into two small rooms. One room contained a bed and shelves, all destroyed. The other room was empty, save for rows of twine drawn across the beams from front to back. It smelt of rabbit.

I walked out into the sunshine. 'It is not the cow that made this mess. The back rooms are as bad as the front, yet the doorway is too narrow for the cow and I see no dung.'

Dowling extracted his head from betwixt the cow's ribs. A maggot wriggled on his hair. 'Mary Hancock told me someone has been taking what they will from the houses of dead men.'

I was shocked. 'Surely Elks could find out who is doing it.'

Dowling hacked at the cow's spine with the cleaver. 'Maybe Elks is in league.'

Which made grim sense. Another motive to dissuade the villagers from leaving their homes.

'Are the Hancocks still intending to leave?' I asked.

'They say not.' Dowling removed the cow's head. 'But I don't know if they told me truth. Mary Hancock is a strong woman, but not her husband. He's terrified of Elks.'

'We must leave too,' I determined, the stink of the house ripe in my nostrils. 'I might sweep that floor a hundred times, but we'll not be able to sleep in there, not without beds.'

Dowling sat up straight and regarded me with strange eyes. 'We took an oath, Harry, before God, that we would not leave afore the plague was gone.'

'Under duress,' I replied, uneasy. 'God will forgive us.'

'As I live, surely mine oath that he hath despised, even will I recompense it upon his own head. Therefore saith the Lord God.' Dowling shook his head. 'We are bound to remain else we will break our vow. Surely the plague shall be unleashed upon us.'

He was serious, I realised. 'We might be here for months,' I pointed out. 'In which case we will die of the plague, anyway.' And I would lose my shop.

Dowling wiped the blade of his knife against his trousers. 'In God shall we put our trust.'

I felt my throat constrict. 'In God shall you put your trust, Davy. I share not your faith.'

Dowling laid the cleaver upon the ground and clambered to his feet. He wiped his hands on the front of his shirt and rubbed them briskly. 'I have known it since we met, Harry,' he said. 'You think you don't believe in God, so you say, yet how many times do you call upon him?'

'It's a habit,' I replied. 'God knows.'

Dowling laughed aloud. 'So he does, Harry, if you do not.' He folded his arms and stood afore me like a small mountain, bestowing upon me a saintly gaze.

If God sent a second son to this earth, why not a butcher this time instead of a carpenter? Surely he wouldn't look like Dowling, though.

'I will not stay in Shyam to *avoid* the plague,' I said. 'God or no God, it would be a nonsense.'

Dowling scowled. 'God shall smite you down.'

'With luck he shall overlook my innocent slight,' I replied. 'For the list of the condemned must be long by now. God is old, anyway; perhaps he will forget.'

'God is not mocked,' Dowling's nose coloured. 'For whatsoever a man soweth, that shall he also reap.'

I turned away. 'Whatever God's will, we cannot sit here waiting for death. Tonight we will search again for Josselin. Wherever Elks has been staying these last few nights, that's where we will find James Josselin. He has taken him to a place where none will find him, the house of one already killed by plague.'

'Aye,' Dowling nodded. 'And since two-thirds of the village is dead, that leaves many houses to search.'

'As well the Hancocks explained where we might best focus our efforts.' I calculated in my head. 'If there are two hundred dead, then that is likely no more than fifty households. Of those no more than ten would suit Elks' purpose.'

Though the sky was clear that night and the fields brightly lit by a well-fed moon, it was not so easy to navigate through the forest. The tunnel afore us was black as coal, oblivious to the moon's fine efforts. A light wind rustled the leaves of the trees, whispering in our ears, imploring us to enter.

'The house of Adam and Alice Hawkesworth,' Dowling told me again. 'Their cottage stands about a mile into the forest down this path, in a small clearing. They died there nine months ago. It was a while afore they were discovered. The man that found them was a farmer called John Wood. He died a week later, but not before recounting the horror he stumbled upon. The animals of the forest had already begun to dispose of the bodies.'

It could be no worse than Buxton's cottage.

'There are two more houses we may come to first,' Dowling said. 'The Mortens and the Frythes. They still live.'

'Then we should count our footsteps,' I suggested. 'A mile is about two thousand paces.'

Dowling snorted. 'The Mortens and Frythes will have candles in their windows. I think we'll find our way easily enough.'

Stepping into the darkness was like taking off my clothes, so vulnerable I felt. I stared wide-eyed and unblinking yet saw nothing. A man might stand silent in front of us and we wouldn't see him. Nor he us.

Thirty paces in, the forest canopy fractured, allowing thin shards of light to illuminate the scene about us. A few pale trees framed the way forward into another black void. Sudden rustles in the bushes, the mournful hooting of an owl high above us, only served to cultivate the panic that threatened to undo me.

Dowling pointed into the trees. 'A flame.' A small fire burning on level ground in front of a squat wooden cabin. What strangeness compelled a man to live in such isolation? I imagined all the creatures of the night poised in a wide circle about the dwelling, all sat just out of the light. We stayed on the path, crossing the front of the small house, behind a clump patch of trees. Our footsteps shattered the silence no matter where we placed our feet.

'Hold!' Dowling beckoned me again, crouched behind a thick bush. 'Someone is busy.'

A hulking giant, broad and crouching, moved across a small square window.

'Mary Hancock described the Mortens as an old couple without children,' Dowling whispered, 'I reckon this is their house.'

'Then that is not Morten,' I concluded.

A loud crash sounded from within the cabin, like a boulder fell through the roof, then three muffled blows sounded against the wall or the floor.

Dowling stretched his neck out further. 'I think we have found our vandal,' he murmured.

We sat listening to the violence, while I pictured the inside of Buxton's house. The man I glimpsed was a giant, fully capable of pushing over a dresser or throwing a cot against the wall. A man to be avoided.

Then at last, peace. An unnatural silence while we waited for something to happen.

The front door opened and the big man emerged, leaning forwards, carrying a lamp in his left hand, tugging on a rope stretched over his right shoulder. I ducked behind the bush as he stepped into the clearing, facing in our direction. I heard a strange slithering noise, loud and rough, like a giant serpent wriggling on its belly.

A light shone between the branches of my bush, the lamp, flickering, swinging from side to side. As I watched, unbreathing, the giant walked past us, twenty yards to our left, pulling on the rope. Attached to the rope was a corpse, the body of a woman with a noose tied round her neck. I watched aghast, the vile beast tugging her body through the dirt.

The woman was old, her long grey hair spread loose. Her head strained against the rope as if her neck might snap off from her body at any moment. Her face was scarlet, eyes black and protruding.

'What in God's name,' I whispered, my voice protected by the sound of the woman's body sliding over the ground.

'Marshall Howe,' Dowling said. 'He who buries the last corpse of every household. He ties the rope about their necks so he doesn't have to touch their bodies.'

Marshall Howe dragged the dead woman six feet behind, her body shrouded in darkness.

'How do you deduce that?' I challenged him. 'The fellow is a brute and a beast. How do you know he hasn't simply robbed her of her

165

belongings and takes the body away for some nefarious motive?'

'It's Marshall Howe,' Dowling repeated. 'When Mary Hancock mentioned his name the boy cried. He ransacks the houses to claim his reward.'

'A scavenger, then,' I said. 'The villagers praise him for his heroic deeds, yet he does it only for greed. Another evil demon with a black heart. He smashes dressers onto the floor when all he need do is open a drawer.'

'He doesn't want to touch the furniture,' suggested Dowling, standing up and brushing the debris from his trousers. 'Perhaps he is a good fellow, perhaps not. Only God knows which, for the dead do not miss their possessions.'

Howe plodded off into the distance, back towards the village. I watched the lamp swing and lurch, my courage wobbling with it.

Dowling headed off the other way, into darkness. 'Come on, Harry.'

I hurried after him before we reached another black tunnel. This time I gripped a handful of sleeve. To bump into Dowling would be no less painful than bumping into a tree.

I counted aloud, another hundred paces before we again emerged into a ghostly circle. I breathed deep and placed my palm upon my beating heart. It was not the dark I feared, rather what lay beneath.

Dowling stared into the trees, eyes watchful, face unmoving. He leant forwards, nose twitching. 'They grope in the dark without light and he maketh them to stagger like a drunken man.' He thumped me on the back, his attempt to encourage me.

The track sloped gently downwards in a long curve. We stepped off the path into low, spiny bushes, thorns stabbing at my legs. If the house stood in a clearing, there must be an expanse of sky above it.

It shouldn't be possible to walk past it in the dark. I couldn't bear the thought we might get lost. How did we know we hadn't passed a fork in the path that might lead us astray? A thick ball of fear threatened to burst inside my chest.

'Ahead,' Dowling exclaimed, excited.

I prayed his enthusiasm was not misplaced. Tears welled up in my eyes when I saw he was right. The cottage was a tiny grim abode, shrouded in shadow, sinister and mysterious. Yet I was delighted to see it.

Dowling pulled me forwards, faster than I wanted to walk. 'Hurry.'

I dragged my heels in the dirt. 'Why?'

'Someone else is with us,' he said, jerking me so hard I almost stumbled.

I flung myself behind the wall and stared across the grass. Nothing. I strained my ears, but again could hear nothing above the sound of Dowling's heavy breathing.

I placed a hand against the stone wall of the cottage, cold as ice despite the warmth of the breeze that swelled through the forest. No sound from within, nor the slightest shard of light. If Elks lived here, why no light, no candle in the window to guide him?

Then a branch snapped, like a musket shot, clear and loud, cracking against the silent backdrop. Whoever followed tracked us by the sound of our footsteps. Elks wouldn't be so subtle.

'One of them and two of us,' Dowling growled. 'He's followed us from the Morten house. I heard him when Howe reached the treeline.'

'You didn't tell me,' I grumbled.

'It wouldn't have helped,' he said. 'You were shaking like an old woman.'

I clenched my jaw and scowled, furious.

Something rustled across the clearing on the other side of the path, an animal, something small.

I stared ahead while my mind absorbed the quietness of the surrounds, the likelihood we were at the wrong house. The possibility that this nightmare trek was in vain. I felt like punching something. Dowling's chin.

'See,' Dowling hissed, grabbing again at my sleeve. I wrenched his hand free and bent round to peer past his great arse.

It was the same fellow we saw earlier in the day. A skinny man with naked bony head, attempting to hide himself in the shadows of the trees as he sidled about the edge of the clearing. He carried a sword in his left hand, held afore him as if he expected to be ambushed at any moment.

'You think Elks and his dogs again?' I whispered.

'I doubt it,' Dowling answered. 'Six of them patrol the village, and all must sleep sometime. So I suspect no more than three of them come out at night, determined to guard the main roads in and out.'

The thin man stopped and cocked his head, no more than twenty paces away. Dowling crouched, muscles taut. He clearly intended to throw himself upon the poor unfortunate, sword or no sword. His only chance was to run for it, for Dowling was slow, yet he kept advancing. Then he made a dash across the blue terrain, towards the front door of the house and out of our view.

Dowling stepped about the side of the house and I followed, scanning the ground as we tiptoed. A small pile of logs sat at the front of the cottage, left over from winter. Dowling lifted two logs from the heap, handing one to me. A weapon.

The front door stood ajar. Inside I heard shuffling, the sound of our pursuer stumbling in the dark. Dowling put a finger to his lip, and slipped inside. I followed, darting quickly to my right into the depths of the deepest shadow. A floorboard creaked. Then a much quieter sound; the deft step of a lighter man. Dowling's head appeared in the moonlight shining through the window and I saw a flash of silver. I leapt forward and aimed my log at a black shadow to my left. A man shouted and so I hit again at the same space. Something hit the floor with a heavy thud.

'Why did you do that?' Dowling exclaimed, furious.

'You have the ears of an elephant,' I replied, 'but you walk like one too. He would have run you through before you blinked.'

'Nonsense.' He gripped the man's shirt and dragged him out into the moonlight, practically choking the fellow.

I picked up the fallen sword then knelt next to the intruder. 'You are old and heavy, Dowling, which is why he heard you and didn't hear me.'

'It was the noise you made attracted him to the door,' Dowling protested.

'Look in a mirror,' I snapped. 'You are what you see.'

I had hit the man just above the ear, and on the back of the head. Both wounds bled freely, but he was still conscious, though pained. He rolled onto his back and opened his eyes.

'Who are you?' I demanded.

'Who are you?' he slurred, dribbling from the corner of his mouth.

He was quite young, about the same age as me. A layer of black stubble carpeted his head. His eyes were clear and blue, his demeanour sharp and determined.

'I asked you first,' I replied, 'and if you don't answer, then Dowling will rip your arms off.'

'Galileo,' he said, which was obviously a lie.

Dowling looked suitably annoyed, but the young man eyed him dispassionately, seemingly unafraid.

I fingered his fine-cut shirt. The look in his eye was that of a seasoned campaigner, one experienced in the ways of the court. 'You are not of this village,' I said. 'So I wonder how you walk so freely? Elks' men trailed you with their dogs earlier. How did they not find you?'

'I walked up the stream,' he replied, disdainfully. 'Dogs have sharp noses, but these villagers have dull brains.'

He levered himself onto his elbows and looked about, assessing the situation calmly, despite the blood dripping down his cheek. 'Why did you hit me twice?' he complained, wiping at the blood with his palm.

'You were about to stab Davy in the stomach,' I replied. 'Of course I hit you twice. You are lucky to be alive.'

'Hah!' he exclaimed, sitting up straight. 'So you say.'

He clambered to his feet, much to my alarm. I jumped up before him and held the sword towards his chest.

He held up a hand before turning back into the cottage. 'I am looking for a cloth, to hold to my skull where you hit me with that log.'

'Marshall Howe has been here,' he remarked, picking his way carefully through the debris. He stopped, attracted by the edge of a tablecloth. 'Someone's finest,' he said, jerking it clear of the table that lay atop of it.

'Do you work for Lord Arlington?' I asked, for he had the arrogance of another Withypoll.

'Not I,' he replied. 'Nor you, judging by your appearance. Yet if you speak of him you must have some connection with the court.' He wiped at his head. 'For my part I intend to tell you nothing.'

I handed the sword to Dowling. 'Tell us at least how you walk so freely.'

'I didn't tell them I arrived.' He shrugged. 'You two wandered into the middle of the village and stood waiting for them to find you.' He laughed and shook his head. 'Simple fellows, I told myself, but I would understand your intentions.'

'Not so simple we didn't spot you following us this morning,' I pointed out. 'And relieve you of your sword tonight.'

'Aye,' he grimaced. 'I am simpler than you.'

'If you have no connection with Elks then we have nothing to hide,' Dowling growled, 'and since we are so simple, why would you seek to hide anything from us?'

'A good point,' Galileo said. 'And I am feeling dizzy. Would that Howe might leave furniture to sit on.'

'We are here to find James Josselin,' Dowling said. 'I think you are too.'

'True enough,' he replied. 'Though I have been unable to find him. This was a likely place to look.' He nodded, impressed. 'Though not the right place. Why did you come here?'

'If you have travelled the whole journey as cautiously as you entered Shyam, then you have not spoken to the same folks we have,' Dowling replied. 'We are confident we know where he stays.'

'He doesn't stay here.' Galileo waved a hand at the silent shadows. 'So why come all the way out here in the middle of the night?'

'No more questions,' Dowling said. 'Not until you tell us something of yourself.'

Galileo shrugged. The blood on his head formed a thick clot. 'Since you have been so open with me I will be open with you. Tell it to Arlington, though, or indeed any other, then you will be killed. Not by me, you understand. By Arlington.'

'Go on,' Dowling urged.

Galileo dabbed at his head one last time before throwing the cloth to the floor. 'Josselin didn't kill the Earl of Berkshire. They were best friends.'

I frowned. 'We know that already. Josselin's mother told us.'

'They were both part of the mission that went to Holland to negotiate a peace,' said Galileo.

'I didn't know there was a peace process,' I exclaimed. 'Arlington told us Josselin sabotaged any chance of peace.'

'The peace mission was not public knowledge,' said Galileo. 'Nor was Arlington sincere in pushing for it. His fondest wish was that the House of Orange would rise up and depose De Witt, and make peace with England on our terms.'

It seemed complicated to me.

'And yes,' he jabbed a finger at my chest, 'Arlington is telling everyone that Josselin sabotaged the peace process, which makes no sense, for Josselin was personally committed to it, believed in the coming together of two Protestant nations. Which is why I must find Josselin, to discover the truth of it, to know what he knows.'

'And you work for the Earl of Clarendon,' I surmised, my own head as thick as his.

He nodded.

'Then we are on the same side,' I worked out. 'All of us working for the King.'

He cast upon me a withering glance. 'No man is so simple as that.'

'No, indeed,' I winced. As well the darkness hid my red face. 'Whether we be on the same side or not, we are as keen as you to discover the truth. Though no one seems to know Josselin is here, we found his boots and coat in a chest in Elks' house.'

Galileo stood away from the wall. 'Elks has him imprisoned, and you came here because this place is remote.'

'Aye.' Dowling agreed. 'And there cannot be many cottages so remote, where the occupants are dead.'

There didn't need to be many if it took us all night to visit every one. Yet Galileo seemed impressed. 'Then we shall find him soon,' he declared, resolute. 'Now, shall we return to Shyam or do you have more houses to visit tonight?'

He walked the fastest of the three of us, pausing impatiently when he approached the pond. He squinted as if blinded, the purple lump upon the side of his head swollen to the size of a tennis ball.

'I will meet you at the cottage where you are staying, sometime in the morning.' He touched the bump gingerly. 'Don't follow me.' With which he slipped into the undergrowth and was gone.

'He seems like a worthy fellow beneath it all,' I reflected.

'Bright-eyed and full of intent,' Dowling replied. 'That doesn't make him a worthy fellow.'

'Aye, then.' I was too tired to debate the matter further. 'I am glad he is gone, though, for we have work to do.'

Chapter Seventeen

The Moon applying into Mars prenotes the degrading, or lessening the honours of some in Authority.

The water on the pond lay flat, polished black and blue beneath the moonlight, not a ripple upon its surface. The gibbets on their posts stood black against the pale night sky. In the cage ahead I made out five bodies. Two sat huddled, moving occasionally, the other three lay motionless next to each other, in a row. A goatsucker sang loud from somewhere to our right, a strange trilling sound, like a giant grasshopper. Some called it the corpse bird.

I sighed and stared out upon the quiet scene afore me. We watched from beneath a tall hedge that marked the boundary with the field behind. It was my idea to wait here for Elks. I had no desire to spend another day in this infected hole and was determined to leave as soon as we were able, no matter Dowling's objections. Elks was at home or at the barricades tonight, which meant that sometime around dawn he would likely arrive or leave. If we could establish the direction of his coming or going then it would greatly help our search. The darkness was a mercy, a comforting blanket beneath which to hide. Then Dowling began to snore.

Rather than disturb him I took off my jacket and laid it over his face. The chill helped me stay awake. I wearied of sneaking about this village. I wearied of the fear that suffocated my heart and froze my wits. I struggled to dismiss the presence of Death from my thoughts, but it was impossible.

I shivered. What I wouldn't pay now to walk into the Mermaid and sit myself by the fireplace with a cup of wine and a plate of oysters. I thought again of Jane and her strange behaviour. I recalled the softness of her skin, wide green eyes and open face, glimpsed only for a moment in Cocksmouth. After we recovered from the discharging of our carnal lusts, she regarded me with renewed ferocity, angrier than before. It was like I was the thief and she the victim, which seemed to me like the spider blaming the fly for giving it a stomach ache. But since we returned to London she was different, like she entertained the notion of a different way of being.

I was too cold to sleep. I marvelled at Dowling, lain upon his back, my coat upon his face, gently rumbling. He was not a fat man. To touch his body was like prodding a rock. What kept him warm? His faith, would be his reply. Thick hide and a fat head would be my guess.

First light crept over the horizon just as I thought I would freeze. New birds sang lustily, to warm themselves up, obscuring the jarring song of the goatsucker. At their cue the first strands of red crept above the horizon, slowly infiltrating the skies above us.

A scream rent the air, shrill and piercing. Dowling made a sequence of foul noises like he was kissing himself. I tugged the jacket from his face and prodded him in the ribs. He opened his eyes and stared about him, disoriented. I wriggled forwards, deeper into the hedge, to seek from where the noise came. Two men in the cage climbed to their feet, stood with their hands clutching the bars, staring towards the church.

A slight figure appeared at the far side of the pond, running from the canopied track that led east, naked body white against the grey surroundings. She ran with arms held out straight as if she sought to rid herself of her own hands. When she saw the gibbets she stopped, staring with wild eyes, body jerking in rhythm with her staccato cries. Then she screamed again and leapt into the pond.

Two figures ran out of the woods behind her, Elks and the bald man we met earlier that day. They stopped at the edge of the pond where the woman stood up to her waist splashing water upon her chest, face contorted in agonised grimace. A third figure lumbered slow behind, short stumpy legs struggling beneath a hulking torso, rope curled about his shoulder. The giant Marshall Howe, wearing but a thin shirt with sleeves rolled up as far as they would go. He reminded me of Dowling.

Dowling fidgeted. 'If they don't pull her out soon she'll die of cold.'

I had seen the symptoms too many times before. 'She will die of plague before she dies of cold.'

Elks laid a hand upon the bald man's shoulder before turning to Marshall Howe. He talked quickly while Howe listened, head bowed. Then the giant nodded and let the rope from his shoulder fall to the floor. He tied one end into a noose then waded out into the water behind the woman. He paused a moment before lowering the rope over her head and jerking it tight. She fell backwards, clutching at her throat. Howe pushed her head down into the pond while she kicked and splashed. When the thrashing ceased, Howe stood up straight and attempted to pull her onto the bank. He reached halfway, breathing heavily, before turning for help. The bald man stepped gingerly into the water to join him, taking a piece of rope from Howe's huge hands. They then pulled together, tugging hard, digging their heels into the soft mud. At last they succeeded, jerking the corpse from the bottom of the pond where it must have got stuck, depositing it onto the grass.

The whole world fell silent, holding its breath in disbelief. I blinked and waited for the corpse to move. Dowling stared, white-faced, jaw loose. What could we have done to prevent it? It happened too quick. My heart was beating so hard it would explode.

Howe picked up the rope from where he dropped it and pulled her dead body along the grass towards the forest. Elks pushed a lock of lank hair behind his ear, touched the bald man on the shoulder, and headed after Howe. The bald man headed off in the opposite direction towards Fiddler's Bridge. The sky seemed to sigh, casting upon us another degree of light. We witnessed a savage murder, no less, whatever their casual demeanour.

Dowling clambered to his feet. 'We follow.'

I took his lead, head heavy with lack of sleep and numbed shock. I had no desire to follow Elks lest it was to find out where he lived, but could find no words to debate the case.

We paused at the stile afore hurrying about the perimeter of the pond. Two clerics stood at the bars of the cage, their heaving sobs betraying the shattered ruins of their faith. Dowling didn't spare them even a glance, marching forward with grim determination.

Howe and Elks were easy to follow, the steady slithering of the corpse upon the forest floor marking their journey. We followed at a distance, sticking to the early morning shadow at the side of the path. Daylight stabbed through the treetops as if searching for the perpetrators of the terrible sin.

Halfway to Buxton's house the noise stopped. Elks said something to Howe afore disappearing into the trees to our left and Howe resumed his steady trudge up the main track. We ran to the point where Elks departed, as fast as we could without making a noise, not daring to attract Howe's attentions. I put my fingers in my ears, unable to bear the sound of the woman's feet bumping off tree roots and broken branches.

At last we reached the bend. The path to our left wound down through thick undergrowth like a ribbon, between beech tree and birch, into a gloomy basin where the young, morning light struggled to penetrate. We stepped down the hill as fast as we could, wary now we had no sense where Elks might be. A branch hit me hard across the forehead.

Dowling walked faster, nose thrust forward like a sniffing dog. He pointed out a narrow opening in the undergrowth I would scarce have noticed, a narrow track sheltered by giant fern. 'He turned off again here,' he whispered.

'How do you know?' I asked.

'He is headed towards Isaak Wilson's house,' Dowling replied. 'The house sits another hundred paces down this path, and Wilson died twelve months ago.'

'The plague found him here?'

'Don't talk of the plague,' Dowling snapped, voice tight.

My foot slipped upon the rolling earth and I nearly fell, grasping at Dowling to stop myself falling.

'You walk like an infant,' Dowling growled, righting me roughly then letting me go. 'Be mindful, else he will hear you.'

I clenched my jaw and concentrated on the ground beneath my feet, paying attention to the roots protruding from the dirt. At last the ground flattened. We came to the edge of a small clearing, in the middle of which stood another stone house and two wooden outhouses. Elks was gone, but light shone from the main window.

'Isaak Wilson's house,' Dowling muttered. 'With someone else's candle in the window.'

We burrowed into the thick undergrowth, easing our way through the clutching bramble. Elks had not had the dog with him, I realised, heart suddenly cold. Was the dog here? It couldn't be; why would he have left it at the house? He must have been on his way home when he came across the affected woman. The dog would be at the barricades with the other wardens. I prayed it was so and made extra effort to tread silently.

We found a trunk so thick we could both lean against it. The candle danced, flickered and eventually died. Colours came to life as the sun climbed high, and the earth warmed up. I fell asleep, at last, head rested against Dowling's heavy shoulder.

I woke alone, lain upon my side, hungry. Sitting bolt upright I looked for Dowling, finding only flattened ground, cold to the touch. Staggering to my feet I saw the house through the hedge. To my left now led a long trail of flattened gorse, lined on either side by low bushes, branches broken off and snapped by a beast the size of a great bull. I followed the trail of debris and found Dowling stood next to a tree, peering towards the back of the house.

'Is he in there?' I whispered, stretching my stiff limbs.

'Aye,' said Dowling. 'He stirred himself a few minutes ago. I reckon he's about to leave.'

'What else have you found?'

Dowling rubbed his neck. 'One of the outhouses is derelict, the other is secured with a new lock.' He turned. 'Move. Back to where we were. Quickly.' He pushed me up the path, towards the giant tree trunk.

The door opened and Elks strode forth, swinging a club like he expected to use it, brown hair hanging heavy about his ears, long face bereft of mercy. He looked fresh and well rested, full of vigorous intent. I tucked myself deeper into the cover as he strode past, up the slope and away into the woods. Once he was gone I shuffled to my feet and forced myself to stand straight.

'He won't be gone long,' I predicted. 'He'll go straight to Buxton's house to check on us. When he finds us gone he'll track us down with his dogs.'

'If Josselin is here, then he is in the outhouse,' said Dowling. He led the way to a low wooden building without windows, wide heavy door bolted from the outside.

'Built strong,' I remarked, rubbing my hand against the rough planks.

'Aye,' Dowling agreed, 'but a long time ago.' He pulled at the padlock, a squat heavy beast with a flap over the keyhole. 'The lock is strong, but not the hinges.'

He let the lock drop against the door and pointed to the top hinge, a simple dovetail with six screws, all rusted. The wood was brittle and dry. 'We just need a lever.'

He strode across the clearing to the house. No lock to contend with here, for the door was open. The air was musty, the light poor. A heavy table occupied the middle of the room, with four chairs, three of which sat flush against the side of it. Of more interest were the two loaves of bread and a plate of dried beef.

I poked my head into the back room while chewing. Elks wasn't a clean man. A chamber pot stood full in the middle of the floor and the bed stank most foul.

Dowling turned from the unlit fireplace with a poker in his hand. 'Here.'

'What will we find?' I wondered aloud, approaching the outhouse once more.

'There is little point in guessing.' Dowling sighed. 'Though if Wilson died without releasing his animals, we should be able to smell it from Shyam. I reckon this is Elks' work.'

He stabbed at the wood about the top hinge with the end of the poker. I prayed it wouldn't take long, still fearful of Elks and his dogs. Nor did it, for Dowling worked in a mad frenzy, chopping at a crack in the door with the blunt iron bar until it widened enough for him to jam the poker in and tear the wood apart. Once the top hinge was loose, he prised the door far enough away from the jamb to grip it in his hands. He pulled with all his weight, grunting red-faced. When the bottom hinge gave way with a shriek, we were through, into another pocket of Hell.

The room was bare, floor strewn with rotting straw, tiny shards of light providing scant illumination from between the weathered planks. At the end of the room squatted a man, chained to a low iron bar running the width of the outhouse, in front of two long troughs.

'Mind the hole,' he grinned, wrists manacled to his waist, nodding to our right. 'That is to be my grave.'

Someone had dug a large hole, six feet long and a yard across.

He leant forwards, legs crossed, naked body filthy, the tip of his yard resting limp against the straw. A chain connected the iron band at his waist to a four-foot iron bar. The stench of piss and faeces soaked the air. He stared with bright eyes, mouth fixed in a broad smile, sinister and humourless. Long dark hair hung wet about his shoulders and plastered his forehead, yet the eyes burnt.

I took care not to approach closer than the length of the chain. 'Your grave, you say?'

'Aye,' he replied, leery. 'Elks dug it for me. He thinks the sight of it will drive me mad.' He snorted. 'I enjoyed watching him dig it. The ground is hard.'

'You are James Josselin?' I surmised.

He nodded. 'And you are spies.'

Unfolded he would stand uncommonly tall, I reckoned, more than six feet. Or perhaps he just seemed that way because he was so awfully thin. His ribs stood out like the claws of a demon. I looked about for signs of food and water, but found none.

'When did you last eat?' I asked.

'A week ago,' Josselin replied. 'The devil doesn't feed me. I suck straw for water.' I felt my guts churn, for the straw was yellow and soft, weeks old and creeping with insects.

The flesh about his eyes and cheeks was purple and blue. A long ugly welt wound its way from below his ribcage to beneath his arm. Someone had kicked him, else beaten him with a stick. He eyed Dowling's poker like it was an old adversary.

'How long have you been here?' I asked.

'Since I came,' Josselin replied. 'Elks was first to meet me. My bad luck.' He stared at me once more, small brown eyes unmoving, lips drawn back to reveal bright white teeth. The flesh about his wrists was red and festering and he smelt like he was rotting. This, then, was the 'great man'.

I pulled from my pocket a hunk of bread I was saving for later. He took it with grace and chewed, unhurried. He squinted. 'Methinks you came to fetch me back to London, but you cannot take me back.' He held up his chained wrists. 'Less you have the key.' He laughed, a sad abrasive noise tinged with lunacy. 'Did Arlington send you here, or was it Clarendon?'

I tried not to gaze upon his genitals.

'Why say you Arlington or Clarendon?' Dowling demanded, wandering dangerously close.

Josselin eyed Dowling out the corner of his eye. 'Arlington says I betrayed England to the Dutch. Clarendon is the most determined to make peace.'

'We work for Arlington,' I said. 'Though not willingly. He says you killed your best friend.'

Josselin breathed slow and steady through his nose, his face turning a violent shade of crimson. He clambered painfully to his feet and stood erect, bashed and bruised, covered in a thick layer of dirt and sweat. I edged backwards. Though his arms were chained to his waist, still I feared the look in his eyes. I didn't trust him not to bite me.

He shuffled forwards, as far as the chains would allow and jerked his wrists away from his iron girdle, succeeding only in making them bleed. 'I am not a traitor nor a murderer.' He let his head roll back and stared at the ceiling, stood silent, trembling.

'We found your book,' I said nervously. 'On the way to Shyam.'

'My book?' He lowered his chin and blinked. 'You have my book?'

'I do,' I remembered, digging into the folds of my jacket.

'Keep it,' he snapped. 'Charlatan words writ by devious agents. Believe nothing you read.'

'You circled passages pertaining to the Dutch.'

'The book is written by a charlatan. It tells of the demise of the Dutch forces.' He stepped towards me, restrained only by the chain. 'Ask yourself why the Dutch must fall.'

'We are at war,' I replied, bewildered. 'Of course the Dutch must fall.'

Josselin bared his teeth. 'And why did Charles have to die?'

I blinked 'Berkshire? I don't know why he had to die. Arlington said you killed him.'

'My best friend,' he said, clenching his fists. 'Why did I kill my best friend?'

'Do you know who did?' I asked, nervous.

'Aye, I know,' he replied. 'At least I know who ordered it.' He clamped his mouth closed and glared.

Dowling took another step closer. 'Everyone has told us what you did in Colchester when you were a child,' he said.

I cursed him silently for distracting Josselin. I wanted to know who killed Berkshire, not listen to old stories, embellished and re-embellished with the passing of two decades.

Josselin bowed his head. 'Josselin the hero,' he said. 'Who tried to save Colchester from the barbaric hordes of General Fairfax.' He nodded to himself. 'You know Fairfax still lives? Black Tom. Forgiven all his trespasses because he helped Monck bring the King out of exile.' He clenched his fists again and grimaced, a thick blood vessel standing prominent upon his brow. 'My mother was one of the five hundred brave women that pleaded for food, once the soap and candles ran out,' he said. 'They stripped her of her clothes like the other four hundred and ninety-nine. Then they chased her about the fields on horseback until at last they allowed them to return inside the town walls. Most of them, anyway.'

'They say you didn't talk even when they tortured you.'

Josselin sucked the air in through his teeth then closed his eyes. 'They said they would hang me unless I told them the message I carried and who it was for.'

'You were just a boy,' I exclaimed. 'Any boy would have confessed it, any man would have confessed it. They were soldiers that tortured you.'

'I know who they were,' Josselin murmured, eyes tight closed. 'And I saw what they did. I would have told them the message the moment they asked, but I forgot it.' His eyes were moist. 'Each time they held a match to my finger I begged them to stop, but they would not.'

I looked at his hands. The skin on his fingertips was ridged and rutted, like the landlady said.

'You are a hero to these people,' I said. 'Every man in Essex talks of you with fondness.'

'I don't know these people,' Josselin retorted. 'I was a child. I left when I was a young man. They say I am a hero because I wouldn't speak, yet I knew not what to say. They are not interested in the truth. Not now, not then.'

'Then why did you come here?'

'To escape Arlington,' he replied. 'I knew he wouldn't follow, not into Shyam.'

Now he stood naked in a cowshed wrapped in chains, deep in the heart of plague country.

'Who killed Berkshire?' I asked.

A dog barked, close by. I turned to Dowling. 'Elks!'

Josselin again strained to pull his wrists away from the chain that bound them to his waist, roaring with frustration and pain. The iron cut into his flesh, releasing a fresh tide of blood and pus to pour over the palms of his hands.

'Come!' I urged Dowling. 'It's our scent they are following.'

'We cannot leave him here,' Dowling protested.

'We'll come back,' I hissed. I raced towards the forest, then stopped and cut back, running across the track that led from the village, diving into a low cluster of bracken.

'What are you doing?' Dowling demanded, panting, towering above me. 'You think the dogs won't find you?'

'Lie down!' I croaked, hoarse, burying my head. The barking was close now.

He lowered himself gracelessly to the ground, grumbling.

'We won't escape the dogs,' I whispered. 'There is no point in running. I want to see what Elks does.'

Dowling frowned and shook his head as the first of our pursuers burst into the clearing. It was Elks, black dog straining at its leash before him. He flicked at his lank hair with one hand, glowering at the broken outhouse door. He scanned the clearing quickly afore hurrying to the barn, allowing his dog to pull him forwards. Staring into the black void, he jerked back the leash, refusing the hound liberty to prowl further. Then the dog found our new scent and tried to pull away again, but Elks held his ground. Four more men arrived, three dogs between them, yapping loud in their desire

186

to be let loose, strangulated barking peppered with intermittent squeals.

'That way,' Elks pointed away from the barn. 'The scent goes that way.'

I leapt up. 'No need!' I shouted, lifting my hands above my head. 'We are here.'

Dowling scrambled to his feet and joined me, pained expression on his face showing he doubted my sanity.

Elks scowled, face scarlet, with the exertion of running ahead, I wagered. What had he thought, I wondered, as the dogs led him closer and closer to Wilson's house? I heard anger in his snarl and saw the fear in his eyes.

'James Josselin is in that outhouse,' I cried. 'We weren't trying to escape. We came to Shyam to find James Josselin and we found him in that barn.'

The bald man laughed. 'James Josselin hiding in Shyam,' he snorted. Yet he let his hound pull him towards the broken door.

'Keep out of there,' Elks warned, edging sideways. 'Take these two to the cage and we will deal with them later.'

'I tell you Josselin is inside the barn,' I said again. 'Chained and manacled. Elks has held him there this last week, planning to bury him alive. There is a grave there. Just look.'

The bald man stepped about Elks, assessing him warily as he did so. I stepped sideways, hands still raised, so I could see inside the barn. Josselin stood stiff, watching the bald man approach with imperious disdain.

'This cannot be James Josselin,' the bald man exclaimed, regarding Josselin's filthy naked body with disgust. 'This is some lunatic.'

'If I wasn't chained I would bite off your face,' Josselin growled, eyes blazing. Blood covered his shoulders, thick and sticky. 'You are John Smythe and I will not forget it.'

The bald man took a quick step backwards, like he trod on a snake.

'Enough!' Elks roared. 'This man is indeed a lunatic. I caught him trying to enter the village last night and imprisoned him. He had no clothes when I discovered him.'

'You didn't tell us,' Smythe replied.

'No,' I said. 'Nor did he tell you he has James Josselin's clothes hidden in a chest in his house.'

Elks turned to me furious, then threw the leash from his hand. The dog stood motionless for a moment, shoulders hunched, head lowered, teeth bared. It crept forward, eyeing first Dowling then me. Then it sprang at Dowling. Dowling threw up an arm to protect himself and the dog sunk its teeth into his flesh. He opened his mouth but didn't scream, just grabbed at the dog's nose with his free hand. I grabbed the dog's shoulders but it wouldn't move, hard muscle oblivious to my feeble pawings.

'Release your dogs,' Elks shouted.

I turned to see the ginger-haired man pull in his hound and reach for its collar, preparing to set it upon me. I froze, torn between the sound of frenzied snarling behind and the sight of two furious beasts, slavering for my blood.

'No,' called Smythe. 'Hold them.' He glowered at Elks. 'First we find out what this is all about.'

'Call the dog off!' I yelled at Smythe. 'Call it off now!'

The bald man whistled, sharp. The hound released its grip immediately and trotted away, head bowed, tail between its legs. The ginger-haired man grabbed at its collar.

Black holes peppered Dowling's arm, from which leaked long

scarlet streams. He stared at the mess, pale-faced, and cradled it against his chest.

Elks pulled the club from his belt and strode into the barn. He drew back his arm and aimed a mighty blow at Josselin's skull. Josselin turned and took the force of it across his spine, falling to the ground with a groan.

'Put down the club, Thomas,' Smythe commanded.

Elks turned, fury seething from every pore of his skin. 'What did you say to me?'

Smythe stood his ground. 'How long have you held him here, Thomas?' he asked, quiet.

'A week,' I replied, when Elks did not.

'A week,' Smythe repeated. 'And in that time more than forty people have died.'

Elks looked ready to erupt, red face now white. 'What are you saying, Smythe?' he hissed.

'I'm saying that the Reverend needs to be told what you have done,' Smythe replied. 'You shall not kill James Josselin, for that would be the work of the Devil.'

'The Devil!' Elks exclaimed, swinging about to face Josselin again, who had somehow managed to regain his feet. '*Josselin* is the Devil, and I shall slay him!' He marched forwards, club held high and swung again.

This time Josselin stepped neatly aside, evading the lunge, swivelling, and kicking at Elks with his right leg, catching him on the ribs. Elks tripped and fell to the ground. He rolled onto his back, dazed. Josselin leapt onto his chest, straddling him, placing the chain between his wrists across Elks' throat.

'So, Thomas,' Josselin whispered. 'My grave or yours?'

189

Elks tried to reach him with his club, but Josselin pinned his biceps with his knees, denying him leverage.

I waited for someone to intervene, but no one did. Josselin pulled the chain tighter and pushed harder. Elks struggled to breathe, face purple. Josselin watched him squirm, intent, breathing steady, tongue between his teeth.

'Take the club,' he whispered.

No one moved.

'Someone take the club,' he repeated.

Elks' eyes protruded from his skull and he gritted his teeth. I stepped forwards and caught the club before it hit the ground.

Josselin sat up straight, relieving the pressure on Elks' neck. Then he leant backwards to address the men behind, allowing his groin to slide forward onto Elks' face. 'Some clothes please, gentlemen,' he requested. 'I imagine Elks has the keys to my chains inside his coat.'

With a last wriggle on Elks' mouth and nose, he stood up straight. 'I shall need a wash, besides,' he said. 'I stink.'

Smythe found the keys in Elks' pocket, releasing Josselin from the chains, using them to shackle Elks. Josselin inspected the sores upon his wrists and about his waist with detached curiosity afore turning his attention to Elks once more.

'You are a bad man, Thomas,' he said quietly.

Elks glared but did not reply.

He bowed to me and to Dowling. 'To you two gentlemen I am in debt.'

He stuck out his chest and drew back his filthy, matted hair with both hands, oblivious to his nakedness. He watched Elks test his shackles, red-faced and rigid, before shaking a finger at a pile of old clothes the bald man offered him. 'Upon reflection I think it best to wash in the river while one of you fetch my clothes from the chest in Elks' house.'

He turned away and strode most royally in the direction of the village, followed by a short procession, Elks at its tail, on his own leash now, walking with the dogs.

Dowling and I walked ten paces behind, my heart full of hope that we might walk straight out of Shyam and back to Colchester, there to find Withypoll died of plague.

Chapter Eighteen

And at other times, it declares the willingness of the people to alter and change both Governors, and Government.

The procession stopped at the river for Josselin to wash. He stepped into the water up to his groin and cleansed himself of filth, prising cakes of blood and straw from his arms with long fingernails, washing the grime from his face and tending to his wounds. When he plunged his hair into the slow-moving water, a brown stain formed, covering the surface of the stream. The wardens watched entranced as a handsome young man emerged from beneath the grime; white-skinned and angular. Red sores coated his legs and forearms.

Elks approached Smythe while all watched Josselin, transfixed. Elks whispered, hands held forward, but Smythe moved away without meeting his eye.

The ginger-haired man arrived, panting, with Josselin's clothes, just as Josselin clambered onto the bank. Josselin pulled on his drawers as if no one watched, then a flowing, silk shirt and blue, silk breeches. The sun reached halfway up the sky and the air was warm. Josselin handed his long black coat back to the ginger-haired man, who took it like his servant. With his long, dark hair pulled back off his face and tied behind his shoulders, Josselin resembled the King himself.

Smythe ducked his head as if tempted to bow. 'Would you like something to eat?'

'To drink.' Josselin turned on his heel and headed up the track. 'Wine, if you have it.'

Smythe exchanged glances with his companions and shrugged. 'We have ale.'

'Ale, then.' Josselin waved an arm and lengthened his stride. 'This cage.' He turned to look at Smythe. 'Is that where you will imprison Mr Elks?'

Elks glowered, stumbling when the ginger man shoved him.

'He hasn't eaten for a week and he asks for ale?' I whispered at Dowling.

'I fear for the health of any man that spends a week in the conditions we witnessed,' Dowling replied. 'Stay alert, Harry.'

Josselin stood with hands on hips, face contorted in ripe disgust as he surveyed the circle of iron gibbets, decomposing corpses grown another day more rotten. He turned to Smythe. 'Who are all these people?'

'The village swore an oath to stay and they tried to leave,' Smythe replied, avoiding Josselin's horrified stare. 'The Reverend Mompesson commanded it, and Elks enforced it.'

'We all enforced it,' Elks interrupted, angry. 'As God is your witness, you dare deny it?'

Smythe muttered and ducked his head.

Josselin caught sight of the cage at the edge of the pond. 'Who are those wretches?'

'Four clerics.' Smythe traipsed in his wake, shoulders slumped. 'They came in two days ago on donkeys. Said they would tend to our souls then return to Colchester. Thomas said we should lock them away as well.'

Elks snorted, as the rest of the group followed Josselin to the bars of the cage.

'Good,' exclaimed Josselin leaning forwards. 'I'm glad you did, for these are not clerics.'

Smythe opened his mouth as if to say something, but settled instead for exchanging glances with his mystified colleagues.

I approached close enough to see the spark of excitement in Josselin's eyes, the tip of his tongue dance quickly between his teeth. The two clerics that lived quaked beneath his gaze, sensing there was something wrong. They looked to me as if in search of explanation.

'Godfrey Allen and John Ansty,' Josselin declared triumphant. 'The dead men are Greenleafe and Meshman. Spies. If it were up to me I would put them to death.' He turned away. 'Where's that ale?'

Smythe wiped his palms on his arse. 'At my house,' he replied, attempting to smile. 'Over the bridge.'

'Away, then!' Josselin declared, pointing at the sky. His dark eyes settled on me. 'Come, Arlington's men. You I trust. Come with me.'

The clerics gazed at me with pleading eyes, hands clasping the bars. 'What does he say?' one of them whispered. 'I have never heard those names before. We are clerics from Colchester. Ask Mayor Flanner.'

I raised my head and saw Marshall Howe stood behind the cage, glowering with murderous intent. My throat constricted and I turned quickly to Josselin. 'You are sure they are spies?'

He rattled the tip of his boot against the bars. 'Of course. Arlington's scum. Murderers and thieves.'

The two clerics shook their heads silently, clasping their hands and biting their lips.

'Marshall Howe.' Josselin raised his chin. 'Stop staring at my good friends. Lock Elks in the cage and take down all these bodies. Take them to the church.'

Howe's expression didn't change, nor did he move a muscle of his body.

'Don't worry about Mompesson,' Josselin mouthed the words with exaggerated care. 'I will go and speak with him after I have visited Smythe at his humble abode.' He nodded his head and showed his teeth. 'Come, Arlington's men.'

I chased after him. 'What will you do to the clerics?'

'I have no idea,' Josselin replied, looking over his shoulder. 'I cannot release them, for those two dead men are plagued. We should leave them there for forty days, I think.'

Dowling scowled and scratched at his head, unable to tell if Josselin was serious and reluctant to ask. Smythe ran ahead, while Elks protested loudly behind us, Howe bundling him into the cage with the clerics.

A pale face peeked out from the window of a small cottage just the other side of Fiddler's Bridge, a narrow walkway of wooden planks bound together with twine. A young woman with dark hair, wide-eyed and hesitant. She disappeared once she set eyes on Josselin.

Smythe emerged carrying a large stone flagon and three cups. He offered the cups to Josselin and to us. Dowling shook his head and I refused, determined to retain my wits.

195

Josselin pushed two of the cups against my chest. 'You would have me drink alone? Drink.'

We complied, me more willing than Dowling. Much to my surprise it tasted pleasant, like fresh apple. Josselin enjoyed it even more than I, for he sank the first cup in two draughts, nodding at Smythe for a refill.

He breathed deep and inspected his surrounds as if with fresh eyes, gazing into the boughs of the trees. 'Difficult to believe this place is plagued. Such a beautiful place, I always thought.' He finished his second cup barely slower than the first and belched softly. 'Now I want to talk to the Reverend. Bring the flagon.'

A row of wild, yellow roses spread across the front of the rectory, tended lovingly. The door and windows were closed. Josselin kicked open the gate and staggered up the path, eyes half lidded. The village wardens watched from behind the low stone wall, fidgeting. Half a dozen other villagers emerged from the quiet to watch from a distance.

Josselin banged his fist upon the door. 'Mompesson!' he shouted, slurring.

A face appeared at the top window, craggy and heavy with a large straight nose. The man's eyes were big and brown, unusually melancholic. He opened the window and leant out, hair hanging down his back, tied and clean, brushed of all knots. His elegant white linen shirt bore a plain broad collar. 'My wife is asleep,' he protested, staring down at Josselin. 'Can ye not talk quietly?'

'Certainly.' Josselin waved an arm and staggered, before taking another swig from the flagon. 'Come downstairs and we shall talk quietly.'

Mompesson didn't move. 'Who are you?' he asked, eyeing the small gathering.

'I am James Josselin,' Josselin bowed. 'Known to all for my exploits as a young boy.' He held his hand up to his face and stared at the ridges on his fingers as if they were new.

Mompesson frowned. 'Why do you come to Shyam, Mr Josselin? Our village is quarantined.'

'I have been here some time, Reverend,' said Josselin. 'Your friend Thomas Elks locked me in a barn.'

Mompesson leant further out of the window in an attempt to read Josselin's expression. But Josselin was drunk, swaying from side to side and licking his lips.

'It's true, Reverend,' Smythe affirmed. 'We found him ourselves.'

Josselin stepped in front of him. 'How many have died, Reverend?' he cried. 'More than half the village. And what in God's name inspired you to squeeze your own people into gibbets? What barbaric practice is that? Are they not your flock?' He threw back his arms, legs splayed.

'That was Elks' decision,' Mompesson replied, keeping his voice down. 'We all decided, together, to remain within the parish boundaries until the plague abated.'

Josselin pointed an unsteady finger. 'Not all, Reverend,' he said. 'Else there would be no need to place men in gibbets. Where is the rock upon whom these good people depend? Thou art great, O Lord God: for there is none like thee. I hear you lock yourself inside your church.'

'God is with us,' Mompesson growled.

'The *plague* is with us, Reverend,' Josselin replied. 'God, I am not so sure. Perhaps he stays away? Else how did Elks come to earn such trust?'

Mompesson retreated, shadow falling upon his face. 'If what you say is true, then he deceived us all.'

Josselin snorted. 'He deceived you, you say, though his deception

197

was clear enough. You saw the gibbets, did you not? Now will God punish you for it, do you think? Does God punish everyone in this village for your errors?'

Mompesson thrust his head through the window, red-faced, the skin upon his neck pulsating in rhythm with his heart. 'You are not a man of God, sir. I have heard stories of your heroism and applaud you for it. But you are not a man of God, nor will the people of this parish mistake you for one.'

'I make no claim to be a man of God,' Josselin shrugged. 'You are the one who makes that claim.'

He turned away, distracted by the low murmuring of gathering villagers. Mary Hancock stood twenty paces away, watching wide-eyed.

'And in the cage, four clerics,' Josselin muttered, too low for the villagers to hear. 'Come to spy upon me.'

Mompesson's brows lifted in surprise. Josselin blinked, as if struggling to see straight. He attempted to smile, lips wet and eyes hooded.

He beckoned Mary Hancock. She walked towards him with short tentative steps. She was alone this morning.

'Good sir,' she exclaimed, eyes bright, falling to her knees. 'How blessed are we that you should visit us in our hour of need.'

'Think nothing of it,' Josselin grinned. 'Have we met before?'

'No, sir,' she replied. 'Though I remember you. Everyone knows of your bravery at the Siege of Colchester.'

Josselin's smile faded.

Mary Hancock didn't seem to notice. 'You proved Hugh Elks murdered Elizabeth Braine besides, I remember that too.'

'Aye,' Josselin replied, pensive. 'So I did.'

Mary Hancock looked up at Mompesson, then at Josselin. 'May we now leave Shyam?' She clasped her hands together. 'Many took the oath to stay, yet it seems we are punished for it. Perhaps it is God's will that we leave.'

I held my breath.

'God's will?' Mompesson spluttered from his window. 'You presume to interpret God's will? Get thee back to your house, Mary Hancock. Get down on your knees and pray hard. Pray you might be forgiven your ingratitude, that you and your family are all living. Is that not proof enough of God's good intent?'

Mary Hancock bowed her head, yet maintained her gaze upon Josselin.

Josselin pursed his lips and frowned in concentration, scratching at his scalp. 'I think we must remain in Shyam just a while longer,' he said at last. He scanned the faces of those that circled him, eyes glinting and sharp.

Of course, I realised, heart sinking. He could hardly sanction the opening of the parish boundaries, when it was the quarantine that helped him avoid capture.

Mary Hancock's shoulders slumped, and she stared at the ground.

'Just a little while longer.' Josselin laid a hand on her head. 'Perhaps not very much longer.'

'On whose authority do you issue instructions?' Mompesson barked. 'I am reverend of this parish. You are but a visitor!'

Josselin cocked his head, as if paying the Reverend's words due respect. 'A visitor, you say?' he said at last. 'More prodigal son. What say you, Smythe?' He turned to the bald man.

Smythe nodded slowly. 'More than a visitor, I would say,' he replied, avoiding Mompesson's eye.

Mompesson scanned the gathering audience. There were nearly fifteen people now, almost a quarter of the remaining population. I stepped backwards, fear gathering in my chest as I sensed the presence of plague.

'Every man took an oath,' Mompesson reminded the group, solemnly. 'That no man would leave here, that we would trust unto God.' He paused for affirmation, but no one spoke. 'God tests us.' He slammed his fist suddenly into the palm of his hand. 'If we give way unto temptation, then we are surely condemned.'

'I agree, Reverend.' Josselin waved a hand like he bestowed a royal favour. 'An oath has been sworn, and God would not forgive you were you to break that oath. But that was the only oath that was sworn, was it not?' He sought confirmation from those about, readily granted. 'None here swore to hunt each other with dogs? None here swore to kill each other and display each other's corpses for all to see?'

'I told you,' Mompesson replied through clenched teeth. 'Those were Elks' decisions.'

'Then rest assured, Reverend,' Josselin bowed his head, 'I shall make different decisions. Meantime we shall maintain the quarantine and imprison only the spies.'

He scanned the faces before him, spotting Marshall Howe stood attentively at the back, shovel on his shoulder. 'Be not merciful to wicked transgressors, spies and traitors.' He waved his mug in the air in Howe's general direction.

Howe nodded.

A tired face appeared at Mompesson's side, the face of a woman, red hair drawn back behind her shoulders. Her eyes widened and she buried her head upon his shoulder.

'I will see you all tomorrow,' Mompesson's voice boomed, before he drew a curtain across the window and disappeared from view.

'What is tomorrow?' I asked Smythe.

'Since the plague, there are two services a week,' Smythe mumbled, scowling.

'For which we must all be present,' Josselin added, hearing our conversation. He placed an arm about my shoulders and belched. 'Meantime I will talk to Smythe.' He dropped his arm and hurried Smythe back towards the bridge.

Dowling drew up to my side. 'That man is troubled,' he said. 'He drinketh strong drink rather than pour out his soul before the Lord.'

'Indeed,' I sighed.

I lifted my heavy soul from where it had fallen upon the path and dragged my feet back in the direction of Buxton's house. Prisoners still. While Josselin drank I would smoke. I felt for my pipe in my pocket.

Dowling said nothing on our way back to the cottage, his face wreathed in lines of misery and concern. I felt his faith, collapsed upon one knee, struggling to avoid being crushed beneath the weight of selfishness and evil. Whatever game God played, he played it strange.

Chapter Nineteen

The Moon is hastening unto the body of Mars in the
barren sign Virgo, which naturally signifieth Wars,
Slaughters of men, many Discords.

Buxton's house stank so bad we slept the night on a grassy bed in a
small hollow at the fringe of the Delf, close to the river. Though it was
comfortable enough and my head was tired, sleep evaded me. Three
days until Culpepper's deadline expired.

Now we found Josselin I didn't know what to do next. Arlington
told us to fetch him out, yet I didn't see how. The villagers were on
his side. He would plot his own journey, whatever that might be. In
many ways he seemed an honourable fellow, yet there was indeed a
hint of strangeness about him, as Jefferies warned us at Chelmsford.
A demon of some description hid betwixt his ears, born of his
suffering all those years ago at Colchester. He strode about Shyam
as if he owned it, yet what for him now? Stay here and die, else face

Arlington's wrath. It was no more palatable predicament than ours. Did he see us as colleagues, useful collaborators, or else spies? The four men in the cage were clergy, I saw it in their eyes, yet he saw them as infiltrators, out to get him. How safe were we? Thoughts came and went, then returned unsatisfied. At some point I must have fallen into a slumber, for Dowling shook me awake next morning.

'So much shuffling,' he complained. 'And what conclusions did you come to as a consequence?'

'We must persuade Josselin to leave,' I slurred, heavy-headed. 'Whatever your oath to God. Elks forced us to make those oaths. God knows that.'

'God will guide us,' Dowling replied, unperturbed. The usual nonsense.

I brushed the debris from my breeches and descended the riverbank to bathe my face and drink the water. 'I am hungry again,' I realised. 'Now Elks is in the cage, we can go seek food openly.'

'Man shall not live by bread alone, but by every word of God.' Dowling pointed back towards the path. 'This morning they hold their church service. Through the trees and over the rise.'

'We still need bread,' I grumbled, 'and I must smoke a pipe before I subject myself to another crowd.' I dug into my pocket for pipe and leaves. If the whole village was going to be there, then so would the Pest.

'What will you light it with?' Dowling asked, tramping through the undergrowth.

Damnation. I pushed the pipe back into my pocket and placed a pinch of leaves onto my tongue. They tasted like mint. I set about chewing.

We stopped afore we reached the path. A man and a woman

trudged miserably, followed by a gaggle of children, jostling against each other like baby geese.

Dowling placed a hand on my shoulder and spoke low. 'They wear their best clothes.'

How could he know that, I wondered, irritated. Had he inspected their wardrobe? If we kept going we would end up in Colchester, I thought, wistful.

A break in the hedgerow led out upon an undulating meadow and down into a wide basin, a natural amphitheatre. Among the first to arrive, we made our way to the far side of the hill and settled ourselves upon the moist grass. More families materialised, cautious and silent, signalling to neighbours discreetly, but talking to no one. Each family found its own isolated spot, away from others. Mary Hancock led her brood to a spot halfway down the bank, barely acknowledging us with a dart of her eyes. She scanned the assembled ranks before sitting. John Hancock clasped his hands and stared at his feet.

Mompesson arrived accompanied by the same slender woman we saw the day before, unusually pale of complexion. She held herself stiff, back to the congregation, and sat at the bottom of the bank where she might be closest to her husband. Mompesson wrung his hands, nervous, scanning carefully the assembled throng. To see who was left.

He cleared his throat and held his arms up ready to speak just as Josselin strode out of the bushes. Every head turned. Mompesson lowered his arms again and scowled. Josselin saw his anger and tossed his head, oblivious, enjoying the attention. He appeared as pale as Mompesson's wife, but sober. He waved a hand to all assembled and settled himself at the top of the bank right in

Mompesson's line of sight. He lifted his chin, staring forwards, and again I wondered what thoughts hid behind that mask.

'Rend your heart and not your garments,' proclaimed Mompesson, deep, tremulous voice filling the vale. 'Turn unto the Lord your God.' He paused, arms wide and lifted his head slow, like he wore a leaden hat. 'For he is gracious and merciful, slow to anger, and of great kindness, and repenteth him of the evil.' He stepped sideways to the right, then back to the left, hands raised as if expecting to be engulfed in a great wave. 'If we say we have no sin, we deceive ourselves. Repent ye!' he exclaimed, voice fearful. 'For the Kingdom of Heaven is at hand.'

Josselin watched calm, like a cat watches a mouse. Yet the flush upon his cheekbones spoke of some inner turmoil.

'Now shall we remember those who died these last three days,' Mompesson spoke gruff. 'They brought nothing into this world, and it is certain they will carry nothing out. The Lord gave, and the Lord hath taken away; blessed be the name of the Lord.' He bowed his head and pulled a piece of paper from his pocket. 'We remember this day; Thomas Frythe, Elizabeth Frythe and Francis Frythe.'

Quiet weeping broke the hush, soft and subdued, from different places about the hill. For lost friends, no doubt, but also in fear of their own lives.

'Samuel Morten and Margaret Morten.'

Children started to cry, frightened to witness their parents' grief. The list of names continued, more than twenty of them, all of whom would have been present last Sunday. Who will still be here next Sunday, I wondered? I imagined Mompesson reading out the names of Harry Lytle and David Dowling, a shiver running down my spine.

I grasped Dowling's sleeve. 'Look!' I whispered. Up, away to our

205

left, emerged Galileo, the Earl of Clarendon's man. I had forgotten all about him. Had we agreed to meet at Buxton's cottage? I struggled to recall. The side of his head bulged purple and yellow, the wound I inflicted matured to full splendour.

'He shows himself,' Dowling murmured. 'A bold move.'

Indeed, I considered. Though he couldn't yet know how uncertain was Josselin's temper. I watched out the corner of my eye as he crouched by Josselin's elbow, speaking purposefully into his ear. Josselin's expression didn't change. He just kept nodding.

Mompesson began to read Psalm thirty-nine. 'Lord, let me know mine end, and the number of my days: that I may be certified how long I have to live.'

Amen to that, I thought.

I turned again to Galileo, surprised to see he turned green. Josselin seemed to lunge at him, just missing, and Galileo hopped away, like a giant frog. I wiped my eyes and looked to Dowling to see if he noticed, but the butcher watched Mompesson intently.

The loudest weeping came from below. A young woman sat alone, bent over her rounded belly. She wailed soft, oblivious to all, fingers clasped tight about her own golden hair. Her husband must have died. The stark timbre of her woeful mourning struck a chord somewhere beneath my ribs. She seemed to shimmer. Her edges blurred and a fierce strong light shone from the middle of her body, dancing, yellow strands shooting from her midriff like thin flames. I blinked hard, but to no avail. Her hair blazed red, crackling like a bonfire. Then she turned her head and I saw Jane.

'God's teeth,' I exclaimed, too loud, seizing Dowling about the scruff of his neck. A thrill of horror gripped my lungs and stopped me from breathing.

Dowling struggled to unpick my fingers from his neck. 'What is it, Harry?'

A man to my left watched me with white face aghast. 'I am fine,' I croaked, forcing myself to breathe steady again until the man looked away.

'I had a thought,' I whispered to Dowling, a terrible thought. 'What if Jane is with child?'

His big face stared back at me, blank. Then he pursed his lips. I could see him thinking back to the last time he saw Jane, just before we left London. 'Lucy behaved strange when *she* was with child. It is a thing women go through,' he mused. 'All sense and reason deserts them.'

'You have a child?' I asked, distracted. 'You never told me you had children.'

'You didn't ask and I didn't tell.' He scowled. 'Nor am I about to tell you of it in the middle of morning prayer.'

Which was not the soft ear I sought. I tried to remember what Jane's belly looked like before we left, whether it was unusually large. She had not seemed misshapen. I attempted to quell the crashing waves that surged within my own belly. I didn't know for certain she was with child, I reminded myself. Many things might drive a woman to strange behaviour besides pregnancy, especially Jane. Surely she would have told me if she fell pregnant? Blamed me for it, hit me about the head with a saucepan; she would not have kept it quiet – she kept nothing quiet. I determined to focus my attentions back onto Mompesson, give my mind time to reflect upon the terrifying idea.

'And we have done those things we ought not to have done,' Mompesson read, 'but thou, O Lord, have mercy upon us miserable offenders.'

The miserable offenders were miserable indeed, heads bowed, hope sickly. I scanned the hill quickly, leaning forwards. Galileo was gone.

A woman gasped. Another screamed. Mompesson stopped talking, stood frozen. His wife lay prone upon the grass at the base of the bank. Even from a distance I saw the dark circle about her neck against the paleness of her skin. Mompesson dropped to his knees, cradled her head in his arm and cupped her face, calling her name, again and again. Several of the congregation fled, running for the safety of the forest. The rest edged backwards and away. None stepped forwards to help.

'Come on, Harry,' Dowling muttered, ever conscientious. I followed him, reluctant, down the hill.

Mompesson huddled over her chest, holding one of her hands in both of his, a strangulated wail leaking from his mouth. Dowling laid a hand upon his arm, leaning over his shoulder to inspect the woman. No need, for she was dead. Her mouth lolled open, face contorted into a twisted mask. A black bubo protruded upon her neck, tight and round.

'It is a judgement,' Mompesson whispered. Tears glistened upon his cheeks and along the ridge of his great nose.

I thought of Josselin's words the day before and wondered for a moment if he might be right.

'A judgement upon us all, Reverend.' Dowling squeezed his shoulder. 'The seers shall be ashamed, and the diviners confounded, for there is no answer of God.'

Which is not how the villagers would see it.

Catherine Mompesson stared into the blue sky, eyes still bright. The Reverend leant over her, searching for any sign of movement, brushing his hands against her shoulders in a strange, repetitive motion.

'Go home,' Josselin cried from high up on the hill to the few that remained. 'Everyone. Back to your houses.'

A collective sigh settled upon the grassy dell and in just a few minutes we found ourselves alone with Mompesson and his dead wife. Josselin remained aloof at the top of the bank, arms folded across his chest. Then he turned his back on us and walked away. Did we offend him?

Dowling pushed on Mompesson's shoulder to attract his attention. 'We will help you take her home.'

'We need something to carry her upon,' I said, alarmed. The rectory was a walk away, back up the hill and over the bridge.

Dowling stared at me, stern. 'We have carried bodies before, Harry,' he growled.

Aye, but not so many infected with plague. I looked to the heavens and resigned myself to fate. God had better be watching and taking proper notice. I took the woman's ankles, grasped them firm and held them to my hips. Dowling lifted her by the armpits, where usually lurked more buboes. Faith was a dangerous thing and Dowling seemed determined to tempt it.

Her legs were still warm. I let Dowling lead the way and followed him into the copse. Mompesson walked alongside, hand lain upon his dead wife's cheek. She weighed less than a child and we made easy progress.

Outside the rectory Mompesson stood staring as if seeing the house for the first time. 'If you would be so kind . . .' he said, leading us on.

The front room was simply furnished. Three heavy chairs, a cold, empty grate, and the stone floor swept clean. Mompesson hurried us into the kitchen, gesturing at a sturdy wooden table. 'If you would lay her down here.'

'Where will you bury her?' Dowling grunted, lowering her with care. Not a gentle question.

Mompesson began to weep, unrestrained, stretching out a hand to her still staring eyes. He paused for one final moment of intimacy afore closing her eyelids.

I tugged at Dowling's sleeve. He lingered, reluctant, but Mompesson was oblivious. The bubo was bigger now, black as coal. Though her body was dead, the infection still grew. Mompesson wiped his hands upon her face and pushed his cheek next to hers, trying to climb inside her, so it looked.

I regarded his face, tears covering his cheeks, nose red and swollen. Difficult to imagine this was the man that rallied the courage of a village. I felt like a trespasser and headed back out into the sunshine.

I looked at my hands and prayed the plague did not already creep upon them, silent and invisible. 'We must be more careful, Davy,' I said, the words sounding ridiculous even as I spoke them. 'If we will see London again we should be more discreet.'

'Have faith, Harry,' Dowling replied, so quiet I could barely hear him.

'Good morning,' Josselin's throaty growl spoke from beyond the low stone wall. He stood upon the street alone, hands in pockets. 'How fares the Reverend?'

'Not so well,' I replied, thinking to wipe my hands upon his cheeks.

'I think you should leave him alone now,' Josselin warned. 'God is jealous, and the Lord revengeth. The Lord will take vengeance on his adversaries.'

'Why do you dislike him so much?' I asked. 'I thought you hadn't met him before.'

'I haven't.' Josselin smiled his terrible smile, eyes gleaming bright. 'Yet he nestled beneath Elks' wing like a small chicken. For that he should be punished.'

Mompesson and the spies.

I looked left and right down the street, searching for Smythe. 'You are alone,' I observed.

'I have no friends here,' Josselin snapped. 'I told you before, I don't know these people. The villagers will suffer what fate God plans for them, and the spies shall be dealt with.' He extracted his hands from his pockets and lay them upon the top of the wall. 'You are spies, but you are agents of God besides. He sent you to release me of my chains.' He cocked his head as if expecting a reply.

'What of the man you spoke to at the service?' I asked. 'Is he not another of Clarendon's men, a friend of yours?'

'Clarendon employs a small army,' Josselin replied. 'Galileo is just another spy that asks questions and promises redemption.' His eyes seemed to fix upon a point distant. 'The less I speak, the more I learn. No man can resist speaking. If you would know what lies in a man's heart ask nothing, for he will reveal it readily. Ask him a question, and he will protect even the most fleeting thought as if it were a great secret.'

I thought again of Dowling's children and Jane's pregnancy. Ask nothing was Josselin's advice. It hadn't worked thus far.

Josselin continued to stare. 'I have a lot to do today. Later we will talk, for we must decide what to do next.' He turned his attention to me, searching, like I was the harbinger of some great secret. I thought of Withypoll. We hadn't told him about Withypoll yet.

He nodded slowly. 'Tomorrow, then,' he said. 'If not before.'

Another day in Hell, but I couldn't think how to protest. 'We must eat.' My stomach reminded me.

'Go to Buxton's house,' said Josselin. 'I will send Smythe with food.' He waved a hand, again most royally, and headed off back towards the pond.

'Back to the cottage, then,' I said, watching him walk away, striding long like he owned all of Essex. 'We should see how the Hancocks fare, anyway,' I said to Dowling. 'Now would not be a good time to plot an escape.'

The track back into the woods was once more deserted, all the villagers having hurried home despite their licence to wander.

Only the birds sang sweet.

Chapter Twenty

All the family being dead of the Plague, by reason thereof, I cannot come by them.

I heard the sound of wailing even before we reached the cottage. I thought I recognised the voice of Mary Hancock, desolation wracking her brittle soul. There was no end to it, it seemed, no escape. We could stop, turn, and walk the other way, but we would find misery there too. Death was all around.

The Hancock's house nestled deep in the grass, just below the line of the road, sinking beneath a mound of creeping ivy. Loud weeping sounded from the window, the lament of a mother that discovers she may lose a child. Too late then for the Hancocks to think of leaving. Was it late for us too? My chest constricted and I struggled to breathe. Not the plague, I told myself, just naked fear.

I stepped to the small glass window and peered in, Dowling at my elbow. Six people knelt about a bed upon which lay two figures; one still and quiet, the other feverish. Mary Hancock knelt upon the floor wiping a child's brow, the boy we met on our first day. She watched his every move from behind her black hair, fallen wild across her face. The boy writhed and twitched, eyes closed, body glistening, moaning quietly.

One of the girls tended to the father, dabbing at his forehead while tears rolled slowly down her cheeks. I would have thought him dead already were it not for the colour of his skin, a fierce burning scarlet. The boy bared his teeth and dug his fingers into the flesh of his own chest.

The children all looked to their mother constantly, biting their lips and fighting the tears, realising something was wrong, yet not wanting to distress their mother further. Then one of the younger girls screamed, pointing at me. 'Marshall Howe,' she shrieked, composure shattered.

Mary Hancock looked straight at me, cloth held suspended above her child's face. For a moment I sensed the same horror I saw in her daughter, but she quickly recovered her wits and rose, striding to the door, furious.

'Why are you here?' she demanded, throwing the door wide open. 'Why do you come?'

'We heard weeping,' Dowling explained, stepping away. 'We came to see if we might help.'

'We help each other by leaving each other alone,' she beseeched him, bitterness in her voice. 'That way we make sure the plague doesn't spread. Do you not understand? That is what we were told.'

I understood well enough, though I reckoned it was nonsense. It hadn't stopped the Pest in London and hadn't stopped it here. The whole village hid behind closed doors for fear of spreading the plague, yet the plague killed two of every three already.

'I have some leaves.' I pulled the packet from my pocket. 'And a pipe.'

She glowered, furious, then slammed the door closed. Nine of them snuggled together in their little nest, two adults, six children and the Pestilence.

'Who will dig the graves?' I realised. 'Marshall Howe digs only the last.'

Dowling didn't reply, just stared, eyes soft, jaw loose.

'And we may be leaving soon,' I reminded him, whatever his oath.

'I will build them a fire,' Dowling replied, teeth clenched, 'and find vitriol or vinegar. Then we will dig graves where they cannot be seen.'

We hadn't yet succeeded in finding bread, let alone vitriol and vinegar, and whilst I admired his sensitivity, I wondered how Mary Hancock would know we had dug holes for her if she couldn't see them.

'I will fetch vitriol and vinegar,' I said. 'You start building the fire and fetch the shovel from Buxton's house.'

I headed back towards the centre of the village, back the way we came. In the distance a familiar figure approached.

Smythe stepped sideways, blocking my path. Though most of his head was bald, still he sported a short ginger tuft upon his forehead. He carried a bag. 'Where are you going? You were told to stop at Buxton's house.'

'I came to find you,' I replied. 'Josselin said you would bring us food.'

'Aye,' he growled. 'Am I not here?' He handed me the bag. Inside was a loaf of bread, some sausages and a pie.

'Do you have vitriol and vinegar?' I asked him. 'Or pitch, tar, frankincense?'

215

He screwed up his face like I was a lunatic. 'Why do you want vitriol and vinegar?'

'John Hancock is infected,' I told him. 'His son besides. We want to light a fire to fumigate the house.'

'Ah,' he groaned, like he was punched in the guts. 'I've known Mary all my life.' He bowed his head and placed his hands on his hips. 'What use is a fire?'

'They lit fires in London to keep away the plague,' I explained, though they didn't seem to work.

'You think it will help the Hancocks?' he demanded, sceptical.

More likely it would help us think we were being useful. I shrugged.

He turned on his heel and beckoned me back towards the pond. 'Vitriol and vinegar I can fetch you,' he said. 'Not the rest of it. Your fire will still work?'

'Some people used only vitriol and vinegar,' I replied. The poor mostly. 'It works as well as any other remedy.' Which was not at all.

He nodded to himself, striding onward.

'You have lived here all your life,' I guessed, struggling to keep up.

'Aye,' Smythe replied, staring ahead.

'Are you not afraid to wander the village, now it is plagued?'

He turned, mouth drawn into a tight sneer. 'Would you have me cower in a corner while every man I know dies? Makes no difference, anyhow; the Pest still claims its victims.'

'It was the same in London,' I said. 'When plague took a man, the whole house was shut up until all were recovered, then forty days more. The plague still spread.'

He eyed me with suspicion. 'You live, though.'

'I left for the country,' I replied, wary. 'As did every man that had the means. We waited for the plague to leave, then returned. I stayed in London longer than most, but was ultimately persuaded by the voice of the majority.'

'What voice?' he scowled.

'Save thyself,' I answered. 'It is the only sure way to avoid death.'

His cheeks flushed, and I thought he would strike me.

'I'm just agreeing with your sentiment,' I protested. 'That there be no purpose in locking thyself behind closed door.'

'Aye,' he growled, 'but you say there be no purpose in locking ourselves behind closed boundary, neither.'

'I am one man,' I replied. 'You had this debate already, I assume.'

'There was little debate,' Smythe grumbled. 'It was Mompesson's idea. The rest of us went along with it because he said God would look favourably upon us.' He snorted. 'Which he has not.'

'You live,' I pointed out.

'So far,' he replied, marching on down the stony track.

We emerged into the clearing by the pond. A hand clutched at my heart. Marshall Howe was chopping wood with a great axe. I caught a glimpse of three shadows in the cage, but hurried along towards the bridge. 'What is he doing?' I asked Smythe.

He cast Howe a cursory glance. 'Something for Josselin. Great oaf. What do you do in London?'

'My father made shoes,' I answered, truthfully. 'I was a clerk. Now I would be an apothecary.'

'An apothecary?' he exclaimed. 'No apothecary has visited here since we closed the boundaries. I heard they have cures for the plague in London. You can cure us?'

'I shared with you the only cure I know of, and it be preventive,' I replied. 'Though there are many remedies you might try. A warm poultice of butter, onion and garlic, perhaps. I knew of a medic once who swore by nutmeg, boiled meat and pickles.'

'What happened to him?'

'He died.' Fell face first into his dinner, I recalled.

Smythe glanced sideways. 'What remedies do you take?'

I dug into my pocket. 'My leaves and pipe.' I showed him.

He eyed the leaves eagerly. 'Do they work?'

'I am not dead yet,' I answered. 'Though I think more by good fortune. Here.' I offered him the packet. 'Take some.'

'I will try it,' Smythe resolved. 'Keep the packet until we reach my home.' He shook his head, as if trying to shake a thought out his ear. 'Why come to Shyam? Save thyself, you say. Flee the plague while you may. Yet you come to Shyam?'

'That's right,' I nodded. 'Not willingly, neither. We were sent to see if Josselin still lives. He you all adore.'

'So you are not Buxton's brother?'

'No,' I confessed. 'That was a lie, for Elks' benefit.'

'A lie,' Smythe repeated to himself, between clenched teeth.

Once we crossed Fiddler's Bridge, Smythe issued an instruction to wait while he disappeared into his home, taking my packet with him. It felt strange, like he took my hand, or a foot. He emerged soon after with two bottles, one large, one smaller. 'Why come after James Josselin?' he demanded.

'He is an important man,' I replied. 'He works for the King.'

Smythe handed me the bottles. 'Well now you can tell them where he is, if you survive the plague yourself.'

'How do you all know him so well?' I asked. 'He has visited only once, has he not? And did he not offend Thomas Elks? I thought Elks had many friends amongst the villagers.'

'Elks had friends,' Smythe agreed, 'though many are now dead.

Josselin was one of them once, for he came here oftentimes to collect taxes and pay for the goods we sent to market. We all knew him, Elks more than most, for his father leased a big holding west of Town Head.'

'You all loved the tax collector?'

'Aye,' Smythe nodded vigorously. 'He gave what was owed, and turned a blind eye when he saw folks had not the means to contribute. I know for a fact he made up the difference out of his own estate when it was necessary.'

I frowned. 'He *was* a hero then.'

'Aye,' Smythe nodded again. 'Which is why so many of us was ashamed the way he was treated in return.'

'What do you mean?'

Smythe scratched his head and grimaced. 'Hugh Elks was a violent man and everyone knew it. That's why Josselin went first to his house when Lizzy Braine was found dead. His own family disowned him, all except Thomas. Even Thomas tried to talk to him, but Hugh wouldn't be talked to. He wouldn't watch your eyes for more than a few seconds afore he was distracted by something else.'

'Hugh Elks did kill Lizzy Braine?'

Smythe scratched the back of his head. 'He killed her, and deserved what he got. None resented Josselin for it, none except Thomas Elks. Elks bided his time, waited for nightfall. Then he and some others went round to the rectory and dragged Josselin out by the boots. First they tried to hang him, then they tried to burn him.' He rubbed his hands upon his face. 'The Reverend did nothing about it, just locked himself behind his own door. Not Mompesson, he wasn't here then. None of the villagers did owt about it either, though few were around to witness it. Josselin saved himself, it's said. Found some

219

Godly strength when he saw the fire, kicked and punched his way free. Ran all the way back to Colchester and never been back since, not till we found him in the barn.'

'Does he not resent you all?' I asked, aghast.

'He never came back to discuss it,' Smythe replied. 'Though he seems much changed. Difficult to tell what he thinks, but we saved him from Elks this time, didn't we?' He turned to face me, eyes anxious.

'Aye,' I agreed. 'Elks told you to release the dogs, and you chose not to.'

Smythe sighed. 'Perhaps God will look upon us more kindly now.' He looked me in the eye and nodded. 'You have your food, you have your vitriol and vinegar. Now be on your way.'

'Where is Josselin?' I asked.

'Snoring his head off on my bed,' Smythe replied. 'Drunk himself into a stupor.'

I put out my hand for the rest of my leaves. How would we get Josselin out of Shyam if he was drunk all the time?

Chapter Twenty-One

*Those Comets which are carried against the order of the signs, do
ever intimate a change of Laws.*

We lit the fire and dug the graves, just two of them, well away from
the cottage. It took most of the afternoon, for the ground was hard
and my muscles soft. By the time we finished, I stank worse than the
dead cow.

We barely spoke, for if Dowling's thoughts were as morbid
as mine, there was little to be served in sharing such gloomy
forebodings. We had to leave Shyam; that was the answer to
everything. And if we succeeded in taking Josselin with us, perhaps
this village might reassess its commitment to die alone. Colchester
was plagued besides; it was not as if their isolation served any real
purpose.

The fire burnt brighter as the skies darkened. The birds sang
frantic, like they feared the dusk.

'I am going to wash at the pond,' I said, once we finished. 'We'll remind Smythe to feed the Hancocks.' And I wanted to see if Josselin had surfaced – take advantage of the opportunity to talk to him sober.

The Hancocks' house was quieter now. Peering in discreetly I saw the family gathered as they were before, one of the girls curled up asleep upon the floor. The boy still wriggled, restless, but not so much.

We trudged back towards the pond, counting the windows lit by candle. Most were dark. A chill breeze froze my damp skin. What I wouldn't do for something hot to eat, a mug of beer and a comfortable bed. I thought again of Jane, wondered what she was doing right now. I wondered if she thought of me, worried even. What a strange notion that was.

The gibbets were all removed, but in their place an awful, black, shadow against the cobalt sky, slashed with dark streaks of cyan. My bowels melted and my legs trembled. Marshall Howe had been building a gallows, and from the gallows hung five bodies.

We approached cautious, the night air silent. Someone lay prostrate on the ground afore the swinging corpses. Two poles, driven deep into the ground, supported one long beam from which the bodies dangled. Across the beam someone wrote in dripping paint:

BE NOT MERCIFUL TO WICKED TRANSGRESSORS – SPIES AND TRAITORS.

The words seemed familiar.

'In the name of God, what wickedness is this?' Dowling exclaimed,

222

staring at the corpses, swinging gently in the slight breeze. 'They have murdered men of God!'

'Not men of God,' a low voice sounded from beneath our feet. The long bundle unravelled itself and Josselin emerged, eyes dead, face pallid. 'Yet they did not deserve this.'

'Those are your words,' I said. 'You used those very words in front of the rectory.' At that moment I felt utterly sick of that place, sick of the people, sick of the world. Flies covered the two corpses upon the left, crawling with great intent. Flesh peeled already from the cheekbone of the first, wet and grey. A magpie perched upon the second man's head, pecking at his scalp. 'You hang dead bodies?'

'I didn't do it,' Josselin croaked. 'Marshall Howe did it. He heard my words and thought I instructed him.'

Elks seemed to be looking at me, eyes open wide, bulging from their sockets, mouth affixed in a permanent sneer, black tongue protruding.

'You didn't stop him?' Dowling snorted, incredulous.

'I was asleep,' Josselin protested. 'I heard nothing.' He looked up at me, his expression similar to that upon the clerics' faces afore we left them in the cage to go to Smythe's house. 'Someone else should have stopped it.'

'Why?' Dowling snapped. 'You told the village you were in charge.' He pointed to the writing on the beam. 'Those are your words. This is your will.'

'I was drunk!' Josselin cried. 'I was locked up in a shed for five days without food nor water.'

Despite the atrocity I felt some sympathy as I gazed down upon his young face. The face of a young boy bewildered by someone else's cruelty. He dug into the dirt with his deformed fingers. I reminded myself he was chased here by Arlington, accused of a crime he likely did not commit.

'You still say they were spies?' Dowling said, low.

Josselin pointed at each of the bodies in turn. 'Greenleafe, Meshman, Ansty, Allen,' he recited. 'I know them, though I did not wish for this.'

I scanned the five contorted faces. Was it possible? Certainly it was the kind of scheme Arlington would relish, but would four spies allow themselves to be so easily snared?

The ground shook to our left. Framed by the outline of the church, the figure of Marshall Howe, striding slowly in our direction.

'Have you talked to him?' I asked Josselin.

Josselin shook his head and climbed to his feet, wiping his cheeks with his palms, succeeding only in smearing them with dirt.

Howe stared blankly at Josselin, frowning slightly as if he couldn't understand why no one patted him on the head.

'Howe,' Josselin said, rubbing the back of his head. 'Did you hang these men?'

The big man nodded, slowly, frown deepening.

'You did a thorough job,' Josselin turned away. 'For which I shall be commended.'

Howe continued to look puzzled.

Josselin sighed. 'I need to go for a walk. Cut down the bodies, Howe, and take down this gallows.'

He turned to me. 'You stay here with him. Make sure it is done. I will be back soon.'

With which he marched off into the descending darkness, red skies casting a funereal aspect upon the scene afore us. Marshall Howe folded his arms and gazed stern, growling beneath his breath as if he blamed us for his master's foul mood. We sat ourselves down upon the softest grass we could find, away from the gallows, and settled down to another night in paradise. If we didn't leave tomorrow I would lose my shop.

Chapter Twenty-Two

People subject to the Aiery, Earthly, and Fiery Triplicity, shall suffer many Enormities, as death of Inhabitants.

Night fell and the forest quietened. Here upon the green we huddled at the heart of the village. More sounds of pain and distress could be heard, faint but unmistakable. I tried to rid myself of the notion it was the corpses bewailing their fate. It was hard to think of sleeping. Each time the wind picked up, the ropes creaked, swinging in harmony with the cooling breeze. Howe disappeared to find his tools.

I thought of Jane, her soft warm body. Tears pricked my eyes and I sought to shake the memory from my head for fear I would ne'er find her again.

Sleep came when I focussed upon Dowling's breathing, imagined myself rising and falling in time with his gentle snoring. I told myself I would be walking out of Shyam tomorrow morning, come what may. I dreamt of a river, briskly flowing. It picked up my boat and swept it back to London in a long straight line. I stared ahead, trying not to look aside at the men and women running down to the banks, flinging themselves into the water to be rid of the burning fevers. But I couldn't avoid John Hancock, black hair pressed down about his gaping, white face, eyes fixed upon my boat. He slid into the water and swum towards me, faster and faster. Then he disappeared beneath the surface and reappeared at the bow. He gripped the front of the boat and heaved it downwards, trying to sink me. The boat rocked wildly as I prised off his fingers.

'Wake up, Harry.' Dowling shook me hard. 'Wake up!'

I opened my eyes to see his huge face hanging close above mine like he thought to kiss me. I suppressed a scream of terror and pushed him aside, trying to collect my scattered thoughts. Marshall Howe lay flat upon the ground facing the sky, chest heaving in steady rhythm.

'He's asleep, Harry,' Dowling whispered. 'He took down the corpses.'

I looked to the scaffold. Five short ropes tied to the beam, but no bodies.

'Where did he put them?' I asked, thick-headed.

'I don't know,' Dowling whispered. 'But Josselin has not come back.'

I eased myself to my feet, one eye on Marshall Howe, and peered into the blue darkness. No one else around. 'We should try the church.'

We trod quiet as we could towards the churchyard. I pointed to the rectory. 'A candle in the window. Perhaps the Reverend has seen something.'

Apart from the candle, the building stood silent and dark, a square shadow crouching with malintent. I stood at the gate, unwilling to approach closer. We didn't even know if he buried his wife yet.

Dowling sniffed the air with vague unease. He nudged me aside and pushed the gate too hard, so it swung against the short stone wall with a sharp crash. I cursed him silently and squeezed my hands so tight I could barely open them again.

The roses appeared black in the gloom, as if the flowers were strange receptacles, night harbingers of plague. Dowling sneezed, which violent noise sent fear stabbing through my heart. He eased open the front door and poked his head through into the darkness.

'Mompesson?' he whispered, so hoarse he made himself cough.

I felt like pushing him inside and closing the door behind, so loud and unnatural he sounded in the balmy night. He received no reply and stepped inside, still crouched. I waited in the night air, senses attuned to the sound of footsteps. I heard clear his passage about the house, heavy boots marking his passage from room to room.

'Not at home,' he announced, upon finally emerging. 'Nor his wife.' He cleared his throat, placed his paws upon his shaggy hips and regarded the surrounds with grey perplexity.

'Unless he heard you coming from the other side of Shyam and is hiding under the bed,' I said.

He shook his head. 'I looked under the bed and in the cupboards too.'

A fleeting picture of Mompesson flickered across my mind, stood upright in a cupboard with his dead wife held tight to his chest. Never had I felt so attuned to the world about me. 'The church,' I suggested.

We headed towards the ring of linden trees marking the boundary of the churchyard. A path cut through the shadow, dark and winding, offering every opportunity for ambush, but all we encountered was the wind, rustling the tops of the bushes.

The squat square tower stood stark against the blue night sky, the height of twelve men. Afront of it a tall stone cross with strange etchings. Gravestones shone ghostly luminous in the moonlight, the walls beyond casting sinister shadows about the periphery.

'Look there.' Dowling pointed at a dark oblong, not ten paces from the cross.

It was a long hole, freshly dug. 'It can only be for Catherine Mompesson if none others are permitted burial.' I walked close enough to gaze within. 'It's empty.'

'She lies somewhere,' Dowling grunted, before heading towards the chancel door. It was unlocked.

Inside was dark, as we expected, but not ahead. Candles flickered, drawing us forward like reluctant pilgrims. Also a noise, a muffled sound of anguished muttering, mournful and angry. My every instinct bid me leave, yet my head told me we neared a secret, one we needed to understand.

The chancel was clearly built new, for the stone was bright and plain and smooth. Ahead of us a grand arch, and beyond that the nave. I stepped stealthily ahead of Dowling, bidding him be silent with a sharp chopping of my hand. He seemed to understand, for his heavy breathing quieted and he trod softer than I thought possible.

I stopped at the edge of darkness, unable to suppress a gasp of horror. The groaning came from a figure lain prone upon the floor, on its belly, feet towards us and head away, making such dark and awful noises that it didn't hear my unwitting exclamation. It was Mompesson. Most dreadful though was the nature of the congregation.

Catherine Mompesson sat on the front pew, leaning slightly to one side, head lolling on her left shoulder, white dress soiled with dark stains about her bodice and the ends of her flowing skirts. Though her eyes were closed her mouth was not, jaw dropped upon her chest like she died of thirst. Upon either side of her, though not touching, sat two more women and a child, clothes torn and ragged, skin whiter even than Catherine Mompesson. All dead.

Elks and the clerics sat in the pew behind wearing grisly necklaces of thick rope, skin black in contrast to the pallid complexion of Catherine Mompesson. Those from the gibbets who had started to rot slumped in a line three pews behind. A sickly sweet smell hung in the air, the unmistakable perfume of death and decay. Mompesson lay in front of them all, sobbing loudly.

I stole a glance at Dowling's big head and saw the fear writ plain upon his face, the death of something within his soul. I fancied he saw a part of himself in Mompesson, as he saw in every man, with that detached compassion that distinguished him from most others who professed a love of God.

Mompesson begged forgiveness, I supposed. His wife slipped further to one side, a crooked mannequin. No doubt he saw her death as judgement upon his own worthiness, for Godly men saw significance in everything that happened in their lives, a commentary upon their own conduct, as if God had nothing better to do.

We stood frozen, Dowling and I, not knowing what to do. I feared the consequence of our discovery, for the sounds emanating from Mompesson were so raw and violent, I feared he truly lost his mind.

Something slithered away to our right, like a bag of coal being hauled across the floor. It moved in the shadows, sliding towards us from the direction of the north wall. I couldn't move, imagining a figure with no legs, dragging itself by the arms. A black face emerged into the passage of dim light afforded by the candles, eyes ranging the altar to our side, unseeing. My heart froze against my ribs, a block of ice.

'God help us!' I whispered too loud, for it jerked its head immediately in our direction, searching for the source of my utterance. I held my breath, for its appearance was fearsome, face soiled, eyes staring. It was a man, I had to remind myself. He pulled himself forwards across the stone floor again, unable to stand upon his legs it seemed.

Another groan and I blinked to clear my tired eyes, for I thought I saw another of the dead figures stir. Mompesson heard it too, and pushed himself up onto his knees. He knelt there still a moment, ears pricking, until he noticed as I did a movement upon the second pew of the far aisle. Not all these folks were dead.

He clambered to his feet, body bent, attention fixed upon the movement, feet shuffling sharp upon the floor. A barely suppressed excitement plucked upon his arms and legs, as if he believed his own prayers brought the fellow back to life. Then he strode across to his wife and took her head in his hands, as if he checked to see if his efforts worked with her besides. But there would be no resurrection that night, for her skin greyed since last we saw her and the bubo stood out hard and black despite the poor illumination.

The figure on the ground turned its head to Mompesson, and groaned out loud. Mompesson turned, then fell backwards to the floor when he saw the man for the first time. His face sagged as he seemed to recognise the figure. He knelt down at its side afore turning his head towards us. I stood stock-still, praying he hadn't heard us, and he looked away again afore striding towards the font. His footsteps sounded loud upon the stone floor, as they walked away and then returned, fetching a small cup of water.

He seemed calm enough now as he knelt again and held the cup to the man's mouth. The blackened figure drank noisily, thrusting forwards with his head like he would swallow the cup whole. Once he relaxed, so Mompesson's attention once more switched to his wife, staring at her with sweet longing.

'Reverend!' called a voice from the shadows at the back of the church.

Mompesson leapt to his feet.

'You have taken the transgressors and brought them into God's house,' the voice called. Josselin stepped out of the shadows, arms held aloft in wonderment as if he had never been in a church before. 'To the Lord our God belong mercies and forgivenesses. Have they all confessed their sins?'

Mompesson stopped to stare at his wife again, as if the notion she might be a sinner was new.

Josselin sat upon the second pew, well away from Elks. 'I ask God's forgiveness, for I am ashamed.'

Mompesson stared with wide, white eyes. His nose was covered in blood. He must have hit it on the floor when he lay face first.

'I was sinned against,' Josselin said. 'Betrayed. Not once, not twice, but three times. I gave way to vengeance, when I should have sought guidance of the Lord my God. For that I am truly sorry.' He bowed his head.

Mompesson's jaw twitched. 'If the Lord do not help me, whence shall thee help me?' he whispered, pitiful. 'When the Lord thy God shall enlarge thy border, I will eat flesh, because thy soul longeth to eat flesh; thou mayest eat flesh, whatsoever thy soul lusteth after.' He looked again at his wife. 'Would that I could eat her flesh.'

Which proclamation baffled me. Did he crave to be one with her once more, resenting her parting? Or was he merely hungry? I looked to Dowling for some enlightenment, but he averted his gaze.

'The Lord thy God will raise up unto thee a prophet from the midst

232

of thee, of thy brethren, like unto me. Unto him ye shall hearken,' Mompesson proclaimed, voice distant. 'A good man obtaineth favour of the Lord, but a man of wicked devices will he condemn. That is how it is supposed to be.' He sighed. 'I thought I acted in the service of the Lord.'

'So you did,' Josselin assured him. 'I blamed you for the sins of Thomas Elks, but that was wrong. *He* betrayed me, not you, nor God.'

Mompesson shook his head, a tear gathering at the corner of his eye. 'Lead us not into temptation, but deliver us from evil. The Devil appeared before me in familiar form, yet I did not recognise him.' He froze, blinked, then looked at Josselin with fresh eyes. 'What are you doing here?' He looked upon the corpses as if seeing them for the first time. 'You should not be here, James Josselin. This is God's house.' He staggered to his feet and drew a deep breath. I feared he was about to shout.

'I am leaving tomorrow,' Josselin said, calm.

'You cannot leave,' Mompesson replied, frowning like he didn't understand. 'No one may leave until the plague is gone.'

'I am leaving.' Josselin approached him closer. 'For I have further reparations to make. If you fear God has forsaken you then listen to what he is trying to tell you. Rebellion is as the sin of witchcraft, and stubbornness is as iniquity and idolatry.'

Mompesson fell to his knees and his face sunk beneath a lake of tears. 'You think Catherine is dead because I did not listen to God?'

Josselin placed a hand upon Mompesson's head. 'If it were only sinners that died of plague then we would have been the first to die, yet we live. It is not our place to question the wisdom of God, rather it rests upon us to . . .' He frowned. 'I came here in search of forgiveness,

233

Mompesson, yet I am stood here with my hand upon *your* head.'

Mompesson took one of Josselin's hands in both of his own. 'Pray to God and he will forgive you, if you be truly repentant.'

'Which advice you should follow yourself,' Josselin replied. 'For it is the answer to your anguish. You still have a flock.' He cast his eye upon the grisly scene. 'A living flock. All these people must be buried.'

'Aye,' Mompesson sighed, pale and limp, the frantic scrabblings of his former feverish state now dissipated. 'And may God have pity upon us miserable sinners, who are now visited with great sickness and mortality.'

'Amen to that.' Josselin wiped his palm upon the seat of his trousers and headed out towards the chancel.

Mompesson knelt before his wife and laid his large head in her small lap, a moment of intimacy upon which we were trespassing again. Dowling shuffled backwards into the chancel, and I followed, keen to be away. We reached the door without being heard, and stepped out into the night, straight into the arms of Marshall Howe.

Josselin leant against the wall of the church, arms folded. 'Spying again.' He clicked his tongue and shook his head sadly. 'You didn't tell me you worked with Withypoll.'

The hairs on the back of my neck stood erect. 'What do you know of Withypoll?'

'He stands at the barricades asking for you,' Josselin replied. 'Says you will betray me.' He turned to Howe. 'Lock them in the cage.'

Chapter Twenty-Three

The degree of the last conjunction of Saturn and Jupiter intimates
many unhappy disasters unto the vulgar man.

We sat huddled in the far corner of the cage. The opposite side of our prison smelt worse. A thin layer of slime covered the space where the two bodies had lain, like the trail of a giant slug. We leant against the bars beneath a cloudless sky.

'Withypoll is alive, then,' I reflected, staring up at a swarm of shining stars.

'He knew we came here under false names,' said Dowling. 'He wants us to die here.'

The moon grew fatter tonight, casting a ghostly sheen upon the pond and the linden trees. Josselin told Mompesson he was leaving next day. If we didn't get out of this cage before he went, I doubted we would ever leave Shyam alive.

'If Josselin leaves, then Mompesson will enforce the quarantine,' I said. 'Else Withypoll will invade with his soldiers.'

Dowling made a strange noise. I turned about and saw that he was crying. Ne'er had I been more surprised in all my life. I gripped his shoulder and squeezed hard as I could.

'Where is God?' he whispered.

'Everywhere,' I assured him, wishing he would stop, but he just buried his face in his hands.

'Dowling!' I attempted to rouse him. 'If God doesn't exist then he never has existed, and you have become who you are with no one's help.'

He seized my hand and turned his wet eyes to mine. 'I am alone.'

'You have me,' I said. He started to cry again, this time louder.

I prayed fervently to God to send him some message just as a figure emerged from out the shadows of the church, striding towards us. Josselin by himself, a satchel hanging from his shoulder.

'Tell me about Withypoll,' he demanded, as he marched to the cage. Thick fumes of ale escaped his mouth and nose.

'He is no friend of ours,' I replied, pulling my hand from Dowling's grasp.

He pushed his face against the bars. 'What will he do when he finds me gone and you in the cage?'

'He will tell Howe to rebuild his gallows,' I replied. 'If it satisfies his desire to see us die in agony.'

Josselin dug into his pocket for a key with which he opened the cage door. 'You saved my life. You should have reminded me.' He stood aside to let us out. 'I trust you, remember? And I need your help.'

I looked for Marshall Howe, but he was nowhere to be seen. Thank you, God.

'We make our own ways back to London,' Josselin spoke low, eyes wide. 'But once there I want you to arrange for me to meet with Arlington.'

'Why?' I asked.

'He murdered my best friend.' Josselin's voice trembled. 'Charles Howard was my brother. I watched for him and he watched for me. I trusted him as I trust myself. I ran because I couldn't think what else to do, but now I am ashamed.'

'What will you do when you meet him?' I demanded. 'He will hurry you to the executioner's block before you finish speaking.'

Josselin snorted. 'I know Arlington, which is why I fled, like the coward I am. But I have something of his. Not upon my person, but hidden where he cannot find it. Something he doesn't know I have, something he must be looking for. You tell him I will meet with him.'

'He won't come,' I protested. 'He will send soldiers.'

'Then tell him I have his letter,' Josselin whispered, hoarse. 'Not Withypoll, only Arlington. Tell him I have his letter and would meet with him to discuss its contents. Then he will meet with me.'

'What letter?' Dowling growled, wiping his eyes.

Josselin shook his head and raised a finger. 'I trust you,' he said. 'So trust me when I say you don't want to know. If I hadn't read that letter then I wouldn't be here now, and Charles wouldn't be dead. The letter is my business. You go to Arlington and tell him you have done your duty, that you found me and carry my message. If the meeting goes well, then you will have nothing to fear from Arlington. I will ensure it.'

I held my breath to protect against the stink on his breath. He stared, yet his eyes seemed unfocussed. 'Well, then,' I sighed. 'Where would you like to meet him?'

'Discuss that with him,' Josselin replied. 'When you want to find me, go to Aldgate. To Red Rose Lane. I will find you.'

'That is your plan?' Dowling exclaimed. 'According to you, you killed four of his agents, the clerics. You think he will forgive you that?'

Josselin shrugged. 'I don't think he could care less.'

'What if he refuses your invitation?' I asked.

Josselin rubbed his hands together. 'Then I will go to Clarendon. Indeed I will try and seek audience with him first, if I can. He may help.'

It seemed a poor plan to me, but at least it was our chance to escape this accursed village. If we got back to London before dusk tomorrow I could just meet Culpepper's deadline besides, and secure my shop.

'How do we avoid Withypoll?' I asked. 'Likely he brings soldiers with him.'

'So he does,' Josselin agreed. 'We will leave through the Delf. I will go now; you follow in an hour.' He looked Dowling up and down. 'If you are wise, you two might also travel alone, at least until you clear Colchester.'

Josselin stood silent, as if waiting.

'Very well,' I said, for I could think of little else to say. 'See you in London.'

'Good fortune.' Josselin rubbed his hands together and turned towards the church. 'Red Rose Lane,' he said again, waving a hand as he blended into the darkness.

I turned to Dowling. 'I cannot wait an hour.'

'They'll discover the Delf afore that,' said Dowling, tense. 'Withypoll is no fool. Likely he will smell Josselin coming.' He wiped a hand across his mouth. 'Mary Hancock showed me another path. I say we go east.'

I looked again for Marshall Howe, recalling the hatred on his face, and hurried after Dowling into the woods. Dowling walked quickly, stopping only when he reached the mouth of the track that supposedly led out of the village. All was quiet, an eerie silence.

'He asked us to wait an hour,' I whispered.

'It may take an hour to find our way to the road,' Dowling replied, peering into the black tunnel. 'We can wait at the other end.'

As the path led upwards the ground became stonier, the trees sparse and the terrain more open. I prayed the track led where we hoped, and not in a great circle around Shyam. I glanced over my shoulder every few paces to check we weren't followed, feeling naked beneath the stars. At the top of the rise we descended. The ground softened and branches formed a new canopy above our heads. Soon it was impossible to see anything, darkness enveloping us.

I stepped into boggy marsh, a low ditch full of rotting leaves. Water seeped over the top of my boots. I pulled myself up by the root of a tree and realised we reached the road.

'How long do you think that took us?' I wondered. It felt like half the night.

Dowling cocked his head then grabbed my sleeve and pulled me deeper into the undergrowth. The sound of horses' hooves beat a drum from the direction of Shyam.

Five horses cantered from our left, four brown, and a great white steed with Withypoll upon it, narrow-eyed, scanning either side of the road. He looked fit and healthy, no sign of the fever he suffered before. I ducked my head into the ground and held my breath. Once they passed, I brushed twigs and old leaf from my shirt. 'Now what do we do? They'll post soldiers at the gate into Colchester.'

'We get closer,' Dowling replied.

We walked through the scrub another hundred yards before we heard the horses again. We dived into the bushes. Three horses this time, Withypoll at the lead, trotting slow.

'They know we're on the road,' I whispered.

'Josselin too,' said Dowling. 'Else Withypoll wouldn't be out here. He'd be peeling off Josselin's fingernails.'

I shivered. This time I stayed behind my tree. Withypoll was cunning. He would pull off the path and wait. I prayed they didn't fetch out dogs.

An hour later they returned, spread further apart, riding fast. Withypoll leant forward between the ears of his horse, staring unblinking into the forest, with more energy than last time we saw him. The soldiers behind yelled loud obscenities, and waved their hands in the air. The last horse dragged a body behind it, bouncing on the earth like a sack of coal. I watched, paralysed, praying it was not Josselin. It was a lean man without much hair. Though his face was covered with blood, still I recognised Galileo.

'They are all as evil as Withypoll,' I whispered, hating them for their revelry.

I wondered if this display was for our benefit; for Josselin as well, to terrorise us into submission. Instead we burrowed deeper into the undergrowth, far enough from the road we couldn't be seen, close enough we could see the horses whene'er they passed. I strained my ears for every sound, terrified Withypoll might come crashing through the trees at any moment, or that we'd hear the baying of hounds. We made our way so slow even the sun travelled faster than us, climbing to the top of the sky and sinking down again before we reached Colchester. Galileo's face stuck in my mind's eye, the lump on his head where I hit him with a log. I had liked him.

At last the grey, stone wall came into view through the trees, fifty yards away. Between us and the wall was marshland, the treeline finishing short. The great gate stood open. Two soldiers talked together, stood apart from four sentries. They watched the soldiers warily.

We heard horses again, loud galloping from the direction of Shyam. Withypoll and two of his associates rode into view, then drew their horses up sharp in front of the gate. Withypoll leapt from his charge and drew his sword, sticking the tip of it against the throat of one of the sentries, leaning forwards, shoulder tensed, jaw clenched. Then he remounted, reined his horse around and kicked it forwards into Colchester, followed by all the soldiers except one, who lingered a few minutes longer, waving his arms at the sentries and making various loud noises.

Dowling peered into the gathering gloom. 'Josselin is inside the town walls.'

'How do you know?'

'They've been out all day,' Dowling whispered. 'So why the hurry? Something has happened.'

'Josselin is caught?'

'I don't think so,' Dowling growled. 'Else Withypoll wouldn't have stopped. Question is, how did Josselin get in?'

The four sentries gathered in a circle, gesticulating, the man

241

attacked by Withypoll standing at the centre.

'They let him in,' I realised. 'That's what Withypoll suspects. Their allegiance lies with Josselin, not with Withypoll. If Josselin asked them for passage, they would ne'er refuse him. He must have approached while the soldiers were on the road.'

'Then we must follow,' Dowling said. 'Before Withypoll thinks to send soldiers back to the gate. I don't think he realises all the soldiers followed him.'

'You must be joking,' I replied.

'What else would you do, Harry?' Dowling shrilled. 'That is the only way in, and soon it will be guarded by Withypoll's men.'

He was right. Withypoll and his band just humiliated the local sentries. If there was ever a time to persuade them, now was it, whilst they still felt most contrary.

Dowling raised his stiff body and stepped out onto the road. At first no one noticed. We hurried across the bare terrain, my heart beating so loud I thought my ears would burst. Then one man noticed. He held his hand against another man's chest and reached for a wooden club.

'Hold!' Dowling cried, managing a terse smile. 'We are friends of Josselin.'

'You cannot pass,' the leader replied, holding forth his stick. Dark hair grew long down each cheek and he wore a shapeless green felt hat. 'You are the murderers out of Shyam the soldiers are looking for.'

Dowling held up his hands. 'Withypoll told you that, but it isn't true. We work for the King and we are friends of Josselin. Those soldiers are under Withypoll's command, and he is a treacherous dog.'

The man grunted and looked to his colleagues.

Dowling dug into his pocket for the royal seal. 'Withypoll will do all he can to stop us, which is why he tells lies. You must admit us in the name of the King. It is our job to save Josselin from Withypoll.'

The leader stretched out a hand to receive the seal, over which he rubbed a dirty forefinger.

'The King will reward you if you assist,' Dowling assured them.

'If not, he will stick your heads up on poles above Nonsuch House,' I added.

'Take off your shirts,' the man ordered, nervous. 'I must make sure you got no buboes nor tokens.'

I whipped off my shirt quick, then examined my skin as carefully as he.

'Did ye come into contact with those that are infected?' he asked, squinting from afar.

'We went to Shyam to rescue James Josselin,' I replied, 'not to tend the sick.' I felt guilty uttering the words. We couldn't be certain we were not infected. The sooner we passed through the city walls and out the other side, the better for my conscience.

The man sighed. 'Then pass, but in God's name tell no one we allowed you through.'

God did watch over us. I could scarcely believe our good fortune. 'Thank you,' I said calm, suppressing an urge to run. We hurried through the gate and up East Hill. Dusk drove men from the streets. Those remaining went about their business with grim intent, coats flapping in the warm breeze.

'We must find somewhere to hide until it is dark,' said Dowling.

I gazed up at the castle. 'We don't know Josselin will go straight to London, or even if he will go to London at all. He said he would meet with Arlington, but what if he has business here first? We still haven't worked out what Shrewsbury was doing here talking to Dutchmen. We should at least establish Josselin is not gone to the Dutch Quarter.'

'How?' Dowling said, raising his voice. 'Shall we knock upon every door and ask if anyone has seen him?'

'No,' I replied. 'We must be more discreet.'

Dowling protested, eyeing the relative safety of the shadowy wasteland to the east of the castle. 'To get to the Dutch Quarter we must walk through the middle of Colchester.'

'We can't set off to London without horses anyway, Davy,' I replied, 'and we won't find horses at Grey Friars.'

'We will find them outside the town walls,' said Dowling. 'No one cares who we are out there. It's in here they watch for strangers.'

I led us into the grounds of All Saints and leant against a wall. 'And in here that soldiers roam, when before they were locked outside. What spells Withypoll must have cast to persuade Mayor Flanner.'

I heard shouting and peered over the wall and across the high street into the castle grounds. A disorderly mob of a dozen soldiers or more staggered down the hill from the castle itself. They walked unsteadily, still happily complying with Captain Scotschurch's mandate to stay drunk.

As the sun finally disappeared behind the horizon, so candlelight appeared in the windows of the houses.

'Follow the lights,' Dowling pointed. Torches shone from the direction of St Runwald's and the marketplace.

'Withypoll must be at the Moot Hall,' I guessed. 'Now is as good a time as any.'

I led us north towards the Dutch Quarter, Dowling following

reluctant. I had no plan, other than to retrace our steps of four nights ago. Two men watched as we struggled to remember the route. One tapped the other on the elbow and they touched foreheads. They weren't soldiers, but watched just as careful, before disappearing into the darkness.

'We have to hurry,' I said, dry-mouthed.

Dowling beckoned. 'This way.'

We hurried beneath the eaves, then headed left. The big house, in which I saw Shrewsbury, stood at the end of the street. Dark, lifeless windows stared back.

'Shrewsbury cannot be far away,' was all I could think to say.

Dowling laid a hand upon my shoulder. 'We have to leave, Harry.'

Voices sounded from the end of the same alley we just passed through. Then more voices from the street behind, laced with the excitement of the hunter. The alley brightened with the light of torches as the noise grew louder.

Too late to retreat. I ran up to the house and tried the door. It was unlocked.

'Come,' I hissed at Dowling, who still stood motionless.

He bounded after me with long loping strides, and I closed the door just before the first pursuer emerged from the alley. The house smelt dusty, hollow and deserted. We crouched before the long bay window and peered out into the night. A small crowd gathered. Soon the cobbled street was full, a dozen soldiers or more, all carrying torches. They chattered amongst themselves, pointing in all directions, until Withypoll appeared and the noise subsided.

He stared at the ground and walked slowly towards us. Then, to my blessed relief, he turned aside, waving a hand left, directing half the soldiers away towards the north and the other half back towards the castle. He lifted his torch, illuminating his long, cruel face, afore following the soldiers north.

I turned from the window and slumped backwards against the wall.

Dowling still crouched, facing outwards. 'We're safe for now. A dozen drunkard soldiers can search only slowly at night. We have until dawn to find a way out.'

'Withypoll will not make the same mistake twice,' I worried. 'Every gate will be guarded from the inside.'

'What would Josselin do?' said Dowling.

'Climb the wall?' I wondered. 'Dig beneath it? Find a breach?'

'I reckon he'll have prepared already his escape,' Dowling replied. 'There'll be a house somewhere, close to the wall, whose occupants will help him.'

'Fairfax bombarded the west wall with cannon,' I said. 'St Mary's was destroyed. There must be an easy route out somewhere about Head Gate or the Balkerne Gate.'

Dowling nodded. 'Since half Withypoll's men have gone north, we should go south, but we'll have to cross the centre of town.'

'Not if we go direct west through St Peter's,' I said. 'Then make our way south across the corn market.' I turned to peer out of the window again, feeling more cheerful.

Something moved at the far end of the street, a flash of white.

I elbowed Dowling in the ribs. 'Did you see that?'

'See what?' Dowling muttered.

I watched so hard, my eyes hurt. Someone darted from one side of the road to the other and now stood in a doorway, deep in shadow. I could still make out a sliver of white against the black shadow. Whoever it was stood still, waiting for something, or someone.

'We cannot stay here,' said Dowling.

'Someone hides in the shadow,' I insisted. 'What if it is Josselin?'

I stood up and headed for the door. I put my ear to the wood, but all was silent. Then I opened it slow, felt the night brush gently against my cheek. Then I looked down and saw our footprints, clear, edged with flakes of dried mud.

'This is what Withypoll was looking at,' I whispered to Dowling, eyes fixed upon the doorway where I saw the white shape.

'Aye, and Withypoll is not a fool,' said a gruff voice.

I spun to my left, hands raised, too late. The club hit me square above the forehead. My knees buckled. Two soldiers jumped on Dowling, dragging him to the floor. I heard the crack of his skull beneath someone's thick boot. I lay on my side, a warm river of blood trickling down my nose.

The white shape floated out onto the street, a tall majestic figure, yellow skin drawn like parchment. The Earl of Shrewsbury?

'You were told to fetch Josselin,' Withypoll said from somewhere above my head. 'I don't see him.'

I tried to look up, but my head wouldn't move.

Someone pulled at my hair, and something cold rubbed against my throat. 'I would *like* to kill you, Lytle,' Withypoll whispered in my ear. 'First tell me where is Josselin?'

So he didn't have him.

'He is a hero here,' I slurred. 'They do as he commands.'

'I will find him,' hissed Withypoll. 'Make no mistake. Then will I cut his lips from his face.' The blade pressed against my windpipe. 'As I will do to you one day, but Arlington insists upon seeing you first.'

My stomach cramped, and my guts churned, forcing me to vomit.

247

I panted, sucking in cool air, retching nothing, for we hadn't eaten properly in three days.

'Take them,' Withypoll commanded. 'Tell Lord Arlington to save them for me.'

I searched again for the ghostly shape of Shrewsbury before someone punched me flush on one cheek with what felt like a hammer. I remember nothing else until we were well past Brentwood.

Chapter Twenty-Four

*As unto the Spanish Dominions, they are like to be much concerned
in their Leagues with their Allies and Friends.*

Dowling's forehead bore a clearly discernible boot print stamped into
his skin. He lay with arms bound behind his back, staring at the same
instrument as I did. In the same dingy room in the Develin Tower
where this all started. Back in London.

Arlington stroked the black hair of a dead donkey's head,
impaled upon a wooden spike. 'A friend of mine told me about this.
He saw one in Spain. I had this one built especially.' He ran a finger
along the line of its cranium then pulled one of its ears out straight,
smiling in grim satisfaction. 'I have not had the pleasure of using it
yet.' He turned to me, the edges of the black plaster upon his nose
gently peeling.

'Untie him,' he demanded.

Two soldiers stepped forward, hesitant, like they feared for their own lives. They picked at the knots hastily, muttering under their breath as they worked. Then my wrists were free.

'Place him on the donkey,' Arlington ordered.

The head and spike attached to a long piece of wood, running across the top of a four-legged frame. The saddle of the beast was planed sharp as a razor, stuck straight up into the air. As they lowered me onto its back, the edge of it cut into my arse. I leant forwards in an attempt to relieve the pressure.

Arlington lifted a finger. 'Bind him again.' The soldier jerked my hands behind my back and the wood bit deeper into my flesh.

'The Spanish military use this in the field,' Arlington announced, brightly. He pointed to a pile of iron balls, heaped in the corner, then fetched a pair of manacles and closed them around my ankles. The chains falling from the manacles were covered in hooks. 'It is a most ingenious device.'

He picked up two balls, each of which had a loop embedded within it, and hooked one onto each of my feet. The manacles pulled me down even harder upon the blade of the wooden frame and the wood ground against my bone. I gritted my teeth and wriggled desperately in an attempt to relieve the pain.

'What do you think, butcher?' he asked Dowling. 'Would you like to join him?'

'Why torture him?' Dowling barked. 'We have no secrets from you.'

'Every man has secrets,' Arlington answered, calm. 'Now I would attach more and more balls to each leg until the weight pulls the man down so hard against the edge that it cuts him in half.'

It felt already like my body was torn in two, fire shooting through my anus.

'It seems to work.' I heard Arlington's voice, full of wonder. I stared upwards at the ceiling, tears filling my eyes.

'What do you want?' Dowling shouted.

'I don't know,' Arlington replied, voice distant. 'Perhaps nothing. Perhaps I will try another two balls.'

'He saved your life,' Dowling bellowed. 'You were writhing upon the ground, barely conscious. Wharton held his sword with both fists, ready to drive it into the back of your neck. Harry saved your life.'

'That is not how it happened.' Arlington blinked, turning to the soldiers. 'I was locked in deadly combat with the Earl of St Albans and was about to slay him, when this fellow intervened, plunging a butcher's knife into the back of his head.'

I tried to hold my body still, fearing if I moved the sharp edge would cut deeper into my body. I opened my eyes and looked down to my left without moving my head. The soldiers cowered.

'He saved your life.' Dowling tried to stand, back bent. 'And would do it again.'

I wished he would sit still.

Arlington stepped forward and pushed Dowling back onto the stone floor. 'I should hope he would,' he declared. 'I serve my King to the best of my ability, and reward those who are similarly loyal.'

'Then take him down,' Dowling begged, eyes wide.

Arlington waved a hand. 'Take him down,' he said, much to my amazement. 'I had no intention of torturing him,' he explained to the soldiers as they lifted me from the wooden donkey. 'Not yet, anyway. Throw him back onto the floor.'

Though they lifted me off the cursed contraption, the pain didn't subside. I staggered back to my place with legs bowed. Dowling breathed low and shallow.

Arlington leant backwards against the donkey, tossing a heavy ball from one hand to the other. 'What happened in Shyam?'

'James Josselin sought refuge,' I answered quickly, determined not to end up back on the device. 'He was apprehended by a man named Thomas Elks who hid him away with the intention of killing him. We found him.'

'Where is he now?'

'If Withypoll doesn't have him, then he is on his way back to London.'

'Back to London?' Arlington grimaced. 'He runs away. Now you say he plans to run back?'

'He wants to talk to you,' I replied. 'He asked us to arrange a meeting with you. He says he has something of yours, something you may not know he owns.'

'The traitor has a secret.' Arlington lifted his arms in an attempt at humour. But his brow furrowed. 'What does he have of mine?'

'He said a letter,' I replied, feeling the sweat upon my palms. 'Though he wouldn't say what was in it.'

Arlington pursed his lips strangely and stared so hard his eyelids disappeared. He turned to face one corner of the dark and dingy turret, biting at the fingers of one hand, muttering. Then he tore at his wig and threw it on the floor. He stood over it, red-faced, breathing deep. The two soldiers looked at each other and then the door.

He swivelled on one heel and screamed. 'Go!'

They hurried out the room, closing the door carefully behind. I listened to their footsteps dance down the stone staircase.

'I have had enough!' Arlington yelled, face red and moist against the whiteness of his shaven head. 'I asked you to go to Shyam and fetch Josselin. Yet instead you take it upon yourself to arrange a *meeting*!'

252

He stood bent, head craned forward, seeking some response. It seemed prudent to remain quiet.

'What were you doing sneaking about Colchester, hiding in an empty house – in the Dutch Quarter?' Saliva flew in all directions.

'I saw Shrewsbury there, talking to some Dutchmen,' I explained. 'Before we went to Shyam.'

Arlington's face turned a shade of deep purple. 'What?'

'The Earl of Shrewsbury,' I said, praying his twitching fingers would not alight upon a knife.

Arlington's face twisted into a mask of livid incomprehension. 'You saw the Earl of Shrewsbury in the Dutch Quarter at Colchester,' he choked. 'The Earl of Shrewsbury in England.' He looked to Dowling, who bowed his head.

'*I* saw him,' I said. 'Before we went to Shyam. In the same house we were arrested by Withypoll. We went to see if he was still there, for it seemed likely there might be some connection. The Earl of Shrewsbury fled to Holland. So it seemed to us . . .' Dowling looked like he would weep. 'It seemed to *me* . . .'

Arlington's face became pink again, as the blood drained back from his cheeks. 'You told Withypoll this?'

'I told him the same night,' I replied. 'Before we left for Shyam, but I don't think he believed me.'

'I am not surprised,' Arlington exclaimed, voice weak. 'The Earl of Shrewsbury was killed two months ago. Killed by agents of De Witt, who suspected he conspired with the House of Orange. They did not mean to kill him, they said, though I don't know how you kill a man by accident. They were keen for us to know how apologetic they were.'

I shook my head firmly. 'I know the Earl of Shrewsbury well.'

253

'You saw a dead man.'

'Did you see his body?' I demanded, stubborn.

Arlington sighed, looking to the ceiling. 'No, I did not see his body. Why should I want to see the old fool's dead body? He stank when he was alive; God knows what state he would be in if they sent his rotten corpse back to England.'

'Then you don't know he is dead.'

'You doubt my intelligence?' Arlington glared, cheeks glowing again.

'Perhaps I was mistaken,' I replied, though I knew I was not.

'Ah!' Arlington exclaimed, throwing his arms in the air and turning away. 'Withypoll would like to cut off your balls,' he cried. 'And I would like to watch.'

'Josselin was imprisoned,' I said. 'Elks locked him up and we found him.' I stopped. Perhaps I should not reveal how we saved Josselin's life. It occurred to me most of our troubles could be traced back to saving people's lives.

'You found him, released him, then sat back and watched him go,' Arlington whispered. 'Is that what you are telling me?'

'He is a hero in Shyam,' I replied. 'Had we tried to arrest him we would have been lynched. Instead we thought to escape the village and seek out Withypoll's assistance. But Josselin locked us in a cage from which we escaped. We followed him to Colchester, close behind. We were looking for him in the Dutch Quarter.'

Arlington trembled with anger. I wished he would pull back his face from mine, for his breath was rank, and my face was wet.

He clenched his fist in front of my eyes. 'Why? They are all weavers and wool merchants.' He turned his back and retreated to the corner of the room to retrieve his wig. He dusted it against the leg of his breeches and pulled it back over his head.

'Since we are alone, *gentlemen*,' he spoke the last word as if to children. 'I will concede that you did indeed save my life in St Albans.' He adjusted the hairpiece carefully. 'Which is of no value to you at all, since I cannot have it known that I allowed myself to be rescued by a butcher and a clerk. So forget it happened.' He smacked his hands together to be rid of the dirt. 'It's just another reason to be rid of you.'

Which did not seem fair.

'I sent you to Shyam to do a job and you failed.' He waved a hand at the donkey. 'Which is yet another reason to be rid of you. Withypoll would do me the honour without needing to be persuaded.' He drew a short blade from his jacket. 'Nonetheless I will give you one last opportunity.' He sliced at the ropes binding my wrists. 'Not because I am a generous man, nor a kind-hearted man, for we all know I am none of those things.' He slipped the knife back into the folds of his coat and stood in front of us, hands on hips.

'Josselin must be apprehended,' he said, quietly. 'He is a traitor, and is therefore dangerous. You know what he looks like and have been exposed to him already.' He turned back to the dark corner, and returned with a twisted iron contraption. 'I don't want others talking to him, so I must trust in you.'

He held the tool up in the air. It was like a pair of tongs with the edges turned in and sharpened, thin metal hooks upon their extremities.

'If he is in London then you must find him,' he said, calm. 'How were you to arrange this meeting?'

'We were to leave message for him at the Mermaid,' I lied.

'Then leave your message, arrange the rendezvous, and tell me where to find him.' He thrust the tongs into my face. 'If you fail again then it is

255

not only you who will suffer.' He looked at Dowling. 'You have a wife.' Then turned his attention to me. 'You do not, but I hear you are fond of your housemaid. You took her away with you to escape the plague, did you not?'

I nodded, dumb, for I recognised the instrument he brandished. It was an ancient breast ripper, a tool used by the inquisitor in days gone by, to shred a woman's breasts.

'Do you understand now, gentlemen, how serious is your mission?' he asked, lowering the device.

'There is no need . . .' Dowling said, weak.

I looked at the donkey and imagined Dowling and I placing Arlington upon its blade.

'I see what you are thinking, Lytle,' Arlington leered. 'I would think the same if I were in your shoes. But if I am found dead, then you will be held culpable. You and your families will be punished.'

He tossed the cruel instrument into the corner. He would never use it himself. He would send apprentices to commit the deed with their own blunt devices. It was a common enough occurrence and would ensure the deed could never be traced to him.

'Did Josselin tell you he worked with Clarendon?' Arlington asked matter-of-factly.

We both nodded quickly.

Arlington rubbed his nose. 'I cannot think why he would return were it not to seek help from the good Earl. I must know the moment he attempts to make contact, for it would be convenient to be able to arrest him in the presence of the Earl. In the Earl's private closet if necessary.' He clicked his fingers. 'But the timing must be perfect. If I send men too early he will never arrive, and Clarendon will be most offended. If I send men too late, then Josselin will be gone.' He turned to point at both of us, one with each hand. 'From tonight you will stand watch at Clarendon's residence on Piccadilly. Watch where he goes and follow. Josselin may attempt to contact him. If you see Josselin, then one of you will inform me personally. Is that clear?'

'Aye,' we replied in unison.

My heart ached, and any suspicion I still harboured that this devil was a man, was assuaged. 'What about the meeting?'

'Tomorrow,' Arlington spat. He blew out his cheeks and took a deep breath. 'It has been an entertaining evening,' he proclaimed, taking up a position next to one of the narrow windows, there to watch the red sun dying. 'For which I doth sincerely thank you. Now be gone.'

I couldn't believe we were free to go. Time to see Jane.

Chapter Twenty-Five

*There will therefore be expected the clearest of our endeavours to
satisfie the Curious in their more than moderate expectancies.*

I knocked loudly before stepping back to the middle of the street.
When she opened the door I spotted the flash of delight upon her face
before she hid it behind a scowl.

'I'm back,' I said.

'So you are.' She looked up and down Bread Street. 'Why are you
standing over there?'

'I've come from Colchester,' I whispered hoarse, so none else might
hear.

Her belly was definitely rounder than I remembered, but I had not
the expertise to tell if it was sign of a child, else the consequence of
eating too much pudding. She always ate more when I was away. She
said my presence affected her appetite. The smell of incense drifted
out from inside the house.

She scanned my filthy clothes from foot to head with sharp green eyes. 'You've been to Essex and now you're returned?' she asked, eyes narrowed. 'What be that black mark?' she pointed at my forehead.

'A bruise,' I replied.

'A big bruise,' she said, suspicious. 'And what is that in your pocket? A pipe?'

I dug out the leaves and held them up in the air. 'To protect me from plague.'

She leant forward, squinting. 'Where did you get them?'

'Culpepper gave them to me. The apothecary.'

She peered. 'You smoked that in your pipe?'

I nodded.

'Looks like seer sage to me.' She stood straight, arms folded. 'Have you been seeing things?'

'What sort of things?'

She watched me close. 'You have, haven't you? Bright lights? Shimmering shapes?'

'Perhaps,' I said, slowly. I looked down at the innocent looking pile of dry foliage in my palm.

She smiled, and I saw the end of her tongue. 'You said you knew about plants.'

Enough. I tucked the leaves back into my pocket. 'I came to see how you are.' She opened her mouth to say something, but I dared to interrupt. 'Are you with child?'

Her arms fell to her sides, all thought of plague forgot. 'You noticed that yourself?'

'Aye,' I replied. '*Is* it a child?'

'Yes,' she replied, eyes wet.

A tennis ball appeared from nowhere and stuck in my throat. I wanted to take her in my arms, but dared not approach closer. 'I am glad,' I said, fighting back the tears.

'*Glad?*' she exclaimed, lines furrowing her brow. 'What are you glad about? You have no job and spend every day in the Mermaid.'

'I have decided to become an apothecary,' I replied. 'That's why I've been seeing Culpepper. He's going to sell me his shop. I will be a good father.'

She gaped in most sarcastic fashion, ducking her head and staring from beneath her brow. 'You will share with him your worldly wisdom, no doubt,' she blustered, trying to hide the wetness of her cheeks. 'Teach him a trade and set a fine example of outstanding moral behaviour.'

'It might be a girl,' I muttered.

'Boy or girl.' She wiped her face and lifted her chin. 'Do you plan to marry me?'

'I . . .' It seemed a silly question. I shrugged. 'Would you *want* to marry me?'

'How can you ask?' she sobbed, wringing her apron between her hands, staring at me with a wistful expression I had ne'er seen before.

I wasn't sure if she meant yes or no, but her gaze was so tender I could only assume she quite liked the idea. Now seemed like the time to embrace, but fear I might carry the Pest prevented it.

'I don't know what to do,' I confessed.

'Sort out your affairs with Lord Arlington and come back to me healthy,' she cried. Then she clasped her hands to her mouth, turned and slammed the door closed.

It was a good thing, I screamed silently. Imagine how worried I would be had she ran across the street and thrown her arms about my neck. Who knows what might have happened to the baby? Yet I yearned to hold her tight.

Her face appeared at the window and she waved. I thought to tell her I loved her, but decided to leave that until next time. I waved back and hurried to meet Dowling at Clarendon's house.

Chapter Twenty-Six

If we allow one sign to signifie one year, than it is manifest, that from the time of first commencing the Wars, until full three years, the Hollanders will not be in denomination high and might Lords, but a clowded, impoverished people.

The Earl was getting old. Once advisor to Charles I, then Lord Chancellor to Charles II in exile, he paraded the court like the King's own father. He built himself a magnificent house on Piccadilly, casting a long shadow all the way to the palace itself, a mark of his influence. It was a bigger house than any man could need. Built three storeys high with two long wings, Clarendon could house the entire court inside its walls if he so wished.

Some called it 'Holland House', for they suspected it was built from the proceeds of Dutch bribes. The taller rose the house, so further crumbled what popularity the Earl still enjoyed. The years had passed, and Charles was no longer a boy. Where once the King relied upon his older mentor, now he resented the moralising and nagging. Some at court even dared mock the old man, though not to his face. Clarendon's star was on the wane.

Piccadilly was wide and paved, a quiet oasis ploughing a furrow through green parkland. People paraded on Pall Mall, waved their mouchoirs and exchanged vain pleasantries. Others sat and enjoyed the morning sun. Dowling waited for me hid behind a tree.

'What news?' he asked.

'She's pregnant,' I replied, sitting next to him.

He pounced, smothering me against his sweaty chest. I pushed myself away and escaped his flailing arms. He smiled wetly, like an old woman regarding young lovers.

'Have you seen Josselin?' I asked, seeking to distract his attention.

'He's not come out,' Dowling replied awkwardly, settling himself.

It was easy to see who came and went, for the path from door to gate stretched fifty yards. We sat across the road, with fine view between the gateposts.

'Do you want to go and see Lucy?' I offered.

'Later,' he replied, more sober. 'When I have worked out what to tell her.'

Unlike him, I thought. He hadn't seen her for a week.

Two servants hovered outside Clarendon's front gate wearing smart, blue suits and tall hats festooned with ribbons. Large, young men, lithe and strong, posturing for the ladies.

'So we sit here all day,' I muttered, watching them preen.

'Else go for a ride upon the Spanish donkey,' said Dowling.

I recalled the horror and disgust upon Jane's face when first I told her of our mission to extract Josselin from Shyam. What would she think of our new mission; to wait for Josselin to step into a trap?

263

'We collude in an innocent man's death.'

'What do you suggest?'

'Speak to Clarendon. Josselin says he is committed to peace.' I thought aloud.

Dowling slapped his hands on his knees. 'Did you not hear what Arlington said? We are to wait for Josselin and report his arrival.'

'I heard,' I answered, standing. 'But if we comply with that instruction, then what next? Kill a man?' I had already severed a man's finger. 'If we fail, then I will take Jane away, out of England if need be.' It sounded desperate even as I said it, yet we could not sit idly by.

'I don't want to leave England,' Dowling protested.

'God will watch over you, won't he? I doubt he is impressed to see you just sitting here.'

Dowling raised himself slowly, face contorted in indecision.

The two servants noticed our approach when we were still but halfway across the street. The tallest watched with a supercilious sneer etched upon thick lips, black brow curled above dark eyes. He raised a wooden cane and pointed it at my chest, as if defining the boundaries of an invisible territory.

I brushed the end of the stick aside. 'We work for Lord Arlington. We have news for Clarendon.'

'What news?' The taller man smirked. 'Get thee gone, vagabonds, before we stick you like pigs.'

My throat constricted and fire smouldered in my belly. 'Tell him we spoke to James Josselin. Tell him Josselin is in London.'

The shorter man regarded me seriously, eyes wandering from my tangled, greasy hair down to the toes of my ruined boots. 'If I deliver such a message and it rouses his interest, then he will throw you into a dark place from where you may never emerge, should you speak false.'

Dowling lurched forwards with clenched fists. 'We don't speak false.'

The guard opened the gate and slipped through, still suspicious. The other guard bid us come closer, afraid we might flee now the message was to be delivered. We waited beneath the climbing sun in silent anticipation. The guard returned but a short time later, beckoning with his sword, brisk and serious.

'I will come with you.' I pointed at Dowling. 'He will stay here.'

Dowling's jaw dropped as he prepared to protest. Then I saw him stop, recognising how important it was that one of us remain outside to watch for Josselin. The tall servant hesitated a moment before harrying me forwards beneath the gaze of forty windows.

'Move along.' The guard shoved me. 'Don't mistake yourself for a guest.'

He opened the door upon the most opulent of interiors. The marble floor sparkled white beneath my feet like a great mirror. Rich, new tapestries hung upon wood-panelled walls, depicting scenes of woodlands and fields, and lots of French peasants. The central staircase twisted an intricate path from the floor up into the shadows of the silent interior.

'What are you waiting for?' growled the guard, poking me in the back. He prodded me left, down the darkest corridor, naked of wood, bare plaster heralding the wing of the house yet to be completed.

I stepped carefully past a pile of planks and a long row of open doorways, until reaching a small plain door tucked around a corner, nestled in a small recess. The guard turned the key in the lock and held it open. Beyond was darkness.

'Is that a dungeon?' I stepped back. 'I came here of my own free will.'

'So you did,' the man replied. 'Now you are subject to his lordship's will. Get inside.'

He raised his sword and his partner appeared behind him, face alive with curiosity. I saw no choice but to step into the bare stone corridor.

Light shone weak from around the corner. To my surprise the sentry followed, pushing me along the curved passage towards a large, square room, bright but damp. An open doorway led outside to a brick stairwell, but it was barred with an iron grille, as were the windows. I stopped upon the threshold, wary, but the guard kicked me in the back of my right knee and shoved me forwards, slamming closed a second iron grille, leaving me trapped, like a bird in a cage.

'Don't worry,' the guard said in low tone. 'If you be telling the truth then you will walk back the way we came. If not.' He shrugged. 'You were warned.'

He slipped back into the gloom, footsteps echoing down the passage.

I touched the wet stone with my fingertips. The staircase outside was straight and narrow. At the top of the stairs grew green bushes and trees. Creeping vines fell down the walls. We were at the base of a damp pit, a strange cell without obvious purpose. I shook the iron grille. It was locked tight. This was Clarendon's house, the place he lived. Why should he build a prison in his own private residence?

More footsteps, again from the corridor behind, heavier this time. A man appeared at the bars, tall and stern, a handsome fellow with shiny, black hair. Green eyes stared like a hungry cat.

'Open the door,' he snapped to someone behind.

The key turned in the lock and he stepped inside, padding softly like a big lion. He descended upon me without fear or caution, stood more than six feet tall, broad and solid. Not old man Clarendon. He went to seize one of my ears, but I slapped him away. He smiled, teeth glinting in the wet sunlight. 'Tell me your name,' he said, utterly at ease.

'Harry Lytle,' I replied quickly, not for a moment contemplating a lie.

'Perhaps I have heard of you,' he frowned slightly. 'Though I cannot recall in what context.' He seized one of my hands in his own before I could move, inspecting my fingers. 'You have soft hands,' he remarked, piercing eyes probing mine with fascinated curiosity. He rubbed the lapel of my jacket between finger and forefinger. 'Why have you come here, Harry Lytle?'

'To talk to Clarendon,' I replied, unable to keep the tremor from my voice. He stood too close. Though his clothes were of the finest quality and every hair upon his head lay in immaculate order, ne'ertheless he gave off a rank odour, like a beast that eats raw meat and makes no effort to cleanse itself.

'Persuade me you deserve his attentions,' he demanded. 'Else I will bury you in his garden.'

I couldn't think. I tried to remember why I came, my objective. 'Has James Josselin come here?'

He cocked his head and frowned, folding his arms behind his back. 'Why do you ask?'

I wished I'd kept my mouth closed.

'Speak,' the man commanded. 'What do you know of James Josselin?'

'I know he is accused of treachery and killing the Earl of Berkshire,'

I answered, nervous. 'He denies both.'

'How do you know?' he asked, eyes dull and angry.

'He told me,' I replied.

The big man regarded me like I was a mysterious puzzle. 'Josselin has fled to Shyam, beyond Colchester. Shyam is plagued.'

'He is no longer in Shyam,' I said. 'He's come back to London. He said he would come here to seek protection. He says only Clarendon shares his desire for peace.'

He reached out a hand to touch my hair. 'We worked on the same deputation, though I work for Clarendon and they worked for Arlington.'

I smacked at his hand. 'Do you think Josselin killed Berkshire?'

'No,' he replied, eyes darkening. 'They were the best of friends. They knew each other since childhood.'

'Who killed Berkshire?' I asked.

'Why didn't you ask Josselin?'

'I did.' I clenched my fists. 'He said it was Arlington.'

He flicked at a fine wisp of hair that had fallen upon his cheek and carefully placed it back behind his ear. 'Arlington's spy walks into Clarendon's house and asks questions. What makes you think anyone will reply?'

'Lord Arlington told us to watch from outside the gate and let him know when Josselin arrived.' Anger welled inside my breast. 'I am not supposed to be here at all.'

'Really?' he exclaimed, doubt clouding his eyes. He watched me like I was a strange animal, something to be feared, or squashed. 'I am supposed to believe that?'

I blew out through my cheeks and dug my fingers into my scalp. 'Whether Josselin killed Berkshire or not, Arlington will see him die for it, and for his treachery besides.'

'I know what Arlington says,' the man said. 'I don't know why you come here to tell me it.'

'Where is James Josselin?' I insisted.

He shrugged. 'I assure you he is not here, nor has he been. You said you spoke to him. If you spoke to him, then you know where he is.'

'I spoke to him in Shyam,' I replied. 'I said I would meet him again here.'

The man stepped away, wiping his palms upon the seat of his breeches. 'You entered Shyam? Then you may be plagued.' He reached for his sword.

'I am not infected,' I replied with a confidence I didn't feel. 'I took precautions.'

'Why are you here?' he barked. 'You barge in here headstrong, like a fool. Is this some crude scheme of Arlington's?'

'Make of me what you will,' I said, raising my voice, 'but don't suspect me of the same malignant treachery with which *you* seem so familiar. Josselin ran from London when he was accused of murder, yet you know he is innocent. Why did Clarendon not protect him?'

He watched me carefully, eyes devouring mine. 'He fled immediately, before anyone could help.' I realised what question he was about to ask just before he asked it. 'Where is Galileo?'

I felt my cheeks burn and I avoided his gaze. 'Withypoll killed him,' I replied. 'On the road out of Colchester. Dragged him behind a horse.'

The man stared like he would punish me for it. 'You left with Josselin?'

'We left by ourselves, after Josselin,' I replied. 'He said he would come here first.'

He cracked his knuckles. 'What else did he tell you?'

'He said we should ask ourselves why the Dutch must fall.'

'They must fall because we are at war,' the tall man answered. 'Peace or war. Now it seems the war will continue.'

'Why so?' I demanded.

He pursed his lips. 'It is no secret, after all,' he considered. 'I am surprised Arlington has not told you himself.'

'He said only that Josselin had sabotaged peace. That he betrayed his country, killed Berkshire and fled.'

Small lines of disdain appeared about the edges of his mouth. 'You have heard of De Buat?'

'No,' I replied, feeling foolish.

'Of course not.' The man smiled without sincerity and glanced at the gate that led back into the house. 'De Buat is a French nobleman who grew up in Holland. He held a post in the Orange court. The Princess Dowager appointed him to represent the House of Orange as envoy to De Witt.'

I was lost and the tall man saw it.

'De Witt is the leader of the Dutch,' he said, as if talking to a small child.

'I know that,' I growled, ears burning. 'I am not a fool.'

'De Witt is determined the provinces shall never again be subject to sovereign rule,' which I also knew. 'The House of Orange is determined that the Prince of Orange shall assume his rightful position. There has always been the possibility of civil war between De Witt and the House of Orange, a possibility that has obsessed Arlington these last few years.'

'And so this Frenchman De Buat runs between Holland and the House of Orange, like you and Josselin ran between England and Holland.'

The tall man bowed as if in deference to my great wit. 'Quite so. We came across De Buat often, for he is the Orangists' ambassador to Holland.'

My head started to spin again.

'Clarendon sought peace with the Dutch; Arlington sought civil war. Arlington sought to provoke the House of Orange into declaring war upon the Dutch so that England might make a treaty with the new government, on terms most favourable.' The tall man spoke seriously now. 'De Buat was in Arlington's confidence. His spy within.'

'What happened?'

He spoke in a low whisper. 'Arlington sent Josselin to Holland with two letters. The first was the official letter De Witt was supposed to receive, intended to placate his suspicions, proclaiming England's commitment to peace with Holland. The second letter was a personal letter for De Buat only, encouraging him to rouse the House of Orange to action, for Arlington became increasingly frustrated with the Princess Dowager, and her indecision.'

'And De Witt read both letters?'

'De Buat *gave* him both letters,' the tall man barked. 'The question is why.'

I let his words settle in my mind. 'Josselin tricked De Buat into giving De Witt both letters?'

The tall man nodded sagely. 'That's what Arlington believes.'

'Why would Josselin do such a thing?'

'I don't know why,' the tall man replied. 'No one does.' He lofted his sword so it pointed at my chest, his stale odour sticking to my face. 'I was hoping you could tell me. You or Galileo.'

I raised my hand to my forehead. 'The Earl of Clarendon and Lord Arlington are both confidants to the King, are they not?'

He shook his head and snorted. 'You don't understand politics, Harry Lytle, nor the relationship between Clarendon and Arlington. It was Arlington who first persuaded the King to go to war with the Dutch, greedy for the rich trade the Dutch enjoy in West India. The King yearns to be independent of Parliament, which he can only achieve with new sources of revenue. Otherwise he is obliged to call Parliament for no other reason than he needs their money. Had England defeated the Dutch early then the King would have been rich.'

'Clarendon would rather see the King beholden?' I frowned, worried I would soon lose the thread.

'Of course not,' he sighed, impatient. 'But Clarendon knew it was folly. Arlington is a risk taker. He has no care for this country, nor for its citizens, people like you.' Which was true enough. 'So he is happy to gamble what is not his, in return for great riches. The Earl knows how flawed is that logic. The cost of war will break this country. We have little chance of beating the Dutch, for our leaders are divided and headstrong. Arlington's policy throughout has been to declare in favour of the House of Orange, so emboldening the Orangists to declare civil war. He will not recognise that the Orangists are more circumspect, that they have seen the consequences of our own infightings. It is a foolhardy policy, but Arlington will not be deterred. Indeed he went so far as to betroth himself to an Orangist.'

'Elisabeth van Nassau-Beverweert,' I struggled to remember.

He nodded. 'Berkshire, Josselin and myself, we are the King's ambassadors to Holland. We have worked for peace since the war started, and in October last year we almost succeeded, until Arlington persuaded the King to make demands so outrageous, the Dutch had no option but to seek an alternative policy.'

'The alliance with Denmark.'

'Signed four months later,' he said. 'Now we hear the Dutch may be talking to the French, but the King will not hear of it. He will not hear of it because Arlington persuades him it is not true. Arlington has given up on the whole idea of making peace with the Dutch. He wants full-scale war, nothing else. Now he has nailed his flag to the mast, any suggestion that his policy is flawed would be a humiliation.'

'You knew all this?'

'No,' said the tall man, lips tight. 'Not until all this happened. I don't know what Josselin and Berkshire knew. They were the ones working for Arlington.'

How curious he must be, I thought. How angry must have been the Earl of Clarendon. No wonder they sent their own man into Shyam to find out what transpired.

'May I go?' I asked.

'To do what?' he asked.

'To find James Josselin, and make him tell me what happened.'

The dark man rubbed his middle finger across his brow, stroking it while he watched me. 'Josselin will tell you nothing and Arlington will kill you.'

I stared back at him and said nothing.

'I shall tell you something, Harry Lytle,' he decided. 'James Josselin *has* returned to London, for our spies have seen him in the City. He won't come here, for he will not be allowed.'

'What do you mean?'

'Withypoll returned from Colchester last night and Arlington posted sentries on every gate. If Josselin attempts to leave the City he will be arrested. Soldiers are scouring the streets now. They will seize him soon, and there is nothing to be done.' His green eyes narrowed. 'You didn't know?'

273

'No.' I replied. What were we doing here if Arlington already knew where Josselin was? 'It was a test, then,' I realised, stomach sinking to my feet. 'Arlington told us to wait outside to see if we would obey. He suspects we are in league with Clarendon. He wanted to know if we would do as he ordered.'

The dark man gazed upon me sorrowfully. If he wouldn't help Josselin, he certainly wouldn't help us. Now I understood why he was so puzzled at our arrival.

'Smuggle us into the City,' I demanded. 'That is all I ask.'

'Why?' he asked.

Because I had to get to Jane before Arlington. Because the City was my home, the place I felt safest, and because Arlington's men would be waiting for us outside. I prayed they did not already have Dowling. 'I will find Josselin and I will find out who killed Berkshire,' I replied. 'Just get us into the City.'

He shrugged. 'Very well. Little good it will do you. Once you are in, you will never get out.'

Chapter Twenty-Seuen

Yet we fear some further continuance of the impending Calamities.

We clung to the tarpaulin to stop it from blowing away; the wind gusted so strong. I lay still, afraid Clarendon might betray us and send us straight to Arlington.

'What did you discover?' Dowling breathed into my ear.

'It was complicated,' I replied. 'The essence of it being that Josselin deliberately handed a letter to the Dutch government intended for the House of Orange. By handing over the letter he betrayed Arlington's treachery and revealed the identity of Arlington's spy to the Dutch.'

'Did you find out why?' Dowling asked.

'Clarendon doesn't know why,' I replied. 'I think that's why he won't help. They're afraid Josselin may have betrayed England of his own accord.'

'They think he killed Berkshire?'

'They're certain he didn't,' I said. 'Though they have no intention of pursuing the issue. Josselin is on his own.'

The canvas stank of potatoes and rotten vegetables. Something cold and sticky attached itself to my cheek. I gritted my teeth and tensed my face.

We dawdled at Ludgate for what seemed an age, the noise of chattering so loud it felt like we were stuck in the middle of a great sprawling crowd. I held my breath, waiting for the cover to be torn asunder, leaving us naked and exposed.

'Clear the way!' the driver demanded, three or four times, voice gruff and impatient. He was a big man without much hair, surly and strong. I couldn't hear any reply; there was too much noise to distinguish voice from voice. Someone tugged at the tarpaulin, but then a loud crack made me jump, as of a whip, and then a scream, and the tugging ceased.

'Touch my load again and I'll slice open your belly,' the driver shouted, his voice closer. 'I'm carrying goods to the Exchange on behalf of the Earl of Clarendon. Woe to any man that gets in my way.'

The din subsided a moment, and the cart jerked forwards. Another man shouted, angry, though I couldn't make out the words. A fight broke out close to my ear. Someone screeched and something heavy landed against the side of the cart, but we kept moving, trundling forwards, leaving the worst of the bedlam behind.

'Out now,' the driver demanded, yanking the tarpaulin away.

I sat up and looked around, wary he delivered us into a trap. But no. He pulled up outside the main gate to St Paul's churchyard, the wind howling about our ears, no one paying us any attention.

The driver showed us a mouth full of yellow stumps. 'Jump out before I break your legs.'

We did as we were told and then looked back to Ludgate. Soldiers stood against apprentices, squaring their shoulders and trying to look calm, poking at the apprentices with swords, or waving muskets, unconvincing. The apprentices danced upon their toes, taunting the older men, daring them to attack, some swinging their blue aprons about their heads, trying to flick the soldiers upon the nose or ear.

'What's new?' I asked the driver, jumping to the ground.

'Apprentices don't like being told what to do,' he replied. 'Soldiers won't let them through.'

'Why not?'

'Because if James Josselin escapes the City, the man who lets him pass will be strung from a gibbet by the balls,' the driver replied. 'They're not letting anyone out.' He clambered back onto the cart, jerked the reins and headed north up Ave Maria Lane.

'Where did this wind come from?' I complained, clutching my jacket about my chest. It wasn't supposed to blow a gale when the sky was blue.

'The wind hath bound him up in her wings,' Dowling replied, thoughtful, still staring at the growing crowd. 'If Josselin wanted to get to Whitehall, this is the way he would come.'

'Or else he would take a boat,' I said. Did soldiers guard the docks too?

The square broken tower of St Paul's soared high above us, the west-side portico just to our right, tall columns standing like prison bars. A steady stream of folk flowed in and out its mouth, oblivious. Two men leant against the Bishop's Palace, watching us intent, long brown coats hiding what they wore beneath. Lazy men with nothing better to do? If Arlington was after Josselin, there would be more than soldiers at the gates; the City would be swarming with spies.

I slapped Dowling on the back. 'I will see you at my house.'

'With horse and wagon,' Dowling nodded, heading north.

I headed east, girding my loins for a mighty battle.

I stood in the middle of the road again.

'Cocksmouth!' Jane exclaimed, arms across her belly, face reddening. 'We have only just come *back* from Cocksmouth. What makes you think I would consider returning to that stinking sty?'

'It's safe,' I whispered. 'No one knows I have relatives at Cocksmouth.' Save those neighbours now listening at their windows.

'Safe from what?' Jane clenched her fists in front of her cheeks like she planned to punch me. 'Safe from you, that's true, and you from me.' The yellow flecks in her eyes sparked like gold.

'Lord Arlington has set his men upon us,' I replied, glum. 'I'm not sure what we're going to do about it, but we must make sure you and the baby are safe, else Arlington will come after you as well as I.'

'Why should Lord Arlington come after me?' Jane blinked. 'I'm a servant. What have you told him?'

'Nothing,' I protested. 'He doesn't need me to tell him anything. He has an army of spies that do that for him. Believe me, he . . .' I found myself frozen, mouth half open, leaning forwards, arms extended. How could I help her understand the enormity of the threat without frightening her out of her wits?

Jane narrowed her eyes and breathed deeply. 'What have you done?' she asked, suddenly quiet.

'I told you he sent us to Shyam to find James Josselin,' I reminded her, bracing myself. 'Well, we found him, but didn't capture him, for there is a good chance he is innocent. Arlington told us to watch for

Josselin outside Holland House but I went inside to see if the Earl of Clarendon might help.'

Jane folded her arms.

'It was a trap. Arlington's men were watching us all the time.'

'Then he will dismiss you,' Jane nodded calmly, 'and not pay you the money he has never paid you anyway.'

I shook my head. 'No. He will cut us in half upon an instrument of torture he calls a Spanish donkey.'

Jane's pale face turned whiter.

I held up my hands. 'Before you ask, I don't know how I got myself involved, but now I am and so are you.'

'What will you do?' she asked, eyes brimming.

'Find James Josselin,' I replied, meeting her gaze. 'We know where he is. We'll talk to him and all will become clear.'

My assurances provoked more tears, but the pool soon emptied and she wiped her nose upon her sleeve.

'Cocksmouth,' she said again, glowering. 'You have no relatives other than your mother?'

'Thank the Lord my mother doesn't live in Shyam,' I replied, sensing her rage simmering once more.

She shook her head. 'You expect me to go to Cocksmouth, by myself, with child.'

'If I come with you it will solve nothing,' I protested. 'We have to find a way of placating Arlington.' Or killing him, I thought, surprising myself. 'Besides, you will not be going by yourself.'

Her fingers tightened about her dress. 'Who?'

'Lucy Dowling,' I tried to smile. 'She is a nice woman.' Attractive too, for her age. Much more attractive than her husband. 'They will be here soon to pick you up. You are leaving in an hour.'

'An hour!' she snorted. 'I cannot leave without saying goodbye to my family.'

'You can,' I said, firmly. 'Your family mustn't know. If they know then they will talk.' For all her family chatted like sparrows. 'I will tell them you will be back soon.'

She shook her head again, angry. 'You are such a liar.'

'Aye.' I wrinkled my nose. 'You are right. But we will be back afore ye know it. Perchance you won't even reach Cocksmouth before we catch you up and bring you back home.'

Her eyes brimmed again. 'I don't want to have my baby in Cocksmouth.'

'Nor do I,' I agreed, heartily. 'We'll be back in London long before that.'

She clenched her fist and pointed it at me. 'You promise me, Harry Lytle.'

'I promise,' I said. 'Now I must go. Next time I see you I will have sorted everything out.' I waved a hand with more confidence than I felt and strode purposefully back towards Newgate.

That went well, I congratulated myself, though my soul felt wooden.

Now all we had to do was find James Josselin.

Chapter Twenty-Eight

Its common unto Comets to bring dryness, and such consequences as proceed from thence, viz. droughts, little rain, the death of fishes, barrenness, Winds, Wars, or Fights.

I had experienced many types of different wind, from the light and fluffy, to the heavy and strong, but never such a wind as this. It blew the heat of the day into men's faces, drying the eyes and throat, carrying a fine mist of dust through the air.

Dowling walked sullen. He hadn't mentioned God for almost an hour, which was some relief, but I worried he saw nothing beyond the end of his nose, so sunk in misery he seemed. We headed west, away from Red Rose Lane. We spent the best part of two hours searching for Josselin, without success.

I attempted to rouse the shaggy beast. 'He'll show up later,' I said. 'No doubt he has errands to run.'

'Who knows what he is plotting?' Dowling replied. 'We both know Josselin is a little mad.'

A small procession turned out of Swithin Lane ahead of us, four soldiers struggling to keep up with a tall, blond man wearing a silly hat.

'Withypoll,' I gasped, flinging myself backwards against the wall of the nearest house, my feet sinking into the teeming gutter. They didn't even glance in our direction, marching with such purpose I wondered if they had trapped Josselin.

'We ought to follow,' I said, though the prospect chilled me.

More lines appeared on Dowling's forehead.

I shook his arm, and extracted a foot from the stinking mess seeping into my shoes. 'Come on.'

They proceeded back down the same streets we had walked earlier this morning. When Withypoll turned onto Friday Street, I hurried my pace, alarmed they ventured so close to my neighbourhood.

Two men loitered upon the corner, neither gentlemen nor vagabonds, just standing there with no obvious intent. The soldiers drew their swords as they turned the corner, chasing behind him. One ran awkwardly, boots too large for his feet. They jogged down the middle of Friday Street, turned left on Watling Street, and into Bread Street, my street.

When a neighbour called my name, I held a finger to my lips, afore I stopped still, not twenty paces from my own house. Withypoll pounded my front door with gloved fist. Jane would be gone already, surely?

'What have you done, Harry?' asked a stout fellow with black bristle covering his face and ears, brow lowered in expression of intense curiosity. 'What *have* you done?' He glanced up at me, half afraid, half amused. 'You robbed the crown jewels?'

'Did you see Jane leave?' I whispered, hoarse.

He stared down at the cobbles and scratched his head.

Withypoll kicked the door, without success. Then he gestured to one of the soldiers and they kicked together, cracking my door down the middle at third attempt. All five of them stormed into my house. I heard crashing, loud noises, the sound of breaking furniture.

Dowling laid a hand upon my shoulder. 'We must go.'

I punched his arm. 'What if Jane is in there?'

'Lucy came hours ago,' Dowling replied, staring ahead.

Withypoll emerged, eyes blazing, cursing loud enough for all of London to hear. He stamped his foot on the ground and kicked the wall of my house. The soldiers appeared behind him, like frightened sheep, heads bowed.

I turned to Clinton, my neighbour. 'William, ask them why they've come,' I whispered. 'Seem willing. If they ask you where I am, tell them you heard I was gone to Colchester. Look simple and they'll believe you.'

'Right enough,' he nodded seriously and set off. I prayed he wouldn't look back for encouragement.

He approached the smallest of the soldiers, and tapped him on the shoulder. He exchanged a few words, then returned towards us, Withypoll's eyes fixed upon his back. I sunk into the doorway, Dowling following my lead.

Clinton winked as he passed, shuffling at his normal pace. Withypoll watched him disappear over the hill before sighing, hands on hips. He spoke sharply to the soldier closest to him and followed after Clinton, towards us. I slipped my hand behind my back and turned the handle of the door behind. Mercifully it opened, and we slipped quickly into the house, closing the door behind us.

'Hello, Harry,' a familiar voice sang out. Clinton's wife, same shape and size as he, but with more hair upon her rounded head. 'You look a mess.'

I surveyed my clothes, stained, torn and misshapen. 'I haven't been home for a while.'

'Why not?' she exclaimed, too loud for my liking. 'Jane will mend those breeches and wash those clothes.' She squinted. 'I don't think she'd be pleased to see you out in such a state.'

I edged to the window and peered onto the street. Withypoll and the soldiers marched by, the soldiers with shoulders slumped, Withypoll strident and furious.

'You're right,' I replied. 'I'll go home now.' I watched Withypoll's party reach Watling Street where they turned right. We would have to follow. 'Thank you, Mrs Clinton,' I said, opening the door to the street.

Half the neighbourhood was out, watching the soldiers, exchanging glorious suppositions. No sooner did my feet touch the cobbles than I was surrounded by inquisitive do-gooders, offering kind words with macabre expression, all wanting to know why King's soldiers broke down my door. I behaved as if innocent, moving slow, holding my face in my hands, watching for Clinton. He returned fast, trotting down the road, eager. I grabbed his collar and pulled him close.

'What did they say?' I whispered.

'They said they were looking for you,' he replied, excited. 'Why would they be looking for you?'

I gripped his jacket harder. 'What did you tell them?'

He opened his mouth wide, revealing blackened gums and green-furred tongue. 'I told them you eloped with Jane!' He laughed loud until he'd had enough, then tried to catch his breath, choking.

I watched, stony-faced.

'I told them you were gone to Colchester,' he gasped, catching my eye. 'Like you said.'

I attempted a smile. 'Thanks, Bill.'

Dowling elbowed me in the chest. 'We must go.' The two men that watched us on Cheapside watched us again, standing beneath the shadow of St Mildred's. They caught our eye and slipped away, in the same direction as Withypoll.

'God's hooks!' I exclaimed. 'What do we do now?'

'Not much point in following,' Dowling replied, 'since he will soon be following us. We would go round in circles. We must make haste. He doesn't know where Josselin is, else he would not be looking for us, and we must be careful not to lead him in that direction.'

So we headed south, down to Thames Street, where the candlemakers clustered together in their cramped yards melting tallow, the great stink carried high into the sky and towards the Fleet by the wind blowing off the river.

'We should hide a while,' said Dowling, looking this way and that, as if conscious of his bulk. 'Until Withypoll gives up on us.'

'Not by the water,' I replied. 'If they have soldiers at the gate they must have soldiers at the docks. In a tavern, perhaps.'

Dowling cast me a sideways glance. 'Or a church.'

'What if Josselin goes to meet us,' I exclaimed. 'I say we go to Red Rose Lane while Withypoll sniffs round here.'

Dowling grimaced.

'We have been unlucky,' I insisted. 'Most spies will be searching for Josselin, not us.' I considered my clothes again. 'I am barely recognisable. Withypoll must have posted just a few spies around our houses to look out for us. Elsewhere we will be safer.'

Dowling stopped and stared, like he saw me for the first time. 'The spies are not looking out for me or you, but both of us together. A big, tall man with white hair, next to a short fellow with dark hair and stubble on his face.'

'Should we split up?' I said, feeling lonely already.

'We must,' said Dowling. 'You, as you say, are already dishevelled. No longer a strange fop, but more discreet. No man could pick you out less he knew you intimately.'

'A fop?' I exclaimed. To a bloodied ogre like Dowling, any man who washed might be called a fop. I decided to consider it a compliment. 'I will go find Josselin,' I said, reluctantly. 'Where will you go?'

'Same,' Dowling replied, 'but not with you. I will follow and try to keep you in sight. If we lose each other I'll meet you again at St Katharine Cree, at three.'

'Very well.' I felt better.

I set off, wondering how it was I led. Though I avoided the main thoroughfares, we kept coming across pockets of soldiers, especially close to the bridge. The crowd spilt back from the mouth of the bridge west and east, along Thames Street and up Fish Street Hill.

'What's news?' I asked a ruddy-faced man standing on tiptoe.

'They've closed the bridge,' he snapped, hopping up and down, neck craned. 'I have to get back to Bankside, my wife is ill.' He clasped his hand upon his forehead in dismay. 'They say there are three Dutch spies in the City.' He breathed deep. 'I pray they find them soon and string them up by the neck. I have to get home.'

His words knifed me in the belly, though they came as no surprise. So now I was a Dutch spy. How quickly that happened, I reflected, bile rising in my throat, feeling the same anger and indignation I imagined Josselin experienced. I rubbed my sweaty palms upon the seat of my trousers as we passed Fish Street Hill and came to the mouth of Red Rose Lane.

This was a narrow thoroughfare where the butchers scalded hogs and made their puddings, throwing their waste out into the street to be taken down to the dung boats. This was the last place to come in the middle of summer, for the blood and offal sat on the street all day afore it was collected, attracting all manner of vermin, cats, dogs and flies. I choked on the stink of rotting blood and trod cautiously. Josselin chose well, for spies and soldiers would avoid this street like the plague.

Despite our agreement I waited for Dowling.

'We cannot hang around,' I said. 'We attracted too much attention last time.'

Dowling stopped halfway up the hill, hands on his hips. 'If Josselin is there, he'll be watching for us, surveying every movement with gimlet eye.'

I scanned the surrounding windows. The light was so poor and the windows so dirty, all I saw were a couple of fleeting shadows, impossible to tell if it was Josselin or not. The rats re-emerged from the shadows to renew their scavenging; fat beasts waddling through the slime like they owned the place.

'I still don't think he's here,' I said at last.

'We have to find him,' Dowling growled.

'Aldgate,' I suggested. 'His mother's house at Duke's Place.'

Dowling scratched his ear. 'You think Arlington will not have had the same idea?'

'We'll make our own ways there,' I said. 'As you suggested before.'

It wasn't often Dowling needed my encouragement. I strode up the hill towards Eastcheap with more determination than I felt. A dozen soldiers lingered about the Boar's Head, tousled and round-shouldered, drunk already, laughing uproariously at poor jokes like they felt the eyes of strangers upon them. I hurried east across Gracechurch Street, a busy thoroughfare, then north up Rood Lane past the churchyard of St Margaret Pattens. I turned every few steps to see who followed, looking not only for spies, but also for Dowling's big, white head bobbing up and down above the crowd like a beacon. If spies followed us, they would follow him, not me.

Turning onto Fenchurch Street I walked headlong into a row of soldiers barring the road on either side of St Gabriel, a small church built in the middle of the road. Too late to turn away, for I had already attracted the attention of one older man, tight-lipped and sullen. Over his shoulder I saw a long line of soldiers, leading all the way up the street to Aldgate. Dowling had been right. This was not the place to come. It swarmed with military.

'Come here,' the old soldier growled.

I stood my ground and prayed Dowling was not close behind.

'What's your name?' he demanded.

'John Fisher,' I replied, thinking of the nearby market. 'I live at Sugar Loaf Alley. Why do you stop me passing?'

'I haven't stopped you passing,' he replied, reaching out to touch my coat, rubbing the stained silk thoughtfully between his fingers. 'You on your own?'

I frowned like I didn't understand the significance of the question. 'Let me pass.'

'Fisher,' he repeated, and eyed me up and down. 'Proceed, John Fisher.'

I snatched my coat from his grubby hands and stalked off like I was offended. By now there were so many soldiers, and so few citizens,

I felt like a soldier myself, else a ghost drifting unseen amongst the living.

The entrance to Duke's Place teemed with excitement, a stinking cloud hovering above the throng below, the smell of too many unwashed men gathered close together. I held my breath and slipped silently between the bodies, reminding myself that Withypoll was far away, scouring the streets west. Arlington would remain above it all, back at Whitehall. None here would recognise me I told myself, again and again.

Every orifice of Josselin's house gaped open, the leaning windows like yawning mouths, belching foulness upon the street below. Soldiers sat upon its doorstep, others passing in and out like it was a barrack. Gone was the quiet grace and dignity of the week before, now besmeared with the loud exuberance of raucous bantering.

I wondered what mess the soldiers made of the delicate interior and where were Mrs Josselin, Eliza and the silent servants. I narrowed my eyes and scoured the house front, searching, until I spied two pale faces, staring out a turret window at the top of the mansion. Too far away to be sure, but they looked like Josselin's mother and betrothed, peering out, frightened and bewildered.

Anger welled up deep inside my belly at the ignorant dolts who sat with their backs to the wall, playing cards, those who stomped across the floor of a house that wasn't theirs. Something of the scene reminded me of Colchester, how it must have been when Fairfax's soldiers surrounded the City, depriving the innocent of food and provisions. I looked for Josselin. If I could find a way, then so could he. If I felt anger, what would he feel? Where was he?

I wandered discreetly about the yard, seeing if he stood as witness in some nook or cranny. I looked to the sky, to surrounding houses, to see if he hid, but nothing. I looked up again at the two women and tried to work out in which direction they stared. What would he do, I wondered? He wouldn't sit idly by, that was certain, yet neither would he charge out into the open with his sword, to be cut down by the small army about him. I tried to think like Josselin, but found it hard.

The sun passed the height of its day's journey. Nearly three o'clock. I wondered what became of Dowling. I imagined he saw me waylaid on Fenchurch Street. He probably proceeded north, to approach by way of Leadenhall. St Katharine Cree was just around the corner.

With one last look at the window high above, I made my way through the crowd back onto the main street, and walked the short distance to the church. The churchyard was tucked down an alley, behind the church itself. Dowling sat upon a bench, hands on knees, white head standing out against the blue sky. He leapt to his feet as soon as I opened the gate and enveloped me in a crushing embrace.

I pushed myself away as soon as his grip slackened, wiping his perspiration from my face.

'You were more circumspect than I, then,' I said. 'No one followed you?'

He shook his head. 'I don't think they'll expect us here, not with so many soldiers. What did that fellow say to you?'

'Asked me my name,' I replied. 'I told him John Fisher.' I thought again of the scene at Duke's Place. 'Soldiers have taken over Josselin's house. Mrs Josselin and Josselin's betrothed stand staring from a top-floor window.'

Dowling grunted.

'Josselin will not stand idly back,' I exclaimed, agitated. 'I cannot think what he'll do, but he will do something. Arlington hasn't read him well. He shouldn't have called him traitor, nor ransacked his house.' I closed my eyes against the wind. 'Josselin is close by,' I said. 'I sense it.'

'Very well, Harry,' sighed Dowling. 'You propose we walk the streets?'

'I am going back to Duke's Place for a while,' I decided. 'We will meet back here at dusk.'

Dowling slouched, brow furrowed, mouth downturned.

'Ask God, Davy.' I patted him on the shoulder. 'He shall guide thee continually and make fat thy bones. Thou shalt be like a watered garden.' Something like that.

I patted him again and headed back to the Josselin house. Something was afoot.

Chapter Twenty-Nine

For in those places shall be Wars, Seditions, and Uproars, strange Winds, Barrenness, and acute diseases, viz. either very strange Feavers, or the Sickness.

I heard the shouting before I reached the court, the singing too, loud and tuneless. Soldiers crowded into the middle of the square, heads thrown back, swilling beer from glass bottles.

All fell silent, then a loud roar, 'Arlington!' Every man lifted a bottle to the blue sky. The first time in Arlington's life he had been toasted so readily.

I thought to inspect one of the bottles, but the soldiers stood in a circle, like a pack of dogs guarding a pile of bones. Unlike Arlington to be so generous.

Josselin's house stood empty; all the soldiers stood outside supping happily. There was enough beer for every man to drink at least two bottles. No sign of Mrs Josselin or Eliza at the window. Their opportunity to feed themselves while the soldiers were distracted.

I walked the perimeter, across the shadow of a great oak growing in one corner, across the front of the other two large houses that bounded the small square. The side of Josselin's house stood in shadow, but something moved, a flash of light catching the sun. I approached closer, wary of a drunken soldier. Before I could explore further, a bottle smashed. I turned towards the revelry to see two men fall to their knees, clutching at their throats. The rest watched, anxious, so quiet I could hear the sound of both men breathing, wracking gasps, like their lungs burnt. A third man held his hands in front of his eyes like claws. Six more pawed at their necks, wide-eyed and terrified. I stepped back into the shadow, pressed against the wall.

Those who didn't succumb stepped nervously through the fallen, inspecting the bottles from which they drank, else throwing them as far away as they could muster. One man thrust his fingers down his throat and forced himself to gag. Others followed his lead, but too late. They too struggled to breathe, collapsing upon the dust, gasping for air. I placed my hands at my own throat, momentarily afraid the plague unveiled itself again.

A hand landed on my shoulder. I startled, and looked round into Josselin's battered face, his naked, shaven head. He wore rough, plain clothes, wide, linen trousers, and flapping, cloth shirt, in the style of a butcher. A good disguise. With bruised face devoid of hair, he looked like any other common fellow. He smiled, calmly.

'You are the apothecary,' he whispered. 'A fiftieth of a grain is deadly. I put half a grain in every bottle.'

I stared, disbelieving.

He gripped harder. 'I wouldn't see them suffer. They will die quick.' He cast me an inquisitive gaze then nodded at a man close to us whose face contorted in agonized grimace. 'First they burn from throat to belly. Then hands and feet, and all their skin. They feel like they are being flayed.' The groans and screams confirmed it, as thirty men lay dying.

Three soldiers stood watching, aghast, and unaffected. The few who chose not to drink. They gathered in a huddle, seeking solace in each other, unable to tear their eyes from the dreadful scene.

'Soon they will lose the power of sight, and will lie there deaf, 'til death comes,' Josselin breathed. 'With a fiftieth of a grain it would take half the day. With half a grain most will be dead before they realise what has happened.'

'Wolfsbane,' I guessed. 'Monkshood.' A plant with medicinal properties, rarely used because it was so poisonous. A white powder that dissolved only in strong drink.

Josselin patted my shoulder. 'Well done, apothecary.'

'Why?' I asked, watching as one man clutched his belly, bending his neck back with eyes closed, a shallow, whining noise escaping his blue lips. An innocent man.

'This is my house,' Josselin said, grimly. 'I didn't invite them, nor did my mother. They invited themselves.'

'Arlington ordered them.' I seized his collar. 'Some of these men had wives and children,' I said. 'Do you not care?'

He placed a hand on my arm and gazed at me, brow furrowed and eyes moist. 'More soldiers will arrive soon.'

I pushed him away. 'Do you not understand what Arlington will do to your mother and betrothed? Have you no idea?'

'He'll do nothing to them,' Josselin answered. He slipped back into the shadows and headed in the direction of Leadenhall. 'I will find him tonight and smite him down.'

'Wait!' I called after him.

'Talk as we walk,' Josselin replied, tossing me the bottle he held in his hand. 'That is the only bottle I did not poison. Drink.'

He laughed loud as I held it at arm's length between two fingers. 'Tell me who killed Berkshire, and tell me about this letter. Give me something I can use.'

'Tut-tut!' he exclaimed.

I tugged at his coat, trying to slow him down as he hurried south, down Lime Street. 'We went to Clarendon on your behalf. We rescued you from Thomas Elks.'

I heard footsteps and turned to see Dowling running behind, stumbling from foot to foot in strange gait, blowing hard.

'You did that for yourselves,' Josselin replied, following my gaze. 'I am not responsible for your poor souls.'

Dowling caught up with us, red-faced, sweat soaking his chest. As we crossed Fenchurch Street, the wind caught me in a sudden gust, nearly knocking me off my feet.

'What news?' he panted, watching Josselin.

'He just poisoned half a garrison.'

Dowling stared at Josselin's back, like he would tear him apart. 'Then we should seize him now. Hand him over to Arlington.'

It would be easy enough to attract the attention of spies and soldiers, I reflected.

Josselin laughed. 'Arlington will thank you with the promise of an earldom then kill you for what you know.' He stopped at the top of Red Rose Lane. 'You are welcome to join me, gentlemen, for I think we are in the same predicament.'

Dowling hesitated.

'There are no spies here,' said Josselin. 'They walk along Eastcheap or Thames Street, peer in, then keep walking. I have my own little place to stay.'

'They will come after you,' I said.

'They will search, but not down here.' He looked about quickly then slipped into the gloom. He led us halfway down the dark narrow street and stopped outside a crooked door. 'Welcome to the house of Farynor.'

He pushed open the door and hurried us over the threshold. A low, squat oven sat to the left of the main fireplace. A bigger oven with smaller mouth sat to the right of it, burning low.

'Where is Farynor?' growled Dowling.

'Upstairs.' Josselin jerked his thumb towards the ceiling. 'Farynor, his son and daughter. I will release them when I leave.' He sat down, threw his legs forward and stretched out his arms. 'Go see them if you wish.'

I stepped cautiously towards the narrow, winding staircase, wary in case he changed his mind, but he just watched, hands rested upon his belly, eyes half lidded. Dowling shuffled forwards, positioning his great bulk between Josselin and the stairs.

The staircase was narrow, wood-warped and twisted. Every board squeaked as I climbed, but upstairs was silent. An open door led to a square room overlooking the alley below. Three sets of eyes watched. A boy and girl huddled either side of a lean fellow with sculpted arms. All three chewed on gags. Their arms were tied behind their back, legs bound with rope, the skin about their ankles red and raw. I thought to pull the gags from their mouths, but to what end? Our need for refuge was equal to Josselin's. I waved a hand and nodded my head in an assuring manner before returning downstairs.

Josselin still slumped in his chair. I stared at his long face, angular and chiselled. His lips were red and seemed to smile. Black hair fell across his forehead and cheeks.

'What's up there?' Dowling demanded.

'The Farynors,' I replied. 'Bound with rope.'

Dowling glowered at Josselin.

'I haven't hurt them,' Josselin protested, pulling himself up straight. 'I don't hurt people.' Which was a great lie. 'But I need somewhere to hide from Arlington. I cannot hide with friends, nor seek lodgings with strangers. Is that not apparent?'

'When were they last fed?' Dowling demanded.

'Fed and watered this morning,' Josselin replied. 'There is dried beef and ale in the kitchen. Feel free to tend to them if you're worried. By all means remove their gags and attempt to have a conversation.'

Dowling strode to the kitchen to fetch provisions, then stomped loudly up the stairs.

'They are not very *interesting* people,' Josselin whispered. 'But then neither is your friend. He is so terribly serious.'

'What now, Josselin?'

'We wait a few hours,' he said. 'The soldiers will swarm to Aldgate and I'll catch a boat from the bridge to Whitehall.'

A precarious plan at best.

'Arlington said he doesn't want to meet you,' I told him.

Josselin closed his eyes. 'He will change his mind.'

'Why did you pass Arlington's second letter to De Buat?' I asked.

He looked up, surprised. 'Clarendon told you that?'

'One of his men. A strange man who insisted on touching me. He said he was a colleague of yours.'

'Thomas Villiers,' Josselin smiled. 'You met Villiers.'

'Why did you pass Arlington's second letter to De Buat?' I asked again.

He stared at the wall. 'And while they abode in Galilee, Jesus said unto them, The Son of man shall be betrayed into the hands of men.'

Did he compare himself to Jesus Christ?

'Arlington destroyed any chance of peace,' said Josselin. 'The man is a beast and he knows I know it. Now I see he cannot harm me, even if he doesn't recognise it yet.'

'If he doesn't recognise it, he will kill you.'

Cold vengeance clouded his eyes. 'He will not get the chance.'

'Nor will you,' Dowling called, clumping down the stairs. 'I think someone else betrayed you today. Two men just walked past in a hurry, peering through the window.'

Josselin jumped to his feet and hurried to the door. 'God's teeth,' he muttered. 'How did they find me?'

I shuffled uncomfortably. Our skills were less well developed than his. It was most likely *we* were followed, not he. The same thought must have occurred to him, for he turned to me with burning cheeks and jabbed a finger in the direction of the street. 'Go and see what is happening.'

I opened my mouth then closed it again, for his eyes burnt too bright. I stepped to the door and opened it a crack. The street was empty. I opened it a little wider and stepped outside. The wind blew a gale down the narrow passage, pushing my breeches tight against my thighs. A small child stood to my left, face covered in dirt and mucus. His mother dashed out, grabbed him by the neck and was gone.

I held up a hand to protect my eyes from the savage dust, peering towards Thames Street. Four soldiers blocked the passage out. I stepped back quickly before they saw me and hurried up the hill until

I reached the turn into Eastcheap. More soldiers. I returned to the house, relieved to be out of the gale.

'Why are there soldiers waiting at each end of the lane?' I slammed the door closed. 'Why do they not simply come down and fetch you?'

Josselin kicked the chair on which he had lounged so casually. 'They will,' he said, 'after nightfall. If they come during the day they run the risk of inciting a riot.'

He paced the small room, as if scouring the emptiness for some magical instrument. With one eye he watched the sliver of sky visible betwixt the house tops. With the other he kept an eye on the baker's oven, occasionally stirring from his stair to throw another log upon the fire. For what reason I couldn't fathom, but by the time two hours passed, he stoked a blazing fire, into which he stared with gleaming dark eyes.

As the sun fell, he blinked and turned to Dowling. 'Time to release the Farynors, butcher.'

Dowling hurried up the stairs. A few moments later the children appeared, cautious and smelling of urine. The father followed close behind, avoiding my eye.

Josselin opened the front door. 'Tell them you left the ovens cold,' he said to Farynor. The baker cast him a glance of disgust afore hurrying the children out into the wind.

Josselin stretched himself to his full height and breathed out deeply. 'I have a plan,' he said to me.

'What plan?'

'You will see.'

Chapter Thirty

When Saturn leaveth one sign, and enters another, there are strange sights or apparitions, or other prodigies of the nature of fire.

Darkness crept down the stairs and enveloped us in dusky embrace. The embers in the oven burnt ever brighter.

'Time to go to work,' Josselin announced after sitting silent for hours.

He stepped to the main oven and extracted several burning logs with tongs, placing them into the smaller oven and the great fireplace, where he packed them with kindling and fresh logs. The fires caught quickly, wood dry as bone, and soon emitted a heat too much to bear, even by the door. Josselin continued stoking the fires, holding his arm across his face, sweat dripping from his chin. Upon his face I discerned strange excitement. Dowling watched his back, every move he made, like he gleaned his intent and was horrified by it.

Josselin turned, red-faced and wet. 'What time do you think it is?'

'Past eight o'clock,' Dowling replied, wary.

Josselin nodded. He picked up an iron from by the grate and poked at the wooden walls, digging the rod into the cleft between floor and walls where the house stood next to its neighbour. In three places, where the wood was soft and green from years of damp, he managed to chisel out small holes, which soon became large holes, big as a man's head. Then he dragged more burning logs from the main oven and began piling them on the floor, in the middle of the new holes.

'What are you doing?' Dowling demanded. 'Would you burn the house down?'

Josselin inspected the smaller oven, poking the logs to see how hot they burnt. 'Not just this house. We'll set a few ablaze. With this wind it should be simple enough to set the house opposite alight besides.'

Dowling grabbed his arm. 'To what end?'

Josselin pushed him away, unconcerned. 'Fret not, butcher. We are surrounded by soldiers, remember? They'll put out the fire soon enough, but not before we cause a grand commotion.' He dragged another log from the fire and kicked it against the back wall. 'I doubt they've cleared the whole lane, just persuaded the occupants to remain behind their doors. Once the house is alight, everyone will come out onto the street to watch what is happening. Their first concern will be for their own property, and they will turn to the soldiers, demanding they assist. We'll split up and join the crowd.' A long thin flame licked high against the side wall, the planks already glowing.

Josselin laughed to himself, head bowed, staring at the flame, arm across his belly. 'They won't recognise us, not in the dark. I will accost a soldier myself and beg him to save my house.' He laughed again, shoulders trembling.

The skin on my face felt like it peeled from my skull.

Josselin kicked at the burning wall separating this house from the next. With five well-placed blows he opened a space wide enough to walk through. He disappeared, stepping through the thin flames, pale shirt glowing angelic white. I dashed for the hole in the wall before the flames grew too high, Dowling at my heels.

Josselin stood by the front door, peering through a crack out onto the lane. 'Here they come,' he exclaimed, eyes wide.

Voices shouted, loud and frightened. I watched up the lane as Josselin looked down. Neighbours emerged upon the street, slow and cautious, staring at Farynor's house next door, terror masking their drawn, lined faces. One man stood twitching, like he yearned to fight the fire with bare fists but knew not where to start. His wife bent over double like she tried to swallow herself whole. Children watched between his legs and round her skirts, open-mouthed and fascinated.

A burly man pushed through the gathering crowd. 'Anyone seen Thomas Farynor?' he shouted.

The wall against which I leant burnt into my back. The flames crackled loud, smoke rolling through the hole in the wall. We could not stay long. Josselin had the same idea, for he stood straight and opened the door wider afore sliding out into the night.

'Follow him,' I cried, almost tripping over my feet in my haste to stop him escaping, but the crowd was thick, and I felt suddenly exposed. Every man knew every man on London's streets, and we were clearly not soldiers. But every man watched transfixed as the front of Farynor's house disappeared behind a wall of flame. The fire crept outwards, beckoning, stroking, testing, and the wind blew stronger than it had all day, stretching the flames, bestowing upon them an unholy strength. The top of the house opposite almost touched the top of the Farynor house, and already the fire reached out, charring the old wood.

I heard heavy boots and more shouting. The first soldiers arrived, as open-mouthed as the children, muskets dragging in the dirt. 'Who has left that house?' demanded one, searching the faces of those about him.

'No one,' shrilled a thin woman, hands clasped to her breast. 'They have two children. What if they are inside?' She turned to the soldier, reaching out. 'You must go inside.'

'Not I,' he snorted. 'The Farynors left their house this afternoon, leaving three guests inside.' He crashed his gun against the ground in an attempt to win the crowd's attention. 'Who saw *anyone* leave that house?'

The house opposite burst into flame, creating a fiery arch above our heads like some celestial sign. Dowling stayed apart, white head clearly visible off to my right. I cursed myself for not chasing after Josselin the moment he vanished. He talked of making his way to the bridge to catch a boat, in which case he had run in the wrong direction, for the river was down the hill, not up. Meantime the crowd pushed backwards as the heat intensified, heaving against a forward swell, as more and more people came to watch. With so many people crammed into such a small space I reckoned I could talk to Dowling discreetly enough, and I edged sideways.

I stretched up to reach his ear. 'What say we go to the river?'

He stooped to listen. 'He won't go to the river, not now. The wharves will be packed, all the boats pressed.'

'Aye,' I reflected. 'So he'll walk the City wall looking for unguarded gates, or . . .' I watched the soldiers pushing the crowd further back. 'What's more likely now?' I thought aloud. 'That Josselin escapes the City to find Arlington at Whitehall, or Arlington comes to the City?'

Dowling's face folded into a study of intense concentration.

'Josselin will wait,' he concluded. 'He'll wait close by, close to Duke's Place.'

I looked around. 'Withypoll will come. We need somewhere safe to watch.'

'If Arlington comes, he'll come by boat,' said Dowling. 'That's where Josselin will go. Not to catch a boat, but to wait for Arlington.'

I tugged at his sleeve. 'Come on, then,' I said. 'We'll go round by Fish Street Hill.'

'Stand aside for the Mayor!' a voice cried from behind. A determined little band of soldiers pushed forwards, pikes lowered, jaws jutting. One man dawdled and was spiked in the arse. They marched steady, resolute and determined.

The crowd squeezed us backwards against the wall. A portly gentleman strode at the middle of the group, soldiers surrounding him on all sides. He struggled to keep pace, determined at the same time to keep his back straight and chin raised. He perspired heavily, a stout fellow unused to exercise. His burgundy coat flowed behind, periwig perched happily on his head. Sir Thomas Bludworth, Mayor of London and pompous windbag.

A tall fellow with wild yellow hair and blackened face stepped forward to meet him. 'We must pull down the neighbouring houses immediately,' he declared.

Bludworth visibly recoiled as if slapped across the face. 'We cannot pull them down else we must pay for them. Put out the fire.'

'It burns too fierce,' the soldier protested. 'The wind is too high. If we pull the houses down now, we can stop the fire. Leave it and it will spread.'

The Mayor stabbed the soldier in the chest with his forefinger. 'Extinguish the fire.' He scanned the crowd quickly, gauging the intent of those that listened. His eyes settled upon a granite-faced woman watching with arms folded, mouth drawn in an angry line. 'Why, this old maid might piss it out.'

The soldier made no attempt to hide his contempt, mouth curled in a great sneer. He watched as Bludworth straightened his jacket and eyed the towering blaze as if it was but a small bonfire.

Bludworth waggled a finger. 'I am going home to bed. Tell me when it's done.' He pivoted on his heel and returned the way he came, his escort accompanying him. I spotted Josselin staring from atop the hill.

'Come on,' I yelled, pushing after Bludworth's entourage. Josselin vanished. The crowd surged in upon us once more as it continued to swell and swarm. More soldiers barged their way through Bludworth's wake, angry and frustrated. There were simply too many people for any man to find another.

We fought our way to the crossroads at Eastcheap from where we could see all the way down the hill to the bridge and beyond. Fish Street Hill was packed from wall to wall, two great streams pushing against each other, creating currents running north and south; one current streaming up the hill to approach Red Rose Lane from the north, the other streaming south to approach from the water. No sign of Josselin.

The wind blew hard from east to west. If they left the house to burn, the fire would spread rapidly west. We stepped into the throng and were swept away towards the riverbank.

A tall, orange flame climbed high above the rooftops, thin and strangely still, lurching left with every gust of wind, then regaining its poise, elegant. Men rushed hither and thither. Soldiers shouted instruction to other soldiers, to citizens and boatmen, but with little evidence of organisation. A long line of coatless citizens passed a slow chain of leather buckets from the river to the bottom of Red Rose Lane, a feeble effort, far too little water to make any impact on the fire we saw. The bells of Magnus Martyr began to peal, stutteringly, a call to the whole City.

We walked up and down the riverside, about the towering wall of the Fishmonger's Hall and the back of Magnus Martyr, searching for Josselin. Then the fire exploded, silencing the whole crowd, who crouched as one, as though fearing the sky would fall upon their heads. Fire leapt from Red Rose Lane to Fish Street Hill, engulfing Star Inn. The crowd cried out 'Fire, Fire!' The wind fanned the flames further, carrying burning embers up into the sky where they flew south, over the river. And still no one appeared to be doing anything.

I kicked my heel and watched frustrated as soldiers continued to fling their arms in the air and shout obscenities at each other. If they didn't start pulling houses down soon, the whole City would catch fire. Star Inn was ablaze within just a few minutes, all three storeys engulfed in fire. The flames reached out and lapped against St Margaret's.

We continued shoving our way through the masses, the grim and the terrified pushing against each other. It would not be long before fighting broke out. Still no sign of Josselin, though I experienced a strong sensation he hid somewhere, watching. After an hour or more of constant jostling we sat apart and watched Fish Street Hill burn.

Then the wind turned, blowing out onto the river, towards us. I feared the heat might burn the brows off my face. The flames reached high into the sky, a magnificent, blazing orange against the black night. The crowd continued to grow, but still no one appeared to exert any effort to quell the fire. More and more people came to gaze in fascination, filling the streets. Every now and again there sounded a great crash, a noise echoed by the great crowd, who seemed to breathe in harmony with the ebbing and flowing of the fire and the gusting of the winds.

Suddenly the fire surged at us, grasping then falling away again, like a wave upon a beach. It was time to retreat.

'This way,' I cried, above the raging din of the panicking masses. I pulled Dowling west, for though east was safer, if Arlington arrived he would land this side of the bridge. Dowling groaned as the flames leapt upon Magnus Martyr, the large square church next to the bridge. I held my hand up against the heat wondering where Bludworth was now, whether he slept soundly in his bed.

'The King!' someone screamed.

Down upon the river his long barge flew through the water, eight oarsmen rowing in perfect synchrony, bow raised, standard flying frantically in the gale. It drew alongside the stairs outside the Fishmongers' Hall, and Charles himself stepped out onto the wharf, throwing his jacket back into the boat. He was followed by two more regal-looking fellows in long wigs: the Duke of York, it looked like, and the Devil himself, Arlington. All three stared up into the flames as if they couldn't believe their eyes. Arlington and the Duke of York followed the King's lead, tossing their coats into the boat, before rolling up their sleeves and heading up to Thames Street, followed by the soldiers that rowed them, fixing swords to their belts as they walked.

'Follow fast,' I urged Dowling, who stood fanning himself with the back of his hand. The King would soon be swamped, impossible to approach, which meant Arlington too would vanish from sight. Arlington was the bait, Josselin the fish.

I hurried forwards, following the King's black hair. He stood lean and energetic, head and shoulders above the throng, walking with an easy grace. Arlington followed at his heels, portly and stiff. The Duke of York, the King's brother, followed them both, more watchful, inspecting his surrounds with sharp eye.

On Thames Street the King stopped, hands on hips, shaking his head. I couldn't hear what he said above the noise, but he beckoned two men towards him, two soldiers I recalled seeing upon Red Rose Lane. He asked questions, waving a hand in the air regally, while the soldiers appeared to mumble, lips moving while they stared at the ground. The King jerked his right hand up and down, clearly demanding why they didn't pull down houses to stop the fire spreading. I wondered if Bludworth would be executed. Then the King pointed west, directing Arlington's attention away from the blaze, waving his hands from side to side above his head. Arlington nodded, before ordering two soldiers to clear a passage towards All Hallows. We waited half a minute before following. It was easy to trail him, for both soldiers carried pikes, which waved in the air above everyone's heads.

He led us past the Steelyard and up Dowgate Hill, our passage lit by an eerie, red glow from which the inhabitants of this busy street retreated, to hide behind closed doors. The crowd was thinner here. Halfway up the street I spotted Josselin, creeping beneath the eaves of the houses ahead. He walked with strange, elongated stride, each step measured and deliberate. I poked Dowling and gestured to him to slow, so Josselin wouldn't see us. We allowed the soldiers to pull fifty paces ahead while we focussed on trailing Josselin instead.

Josselin moved with stealth. We lost him for a minute or more, until his pale breeches reflected the candlelight from a window we passed. I struggled to slow my breath, anxiety impeding my capacity to concentrate on fleeting images of Josselin dancing through the shadows. That anxiety increased when he suddenly stepped out into the street and appeared to stare straight at us. Then he darted across to our side of the hill and disappeared up Cloak Lane, a narrow street shrouded in darkness beneath the imposing presence of St John Baptist.

'Do we follow?' I whispered, for it was a strange route. Assuming Josselin still followed Arlington, why did Arlington travel north-west? Why did he not proceed north up Sopar Lane, broader and better lit?

'Follow not that which is evil, but that which is good,' Dowling answered, staring into the black hole. 'Every fibre of my soul tells me to let them go. Some drama is about to unfold. Yet if we are not witness to it, I don't know how we save ourselves.'

'Now I feel much better,' I grumbled, striding to the mouth of the alley. 'Nothing to see,' I whispered, listening hard. The wind blew like a typhoon down the narrow passageway.

Dowling squeezed my shoulder. 'May God grant you courage.'

I resisted the temptation to slap him about the chops and stepped into the darkness. The gale whistled and screeched. No need to tread softly, so I scuttled forwards, keen to catch a glimpse of Josselin's breeches, feeling with my hands. A curtain flapped furiously out of an open window wrapping itself about my face. I saw something move at the mouth of a tiny alley next to the churchyard of St Thomas Apostle, a crumbling church, bereft of bells. A tiny light shone in the distance. My heart pounded blood through the back of my throat.

I shook my head. 'Why should Arlington come here?'

Dowling said nothing but stepped into the entrance of the alley and out of the wind. I squeezed after him and we edged forwards, eyes fixed upon the light ahead. It was impossible to tell how big it was, or how far the distance.

Behind the wall to our left lay a churchyard. A pale glow marked a break in the brickwork. An iron gate hung crooked upon its hinges, almost closed, swinging gently backwards and forwards. Gravestones glimmered beneath the thinnest sliver of a moon. The light seemed close now, square, like a window.

We resumed our slow shuffle, the window looming afore us. A narrow house emerged from the darkness at the top of the alley, a mean structure with two low storeys and a sagging roof. The alley walls ran into the front of the house, offering no means of escape.

'This is a trap,' I whispered, a growing conviction slowing my feet.

'Aye, so it is,' a bright voice sounded loud from behind us. 'Though it was not you we hoped to snare.'

I swivelled sharp to see Withypoll, rattling a cane against the graveyard wall. 'Keep walking,' he commanded.

There were more shadows behind him, and now a low shuffling and the sound of several men breathing at once.

The door to the house stood ajar. Lord Arlington leant back in a chair, smoking a pipe, legs crossed. His eyes glinted above the black plaster on his nose.

'Well, well,' he said, not troubling to smile. 'My loyal subjects come to pay their respects.' He jerked the pipe at two boxes on the floor. 'Hang them.'

Withypoll grabbed me by the throat. Someone tied my hands, another my ankles, and a rope fell around my neck. Withypoll picked me up by the scruff of the neck and hauled me onto one of the boxes. I heard the rope swish through the air, and the noose jerked tight.

Arlington adjusted his chair so he sat opposite us both. I could see

Dowling out the corner of my eye. If I stood on tiptoe I could just about swallow without choking. Arlington sucked his pipe and blew smoke up at the low wooden ceiling. 'I was hoping for Josselin,' he said. 'Perhaps he will join us later. Meantime you might tell me who you spoke to at Clarendon's house, and what you spoke about.'

'I wanted to know if Josselin was in there,' I croaked, dry-mouthed, watching Withypoll prick the blade of his long knife against his thumb. 'They told us he was spotted in the City.'

Withypoll leered, eyes hungry. Arlington stared through my eyes and into the back of my head, sombre and steel-jawed.

'I told you to watch for Josselin and you sought audience with Clarendon.' He tapped the bowl of the pipe against his knee. 'Then you smuggled yourselves into the City without telling me what you spoke about.' He waved a hand. 'What am I to suppose?'

'That we are endeavouring to find Josselin for you, by whatever means,' I replied.

'No.' Arlington pointed the stem of his pipe at my forehead. 'I am to suppose I cannot trust you.' He grimaced and pulled his coat about his shoulders, like he was cold. 'Something about you both *rankles* with me. I don't know what it is, but I cannot endure it any longer.' He blew more blue smoke. 'It is time for you to die.'

Withypoll grinned so hard I thought his face would break. The rope tightened about my throat, and my face swelled up.

Arlington smiled briefly, showing yellow teeth. 'I promised you the Spanish donkey, Lytle, and I thought to hang the butcher from a meathook by his chin, but this is simpler.' He brushed at his trousers with one hand and stared expectantly, as if awaiting famous last words.

Tears pricked the corners of my eyes. 'We have been loyal to you, done everything you asked of us and tried to do more. It is true Josselin escaped us, but we returned to London as fast as we could, to bring him to justice.' I forced the air into my lungs, my eyes stinging. 'And we have not finished yet. I don't understand why you plan to kill us when still you don't have Josselin, nor what he withholds from you.'

Arlington blinked. 'You found Josselin in the City, then?' He licked his lips. 'What more did he tell you?'

'We found Josselin at Red Rose Lane.'

Arlington frowned. 'Pudding Lane, you mean?'

'Aye, Pudding Lane,' I tried to nod. 'It was he who poisoned your soldiers when he saw how they despoiled his house and frightened his family. We saw him there and followed.'

Arlington leant forwards. 'Did he tell you what of mine he possesses?'

'No,' I said quickly, fearful of the look in his eye. 'He told us only it was a letter of some sort, that he possessed it and wanted to meet with you to discuss it. You won't catch him, for he is cleverer than us.'

Arlington leant back, eyes hooded.

'You don't believe me,' I exclaimed. 'I told you before he wanted to talk to you. How else will you get your letter back? Who else will obtain it for you?' I looked to Withypoll. 'He won't catch him.'

Withypoll glowered, like he plotted to dispense the most pain it was possible to inflict on another human being. His eyes turned a darker shade of black and he stepped close enough to kick away the box beneath my feet.

'We found him at Shyam, we found him at Duke's Place, and we followed him here,' I continued.

Arlington looked to the door. 'Josselin is here?'

'He trailed you from Thames Street. His sole objective is to find you. We saw him enter Cloak Lane, then lost him in our own attempt to remain undetected.'

'Why so?' demanded Arlington. 'Why did you not call ahead? We could have trapped him.'

'Because we know that Withypoll wants to see us dead, your lordship,' I exclaimed. 'Every step we take, he tells us he will see us dead. He seeks revenge and will not forgive us.'

'Nor would I, Lytle,' Arlington said, softly. 'How could any man trust you?'

'We do not leave everyone we find,' I reminded him.

Withypoll pulled a thin-bladed knife from his jacket. 'Enough,' he slurred, crimson-cheeked.

'Hold,' Arlington commanded, holding up one hand. 'You speak well, Lytle. Why then do I not trust you?'

I raised my brow at Withypoll. 'Because this fellow speaks in your ear? And because I saved your life and you don't trust us not to tell anyone.'

Dowling breathed inwards, sharply. Withypoll straightened his back and smiled again, pity vying with evil intent upon his haggard face.

Arlington drew on his pipe and regarded Withypoll with quizzical eye. 'You're right, he does talk in my ear. And he *has* discovered nothing.'

Withypoll's brows shot so far up his head it looked like he swallowed a fly.

Arlington ignored him. 'You say Josselin followed us here. Where is he now?'

'I reckon he hides in the churchyard of Thomas Apostle,' I replied, aware he was testing me.

Withypoll turned, eyes blazing. He and the soldiers had been waiting in the churchyard.

'Or somewhere else we will not find him.'

'Hmm.' Arlington frowned. 'Then how do we catch him?'

'He wants to meet you. I reckon he will meet you only in a public place where he believes he is in control of the surroundings.' Where he *would* be in control, because he was more intelligent than Arlington and Withypoll combined. 'A place with open space and lots of light.'

'You listen to him?' Withypoll snorted. 'Josselin is trapped inside the City walls. He will take whatever opportunity we offer him.'

Arlington stood. 'I have to get back to the fire. The King will be wondering where I am.' He clicked his fingers in Withypoll's face. 'We will give these two another opportunity.'

Withypoll scowled.

'You have until tomorrow to find Josselin.' Arlington turned to face us once more. 'Do not disappoint.'

He opened the door and stepped out into the alley. The sky burnt orange, framing Arlington's squat silhouette. We were left alone with Withypoll.

'Very clever,' he hissed, sitting on Arlington's chair, elbows on knee, staring at the blade of his knife. 'You think you saved yourselves, don't you?'

He eyed the soldiers, growled and shook his head, still furious. Then he went to the door and stuck his head out into the alley. 'The fire is spreading fast,' he called. 'I can hear the flames at the end of Old Fish Street.'

I couldn't hear flames, but I heard the sound of men shouting, women screaming. London was in chaos. Those whose houses burnt would be scrambling to empty their houses. The streets would soon be full of overladen carts filled with people's possessions, most with no obvious place to go. The City gates would be overrun with citizens seeking to fetch their goods away, find somewhere else to stay. The soldiers at the gates would find themselves overwhelmed, not knowing what to do. Men outside the gate would be pushing to get in, to help with the effort to fight the fire. Men and women would be fighting to get out, as far away from the fire as they could get. Josselin had created the perfect world in which to travel unseen.

Withypoll tipped his beaver hat, face empty of all expression. 'Arlington told me to leave you, so we will leave you.' He gestured at the two soldiers to exit the door. 'Good luck,' he said, quietly. 'I think this makes us even.'

With which he closed the door behind and left us to our fate. The key turned in the lock and his footsteps faded away down the alley.

'A prayer, Davy,' I whispered, rope digging into the flesh about my ears. Light shone in from a little window at the top of the far wall. Impossible to say if it was fire or dawn. 'We need a good prayer.'

I realised I forgot to visit Culpepper. The deadline passed.

Chapter Thirty-One

The first Comet had a large tail, full, well fixed; there's much Unity betwixt his Majesty and People.

A tiny muscle in my neck locked in spasm, shooting stabbed pains down the left side of my head. I closed my eyes and tried to ignore the agony. My calf muscles cramped and my toes ached, yet I couldn't relieve the pressure even a fraction, for every time I relaxed, just an inch, the rope tightened a little more.

'How are you, Dowling?' I managed a strangulated whine.

Dowling growled. 'There came a great wind and smote the four corners of the house, and it fell upon the young men, and they are dead.'

'The wind may die down,' I replied, not sure I understood. 'It's been blowing for two days.'

He didn't answer.

'What about God?' I asked. 'Will He not save us?'

'Upon your head the name of blasphemy,' he swallowed.

My eyeballs were popping out of my head. 'If the fire does arrive, then perhaps it will burn the rope first,' I suggested.

'For that we should pray very hard indeed,' Dowling replied, solemn. 'Yet I fear you lack the faith.'

'Well you pray, then,' I retorted. 'For you have the faith of a thousand, do you not?' I felt suddenly hopeless.

'You *are* an atheist, then,' Dowling exclaimed, in shrill triumph.

'Just because I don't live my life as if someone were watching from the sky does not make me an atheist.'

Dowling muttered something while I contemplated the silence and tried to quell the panic and fear. I needed to piss.

Thin wisps of smoke slithered under the door, swallowed up before they reached the ceiling, leaving behind only the acrid smell of burning wood. Then the faintest sound of crackling flames, creeping up to the door with despicable malintent. The air grew cloudy, the door blurry and my eyes began to water. I jerked my wrists despite the tightening cord about my neck, fighting the terror that throttled my heart. A wave of black fog billowed into the room, choking and harsh, drifting to the roof and hanging there. I held my breath and tried not to move, my head dizzy. I closed my eyes. Dowling coughed and coughed again, wheezing until he retched.

I tried to shout, but no words came out. My breath rasped at the back of my throat. Tears streamed and the flesh about my eyes burnt. I tried again to hold my breath, but my mouth burnt and filled with phlegm. I was forced to breathe deep, but nothing happened. Then I coughed so hard it felt like my body conspired to turn itself inside out and my lungs threatened to explode. Strange lights danced in front of my eyes.

Shrewsbury's face floated before my gaze, the bags about his eyes so loose and floppy his eyeballs appeared shrunken. He wore a dark grey cloak about a cadaverous body, thin and bony. The syphilis ate him. He hovered just below the ceiling, forcing his face into mine, grinning like a demon. His face was long like Josselin's. It had ne'er struck me before how alike they appeared. A heavy thud sounded in my ears, like an axe against a block. Had Shrewsbury chopped off Dowling's head? I tried to turn and see, but someone grabbed my ankles and lifted them into the air. I glided across the floor towards a fiery glow. Shrewsbury was dragging me to Hell! I tried to jerk my feet loose, kicking out at the bindings that would not be free. I heard my voice rattle as sputum filled my throat. Smoke snaked into my mouth and nose, my head spun. Then something hit me in the face. A strong wind.

'Stir yourself, Lytle,' someone shouted into my ear.

I opened my eyes to see Dowling's red, sweaty face pressed close against mine. I could hardly see, my eyes were so crusted. I tried to bring a hand round to wipe them, but couldn't move. I turned to see Josselin holding my other arm, the two of them forcing me up the narrow alley. My back burnt so hot I feared my shirt was on fire.

'I'm glad you came,' I tried to say, but succeeded only in spraying Josselin's face with a lungful of green mucus.

He spat on the floor without moving his head, struggling to hold me straight. I stretched my legs and attempted to swing them in rhythm with our slow procession back towards College Hill.

'I can walk myself,' I croaked, afore choking again. I dug my heels in the ground and pulled my arms free, falling backward upon the alley floor. Dowling knelt at my side and peered into my eyes.

'I can walk,' I said again, tugging on his shirt as I staggered to my feet.

'Then walk fast,' Josselin grumbled. 'The fire is closing in on all sides.'

I turned to see our prison ablaze, flames filling the space within, consuming all with voracious appetite. Then the roof collapsed, sending sparks flying up into the sky, where the wind seized them and carried them west, towards the rest of the City.

'God's teeth!' Josselin exclaimed from behind.

I followed his gaze and saw only fire. College Hill disappeared. Josselin watched frozen, eyes wide.

'You did this,' I reminded him, head still giddy. My guts churned and I vomited onto the floor beneath my feet.

'Into the graveyard,' Dowling shouted.

He grabbed me by the collar while I still sat crouched, waiting for another spasm. He dragged me towards the middle of the churchyard, away from the worst of the heat and smoke.

I sat on a gravestone watching the flames surge twenty or thirty feet above our heads, roaring with insane ferocity. Though I sat thirty paces away, still the heat engulfed my face, threatening to burn it from my skull. City bells rang loud from all direction, deafening even amidst the blaze of the fire.

Dowling sat close while Josselin strode off in search of something.

I shouted to be heard above the din. 'Josselin saved us?'

Dowling nodded, twisting the rope about his wrists into giant knots. 'He chopped the walls with an axe.'

I plunged my head between my legs, fighting the nausea. 'That was good of him.'

Josselin prowled the inner wall of the churchyard, everything glowing a fiery orange. The wall encircling us rose eight feet tall, with only one other gate, leading directly inside Thomas Apostle, already lit. The leaves of a large oak tree, stood majestically to our left, flickered and glowed like little candles against the black sky as sparks fell onto its branches and nestled against its dry body.

I struggled to remember. 'Is it day or night?'

Dowling nodded at the horizon to the west. 'Night still.'

'We must climb the wall,' Josselin called, striding through the grass.

'Why?' I asked. 'The fire cannot reach us here, nor can Arlington. The fire will burn itself out by tomorrow.'

Josselin stood with hands on hips, staring at the flames like they were a great inconvenience. 'I have to get to St Paul's.'

'We can go when the fire has diminished,' I replied.

He looked at me as if I were a great fool and stuck his hand up in the air. 'Feel the wind, Lytle. How long do you think it will take this wind to carry the fire down Watling Street?'

God save us, he was right. The idea that Paul's might bow to this fire seemed ludicrous. It had stood for six centuries, had seen off fire, lightning, radical Protestants and Cromwell's Model Army. That it might now fall to the hands of the man that stood before me seemed unthinkable. Yet the fire was already halfway there, in less than a day. 'What is at St Paul's you desire so badly?'

'No.' Josselin stabbed his finger at my forehead. 'Let me ask you a question first. What is your relationship with Arlington? I assumed you played some complex game, that you sought to gain my trust on Arlington's behalf.' He looked at my pocket. 'I have seen you smoke your strange leaves, and watched you emerge from Shyam unscathed. I saw Arlington and Withypoll come out of the house and thought they left you there to trap me. But if I hadn't saved you, you would have died.'

Dowling nodded.

'We performed but lowly duties for Arlington,' I explained. 'Then he asked us to investigate the murder of nobility, Thomas Wharton, the Earl of St Albans.'

'The torturer?'

'So it turned out.' I nodded. 'Arlington conspired with him, and expected us to point the finger at the wrong man, else get ourselves killed. In the event we had to save his life when he betrayed Wharton.'

'And he let you live?' Josselin's eyes narrowed, suspicious.

'Until now,' Dowling replied. 'I don't think he expected us to leave Shyam alive, or if we did, the plan was for Withypoll to kill us. It still is.'

Josselin continued to stare, as if trying to work out the rules of an elaborate game. 'If you betray me I will kill you.'

I shrugged. Arlington, Withypoll and the plague had exhausted my capacity for fear.

Josselin jabbed his finger. 'You will help me.'

'As best we can,' I replied. 'Though our attempt to gain you an audience with Arlington failed. He wants you dead.'

'I must get to St Paul's,' he said. 'Then you must carry a message to Arlington on my behalf.'

'And have him kill us?' I snorted.

'Listen to me,' Josselin snapped. 'When we get to St Paul's I will show you the letter. You can see it for yourself. Arlington will not dare kill you once he knows you have seen it.'

'You have hidden a letter at St Paul's?'

'I could not keep it on my person, for if I am caught with the letter upon me then I am lost.'

'What letter?' Dowling grunted.

Josselin puffed out his chest and gritted his teeth like he contemplated diving into the Thames. 'Arlington told you I sabotaged the chance of peace.'

'Aye. You made sure De Witt saw a letter not intended for him,' I said.

Josselin nodded. 'So I did, but not to sabotage peace. In my view it was the only thing to do if peace was ever to be achieved.'

'By betraying Arlington's true intent to De Witt you hoped that England and Holland would embrace each other in peace and harmony?' I said. 'Arlington is Secretary of State. Once De Witt knew he plotted to spark civil war, there could be no chance of peace.'

'You don't know what you're talking about.' Josselin waved a hand in my face. 'If you work for Arlington then you must know he is Catholic.'

'There are rumours,' Dowling said, slowly.

'You heard right when you heard I betrayed De Buat,' said Josselin, 'and God forgive me for it, but De Buat will be alright. De Witt cannot punish an ambassador of the House of Orange.'

'Why did you do it?' I pressed him.

He clenched his fists. 'Arlington gave me three letters. The first to De Witt pledging peaceful intent, which letter was a lie. The second letter was intended for De Buat only, encouraging him to rouse the House of Orange to fight for the reinstatement of the Prince of Orange. To fight against the Dutch, in other words. He incited them to civil war.' He held up a hand. 'I cannot condemn Arlington for that, for De Witt should have guessed. Indeed it might be a good thing for the States that they confront their differences and resolve them now rather than let them drag on for years. The sooner the States resolve their differences, the sooner will emerge a stronger Protestant state, an ideal ally for England.'

I shook my head. 'I still don't understand why you would betray Arlington. Why distract them from their internal wrangling? By exposing Arlington's deceit—'

'It may unite them, it may not.' Josselin interrupted. 'But there will be no alliance with England for the time being, which is the right thing, for there can be no alliance with England the way things stand.'

'What is in the third letter?' I demanded.

'You will not believe me until you read it yourself,' Josselin answered. 'So you must come with me to St Paul's and I will show it to you.'

'What!' I exclaimed. 'Tell us now!'

Josselin shook his head slowly, staring into the towering wall of flame. 'We must climb the wall.'

The flames crept stealthily south and north. The wall stood eight feet tall.

I clambered to my feet. Iron clamps squeezed at my chest, forcing me to bend over double. I cleared my lungs and spat more phlegm.

'You go first,' Josselin said to me. 'We will help you up.'

They both stood six feet tall, cupping their hands for my feet. It was easy to wriggle up on to the top of the wall where I sat straddled, wondering if I might help Dowling, but he waved me out of the way. I peered down into New Queen Street, where people scurried up and down, emptying their houses of all possessions, stacking them on the street. Three families loaded their goods into wagons; the rest would have to manage without, for now the whole city was panicked.

Dowling heaved himself arthritically upon the wall next to me, his red face sweating by my knees, leaving Josselin to spring up by himself.

'Hey!' a voice cried from the street below.

The shadow beneath the wall was moving. A long line of soldiers stood in a row.

'Jump!' roared Josselin, swinging himself into the air and down onto the street. I followed without thinking and landed on my back, Dowling's huge feet just missing my nose. I felt myself hauled up and turned back to see a line of men stood with legs bent and arms akimbo like giant crabs, faces frozen in disbelief.

'Don't just stand there!' another voice commanded from in the distance. Withypoll's voice.

'Run!' Josselin urged, beckoning us towards Knightrider Street.

Thank God we climbed the wall where we did, I thought, as I urged my short legs to run as fast as they could. Had we chosen a spot away from the corner we would have landed in the middle of Arlington's army. Careless of them not to guard each end of the street, I thought, a sense of gratitude elevating my senses. Withypoll's doing; arrogance ever his downfall. Though they trailed us by just ten yards.

Josselin surged ahead, weaving his way through the crowded street without breaking his stride. He pulled further and further ahead, leaving me to do my best to keep up with Dowling. He ran with longer stride, but my legs moved quicker. Bread Street loomed.

'Turn right,' I shouted.

Dowling heard and made the turn. Bread Street was where I lived. Dowling slowed, allowing me to surge past. Four soldiers followed, the others pursued Josselin. This was my parish; these were my streets. I darted left into a narrow lane that twisted its way onto Friday Street. Two feet wide, the soldiers would have to follow in single file. Then north until we reached St Matthew's. I led Dowling around the churchyard wall and through a tiny opening out onto Cheapside. Then diagonally towards the mouth of Gutter Lane and into the shadow. We stopped, panting hard, my breath rasping against the lining of my throat.

'That was close,' I wheezed.

'Aye, close.' Dowling leant forwards, hands on knees. 'And getting closer. The fire will drive us all up against the wall.'

The wind continued to billow and churn, carrying a sheet of embers above our heads. Some died, others drifted deep into the maze of close-packed houses, dry as dust. I heard the Withypoll shouting in the distance.

'What are you two doing?' a voice cried out from behind. 'Make yourselves useful or clear the way!'

Two fellows pushed a large barrel down the street to which someone had fixed two sets of wheels. A third fellow led the way, parading afore it with great majesty, urging all to stand aside and let it pass, which was hardly necessary given the troubles the two men at the back were having in persuading it to roll against the cobbles.

'Where are your buckets?' the portly fellow bellowed into my face. 'You may save your goods, but what about your property?' His gaze fell to our hands, where still we wore our ropes. Then something caught his eye.

'Stop that man!' he yelled, pointing at a small thin fellow scuttling along Cheapside clasping something to his chest. The thin man cast a frightened gaze over his shoulder and tried to run faster, but whatever he had beneath his shirt slowed him down.

'Stop that Frenchman!' our protagonist shouted again, attracting the attention of all on Cheapside.

Two burly fellows pulling a wagon by hand dropped their load and spread their arms wide, attention fixed upon the poor unfortunate. His hair was straight, black and well oiled, and he wore it pulled back and tied behind his neck. He danced from foot to foot, no chance of escape. As the two big fellows jumped at him, he fell to the cobbles in a ball, knees tucked up to his chest.

The portly fellow rolled his sleeves further up his arms and marched up like a great waddling bulldog to where the little man lay cowering. 'What does he hide in his shirt?' He squinted.

The little fellow peered up. His face was thin and angular. A big black mole sat tucked beneath one nostril. 'My dog,' he exclaimed, pulling forth a small black creature with hair over its eyes. 'It is just my dog.' His accent indeed sounded foreign, but many foreigners lived inside London's city walls. He clambered to his knees and sat crouched, holding up the dog with both hands like it was a sacred offering.

Dowling shoved his way to the front of the small gathering. 'What did you think it was?'

The big ugly fellow stood feet astride, gazing down on the smaller man like he hated him with all his soul. 'They found a Frenchman with a trunk full of fireballs out at Moorfields.'

'You thought he carried fireballs in his shirt?' Dowling snorted. 'He is as frightened as the rest of us. Let him go.'

'Frightened you say?' The portly fellow turned to Dowling, thick black eyebrows halfway to the top of his balding head. 'I am not frightened, nor should any of us be. We must put out this fire.' He turned again to the little man and his dog. 'The only ones that have need to be frightened are those that fear being caught.' He held up a hand high into the air, with great ceremony. One of his colleagues handed him a thick iron bar. 'The French have started fires all over the City and are descending upon us now, an army of French and Papists, four thousand men.'

Before any could stop him he swung the bar through the air and hit the little man hard across the temple. The short fellow fell to the ground instantly, eyes closed and body limp. The little dog landed sideways upon the cobbles before righting itself. It began to bark: short, snapping yelps aimed at no one in particular. The gathering crowd stood in a silent circle watching blood pour from the small man's head, trickling between the cobbles in a meandering stream.

'This is revenge!' the portly fellow snarled, clasping the iron bar tighter in his fist. 'Holmes burnt Westerschelling and now the Dutch are trying to burn London.'

Dowling pushed him in the chest. 'I thought you said it was the French?' he said. 'Dutch or French? Make up your mind.'

The portly fellow recovered his poise and took a step back towards Dowling. 'Who are you, anyway, sir?' he sneered. 'Why do you wear rope?' he nodded at Dowling's wrists. 'What prison have you escaped from?'

The crowd now turned to us, murmuring amongst themselves, faces unfriendly and unsmiling. All were terrified, desperate for assurance that someone might save their homes and possessions, and ready to tear to pieces whosoever it was started the blaze.

Why hadn't we just slunk back into Gutter Lane, I asked myself? Why did we always find ourselves at the midst of every conflagration? Withypoll's soldiers would be here soon, if they weren't already watching at the fringes of the mob now surrounding us.

'We were imprisoned by the Dutch,' I called out, an unformed lie. 'Which is why we know it was not the French.' I waved a hand at the dead man upon the ground. 'This man was guilty of no crime.'

Which speech did nothing to settle the atmosphere. I realised, too late, that to suggest a murder took place was to suggest all were party to it. I would have to work twice as hard.

'We came back from Colchester yesterday.' I held up the rope for all to see. 'The Dutch attempted to land at Hythe but were thwarted. Their spies captured us in the Dutch Quarter, and Lord Arlington's men rescued us. We are members of Lord Arlington's secret service.'

The portly man didn't know what to say. He stood with mouth open, eyes gleaming, still holding his iron bar. I did my best to look like a battle-hardened soldier, staring back, expressionless.

'We don't have time for this,' said Dowling, breaking the silence. 'Stand aside, all of you. The army will root out the perpetrators of this great fire, if perpetrators there be. Gather your possessions and leave, else stay and fight the fire.'

He shoved the portly man aside and strode with great confidence towards the Little Conduit.

'Who speaks of Arlington?' shouted a voice from behind. Withypoll's voice again.

'Fish teeth!' I exclaimed, running fast afore any could think to stop us, diving into the crowd that thronged about the Little Conduit pumping water into buckets.

Opposite the Little Conduit stood a gate, a passageway into St Paul's Churchyard, which swarmed busier than Cheapside. All of London carried their possessions here, it seemed, assuming like me it could never burn down.

'God help the good people of Colchester,' Dowling grumbled,

slowing to a walk, rope bundled in his fists in an attempt to hide it.

'God help the good Dutch people of London,' I retorted. 'What should I have said? Or should I have stood there silent, like a big fish, with my mouth wide open? Like you.'

He muttered something beneath his breath and shook his big head, ruefully, eyes moist. I thought of the poor Frenchman, if Frenchman he was, lain dead upon the street. 'I hope someone looks after his dog,' I said.

'The dumb ass speaking with man's voice forbad the madness of the prophet,' Dowling grumbled.

Did he call me a dumb ass?

No matter; we had to get to St Paul's.

Chapter Thirty-Two

Many Nations are deprived of their Grandees, their best and supreamest Officers and Commanders.

The old cathedral was in a sorry state. Already falling to pieces before the Civil War, Cromwell allowed his military to brick off the choir from the rest of the building, converting the nave into a stable for eight hundred horses. They dismantled the scaffold set up in the south transept and the vaulting collapsed. They destroyed the bishop's throne and the choir stalls and demolished the Bishop's Palace. The walls leant and the tower stood crooked, supported by a complicated trellis of timber.

We entered the nave through the Little North Door with a crowd of others. Huge columns towered high above our heads. Every voice sounded thin and shrill beneath the formidable, vaulted ceiling, blackened arches hanging above our heads like a terrible judgement. A steady stream of men, women and children scuttled about, carrying their possessions into the nave from all directions, hunting for a bare patch of floor to claim for their own. A notice instructed all who passed to deposit a penny into a box for every burden fetched into the building, but the box was empty. The mercers, goldsmiths and booksellers hurried faster than everyone, bustling impatiently, fetching their stock down into St Faith's where they might guard their wares against thieves. We stood, backs against the cold stone wall, searching for Josselin.

'If he was mad before, he'll be lunatic now,' I said in low voice. 'All this destruction because he lit a fire in Pudding Lane. What will that do to his conscience?'

I stepped out across the busy stone floor, picking my way carefully through the melee. So many bodies crammed together created an unnatural warmth, leading all to feel uneasy. A fight broke out away to the left, afront of Bishop Kempe's chapel. Two men squabbling over a square foot of stone floor, anxiety and frustration turned to violence.

'A long time since so many came to church,' I said, crossing the transept into the choir, treading through the rubble beneath the shadow of the four enormous pillars that held up the lead-covered tower.

The Rose Window glowed red and orange, shimmering and flickering, casting a fiery pall upon the walls and ceiling, and upon the marble tomb of Thomas Ewer lain just afore us. Past the bust of Dean Nowell, we entered the Lady Chapel, past the skeletal brass figure of Bishop Braybrooke. Unsettling to walk amidst the fine carved figures of men long dead, across a rubble-covered stone floor glowing red like the pits of Hell.

We returned back the way we came, discouraged, for Josselin was more cunning than us. I feared we might walk straight past him and not recognise him. Yet he knew where we were, I was certain.

The merchants, booksellers and goldsmiths queued at the two entrances to the crypt on either side of the transept. Stairs led down into the bowels of the cathedral, the parish church of St Faith's. Yet these fellows didn't push and shove in order to pray. Their boxes and chests were full of worldly goods. However unlikely it seemed that Josselin would expose himself to the attention of so many, I had no doubt that if the letter was down there, he would be down there too.

We joined the line and stood self-consciously with arms bare. A fog of stinking sweat hung about our heads. These men's faces shone red and wet, despite their fine clothes. We dared not skirt the queue, for tempers simmered, so we descended the steps slow, one at a time, hemmed in the midst of the angry crowd.

At the base of the stairs stood a man with parchment and pen, surrounded by merchants, wearing a frayed dark coat, fingers stained black. A row of five great brutes, each with pike and sword, prevented further passage. The crypt spread the whole length of the church, like a giant warehouse. Crates of books and lines of chests and trunks stood in long, neat lines. The room was bare of furniture. The edges of the space hid in darkness.

The man with the ledger peered up at me through rheumy eyes. 'What do you want?'

'We have come to help,' I replied. 'We were told to come down here and move some books.'

'Told by who?' he asked, looking me up and down.

I remembered a name. 'Edward Taylor.'

He stared. 'Edward Taylor,' he repeated. 'Edward Taylor is here. Is it worth my while fetching him?'

I pursed my lips and shook my head. The man with the ledger shuffled over to whisper into the ear of one of the sentries, pointing at me and making hissing noises. Time to leave. Through more crowds of anxious squirrels, all desperate to hoard their nuts.

'Josselin cannot be there,' I said, once we reached the transept, looking anxiously back over my shoulder.

'Josselin has more wit than you and I put together,' replied Dowling. 'If he wishes not to be found we will not find him.'

I gripped his sleeve. 'We'll try the Chapter House.'

I hurried across the transept and out into a tiny square, surrounded on three sides by a two-storeyed cloister. Here we were alone, for the sky hung heavy above our heads, a dull, dirty orange flecked with grey clouds of wafting smoke speckled with ash.

'Why did Josselin leave his letter here in the first place?' I grumbled, pushing open the door of the Chapter House. It was a strange, round building, ten paces wide, wall to wall.

'He was in a hurry,' said Dowling. 'Accused of murder and treachery. He passed by on his way out east.'

'Why enter the City at all?' I replied. 'Faster to go round the wall.'

'Aye,' Dowling replied. 'Perhaps there is no letter after all.' He wandered back out into the courtyard. 'When a man says he possesses a box and refuses to tell ye what it holds, usually it's because he has only just made up the lie and hasn't had time to finish it.'

The cloisters were shallow, impossible to hide therein without being seen. We toured the square slowly, scrutinising every inch of stonework.

'The roof?' Dowling suggested.

'Why should he hide on the roof?' I spoke as if the idea was ridiculous, for I had no desire to climb such a decrepit structure.

'The roof is covered in timber where they are repairing it. Even if he climbed all the way up where could he have hidden a letter?'

'We've been everywhere else.' Dowling stared upwards. 'Who knows what hiding places there might be.'

I followed his gaze. My head spun, the ceiling was so high. Dowling headed to the door leading to the staircase

'Attention!' shouted a voice from around the corner. 'Attention!' it shouted again, more urgent. 'The fire has spread nearly to the wall,' a soldier pronounced. 'Soon Ludgate will be ablaze. The prisoners have already been moved elsewhere. Everyone must leave now, through the west gate, before it is too late.' The soldier stepped into view out of the choir, repeating his message, bellowing at the top of his lungs.

A low moan filled the air, rising to the top of the ceiling and reverberating about our ears in strange echo. A woman screamed and men began to shout. Soldiers streamed from the choir down into the nave, rousing the inert and forcing everyone to pick up what they could and hurry away to our left.

Dowling and I stayed where we were. Keen to leave, but not before we found Josselin. We allowed ourselves to be swept along by the crowd towards the choir. Soldiers lined the steps, armed and anxious, surveying the crowd that swarmed the nave, nervous and afraid.

'No more time,' shouted another soldier at the merchants that fought against the tide, arms full. 'Take the rest of your goods with you and seal the doors. No more time.'

I ducked my head just in time to avoid being spotted by Arlington and Withypoll.

I tugged at Dowling's sleeve. 'Lower your big head,' I hissed.

He bent his knees and tried his best, but his white head shone like a beacon, glowing in the gloom.

I pulled him sideways, towards a thick wooden door. Behind it a narrow staircase, twisting up into the gloom.

'How did they know where to find us?' I panted, dashing up the first few stairs in case we were followed.

'One of his spies,' said Dowling, close behind. 'Unless it's Josselin's doing.'

'Why should he do that?' I snorted, though I feared he might speak the truth. 'Save us from the flames, then unleash those two beasts upon us.'

'Just climb,' Dowling snapped. 'You'll need every breath you've got.'

I had to stop and rest twice before we finally reached the top of the stairs, five hundred feet above the ground. The wind gusted strong, rattling loose timbers strewn all about, the sky awash with black smoke. My legs felt weak, petrified by the fear of being blown off the top, yet I couldn't help but follow Dowling to the edge to contemplate the horror that played itself out before our eyes.

The whole of London was ablaze. We sat as if upon the mast of a giant ship floating on a small lake, the cathedral protected on all sides by the expanse of the churchyard. It was the only empty space betwixt the City walls, and so the flames below us happily consumed every house and every building, not a single hole in the sheet of fire. All gone. The churches, the halls, Cole Harbour, the Exchange. My little house on Bread Street and Dowling's house and shop. Nothing survived.

Looking west was like looking down a long tunnel, fire on each side all the way to the wall. Only ahead could we still see whole buildings through thick black smoke, and a dark silhouette.

'What are you doing up here?' I shouted, wind carrying my words in his direction above the incessant roar of the blaze.

Josselin turned, face covered in a thin layer of soot. His lips moved but I couldn't hear the words. We moved closer.

'. . . lit the fire, but I didn't send the winds,' he said, a strange brightness in his eyes. 'I will execute judgement: I am the Lord.'

Which seemed a tenuous conclusion to me. God sent the wind every winter; it didn't mean he expected us to put flame to buildings.

'Do you have the letter?' I asked.

'Downstairs,' Josselin replied, transfixed upon the flames, a strange smile upon drawn lips. 'God will not allow its destruction.'

When a man sought assurance from God, it was usually because he faced circumstances he couldn't contemplate managing alone.

'Arlington is downstairs,' I said, at last.

'Arlington?' He raised a slow brow. 'I cannot meet him here, not with the letter upon me. I must take the letter somewhere safe first, then you must talk to him.'

'The soldiers are forcing everyone out through Ludgate,' I said. 'Arlington and Withypoll will be gone soon. We should go too.'

'Look around.' Josselin flung his arms in the air. 'Do you not see we are safe? Ye shall reverence my sanctuary: I am the Lord.'

Now he reckoned he was God. This was not going well. I leant over the balustrade, peering down through the black clouds that gathered about the spire. A steady procession of tiny people streamed out the west porch in a thin, straggled line towards Ludgate. Something told me Withypoll and Arlington would not be among them.

'Look there!' I yelled, pointing. Though the wind blew from east to west, the flames reached out from the City to touch the north-west corner of the building, seizing upon a stray board that covered a hole in the lead. Even as I watched, the fire seemed to skate along the wooden roof, like oil rolling over a polished floor. 'We have to go,' I shouted. 'If the fire takes hold of the nave, we will be trapped.'

Josselin's eyes widened, a look of terror upon his long, dirty face. 'The nave, you say?' He spun to face the door and took off, crashing across planks of timber.

I ran behind him, clattering down the staircase as fast as my legs could manage. Josselin and Dowling might take these steps two at a time, but my legs were too short. My chest constricted, and I stepped aside for a moment to let Dowling pass, before resuming the chase.

Even as we ran I heard flames take hold of the scaffolding about the tower, heard the bricks groan and creak about us. I stepped out into the transept just behind Dowling, to see him chasing Josselin down the nave. Smoke filled the huge cavity above our heads as the roof's giant timbers began to smoulder.

Arlington emerged from the gloom, and Josselin slowed to a halt, arms held up in the air.

'At last!' Arlington declared, clasping his hands together. 'I almost gave up hope. I feared you might be burnt alive.'

Withypoll marched towards me, sword fully extended. I turned and ran towards the Lady Chapel, Dowling and Josselin fast behind. The walls sang out now, the stone screeching like it was being throttled. A great lump of burning metal dropped from the ceiling and hit the pavement in front of me with a great crack. I danced about the debris and kept running, all the way to the Rose Window, arriving just as it shattered into a thousand pieces, glass shards flying through the air, embedding themselves in my hair and on my clothes. I turned to see Withypoll slavering like some great hellhound, unsure who to devour first.

The vast, empty window sucked in fresh air, enraging the fire in the rafters so it ignited in a great ball of flame, momentarily engulfing Withypoll. He fell to one knee, beating at his clothes with his beaver hat. Josselin saw his distraction and hurled himself forwards, grasping for Withypoll's throat. Withypoll reached for his blade, lain discarded on the flagstone, but Josselin saw in time and rolled aside to grab it first. Josselin stood first, sword held aloft.

He jabbed the tip of it into Withypoll's chest. 'It was you killed Berkshire, wasn't it?'

Withypoll clambered to his feet, letting his burning jacket fall to the floor.

'Where are you, Arlington?' Josselin shouted.

Arlington stood ten paces distant, sword still sheathed. He drew his weapon and approached.

Josselin bared his teeth. 'Which one of you was it? Or must I slay you both?'

Arlington lowered his blade. 'Why do you concern yourself with Berkshire? He would not have concerned himself with you.'

'Don't seek to confound me,' Josselin replied, face contorted. 'I am beyond confusion. Just tell me which of you killed Berkshire.'

Arlington pointed at Withypoll. 'He did, because I told him to. I had no choice.'

'Every man has a choice in every deed he does,' said Josselin, slowly, like he had just learnt a difficult lesson.

Arlington waved a finger. 'Not really. You told Berkshire about the third letter, did you not?'

'So I did,' Josselin nodded. 'Which is why you had him killed.'

'Precisely.' Arlington nodded back. 'But how did I find out?'

'You have spies,' Josselin replied, his voice betraying new uncertainty.

'Indeed I do,' Arlington agreed, 'and many of them, but none have yet learnt how to read a man's mind.'

Josselin breathed deep and slow, eyes fixed upon the black plaster across the ridge of Arlington's nose.

Arlington leant forward as if afraid of eavesdroppers. 'Berkshire told me what you did and why you did it. He said you were a traitor.'

'Not true,' said Josselin, though his eyes watered.

'True enough,' said Arlington, sadly. 'It hurt him to tell me of it, but he saw it as his duty. His duty to the King.'

Josselin shook his head.

Arlington shrugged, like he was an innocent player in this fine drama. 'He called you traitor, Josselin, and wanted me to punish you.'

Josselin stamped his foot. 'He would never have betrayed me to you, foul dog. You discovered it then you killed him.'

'Of course I killed him,' snapped Arlington, as if it was obvious. 'The existence of that letter is a state secret. No man may know of it, and Berkshire was a weakling. I sensed he would regret his betrayal and confess all to you.' He waved an arm. 'Rather, Withypoll did.'

'With my sword,' Josselin hissed. 'What sort of cowardly act was that?'

'Whether an act be cowardly or not doesn't depend on whose weapon you use,' Arlington replied. 'He had to die, and the opportunity to blacken your name at the same time proved irresistible.'

The fire inside Josselin's belly seemed to fade before the heat of the inferno in which we stood. The walls exploded inwards, great cracks like cannonballs firing through the air as molten lead poured down the brick. Josselin's shoulders drooped. Withypoll saw his chance, grabbed Arlington's sword and propelled himself at Josselin, the tip of the blade aimed at his neck. Josselin squinted, then blinked, afore lifting his weapon at the last minute, parrying the blow.

I stood helpless, keen to intervene, but lacking the means. Withypoll regained his balance the quicker and thrust his blade once more at Josselin's chest. Josselin danced backwards and seemed to trip over his own feet, stumbling sideways. He landed on one arm and struggled to regain his balance, but his arm stuck, tangled in his coat. Withypoll sighed, face rapt with joyous anticipation as he lifted his sword. I held my breath and the world stood still. Josselin somehow managed to twist his body and kick out at Withypoll's knee, sending him staggering over Josselin's outstretched leg. As Withypoll fell to the ground I saw a flash of steel as Josselin finally succeeded in freeing his trapped arm. Withypoll's legs gave way beneath him. He fell to his knees, head bowed, hands clutching at a small spot of blood spreading from his hip. Josselin extricated himself from beneath Withypoll's prone body and clambered to his feet, sword hung loose from his right hand, short dagger in his left.

Withypoll didn't move. As Josselin stood gasping in great lungs of air, I seized his dagger and knelt down at Withypoll's side, suspecting trickery. He lay with the right side of his face upon the flagstones, eyes open, body unmoving. His sword lay where it fell, well out of reach.

I touched the dagger against his cheek. 'Are you dead?' I whispered into his ear.

He mumbled something I couldn't hear. I leant down closer to his mouth, holding the dagger firmly. His eye moved, focussing upon the end of my nose. His lips moved, and a froth of red blood appeared at the corner of his mouth. He tried to speak again but failed, then he stopped breathing and his eye dulled. A knot unwound itself deep within my belly and I felt a surge of immeasurable happiness. Then his hand jerked up and seized my wrist. I threw myself to one side, heart pounding.

Josselin roared loud, leapt forward to retrieve his knife and plunged it into Withypoll's belly, twisting it until Withypoll lay finally still.

Josselin straightened and turned to Arlington, holding up his blood-smeared palm. 'Well, then. The killer is dead, but not the villain. Will you take back your sword or shall I cut you down where you stand?'

Arlington spread his palms and blew out his cheeks. 'I will take my sword, if you be so generous.'

'We don't have time,' I shouted to Josselin. 'We have to leave, else we shall all die.'

Fire covered every wall as well as the roof, eating steadily through the dry Yorkshire timber. It was only the immense size of the cathedral that meant we could still breathe, but not for much longer. Lead dripped from the ceiling in lethal red globules, splashing onto the floor and smashing the stone.

'Come on, Josselin,' I urged, but he ignored me, stood with legs crouched, ready to do battle with Arlington.

'Your letter,' I whispered into Josselin's ear. 'It will be lost.'

'Go to the Bishop's residence,' he whispered so Arlington couldn't hear. 'Go to his office and look amongst his papers.'

My heart sank even further down my bowels. 'The Bishop of London is involved?'

Arlington cocked his head, trying to listen.

'No,' replied Josselin. 'The Bishop is old and blind, yet he allows no others access to his private correspondence. It was a perfect place to hide the letter. Look for the royal seal.'

Arlington stepped forward, glancing at the ceiling. Josselin scuttled like a great spider, holding his sword in front of him with both hands.

'We haven't long, Josselin,' Arlington warned, placing one hand behind his back.

'A curse to he who will not obey the Lord's commandments,' Josselin replied, face contorted in hatred.

'Aye, well may God turn your curse into a blessing.' Arlington caught my eye and pointed at Dowling. 'Your choice, gentlemen,' he called. 'If you stand aside, it's treachery.'

'I saved you last time,' I retorted. 'Little good it did me.'

'I humbly beg your forgiveness,' said Arlington, eyes fixed upon Josselin's swaying torso. 'Accept my regrets, and I assure you it will not happen again.'

Josselin lifted his sword and brought it down in a chopping motion towards the older man's neck. Arlington swivelled on his toes, avoiding the blade. He stepped aside to give himself room before lunging at Josselin's chest, but Josselin threw himself out of the way.

I watched aghast, uncertain what to do. The fire burnt so loud I couldn't hear their grunts, nor even the sound of their swords clashing. Dowling grabbed my hair in his fist and shouted in my ear for us to depart, but I was loath to leave Josselin to Arlington's mercy.

Josselin lunged once more at Arlington, but tripped before he could connect. Arlington opened his mouth wide then brought his blade down heavily across Josselin's back. Josselin tried to lift himself upon his knees, but failed, crouched afront of Arlington like an old horse, head bowed.

Arlington bared his teeth in cruel satisfaction afore adjusting his breeches and raising his sword two-handed for the final blow. Just as he prepared to swing the sword I picked up a fallen piece of masonry and threw it at his head. He let his sword fall clattering to the floor, and staggered like a drunk, squinting through the smoke as if to see what hit him. My hand burnt, for the rock had smouldered beneath a thin coating of lead. He turned to face me, blood pouring down the right side of his head, arms dangling loose at his sides. His mouth opened and his knees buckled, and he fell face forwards onto the stone floor.

I dashed forwards to where Josselin lay prone. I rolled him onto his back and Dowling lifted his head. A thin layer of soot coated his long nose and gathered among his eyelashes. His eyes dulled, yet looked upon us with peaceful tranquillity. He appeared sane at last. A thin line of saliva dripped from the corner of his mouth. I shook him gently, but his eyes closed.

'I thought he loved me,' he whispered.

'We must go,' Dowling shouted. 'If it is not too late already.'

The smoke descended and lay thick all around so I could see barely twelve inches in front of my nose. 'The Bishop's residence is on our way out,' I yelled, edging forwards into the black inferno.

Dowling grabbed my sleeve, coughing. 'We don't have time.'

I shouted above the din. 'If that letter burns, they will execute us both and Lucy besides.'

'We shall all be executed, anyway,' Dowling grumbled, pulling me forwards.

I crouched down in an attempt to avoid the thickening swirl of choking, black smoke and wished I knew this building better. I knew the door to the Bishop's residence nestled somewhere in the wall back up the nave, beyond the Little North Door. We ran as fast as we could, avoiding the slow-moving river of red metal trickling across the floor. The cathedral writhed in agony, the sound of its bones cracking echoing all around.

Dowling found the door to the Bishop's residence. Great clouds of smothering smoke billowed from within when he opened the door. I staggered backwards and stopped where I stood. Dowling looked over his shoulder to find me, his face as black as Josselin's. I willed my legs to move, but something within me cried out in fear.

'It's just the hall,' Dowling cried out. 'Beyond is clear.'

He grabbed my sleeve before I could protest and hauled me forwards, coughing and spluttering as loud as I. We emerged into an office, bookshelves lining the walls. Through streaming eyes, I saw an ancient chair and large desk, the back of the desk riddled with small drawers, each with its own handle. Papers protruded from the cracks. We pulled all the drawers open and spread the papers upon the desk, looking for the royal seal.

Dowling stood triumphant, letter held up high. 'Here!'

I grabbed it from his hand and plunged it deep into my jacket pocket. Already the broken seal felt sticky, the room hot as an oven; the smell of burning leather filled my nostrils.

Back out in the nave I saw nothing but fire and smoke away to our left, back where we left Arlington and Josselin. The river of lead grew thicker now. A mighty piece of timber fell from above, flaming as it fell, followed by a great splash of molten metal. The stone pavement cracked and the floor beneath our feet shook and trembled. An almighty roar bellowed from the depths as the floor to our left fell in, revealing the crypt below. New flames soared high above our heads. The fire raged below, consuming the piles of books and cloth stored beneath. A wall of flame barred our passage out, towards the portico. Another beam of timber collapsed with a deafening shriek, and hurtled from high above, showering us with a deluge of sparks.

Dowling roared and pushed me into the fire. 'Go, Harry.'

I stumbled and nearly fell, pushing forwards with my right leg just in time. I covered my face with my arms and braced myself to be burnt alive. Instead I rolled through the sheet of fire and out into the warm night air. Dowling staggered behind, waving his hands afore him with eyes closed, dancing on his tiptoes.

A huge explosion erupted from the top of the spire, sending giant chunks of masonry flying through the air. Bricks popped from the walls, as lead continued to drip down the side of the cathedral, shooting across the churchyard like grenades. The west gate stood open afore us, bent and crooked, twisting slowly in the heat of the burning houses. As we ran through the small gap I felt the hair wither on my head. We ran down Ludgate Hill, heading for the small black arch beneath the flaming building. I feared I heard thin wailing as we felt our way through a mist of black smoke, emerging out behind the City wall.

Thirty yards ahead down Fleet Street, behind Fleet Ditch, thick crowds blocked the road, a wall of faces glowing orange. In front of them two horses.

'God's mercy,' called out the foremost rider, sitting confident upon a magnificent white charger. The King. He cantered over to where we stood, charred and smouldering, afore leaning down and regarding us with deep, brown eyes. 'You left it late, good fellows.' He sat up straight, threw a handful of silver upon the ground and waved a majestic hand in the air as if celebrating his own cleverness at somehow having elicited our escape. The crowd cheered while I picked up all the coins. We might need them.

While the King surveyed the scene before him, we slipped away.

Chapter Thirty-Three

*Since that first blazing Star was seen Easterly, and near Sun-rise, the
Calamities attending seem to follow suddenly.*

I sat in a corner of St Bride's chewing on pie crust while Dowling
went in search of a candle. I could barely keep my eyes open, I was
so exhausted.

The church filled fast. I recognised many of the faces from St
Paul's. We couldn't stay here all night, but I planned to take what
opportunity I might. My eyes closed and I fell asleep.

Someone kicked the back of my calf. I awoke instantly, pushing
myself up to see who assailed me. A small boy looked over his
shoulder, scowling, struggling to keep his balance as his mother
marched purposefully towards the choir.

'Be calm,' Dowling growled softly from behind.

He leant against the cool, stone wall, eyes half open. A candle sat upon the floor to his left, wick burnt halfway down.

I breathed deep in an attempt to cool the bile that simmered in my blood and sat up wide awake. I reached for the letter inside my jacket, terrified for a moment it might be gone.

Dowling reached for the candle. 'No one has been near you, though I've been tempted.'

I pulled the parchment from my pocket. 'Why didn't you wake me?'

Dowling shuffled about so he could read over my shoulder. 'You needed the sleep. Now unfold it.'

The royal seal appeared unnaturally large and bloody in the low light of the flame. I unfolded the letter carefully and noticed immediately the name at the bottom: 'Charles R'.

'God save us,' I exclaimed. 'It's written by the King.'

'To the King of France,' Dowling whispered, hoarse, almost poking a hole in the parchment with his thick forefinger. 'We should not be reading this.'

'If we don't read it we won't know what to do,' I said, my curiosity impossible to appease. Ne'ertheless, my heart pounded a heavy beat beneath my ribs.

'Read it aloud,' Dowling hissed into my ear. 'I cannot make out the words in this poor light.'

I held the letter up close to my eyes. 'Know ye that we would welcome entering into a personal friendship, and uniting our interests so for the future there may never be any jealousies between our great nations,' I began.

'A pact with France?' Dowling exclaimed, too loud. 'Impossible.'

I bid him hush before continuing. 'The only matter that hath impeded our relations is the matter of the sea. History would imply that neither one of us might rule the seas alone, for both our nations are too proud and too strong to bow one to the other. As a consequence, we hath allowed others to establish an unnatural presence that serves neither of us well. May God will it that we settle our differences and come to an accord, so it becometh us to honour that obligation. Else God shall surely show his displeasure. Should you consider this testimony give you just cause, then might we enter into discussions of the most secret and confidential kind, for should others learn of the obligations that we shall discuss, it would surely prejudice the potential of our future union.'

'Is that it?' Dowling squinted at the text. 'What of religion in this?' he demanded. 'The only matter that hath impeded our relations is the matter of the sea? Parliament would say otherwise. They would never sanction a *Catholic* union.'

Nor would they, as Charles knew well, for had his father not been executed for the very same crime? If Parliament was to find out he sought a union with Catholic France then he would surely be arrested. I scanned our surrounds to make sure none watched or listened, then read it through again slowly. There could be no doubting its content.

'What was Arlington doing with this?' I wondered.

Dowling huddled up too close. 'Arlington has long been suspected to be a reluctant Protestant, the King besides.'

'It's a draft,' I realised. 'He gave it to Arlington so that Arlington might advise him on how best to proceed. They conspired.'

'And Arlington gave it to Josselin by mistake,' said Dowling wide-eyed. 'The King will execute Arlington on the spot if he discovers his carelessness.'

I sat motionless, staring into the distance. This might be the King's death warrant in my hands. What must Josselin have thought when he read this letter?

'Now I understand,' I whispered. 'Arlington accused Josselin of sabotaging peace. In truth Josselin saw the only *possibility* for peace was to force Arlington's treachery out into the open.'

'What do you mean?' Dowling growled.

'Josselin was staunch Protestant,' I replied, 'but also a loyal subject. If he revealed the contents of the third letter, he knew he condemned the King to imprisonment. If he did not, then he condemned the Dutch to English and French betrayal. Holland could not survive the combined might of England and France. No wonder he fled to Shyam.'

Dowling clasped his hands together, his Scotch accent unusually thick. I had never seen him so panicked. 'And what of us? Where shall we flee to?'

'Think,' I replied. 'What did Josselin plan to do?'

'He ran away to Shyam,' said Dowling.

I tapped my finger upon my thigh. 'So he did,' I said. 'But then he sought to meet with Arlington, and spoke also of talking to Clarendon. He wouldn't meet Arlington without knowing the letter was safe. So he sought safety for himself on the basis of owning the letter.'

'Which didn't work,' Dowling pointed out. 'For Arlington was determined to kill him.'

'Arlington must have been sure Josselin would not have shared the letter with anyone else,' I concluded. 'Why, though, did Josselin want to see Clarendon?'

'Clarendon is not a reluctant Protestant,' said Dowling with approving tone.

'No,' I agreed. 'But he is loyal to the King, and is the greatest advocate for peace with the Dutch.'

I let the idea settle upon my weary brain.

'We take the letter to Clarendon,' said Dowling. 'Clarendon is horrified and at first refuses to believe it can be true.'

'But then he looks at the seal and the signature,' I continued. 'Reminds himself what a vile creature Arlington is, and realises the King has been plotting behind his back.'

'So he shouts and screams, and throws things about Clarendon House,' said Dowling, 'and realises he must do something.'

'Clarendon would never countenance a union with a Catholic state,' I guessed. 'He would hot-foot it to the palace and remonstrate in private with the King, persuading him the idea is wicked folly.' I raised a brow. 'Whereupon the King would be forced to agree, since he could not risk allowing anyone outside his immediate counsel to even suspect him of entertaining the thought.'

'And what of us?'

What of us indeed? 'We would be utterly dependent on Clarendon's whim. If the King were to demand we be put to death, what motive would Clarendon have to argue?' I pondered. 'His own safety, perhaps? They say Charles cannot abide Clarendon, that he preys upon the royal nerves. Were Clarendon to tell him that two of his own men knew the secret and possessed the letter, then the King could not touch him.'

'Which supposes Arlington did not tell the King about us afore he died,' Dowling said.

'If he has told the King, we have no defence at all,' I pointed out. 'Once he discovers Arlington is dead, he will send out his whole army to find us. But I doubt he told the King anything, for to do so he would have to confess to the King what he did with the letter.'

'We should seek Clarendon's help,' Dowling concluded. 'Either way, it is our only chance.'

'And quickly,' I said, rising to my feet. 'Afore we are arrested.'

The roads about Fleet Street and Shoe Lane teemed thick, crowds hurrying somewhere or another with great intent. Soldiers pressed the fit and healthy into passing buckets from Fleet Ditch, forming a chain all the way to Ludgate. At the end of the chain an optimistic fellow threw the contents of every pail in the direction of the roaring fire, without discernible effect.

Some slipped surreptitiously between the shadows, preparing to flee, seeking wagons and horses to carry their possessions away, for fear the fire would escape the City walls. Those already dispossessed got in everyone else's way, wandering aimlessly, silent and confused, else loudly bewailing their plight to all and sundry.

We hurried along The Strand towards Haymarket. By Charing Cross the crowds dissipated and I noticed we were not the only ones walking fast. Three men, wearing brown leather jerkins over their shirts, hurried behind.

'Stop!' one shouted. 'Where are you going?'

We obliged, for they were too close to escape, and all were armed.

'To St Giles' Fields,' I called. 'I would know if my cousin is safe.'

'You take a long route to St Giles' Fields,' one of them panted, pulling up alongside. 'A shorter road to Clarendon House.'

'What do you mean?' I demanded. 'Do I look like the Earl of Clarendon?'

'No,' he smiled. 'You do not. You look like the two fellows Lord Arlington wishes to talk to.'

'Arlington?' I felt my mouth go dry. 'Lord Arlington is dead.'

The three men regarded each other with knowing expressions.

'Not dead, friend,' the leader replied. 'Pan-fried and crispy, perhaps, but not dead.'

Chapter Thirty-four

Tell us, Oh stranger, what Nation of Europe, or almost of the World, shall be in a peaceable condition within three years?

A boat and three more soldiers waited for us at the river. A crowd of angry citizens shouted and threw stones, desperate to cross to the south bank, for now the bridge was inaccessible.

The soldiers bundled us through the crowd, clearing a path without decorum, shoving and waving their swords. A tall man with wild eyes and red cheeks thrust his face towards us, and the soldier stabbed him just beneath the ribs. He stumbled forwards, grasping for my arm, just as I fell into the bottom of the skiff.

I lay there prone while the boat lurched out to the middle of the river. When I looked up, heavy-headed, I saw the whole terrible glory of it all. The entire City blazed, from west wall almost to the Tower, flames pushed left by the swirling gale. Plumes of poisonous smoke blanketed the sky, high as a man could see. Boats covered the water, small and large, many sinking dangerously deep into the river, overburdened with the possessions of those that fled.

I sat frozen, entranced by the sight of it, bewildered by the notion that Arlington could possibly still be alive. How else could he have escaped other than down Ludgate Hill? Yet flames engulfed the hill just minutes after we ran through the gate.

'Have you seen Arlington yourself?' I asked one of the soldiers.

He threw back his head and brayed like a donkey. 'Aye, I saw him. Stood there smoking, shirt and his breeches still smouldering. An angrier man I have not seen in my life.' He laughed again. 'Angry with you, I'll be bound.'

'Are you sure it was him?'

'You will see him yourself, soon enough,' the man replied, smile fading as we neared the Tower.

We rode the current fast through the starlings, past the bridge and out onto stiller waters the other side, before the boat lurched left for the Tower. More soldiers waited at Tower Wharf. As we neared the quay I thought of the Spanish donkey. Today would be the day I rode her, I wagered, unless God affected some unlikely intervention. I pictured Arlington piling up the weights in anticipation of our arrival. My bowels loosened, and I sought Dowling's attention. He frowned so hard I could barely see his eyes.

They dragged us through the Tower Gate and out along the high-walled passage leading to the ruins of the Develin Tower. As we climbed the stone stairs I listened acutely for any sound from above, but all was quiet. What was God thinking, I thought, to save Arlington of all people?

The soldiers in front of us pushed open the door. One burly fellow stepped forward, grim-faced and sombre, but the others hung back.

'At last,' hissed a familiar voice from the far end of the room.

Something flew past my nose, crashing against the stone wall behind my head. Arlington's short stocky frame emerged from the shadow, bristled face foremost, skull covered in a thin layer of tiny, frazzled hairs. The scar upon his nose stood out in an angry, purple welt, black plaster gone. His skin was dull black, as if permanently singed. Patches of angry, red flesh stood out like beacons, weeping upon his cheek. Without eyebrows or eyelashes, yellow teeth bared in fury, he resembled some strange monster climbed from the depths of the Thames.

'Did you find the letter?' he demanded, rounding the frayed head of the Spanish donkey, stood menacingly in the middle of the room.

'Yes,' I replied.

'Show me it.'

I shook my head. 'No.'

'Prove you have it.'

I recited what I could remember from the letter. '*As a consequence, we hath allowed others to establish an unnatural presence that serves neither of us well.*'

'Give it to me.'

'We don't have it with us,' I replied. 'If we had it, you would kill us.'

'Take off your clothes,' Arlington demanded. 'We will see if you speak truth.'

I glanced over my shoulder at the big man, stood stony-faced at the door, arms folded. I took off my jacket, loosened my breeches, peeled off my shirt and lowered my drawers. Dowling followed suit, eyeing me sideways, brow furrowed. We stood naked with our hands covering our yards while the big man rummaged through our clothes.

Arlington kicked our clothes with the tip of his boot, body trembling with rage. 'Tell me where the letter is or I will hang you from the donkey.'

I attempted to look disdainful, my every fibre screaming out in terror. 'You think we didn't predict this event?'

'Of course you didn't,' snapped Arlington. 'You thought I was dead.'

'If not you, then another of the King's lackeys,' I replied. 'You hurt either of us, then the letter will be sent to half a dozen parliamentarians. If they don't kill you, the King will.'

'Liar,' Arlington cried. 'You have not had time.'

I prayed his spies weren't with us at Bride's. 'We had all night,' I answered. 'The letter is safely in the hands of someone who knows not what it contains together with a note that tells where Edward Josselin's body may be found. The body with your strange blade still protruding from its chest.'

Arlington leered. 'I know where you hid Edward Josselin's body, and my spies will find this note.'

I kept my face stiff, determined not to betray my shock. How had he found the body so quick?

'Good luck,' I replied. 'You hurt us or kill us, then the box will be opened and the contents passed to a list of parliamentarians, men who will not hesitate from stringing you up and slicing your guts in front of your face.'

He stared into my face, eyes searching for the truth. His skin smelt like roast pork and his naked burns glistened. 'I don't believe you.'

'Once we read the letter, we realised what danger we were in. What did you think we would do?'

'Run to Clarendon,' replied Arlington. 'Which is where my men found you.'

'This morning,' I pointed out. 'And as you have discovered, neither of us has the letter upon our person.'

Arlington turned his attention to Dowling, moving stiffly. 'What about you, butcher? You've worked for me the longest. Give me the letter and I will ensure your safety. Refuse me and I will destroy you and your family. Starting with Lytle.' He waved a hand in the air, wincing, whereupon the big man lifted me by the arms and placed me once again upon the donkey. I took my weight upon my wrists.

'Torture him,' Dowling said, voice choking. 'You will torture him anyway. We will not give you the letter under any circumstance. To do so would be to sign our own death warrants.'

Arlington threw back his head and roared in frustration, eyes protruding, thick skin upon his head rolling back in a series of fleshy waves. Spittle coated his lips and dripped upon his chin.

'Very well,' he said at last, voice trembling.

He pointed a shaking finger at Dowling's nose. 'You refuse me. What brave fellows you think you are. How would you resolve this situation?'

'Release us,' I replied. 'That's all.'

'I release you and what happens to the letter if you are struck by lightning, or plague, or dropsy, or *old age*?'

'It's unlikely we will die together,' I said, calm. 'While one of us lives, we shall honour our pledge.'

Arlington clenched his fists and stared like he would tear me apart with his hands. 'I must give that letter back to the King.'

'No.' I shook my head. 'You can tell him you destroyed it because you feared its existence.'

Arlington screamed, unleashing his fury upon the donkey's head, knocking its snout askew. 'If the King finds out you have it he will kill you. You know that?'

'We must trust each other, then,' I said. 'Do you not think?'

His mouth smiled but his eyes did not. 'Shall a lord be held to ransom by a butcher and a clerk?' he mused. 'I think not.'

'We want nothing from you, your lordship,' I said quietly. 'Only to be left alone.'

'And you will keep this pact?' he whispered, stepping close. 'No matter what happens?'

I nodded.

He eyed Dowling. 'Remember your loved ones.'

He swept out of the room, footsteps clattering down the stairs, issuing terse instruction to the soldiers who followed. Then all was quiet.

Dowling stared at me like I was a lunatic. 'Where is the letter?'

'In the river,' I said. 'I screwed it up and threw it in the water on the way here.'

'Then we have nothing,' he exclaimed, craggy face aghast.

'Which means Arlington can never find it.'

Dowling shook his head, despondent. 'What if we must produce it?'

'If I hadn't thrown it away we would be dead already,' I replied, impatient. 'How is that not obvious to you?'

Dowling folded his arms. 'You might have asked my opinion.'

'In front of Arlington's men, aye.' As I recovered some peace in my soul, my thoughts turned to others. 'Now we must tell Josselin's mother her son is dead.'

Then we could ride to Cocksmouth and fetch back Lucy and Jane. Our nightmare was over.

Chapter Thirty-Five

People will generally be troubled with sore eyes.

Still Aldgate escaped the fire. We grabbed buckets at the Postern and threaded our way through the throng, a long chain of grim men, sweat pouring from their brows as they fought to save their homes. I dropped my bucket outside the front of Katharine Cree.

Ash coated the house from rooftop to street, a thick blanket of evil, black flakes that fell from the eaves to disintegrate upon our clothes, leaving stains that could never be washed away. The gargoyles peered out from beneath the grime, squinting foul-tempered.

Josselin's betrothed opened the door as before, dressed all in black, pale-headed. As soon as she set eyes on me, she seized both my hands in hers and stared, beseeching. I was suddenly conscious I stank worse than a tannery, but she seemed not to notice.

'We waited for you,' she said in fractured voice, eyes watering.

Thin lines circled her eyes and an ashy halo surrounded her black hair, hanging in the air. Her wide eyes shone, innocent of guile and full of trust. Her hands were warm and I wished I had assigned this task to Dowling, but he stood behind me, silent.

'Where is he?' she asked.

I grimaced, my shoulders slouching, and she saw he was dead.

'You knew him well,' she said soft, as if he was *my* betrothed.

I saw the effort she made to remain composed, lower lip stuck out almost to the tip of her nose, hands gripping mine harder than she realised.

'We got to know each other,' I confessed, grudgingly.

'And you admired him,' she said. 'It was impossible to know him and not to admire him. Wasn't it?'

'He was a unique man,' I said, uneasily. No other man had burnt down London all by himself.

She stared at my lips, opening her own lips so the shape of her mouth matched mine. I felt compelled to continue. 'It was impossible not to . . .'

'Love him,' she finished eagerly. 'Everyone loved him, but I knew him best.'

Yet he never mentioned her.

She squeezed my hands harder. 'You were his friend. You must feel it too. He cannot have died without some sign, else his life is sacrificed for nothing.' Her eyes studied every inch of my face. 'Something must remain. His words, at least.'

I wasn't sure what she meant. 'His words remain, aye.' I nodded sincerely, tugging at my hands.

'And his example,' she whispered, as if to herself.

'True,' I said. 'His example too.'

'Where does he lie?' she asked, tears streaming down her face.

'At St Paul's,' I answered awkwardly. 'I'm afraid his body is burnt.'

She let my hands slip away, turned and wandered into the house, walking in a crooked line. 'I will never see him again, never, never, never.'

I followed her, Dowling at my side.

'He died as he lived,' she said, low.

How did she know? 'His end was worthy of his life,' I said, desperate to be gone.

She bowed her head, an elegant profile with crooked back. 'I was not with him.' Then she wailed, great waves of misery surging from her throat, choking her.

'Don't,' I heard myself protest, unable to bear the grief she exhaled.

She turned with hands clasped, her face awash. 'You were with him to the last?' she asked. 'I think how lonely he must have been. No one to understand him as I understood him. No one to hear.'

I couldn't imagine the two of them together, Josselin the wild spirit and this strange creature.

'I was with him at the end,' I assured her. 'I heard his last words.'

The air froze, and I knew I had said something immeasurably stupid.

'Repeat them,' she pleaded in heartbroken tone. 'I need his words to live with.'

I licked my lips and felt a trickle of sweat meander down my spine.

'The last word he uttered,' I said, slow, 'was your name.'

I prayed she didn't ask me to repeat it, for my mind was a blank and I couldn't remember what her name was.

She sighed lightly then smiled. 'I knew it.' Then she turned around and drifted from the room like a ghost, blown gently by a thin breeze.

Enough. Time to go to Cocksmouth.

Chapter Thirty-Six

What Calamities or bloodshed shall be inflicted?

We took refuge on Tower Hill. I thanked God for the coins the King had tossed upon the street and prayed I would find my little chest again, buried in the garden at Bread Street. Else I was destitute. Culpepper's shop was destroyed besides.

Once we found a spot, Dowling headed off to Cripplegate to find a horse and wagon. Good luck, I reckoned, yet we couldn't walk to Cocksmouth. We needed some form of transport.

When the King rode by at noon, I hid in the crowd. Ne'erless it was a relief he came, for a vile poison infected the masses, a fermenting hatred for all things foreign, incited by rumours of an impending army of Dutchmen and Frenchmen marching upon the City. The King told them the fire was the work of God, which wouldn't have cheered Dowling much. Then he said he would defend England from all its enemies and that we citizens remained safe under his protection.

A loud explosion silenced everyone. New flames of yellow erupted over the top of the wall, a deafening blast in front of the main fire. Word quickly spread they used gunpowder to save the Navy Office, at last blowing up buildings to prevent the fire spreading east, should the wind change. Too little too late for the thousands clustered on the grass bank. When Dowling returned, he found me staring into space, wondering how long it took to rebuild a city.

'Harry,' he gasped, face flushed.

Lucy stood behind him, eyes wide, lips parted, staring. She was supposed to be on her way to Cocksmouth with Jane.

I leapt up. 'Where is she?'

'Davy told me to go to your house to fetch her, but there was no one there,' Lucy replied, wringing her hands. 'I thought she must have gone somewhere else.'

'No one there?' Where would she have gone without telling me? Or did she leave a message at the house before it burnt? I breathed deeply. She wasn't stupid. Once she knew Bread Street was destroyed Jane would know I worried. But how to find her among the fifty thousand displaced, swarming around the walls?

'Did you go inside?' I asked Lucy.

She nodded. 'The door was open. I thought she might be preparing to leave. She left two bags packed by the door, but she wasn't there. I waited an hour.'

My mouth felt dry. 'Did you find anything to tell where she went?'

She shook her head, eyes red, pressing her lips together. 'I looked, Harry. I looked everywhere.'

'What about the neighbours?' I asked. 'Did they see anything?'

She shook her head. 'I came back in the evening. They said soldiers were there, said you were there too.'

Panic clutched my heart. 'That was hours later. Where would she have gone?'

Something was wrong. Even if Jane decided not to go to Cocksmouth, she wouldn't have left Lucy wondering, nor would she have left her bags.

I scanned the crowds surrounding us on all sides. Why would she flee? I thought of Withypoll, but he couldn't have taken her, else why would he have been at our house with soldiers later in the day?

'God help me,' I croaked, realising. 'What if Withypoll came for us, and only for us?' Dowling and Lucy avoided my gaze. They worked it out already.

'Arlington.' It struck me. '*No matter what happens*, he said.'

I gazed into the flames, high above our heads. What destruction did it signify?

'I'm going to the Well, Davy,' I said, blood pounding at the back of my eyes. 'Will you come?'

He laid an arm across my back and said something to Lucy I couldn't hear. She turned and disappeared into the throng.

'You still have the King's credentials?' I asked. 'We won't get into the Tower without them.'

He pulled the battered document from inside his coat. I watched him out the corner of my eye, saw him bite his lip, felt his fingers dig into my shoulder.

Soldiers swarmed behind the Bulwark Gate, scurrying in all directions, fetching gunpowder from deep within the Tower and piling kegs against the wall. Inside the menagerie the lions roared, unsettled by the noise of soldiers yelling and the far off roar of occasional explosion. We hurried across the short bridge spanning the dry moat and dashed across the cobbles towards the Well Tower.

'How did Arlington discover the body so quick?' I fretted, heart pumping.

'Just because he told us to dispose of the body doesn't mean he didn't leave spies to make sure we did it,' Dowling muttered. 'Obvious when you think on it.'

We stood just twenty paces or so east of the Records Office, where I'd toiled all those dreadful tedious years under the employ of William Prynne. How excited I'd been to escape the mind-numbing boredom. What I wouldn't give to turn back the clock.

They boarded up the Well Tower years ago. Originally built to protect against invasion from the Thames and to supply water by means of the two shafts leading from the base of it down to the river, it fell into disuse. It was the first place I'd thought of when Arlington told us to get rid of Edward Josselin's corpse. Conveniently close to the site of the murder, easy to retrieve the body if ever we were able to inform on Arlington. But Arlington anticipated us.

'I'm sure I nailed those boards back,' I said, watching the door swing gently in the dying wind.

'You did,' Dowling growled, pushing it open. 'Someone has been here.'

The round, narrow room was dark and stuffy. Green moss climbed the walls, thriving in the damp air, disappearing up into the blackness of the winding staircase. A smaller staircase led downwards, into the depths where we fetched Edward Josselin. I stood rooted to the floor.

'She'll be safe, Harry,' Dowling assured me. 'You told her we were in danger. We'll find her.'

'We need a torch,' I said. 'A flame shouldn't be hard to find.'

Back out in the passage a torch burnt bright above the Records Office, illuminating the locked door. I strode to fetch it, praying to the God in whom I had so little faith. Just this one time, I prayed, and I will attend church every day. I will renew my studies and spread the word to all parts of England.

As we entered the Tower I heard a steady drip from down below. The stairs led down to a cellar from which led the two shafts, each with a metal grille at the top and at the bottom. We had worked one of the grilles loose and weighted Josselin's body so it sunk down to the second grille, out of sight to the casual observer. A clever hiding place, so I'd thought.

The grille lay crooked, displaced from its mountings and carelessly replaced. I knelt upon the stone flagstones and held the flame to the surface. I peered into the water, desperate to find Josselin's grey head, else nothing at all.

'What do you see?' whispered Dowling over my shoulder.

At first just blackness, as my eyes accustomed to the dark surrounds. Then something long and thick, dancing in the weak current. I pushed the torch down against the grille, and felt my heart break.

A woman's red hair drifting softly up, reaching out, then falling away. I stared, unbelieving, unable to think. Dowling wailed, yet I barely heard his voice above the sound of blood pounding in my ears. Time slowed, as I watched, transfixed, the thick, red strands of Jane's beautiful hair dancing in the still waters. Then a great fist squeezed my heart unbearably hard, sending waves of pain up through my chest and out of my eyes and nose.

Jane was dead. The baby too.

I let my head fall against the grate and fumbled with my fingers, pushing them through the grille, trying to touch the water. I felt Dowling's arm fall across my shoulder pushing me down, felt his wet cheek against my neck.

The end of the world. God's verdict upon my useless soul.

Chapter Thirty-Seven

*Kings and their Allies will promise fair, but still with reservation
or self intentions, taking occasion or advantage when opportunity
serves for their own self-ends.*

'Withypoll's little joke.' Arlington's voice echoed about the cellar
walls. He nodded at the well. 'He wanted to be here when you found
her.'

I stared up at his charred features, unable to read the expression
on his hairless face. I staggered to my feet, the cellar spinning about
my head like a whirligig. Had I killed him in St Albans, none of this
would have happened, which thought stabbed me in the heart once
more. It was my fault Jane died. I reached out for his throat, watching
his eyes open wide in fright.

'It is not her!' he yelled, lifting his arm with difficulty.

I stopped, trying to work out what the words meant. I swivelled on
my heel and fell once more to stare through the lattice. I peered into

368

the water, but couldn't see her face for hair. I tore the grate aside and threw it against the wall. Arlington edged closer to the door.

'Hold him!' I screamed at Dowling.

I reached into the well and found her chin. I lifted it gently upwards, uncertain if I could bear to look upon Jane's beautiful dead face. But this woman's face was rounder, her nose smaller.

I felt an immeasurable wave of relief course through my arteries, a wave of elation and joy. Then guilt. 'Who is she?' I croaked hoarse. Withypoll's 'little joke'.

Arlington wriggled from Dowling's grip. 'I have no idea. Nor do I care.' He rubbed the back of his hand against his mouth. 'Yet I do assure you that if you don't return my letter by tomorrow morning, then I will place your housemaid in one well,' he turned to Dowling, 'and your wife in the other.'

Dowling twisted his shirt between his hands like he wished it was Arlington's neck. I stepped forwards and poked a finger at Arlington's head. 'Then I would send a copy of your letter to every parliamentarian in England. They will hang you.'

'I have thought on it,' Arlington sneered. 'The King will swear the letter is a forgery and none will dare argue otherwise. Memories of the last Republic are too recent.'

'The King might avoid execution, but you wouldn't,' I said. 'You would be his scapegoat.'

I met his gaze, stony eyes unflinching. So the lord decided not to be held ransom by the butcher and a clerk, whatever the cost. Dowling watched me too.

'I can't give you the letter,' I replied, dry-mouthed.

Arlington shook his head. 'Don't say it, Lytle. Don't make that mistake.'

'The original is destroyed,' I said. 'I threw it in the river on the way to the Tower.'

His jaw dropped and his eyes narrowed. I met his stare easily, the hate in my soul providing me with all the strength in the world.

'I will fetch you the copies,' I said.

Arlington's cheeks reddened. 'The copies?'

'Yes, your lordship.' I glanced at Dowling, whose skin was grey as ash. 'Which are in various places. I will fetch them all back to you tomorrow.'

'Why did you make copies?' Arlington asked.

'You threatened several times to kill us,' I replied.

'How many copies?' Arlington whispered.

'Three,' I lied, without thinking if three was better than two or four. 'They are in a safe place. I will bring all three.'

'You had better,' Arlington said slow, brow furrowing. 'How do I know how many copies you made? How do I know you don't still have the original?'

I met his gaze, pressing all my fears down towards my toes. 'As I said, your lordship. I will return all copies to you, tomorrow. I am your loyal subject.'

He sighed and his shoulders slumped. 'You are much cleverer than I thought.' Then his eyes flashed. 'If you speak truth, I need have no fear. I might kill you without fear of reprisal, yet I would not *need* to kill you. If you speak false then you deserve to be killed, yet to kill you would be to sign my own death warrant.' He cocked his head. 'You pose me a riddle, and I cannot see the answer.'

'I speak truth,' I assured him.

His mouth smiled but his eyes did not. I fancied he would like nothing more than to see me floating face first upon the river.

I bid my soul be silent and hid my hatred. 'I am sick of this whole business, your lordship. I just want to open an apothecary. I don't want to work for you any more, nor have anything more to do with murder and treachery. We will give you the copies and walk away.'

Dowling held his breath.

Arlington rubbed a finger upon the new black plaster that bridged his nose. 'I don't think so, Lytle,' he said slowly. 'I would not be able to sleep at night for fear you forged an alliance with the King's enemies, that you still kept a copy of the letter – the original, perhaps.' He shook his head. 'I will *not* be held to ransom by a butcher and a clerk.'

I failed, I realised. My hands trembled and hot tears gathered at the bottom of my eyes.

'No,' Arlington snapped. 'I will keep you close, both of you.' He looked to Dowling, giving me time to wipe the water from my cheek. 'You want to be an apothecary, Lytle, then you will be a royal apothecary, an apothecary to the King. And you, Dowling, will be a royal butcher.'

'What does that signify?' I asked, a tremor in my voice.

'It signifies that the King shall be your patron, and that every man shall know it.' He smiled broadly, showing all his yellow teeth. 'I shall be your patron, besides. You have no shop, Lytle, so the King will lend you money to establish your business, and again every man shall know it. You will attend Whitehall, and attend me, and I will be watching you. Every single day.'

He would pay me to become an apothecary?

'What say you, Lytle?' his voice echoed loud about the walls.

He asked for my soul. 'Very well.'

He smiled, flaking lips cracking on his blackened face. He rubbed his hands together and gazed upon me like I was his favourite dog. 'Then I will think on it, for I have not yet made up my mind.'

'Tell us when you *have* made up your mind,' I replied, voice flat.

The light in his eyes dulled a fraction and he seemed puzzled a moment. He turned to leave, footsteps marking his passage back out into the evening sunshine.

'I will take his money,' I said, lowly. 'Until I punish him for the evil he has committed.' Damn Arlington's soul. I dared look back to the well. The dead woman gazed up with unblinking stare. I knelt down and we pulled her out.

'You cannot play games with him, Harry,' Dowling said quietly, laying her straight upon the stone floor.

I pushed the hair off her face and stood back to look at her. She wore a plain cloth dress, lying heavy upon her body. I took one of her hands and held it gently, turning it over so I saw her red rough palm. 'I couldn't think what else to say,' I answered. 'He left, didn't he?'

Dowling scrabbled in the folds of the sodden material afore extracting a short blade. 'God save us,' he exclaimed. 'Withypoll stabbed her in the side.' He looked up, mouth curled in angry dismay. 'Such a wound would not have killed her.'

I stared into her face again, light freckles on white skin. Her blue lips rested slightly open, eyes wide. 'She drowned?'

Dowling nodded, resting on his knees. He placed the knife on the floor. I picked it up.

'We must go,' I said, thinking of Jane. 'I don't trust Arlington. We will tell the soldiers at the gate about this woman, whoever she may be.'

I helped Dowling to his feet and took one last look about the square cellar. The woman lay motionless upon her back, staring at the ceiling. Dowling climbed the stairs slow, like he carried his wounded soul upon his shoulders, and I followed.

The wooden door swung in the breeze, banging against the frame.

I prodded him in the back. 'Make haste.'

Just as he turned to remonstrate the door crashed open, smashing against the stone. There was a flurry of movement, a flash of steel, then Dowling's face staring over my shoulder, mouth open wide. He stood crouched, clutching at his belly, then fell backwards out onto the cobbles. Behind him stood Arlington, short dagger dripping Dowling's blood.

'You haven't made *any* copies,' he snarled. 'You made it up while you were talking.'

I stepped backwards. He blocked the way like a short fat demon, burning eyes and yellow teeth standing out against his blackened skin.

'I made three copies,' I said, only in a whisper. I lied and he knew it.

He kicked Dowling's prone body to one side and filled the doorway. 'But you will make copies, won't you Lytle? If I let you go.' He took another step closer to me, dagger pointing at my throat.

I took another step back. 'I told you, I am sick of this whole business. I want nothing more to do with it, only to be left alone.'

Arlington smiled, his lashless eyes blinking furiously. 'I *will* leave you alone, Lytle, alone at the bottom of one of those wells.'

He leapt at me from above, blade headed straight to my chest. I twisted to my right so his blade hit the stone and grasped at the hand which grabbed my shirt. He stabbed at me again with savage strength, cutting the skin below my ear. I deflected the next blow with my elbow, then twisted again, sending him sprawling down the stone staircase. Yet he clung onto me with his left hand while he scrambled to his feet. Then he let go, pushing his left hand against the wall to steady himself. He crouched, breathing shallow, pure hatred shining in his black eyes. Stepping up with his right leg, he readied to launch himself again. I watched him coil like a cat preparing to leap at a bird. As he sprang I withdrew Withypoll's knife from inside my jacket and aimed it at his shoulder.

Chapter Thirty-Eight

The Solar Eclips is in Cancer, a moveable and watery sign.

I found them on Tower Hill, Jane holding hands with Lucy, both of them peering anxiously through the crowd. When Jane saw me, her face exploded with delight. She opened her mouth wide and gazed with bright green eyes, waddling towards me with one arm across her little belly.

Lucy brushed the hair from her forehead, half smiling, half afraid. 'Where's Davy?'

'He's been hurt,' I told her. 'Arlington stabbed him in the belly. I fetched him outside the Bulwark Gate, but dared not make him walk further.'

Jane pushed me backwards. 'You made him walk?'

'It wasn't safe to leave him,' I protested, hurrying back the way I came.

Jane followed as quick as she could, while Lucy ran ahead.

'What happened?' Jane demanded, poking me in the ribs. 'Why did he get stabbed and not you?'

I felt my temper beginning to simmer. 'He got stabbed because he was at the top of the stairs when Arlington ambushed us. We didn't know he was there.'

She pulled at my sleeve. 'And what did you do about it?' she asked, scornful.

I stopped, turned, and grabbed both her wrists. 'I stabbed Arlington in the heart, Jane, and left him to die,' I spluttered, holding her hands too tight. Her mouth formed a little 'o' and I released my grip. 'I was aiming at his shoulder, but I missed.'

She took a step away from me while I reflected on how miserable I felt.

'Where were you, anyway?' I asked.

'Locked up at Fleet Prison,' she replied, tears pricking her eyes. 'By a great oaf who said he saw me stealing.' She rolled up her sleeve to reveal an ugly, green bruise upon her arm. 'He said his name was Withypoll and that he was a friend of yours.'

'He's no friend of mine,' I sighed. 'Anyway, he's dead as well.' I turned to follow Lucy.

'How many men *have* you killed?' Jane exclaimed, trotting after me like an angry goose.

'Just one,' I replied. Unless Dowling died. I prayed God had other plans and ran to the Tower wall where Lucy knelt at Dowling's side. He leant against the flint wall where I had left him, gazing about with head still. He attempted to smile when he saw Jane.

Lucy tore at his shirt and exposed the wound for all to see. It was only a small hole, but ugly; purple and swollen.

'How do you fare?' I asked, kneeling next to Lucy.

He sighed and nodded. 'I will be fine,' he said. 'I have a belly like a boulder. God knows it takes more than a prick to kill David Dowling.'

Did he call me a prick? 'It wasn't my fault, you know.'

Jane snorted, and Dowling's eyes widened.

'Of course it wasn't your fault,' he whispered. 'I knew Arlington before you did. If anything, 'tis I who is to blame.'

'Be quiet, Davy,' Lucy scolded.

Jane clicked her tongue and scowled. 'It *is* your fault,' she hissed into my ear.

'How is it my fault?' I hissed back, keen not to disturb Dowling.

'You had a good job at the Tower,' she said. 'Then you gave it all up to go gallivanting about England trying to solve murders.'

'Solving murders cannot be a bad thing.'

'How can it be anything *but* a bad thing?' Jane retorted. 'How many men have you brought back to life? When a man is murdered it is because someone murdered him. You go sticking your great nose into other men's business and what do you expect will happen?' She let loose a great sigh of exasperation and edged closer to Lucy, studying carefully what she did in tending to Dowling's belly.

I sighed too. How had I ever thought of marrying this woman? I might as well cut off my balls and soak them in vinegar.

'We can take him to my aunt's house,' Jane said to Lucy. 'She lives on the bridge. She will not mind us staying there a while.'

Lucy reached out a hand and brushed Jane's cheek. 'Thank you, my dear,' she said. 'Can we take him there now?'

'Of course,' Jane replied, licking her top lip with her tongue.

Lucy smiled gratefully. 'God watches over us.'

'Watches and wonders,' said Jane, casting me another poisonous stare.

Dowling coughed and cleared his throat. 'Harry saved my life, Jane. I thought God forsook us, but instead he worked through Harry. We travelled to Hell and back, men and women falling dead at our feet even as we walked. Ask yourself how it is we return, unharmed. There can be only one explanation.' He closed his eyes and grimaced.

Lucy dabbed at his brow and cast me a quick smile, while Jane sat there stunned. It was one of the nicest things anyone had ever said about me, however fanciful the sentiment. I felt my irritation subside.

'Help me, Harry,' said Lucy, and we pulled the great butcher up onto his feet.

It wasn't a long walk, but the crowds would be thick and impatient. 'Can you manage, Davy?' I asked.

'That I would walk worthy of God, who hath called me unto his kingdom and glory,' Dowling replied, lifting his chin. 'As I said, 'twas but a prick.'

Lucy and I struggled to support him towards the entrance to Thames Street. It would be a long, slow haul.

'Your house burnt down,' said Jane.

'I know,' I nodded. 'We will have to build a new one.'

'We?' she raised an eyebrow. 'What makes you think I will be housemaid to a pauper?'

'I am not a pauper,' I replied. 'I will find my money when it is safe to go back into the City, and I *had* thought you might want to live with me as my wife. Seems I was wrong.'

She pursed her lips. 'You still plan to become an apothecary?'

'Yes,' I replied through gritted teeth, waiting for her to ridicule me again.

Instead she slipped her arm into my spare arm and brushed her cheek against my shoulder.

'Jane,' I said. 'You know I . . .'

She reached up to touch my lips and smiled. 'We can talk later,' she said. 'It'll be many months before you can build a new home. Meantime we can get married at my aunt's house.'

Her aunt's house had but three rooms. 'I think we can do better than that.'

'Don't argue, Harry.' She pinched my wrist. 'Your life is about to change for the better.'

She smiled happily and I wondered what I had let myself in for. I looked up to Dowling for Godly wisdom, but he bit his lip and struggled to keep walking. At first I thought he was in pain until I realised he was laughing.

Historical Notes

This is, of course, a work of historical fiction. For me the rules of the game are that the author is free to take liberties so long as they are informed liberties, purposeful and in service of the plot. I hope there are no written equivalents of a Viking wearing a wristwatch.

Let me point out three areas which I feel merit highlighting. First, Lord Arlington is clearly a bit of a villain in this book. The real Lord Arlington was a close advisor of the King and did have a black plaster across his nose. He also, however, lived until the ripe old age of 67, finally expiring in 1685.

Second, Shyam is modelled on the Derbyshire village of Eyam. I moved it east of London so as to be able to recreate Marlow's journey in Conrad's *Heart of Darkness*, an exercise I had some fun with. I hope fans of Joseph Conrad find it at least a bit entertaining, and are not mortally offended.

Third, the real Fire of London took two days to reach St Paul's cathedral. That really didn't suit the pace of the story, so I speeded it all up. For those frustrated by these tinkerings, I direct you towards the website *harrylytle.com* where I have served my penance by providing short accounts of most of the places and characters that show up in the Harry Lytle Chronicles.

Acknowledgements

With love and thanks again to Ruth, Charlotte, Callum, Cameron and Ashleigh. I'd like to thank everyone who has bought a Harry Lytle book, especially those who have sent lovely letters, or else messages via my Facebook blog page, Goodreads etc . . . and reviews on Amazon.

To Tara Wynne, Annabel Blay and Clair Roberts at Curtis Brown, who have worked hard on my behalf, and to whom I am very grateful indeed. To all the new faces at Allison and Busby – I'm looking forward to working with you into the future!

I'd also like to acknowledge again all the folks at the Well, especially Sharon, Mike, Hope, Benjamin, Basil, Bob, David, Sid, Melinda, Stephen, Jake and Missye. And to William Lilly, author of *Astrological Judgments for the year 1666.*

SHE